The Reconstruction

Rein Raud

THE RECONSTRUCTION

Translated from the Estonian by Adam Cullen

DALKEY ARCHIVE PRESS

Originly published in Estonian by Mustvalge Kirjastus as
Rekonstruktsioon in 2012.

Copyright © 2012 by Rein Raud
Translation copyright © 2017 by Adam Cullen
First Dalkey Archive edition, 2017.

Names: Raud, Rein, author. | Cullen, Adam, 1986- translator.
Title: The reconstruction / Rein Raud ; translated by Adam Cullen.
Other titles: Rekonstruktsioon. English
Description: First Dalkey Archive edition. | Victoria, TX : Dalkey Archive
Press, 2017.
Identifiers: LCCN 2016054356 | ISBN 9780916583804 (pbk. : alk. paper)
Subjects: LCSH: Estonia--Social life and customs--Fiction. | Suicide--Fic-
tion. | Young women--Fiction. | GSAFD: Suspense fiction.
Classification: LCC PH666.28.A74 R4513 2017 | DDC 894/.54533--dc23
LC record available at https://lccn.loc.gov/2016054356

EESTI KULTUURKAPITAL

Published with the support of the Cultural Endowment of Estonia.

www.dalkeyarchive.com
Victoria, TX / McLean, IL / Dublin

Dalkey Archive Press publications are, in part, made possible through
the support of the University of Houston-Victoria and its programs in
creative writing, publishing, and translation.

Printed on permanent/durable acid-free paper

Table of Contents

I DIDN'T KNOW it when I began, but I do now: I don't want to blame anyone or anything; or if I do, then only myself. But I needed clarity. I don't want to find fault; I want to find out—if I only can.

The last six months of my life have been special. I've given thought to very many things that had no meaning to me whatsoever before. When the doctor told me, yes, I've got bad news for you, but there's nothing to be done and it really is cancer, then I actually already knew. He didn't give me all that much hope, saying only that I'd have to decide for myself whether or not I wanted the operation—although the likelihood of it going well, he said, is relatively small in my case. And on top of that, there's no certainty that the tumor won't start flourishing again in a little while. He estimated that, forgoing the operation, I'd have six months to a year.

I knew how I'd have to spend that time—completing what I'd been putting off for too long already. Delaying it out of nothing but cowardice, nothing but doubt over whether I'd be able to live with the knowledge I needed to seek. Knowledge without which I can't live, either.

Now six months have passed, but I hope I still have enough time to put together the notes I've been jotting down in the evenings after my conversations, while everything was still fresh in my mind and for as long as the pain permitted. In that time, I've managed to speak to dozens of people, to traverse most of Estonia, and even to visit France. Some gave the impression that they didn't want to speak to me, while others appeared, conversely, to have been expecting my appearance for quite a long time, wishing to finally get all the things that had been troubling them for years off their chests. And they even allowed me to record them, so that I've been able to go back to those conversations time and again, to allow their intonations to bring alive those moments when I found out many difficult things; so that now, I can detect behind their tiny quavers important meanings, which for whatever reason I hadn't noticed earlier. I got everything I was able to coax out of them, then put together all the small details into the bigger picture, and now I know almost everything, or at least as much as it's conceivable to know. And whatever I don't know, and can never really find out—those things I know all the same, somehow. I'd never have guessed that there's a writer hidden away in me, but I'll admit right off the bat (not that it doesn't show, regardless) that, when I was faced with the choice of either leaving holes where it was impossible to fill in the gaps between facts and interpretation, or else letting my intuition guide me and imagining how things might have been, for the most part I've given in to temptation. Besides, it doesn't change the bigger picture. The bigger picture stays just the way it is. And whatever I don't know, no one knows anymore.

Occasionally, it feels like I'm out of breath in a race against time. The nights I don't vomit are becoming more and more infrequent, and my painkillers are getting stronger and stronger. Even so, sometimes not even they are any help—the pain is so strong then that I'm unable to focus on anything for several days on end. But a clear day or two follows; on some, the disease even manages to recede to the background of my mind for a little while. From now on, though, I'll try not to trouble you with my health issues. This story isn't about me.

You might recall a sad news item that flashed through the papers five years ago about a tragedy in Viljandi County, where four young people died in a fire. They'd been living at a fair distance from the more populated areas, on a lone farmstead that didn't exactly have the best reputation among locals. It wasn't any kind of drunkards' hangout at all—oh, no; these young men and women had lived there relatively quietly, especially in the last year before the tragedy; they were just a little strange, that was all. And the house they were in was old, wooden—when a fire breaks out in a place like that, it's hard to contain.

Since one of the deceased was the son of an up-and-coming politician, not much more than that made it into the papers. The locals talked about it a little more, of course; but they always do—not even the pointless deaths of young men and women can tame the tongues of sensationalist loudmouths. Birchback (that was the name of the farmhouse that burned) had been restored to its former, pre-Occupation owner many years before the incident, and the man's son—a young bohemian artist—had moved there. From then on, it became a gathering point for all kinds of weirdos, UFO-spotters, Buddhists, and other aura-enthusiasts of every fur and feather. And that was where they spent their days, not drinking any more than the rest of the country folk, and never being a nuisance, apart from maybe running naked into the lake or organizing picnics on a meadow from time to time, and, well, perhaps they smoked a little marijuana there in private, who knows. But at some point, the place was frequented more and more by those . . . oddballs, I suppose: seemingly a little religious, and seemingly not.

And that's when it happened. The tragedy, about which I needed to find out as much as I possibly could before my time came. So that I could see the entire chain of events that had led up to it. Because circumstances were actually different, of course. The fire had just started when someone spotted it, and a few locals managed to extinguish the flames right away. Nothing should have stopped the people inside from running out and carrying on with their lives.

Nothing, aside from the fact that they were already dead by

the time the fire started. They were lying side by side on the second floor, in the master bedroom, their bodies contorted, a small packed suitcase lying beside each of them, and a letter crumpled in their fists: "I, so-and-so, have settled all my debts in this world and can go before God with a pure heart." And what's more: an additional, fifth suitcase was found in another room on the first floor, along with a fifth note on the ground next to it. But I'll get to that later—there's no point rushing ahead in the course of events.

Perhaps you're wondering why I know all of this. It's because the relatives of the deceased had a right to find out. And one of those four whose earthly paths ended in that house was Anni-Reelika Padrik. My daughter. My only child. My princess.

Or more like what was left of her.

I

Fish Tracks in Water

1

I'D PULLED ALL strings available to me to make an appointment with the Minister, which wasn't easy. My name didn't mean anything to him and I wasn't professionally connected to his ministry's jurisdiction in any way either, so he received me with a certain degree of surprise and nonplus. The Minister couldn't have been much younger than me, since everyone who'd died in the house (including his son) was more or less the same age, and we'd had Anni-Reelika earlier rather than later. Yet the man staring at me from across the towering desk seemed much more vigorous and vital than I was all the same. It was obvious that he worked out and practiced moderation. He had the eyes of a man who made very quick mental calculations, and they narrowed slightly as he tried to place me in the depths of his memories. Fruitlessly, I might add.

When I told him why I'd come he remembered, of course, and his expression changed. Then he looked at me as the less seasoned among us look at a friend who's suffered a misfortune with irreversible consequences—embarrassed by our utter inability to help him. It was quite clear he had no wish to call the incident to mind—at least not with himself as a part of it, and not in front of others.

"I wanted to thank you for what you did," I said. "It would've been just awful if the papers had started breaking it all down piece by piece."

The tension slightly gave way.

"Yes," he said. "You know how it is with our media. As if it wasn't terrible enough for the relatives already." As if he himself hadn't been one of those relatives, too.

"Exactly," I said, nodding and trying to word the question that I'd actually come to pose. But he beat me to it.

"Is there something I might be able to do for you?"

"Yes, there . . . certainly is, actually," I said, haltingly. "I suspect you were given an even clearer picture of the details than what was told to the rest of their loved ones. Access to the full materials and what have you. I'd like . . . if it's possible—I'd like to see them, too."

"Mm-hmm," the Minister murmured, unable to decide on the spot. "I don't know what all of you were told exactly, you know. The police investigated the matter, of course—spoke to everyone who might have known something, and that file did indeed cross my desk."

"It's not easy for just anyone to gain access to police files," I continued, "even when they're directly connected to the case."

"What do you need it for, though? Aren't you able to move on with your life?"

I told him. He pondered.

"I'll see what I can do," he finally said. "It's clear enough that you don't pose any PR risk."

He kept his word. A couple of days later, I received an e-mail from his assistant, containing the name of the investigator involved in the case, the department's telephone number, and confirmation that the individual had been authorized to answer all of my questions.

2

But as with every story, this one should be told from the beginning. Or even before that.

Sometimes, I imagine how it must feel to be a person with amnesia who has to memorize everything about himself without actually knowing it from within. Others might talk to him like they used to, as if he actually was the same person, but he sees both them and himself from a certain distance—as if it weren't all happening in reality, as if he weren't truly taking part in the process. He has learned how to react to a conspiratorial touch or smile, behind which he senses a tender memory (one that he lacks), and this is how he continues to deceive those who wish to continue being deceived. But he can't deceive himself. No, the amnesiac can wish all he wants to see himself as the person he is to others, and he can talk himself into believing that he's really capable of doing it, even though, instead of genuinely remembered scenes, he has only a learned knowledge that anyone could imagine as well as he does. Sometimes, he does successfully convince himself of some detail, just as children can lodge a foreign memory in their brains. Sooner or later, though, a yawning gap in some important place will slice through his imagined timeline, forcing him to return to the person he is today.

Something similar has happened to me, twice. First when the news of my daughter's death finally sank in. And then after being given the diagnosis. My memory didn't actually disappear, of course—I could still see the past "me" among my loved ones, among familiar things, experiencing joy and sorrow; but for reasons that now left me feeling entirely indifferent. No, it really wasn't me—it was someone else eating from my bowl and sleeping in my bed and answering when my name was called. Or else he *was* the right one, and now I'm merely someone who possesses not only real memories of himself, but the right name as well, and who is forced to accept an unaccustomed life with its own yearnings and disappointments as his own.

So, when I speak here about former times and being present in them, I might as well be speaking about fish behind the glass of an aquarium—their mouths moving soundlessly, breathing in some other element by some other means.

I didn't read all that much when I was younger (or nothing very philosophical, in any case), but over the last few years, I've really picked up the habit. That has changed me, too; there's no point denying it. Nevertheless, I've become more and more convinced of one thing: even though all the great humanists and religious awakeners and authors of self-help books—no matter what other chasms may divide them—unanimously agree that there's no such thing as an ordinary person and that everyone's special, in reality, that's bullshit. I don't at all understand what's so bad about being ordinary. Why reject it? Maybe because people I've gotten to know of late often don't recognize me on the street; apparently, there's nothing even remotely memorable about my appearance—not even the yellowish-tinted glasses I have to wear almost all the time due to a rare hereditary health problem. (I have hemeralopia and my eyes are extremely sensitive to light.) There's also no professional consensus on whether or not I'm actually color-blind. I myself can't say one way or another: the way I see it, all of the tones that other people use various color names for are indeed different, but whether or not I see them the same way others do—that, I just don't know. As you might imagine, I favor the hypothesis that I see just like everyone else does. That is, if it isn't true that each person really does see things differently, meaning that one picture is pretty to one person, and another is to another. And seen through those yellowishtinted glasses, my world is kind of the color of old-fashioned photographs, anyway. I can only take them off when the light is relatively dim. Even so, they don't make me special. Only people I've known for a long time, acquaintances from school and such—they recognize me, even though I've changed in the meantime. For example, I started shaving my head from the time when my hair, which has been sparse since childhood, gradually started to fall out. On the rare occasions when I run into any of these acquaintances, they usually still wave to me first. But, well—who knows whether or not they remember me by name?

My father was a structural engineer and my mother a schoolteacher; I had no brothers or sisters. We had a two-bedroom place in the Mustamäe apartment district, and I was in a special French-language class at Tallinn Secondary School No.1. That latter circumstance wasn't too common, of course, but it wasn't anything out of the ordinary either, since my mother was a French-language teacher. I was a Pioneer and a member of the Komsomol[1] and hated the Soviet regime just like everyone else— not especially believing that it would ever end, but also not of the opinion that it could be served with integrity. Even the tragedies that shook our family's little world to its foundations were altogether ordinary. Back when my father was doing his compulsory Soviet Army service, he was trained to be a dosimetrist because he knew how to play guitar a little and the officers needed him and a couple other more musical soldiers to entertain them sometimes in the evenings while they drank vodka and played cards. Dosimetrists weren't required to haul heavy stones or dig ditches so that their hands

1 The All-Union Leninist Young Communist League—essentially a youth division of the Communist Party of the Soviet Union.

wouldn't hurt and they could strum the right notes on the guitar at night. They had extremely little to do in terms of measuring radioactivity, since not a single one of the unit's dosimeters actually worked. But when Chernobyl's reactor exploded, those who had any knowledge in the field (on paper) were the very first to be summoned to the military commissar's office, and so my father was transported to Ukraine for May Day along with ten or so others like him. This, however, was before anything intelligible about the incident was reported through the official media outlets. He was there for a month. After another month, he was forced to appear on a television talk show and explain that no health problems would result from cleaning up in the aftermath of the accident, even though the traces of radiation poisoning were even then beginning to show on his face.And six months after that, we were standing by his grave.

He would have turned fifty-five two weeks later. Fifty-five appears to be somehow fateful for men in our family. My grandfather, who was born in 1890 and after whom I was named Enn, was executed by the Russians in the final days of the war— on account of his own stupidity, as Grandma believed, because did he really need to admit to them that he was fluent in both Russian and German? While the former was, as the riflemen saw it, a completely understandable skill on every inch of earth where Soviet boots had tread, the latter testified to enemy sympathies. Neither of my father's two older brothers lived very long, as both fell in the war—one on the Russian side, the other on the German. Nothing out of the ordinary. And it's not my business to deviate from the pattern.

Nevertheless, when I look back on my life from where I am now, I have to admit that it's gone rather smoothly in general. True, the greatest dream of my younger days was never achieved—I made it into the final round of auditions for theater school, but no further. But does that mean that the entire rest of my life has just been one big compromise? I didn't become an ambulance driver or the first Estonian to set foot on the moon either, now did I? Nor will I ever, although the latter title is still up for grabs. On top of that, theater hasn't disappeared from my life just yet, and maybe I do actually have more business participating in it as a grateful observer. I had to study for some job all the same, because although the Soviet military wasn't exactly stalking me as a result of my poor eyesight, I felt like I was in debt to my parents for avoiding conscription with their genes. I had no backup plans—I might, perhaps, have considered going on with French, but it was abolished as a field of study in Soviet Estonia, and I had no desire to move to Russia. However, I was also strong in the sciences, having even competed in the ESSR Academic Olympics in chemistry and physics. Thus for a while I debated enrolling in either the Tallinn Polytechnic Institute or the Tartu State University, and finally decided in favor of the latter, if only to get a little farther away from home. At the Institute, I should have immediately had to pick a specific field of study, like bridge- or road-building, but the University allowed me to delay my final decision for some time. All in all, I'm very satisfied with my choice of field and profession. I started in biology, specialized in ecology, and have worked in the same area of expertise my entire life. Today I work at the Ministry of the Environment, going to inspect industrial sites located along bodies of water and checking the levels of toxins in lakes and rivers. I was in the private sector for a little while, too—a couple of friends set up a company and were having environmental studies done for new building commissions, but after a short time I quit, since I wasn't always able to keep mum at the right moments.

I was once told that I have a real knack for science, but the circumstances didn't favor it, and to tell the truth I didn't have the passion for it either. To me, biology has been like a reptile's sheddable skin: at this point, only its delicate pattern actually remains somewhere on the surface of my consciousness—

memories of things I used to know, but which have had no effect on the course of my inner life.

What came next? Marriage, our daughter's birth, the divorce. Nothing out of the ordinary.

I hope I'll be able to write about my marriage without bitterness, despite the fact that it failed. I know very well that no single party is ever to blame for a relationship going sour. If nothing else, the other person can always at least be criticized for making the wrong choices and feeling a need to adhere to them. And it was quite obvious that Maire and I didn't match at all, but in the beginning neither of us would admit it, and later, all kinds of other little details always loomed larger. I think I can say this with a clean conscience. Because now, I know that I've actually always been good at paying attention: wherever I could have merely seen eyes, I also noticed expressions; wherever simple sentences could be heard, I picked up intonations. Still, I wasn't able to grasp the importance of details when I was young, though maybe the problem also lay in the fact that we were always in a hurry (where to, I wonder?), and therefore it really wasn't necessary to peer beneath the surface. Today, however, when I leisurely let my memories wash over me, streaming before my mind's eye, I'm startled to find so many details that might have set things moving in another direction, had I only been capable of reading the message differently as my mind mechanically recorded the instance.

I don't know for certain when it began, exactly. But things were certainly bad when she started wearing high heels again. I knew she liked them, of course, but she'd stopped wearing them for quite a long time after we decided we were an item. Because, well, I'm not especially tall in stature, and I suppose she realized I wasn't very comfortable looking shorter than my partner. I should have taken the heels' return as a sign, but I suppose by then it wasn't all that important to me anymore. And already sometime around when Anni started going to high school, it became clear to both of us that as soon as she'd left the nest, the nest itself would crumble as well. Still, neither of us leapt to breach the topic too early, since, who knew—maybe we would've done something irreversible. Of course, it later turned out that Anni herself had suffered the most from the situation—the very person for whom it would seem we'd stayed together.

To Maire, the chance of being disappointed in me again at every step was more a comfort than a bother. She was probably upset most by my general lack of ambition, by my disinclination to "get ahead" in life and make a career for myself, no matter in what line of work, so that I might be able to ensure for her the status which, in her opinion, she deserved in life. However, I wasn't fit to be a politician, and I likewise lacked any kind of qualifications for entrepreneurship. I certainly took note as my former classmates from school and university set up their own companies one after another and were soon driving around in Mercedes and Audis, but I was dead certain that even if I were to try to get something similar started up, I'd be struck down by failure and bankruptcy sooner or later, and I had no need for that kind of an embarrassment. Neither did Maire.

So, although Maire and I always got along well in principle and on her terms, I probably remained in her eyes a nerd and a loser, whom no one takes seriously. That wasn't true, by the way—my colleagues always respected me, and I appreciated it. Under no circumstances would I have wished to replace it with the disgruntled respect that's shown toward former companions who have jostled their way higher up along the job-ladder; or, I should say, the respect shown towards their armchairs, stripes, and signature-giving pens. I had no need for that.

For that reason, I also got along quite well with my fatherin-law, who was in a similar situation but had yielded to his wife's

demands. He'd apparently risen to a rather high position in
the Soviet hierarchy along some agricultural path, even though
it was clear that he'd have preferred to keep getting his own
hands grubby instead of monitoring others to make sure they
were dirtying theirs in strict accordance with Communist Party
instructions. Being someone who came from relatively humble
beginnings and enjoyed comfort, he naturally didn't turn down
all the luxuries and privileges to which the system entitled its
chosen ones; but at the same time, he wasn't prepared to perform
any exceptional perversions in their name. He was entirely
insouciant about the higher tiers of the power pyramid, and
was satisfied with their decently large house in a suburb close to
the capital and their new black Volga that he drove without a
chauffeur, and, to top it all off, their summer home on the shore
of Lake Võrtsjärv. He always disappeared to the cabin whenever
he had the chance in the summer and fall, because he enjoyed
fishing. I even accompanied him on those trips on a couple
of occasions, even though I wasn't all that interested in staring
at a bobber floating on the water; still, it didn't seem proper
to decline the invitation either. While out on the lake, he was
always laconic and could go without speaking a single word for
hours on end; and even when we were drinking vodka in front
of the fireplace later, he didn't say very much.

On the other hand, Maire's mother was cut from a different
cloth, and basically my wife was just like her mother. Both were
fantastic at home—although in my mother-in-law's case, it
manifested more in the form of her cooking and baking skills.
Maire preferred to organize get-togethers like lunch parties,
where the main emphasis was placed on the correctness of
manners: the right wine being served in the right glass and with
the right dishes, but not on how flavorful those dishes actually
were. Not that she wasn't good in the kitchen—it just didn't
enthuse her. I must admit that, in the beginning, I was very
impressed by her social adeptness. When I was presented to her

parents for the first time, Maire herself had cooked and baked and set the table for the occasion. Everything was like a real dinner party— there was a name card at every seat; the aperitif was followed by a white wine, then a red (one glass per person), and finally a cognac that, by the way, was not Armenian but French, which didn't actually suit my palate at all; yet it was quite the statement in late-1970s Estonia. "Whoever acts like she's with a king at home feels at home when she is with a king," Maire's mother praised her. Maire nodded, but I noticed that her younger sister, Elo, almost snorted openly. That irked me back then. Later, I found out that Maire's childhood dream had been to go into diplomacy—she'd even tried to get into the Moscow Institute of International Relations, albeit unsuccessfully: I suppose her father's contacts hadn't been enough. For in spite of her sheltered position, Maire's life in Estonia still didn't feel quite right. On top of that, while she had to live in a somewhat uncomfortable mental symbiosis with Soviet reality (but nevertheless one that had evolved independently of her will), she generally agreed with the Eastern Bloc's foreign policy. For instance: she supported the war in Afghanistan in principle (at least at first), especially when it came to women's rights, and she regarded Pinochet's junta as more criminal than Jaruzelski's.

All of this didn't impede her from maintaining a clearly nationalist mindset—what's more, one that she believed was entirely genuine. Thanks to her father, their family had access to the special *nomenklatura* shops, where they were able to purchase deficit goods once per week; and in addition to ordinary rubles, they were given certificates that could be redeemed for higherquality clothes and home appliances. And every time she and her mother returned from one of these shops, they never failed to comment on the stupidity, impoliteness, and poor taste of the Russian communist officials' wives; and from there, the talk soon turned to the hordes of Russian immigrants filling ever greater sections of the city, and then to the problem of

Estonians not sticking together enough. And naturally, Maire had been in a folk-dance group when she was younger, even performing at the Youth Dance Festival once. She could also play some guitar and accompany herself singing: *Oh Estonia / Oh the land where I was born / As long as your village lives / So will you also . . .* It seems funny now. But to her family, keeping up the habits of the imagined upper class was almost like a political protest: we aren't them. And they truly weren't.

However, it was actually a lot more about cash than it seemed like to the outside observer. Out of the entire family, Maire's sister Elo was the only one who didn't adopt their attitude towards life; but even she never protested very loudly. Now, when I think back on that time, it seems like Maire's unconditional will to live and act the way the civilized world's strictest rules required (a trait she inherited from her mother) had been self-instilled— foremost as compensation for the fact that their chance to live in that manner had been achieved by serving a regime which they themselves didn't respect. No one wanted to be a collaborator, and neither did they. As soon as it became evident that the old regime was coming to a close (but not a moment sooner), even they started giving that "we-hollowed-it-out-from-within" routine that became so familiar to all of us later; and still, in the summer of 1988, when the whole of Estonia was feverish with the spirit of liberation, Maire's parents vacationed at the government holiday home in Crimea and dragged Elo along with them in spite of her protests. Maire's father had even briefly participated in some kind of a self-governing Estonian agricultural labor group—certainly without ever believing that it might turn into anything.

To their credit, I must say that this kind of behavior wasn't quite faking. Maybe it had been at the beginning, but over the years, it developed into the dominant conduct in their dealings with one another. I know this, because Maire and I lived with her family for close to ten years. At first we were simply visiting, but when Anni was born, Maire was only in her third year of university, it was May, and she missed all of her final exams, understandably. She was able to re-take them all in the summer, chiefly because her mother took charge of looking after Anni. And in the fall she was back taking classes again. In those days, we tried to get out to the suburb (Saue) every weekend. I had my own car by then: an indigo-blue Zhiguli—so what that I bought it used off my father-in-law, but with my own personal money earned from summer construction projects. After Maire's graduation, we sort of naturally moved in with them— temporarily, so to say—because her parents had two free rooms upstairs and I was always having to drive all across Estonia for work, so there wasn't any great difference whether I lived in Tallinn, Tartu, or Pärnu.

I've since wondered whether things would have gone differently for us had we been able to start our life together in total independence. Maybe our marriage would have ended even more quickly if I hadn't been able to provide my family with the kind of life to which Maire was accustomed. But maybe not—perhaps coming into direct contact with real life would have taught Maire to see things slightly differently instead. I can't say that her parents' attitude towards me was in any way improper. At the same time, it was quite clear they didn't regard me as a suitable choice for their daughter. I don't believe they told her that word-forword behind my back; certainly not. But as the years passed, I started to sense it from the general attitude that developed; so, it had to be obvious even to Maire long before it was to me. No doubt that was the reason why she always badgered me to do something with my life—she needed to prove to her parents that she was right. The way I saw it, though, my whole life was still ahead of me and there was time aplenty—I had an interesting job, a precious daughter, and a nice home all the same. So what that it was under my mother- and father-in-law's wing? What was the rush? Maybe she and I should have spoken frankly about it, showing all our cards. It's possible we'd have understood each other more clearly. But as I've said, she wasn't that kind of person.

Anni was already ten years old by the time we moved from Saue to Tallinn. For some time, I'd been fending off hints from my mother-in-law that if I were to ask her husband, he'd supply us with the money to refurbish a cooperative apartment, since my own salary wouldn't enable me to collect that kind of cash; and that if I didn't want that, then he could, in principle, also use his influence to help my position on the official apartment waiting list. I'm glad that she made me asking him a condition. In her opinion, it most likely meant the obligation for me to somehow "position" myself; to truly do something to advance my position in life—but the way I interpreted it, it was a demand to demean myself, to acknowledge my failure; and I naturally didn't intend to do that. I think Maire actually realized this, too, because after one conversation where she naïvely asked why I wasn't asking for her father's assistance in securing an apartment, she never brought the topic up again. Our situation could have been helped along just as well by having a second child, which in general I thought would have been a great idea. But when I broached the subject offhand, Maire resolutely informed me that she was done giving birth in this lifetime, and I simply had to accept the fact. So, that shows you the state our relationship was in.

What kind of a person she actually was, if she was any kind at all—that, I never managed to determine over the course of our marriage.

Out of their entire family, I got along with Maire's sister the best. Elo was a lively and restless spirit who seemed to have somehow ended up in their company by accident; her mother and sister's attempts to coach her on how to behave properly and modestly had come to naught. Something about the way Elo was back then didn't allow you to foresee the entirely different kind of a person she'd become years later. When she was excited about something, she displayed it loudly, and when something got on her nerves, she didn't keep it to herself. She was a voracious reader of poetry and a true star in her school's drama club; her interest in theater was even more expansive than mine. Later, she even gave serious consideration to applying to the theater school, but didn't go for an audition when she found out how many girls always try out in the first round. And it goes without saying that she could be spotted at every performance worth attending. That connected us, even though I myself wasn't going to the theater all that often anymore. She was twelve years old when Anni was born, and our little baby rapidly gained an important place in her life. "She treats her like a living doll," Maire joked, although we were both grateful that Elo agreed to watch Anni whenever necessary— like when Maire's mother invited us to attend an operetta. And she had an interest in everything. Both her parents and her teachers had thought she had no aptitude for mathematics, until one day (it might have been when she was in eighth grade), Elo asked me to explain a problem to her, and it turned out that she was in fact exceptionally bright and could grasp things on the spot. It was simply that up until then, she'd only been told to dully memorize mathematical formulas by rote, without figuring out the system behind them; not to mention without being given an explanation of how it all fit together with reality. From then on, we sat down with her textbooks several times a week in the evenings and picked subjects apart. Instead of the two points out of five that had been looming as her second-quarter grade, she received a full four; her physics and chemistry scores were in good shape already by the end of the third quarter; and she graduated eighth grade with only fours and fives. Our contact was less frequent after Maire and I moved out of Saue, but Elo and Anni still talked, and later, when Elo was living in Sweden, Anni once even visited her there for a full month.

To Maire's parents, however, Elo's lively nature merely resembled misbehavior, and her unbridled interest in all kinds of different things was simply superficiality. She was incredibly social, which in their minds naturally meant she didn't have a single true friend. All the same, she did her best to please them. She never caused any serious problems even during her teenage years, although she didn't always come home at the agreed-upon time and occasionally left her room messy, of course. On such occasions, her mother wouldn't scold or punish Elo; instead, she would simply make some decision for her daughter, on which she would have otherwise conferred with her first. For example, she'd announce they were all taking a family trip to Otepää for the weekend to ski, or would put all of her best clothes in the wash with the exception of a single dress before a class party. Elo always got the message, and for a week, her room would be spotless and she'd be home before ten o'clock. But of course it never stayed that way for long. If you ask me, Elo was simply an ideal child. I could remember all too well what my classmates and I had gotten away with at that age, but once when I tried to reassure my mother-in-law by telling her that, she hissed at me swiftly and uncharacteristically, thank you, but I do not require your advice on how to raise my own daughter, just as I don't intend to instruct you on how you should raise yours.

The last time I saw them was at Anni's funeral. Maire's mother approached me first, giving me a firm, almost masculine handshake, looked me in the eye, and stated clearly and audibly: "My sincere condolences." Then she turned towards Maire, who was standing next to me with her eyes bleary from crying, placed a hand on her shoulder, and said: "Chin up, girl." They spoke some more, but at a whisper so I couldn't hear it. All the while, Maire's father was staring at me and appeared unable to find anything to say, until the pause stretched out to an uncomfortable length because mother and daughter were still conversing. Finally, he invited me to come and visit them again someday, or to perhaps go fishing with him on Lake Võrtsjärv, if I could find the time.

I promised I certainly would.

Yes, it's true: by now, enough time has passed for me to look back. And I now know that I should ask myself more. For example: am I sure that my proposal to Maire was influenced by her mischievous green eyes, her soft and slow kisses, her curves that promised unbelievable journeys, but were off-limits for as long as we fell into the bounds of merely a friendly goodbye? Or was it all out of some dark desire to replace my vista from a Mustamäe apartment with one that looked out across a spacious flower garden, to replace pea soup and cabbage stew with veal and banana pudding, to replace the constant fear of bosses' uninterpretable volitions with refuge behind the shield of an apparatchik's daughter? Like all men at that age, I was confident I could achieve everything I needed to achieve in life with my own two hands. But self-fulfillment required certain conditions. Even so, when I try now to visualize myself then, I can't find any kind of conscious plan to compromise in the name of a more comfortable life. Still, it might well have been the case that the person Maire was in my eyes already inherently included all that came with her—though I suppose we do always contain, to a certain degree, our own history, our own family, as well as the potential forking roads that lie ahead of us.

I had relatively little experience with girls before Maire. One reason for choosing to go to Tartu for university was, of course, the desire to get farther away from home, and my first semester in fact passed almost without a single visit to my mother and father. Naturally not because of my studies. My male classmates and I mainly drank, and from time to time there were girls in our company too. But I was certainly wise enough to figure out that there was no point in looking for flings among the people you're going to have to spend the next five years with, one way or another. On top of that, the prettiest girl in our class paired up with one of my classmates quite early on (I believe they're still together to this day), and I didn't have much of an interest in the other girls. I kept in close touch with my high-school friends—a whole lot of them had gone to study history and Estonian philology, and there was also a guy who went into chemistry and was in a number of the same college classes as me, although we hadn't gotten along especially well before.

But my hormones were raging, naturally. I'd almost lost my virginity already late that October, when some friends and I went to a dance where I met a Russian girl named Viktoria. She was studying sports medicine, was shorter than me and pretty cute, and had curly brown hair and dimpled cheeks. I knew from the other boys' chatter that Russian girls were generally loose and it didn't actually count if you slept with one—however, it paid to be on your guard and not stay for one more smoke in the morning, because if they sensed that you were quarry, they'd sink in their teeth and never let go. The looser they were, the more they felt the urge to marry—that's what we boys believed. Armed with this knowledge, I figured that a little fling with Viktoria wouldn't be at all out of the question. Still, I wasn't prepared for her inviting me up into her dorm room on the very first night I walked her home. We cautiously kissed for a little while in the hallway, and I could tell that more would come. But when Viktoria and I sat down on the edge of her bed, she started undressing purposefully without further ado, and ordered me to do the same. Someone softly snoring rolled over on the other side of the wardrobe divider, while a sleepy voice from another bed asked: "Vika, 's that you?" And the fourth bed next to the door was still empty, so it was possible someone else would be returning at some point. Thus, the situation was anything but romantic. I stopped Viktoria, we hugged a little while longer (quite passionately), and then I whispered that I had to go, but I'd come to see her soon, and I slipped out the door.

I knew that my dorm room would be empty the next weekend, because two of my roommates had both gone home already on Friday morning and the fourth—Andres, who was two years ahead of me—had been on Hiiumaa Island since the previous weekend. He'd gotten sick while he was there, so I could guess he probably wouldn't be coming back to Tartu before Monday morning. So, in the best case, we'd have privacy for the whole weekend. I cleaned the room to be as neat as I could make it, bought a cake and two bottles of red wine just in case, and went to pick up Vika. Luckily, I also remembered to buy a bouquet of flowers on the way—that's what you did back then. I hoped, of course, that none of my friends would spot me, because we tended to joke among ourselves that you could just give a girl dead rats instead of dead flowers—corpses, all the same. I'd never given a girl flowers before, and the shopkeeper looked at me a little strangely when I asked for two carnations and two roses—a considerable cultural faux pas, I soon found out. She asked what they were for, and when I said they were for a girl, she told me to buy three roses, instead. You live, you learn.

Vika didn't have anywhere to go for the weekend—she was from somewhere quite distant (Saratov, if I remember correctly) and was delighted to see me. The flowers were to her liking, too: she kissed me firmly on the cheek right then and there in front of all her girlfriends, at which point I apparently blushed, because they all started to laugh. She would have preferred to go out dancing again instead of straight to my place, but with her greater level of experience, she doubtless read from my face (even through my glasses) that there was no point in postponing the inevitable. I was astonished, however, to find Andres already in the room when we got there. He'd come back early because he needed to hand in a paper no later than Monday, and all the reference materials for writing it were at the library. So I had no other choice but to offer him wine and cake too. Keeping my cool, I tried, even so, to drop Andres the hint that Vika and I had more of a private engagement underway, but she, on the other hand, wouldn't hear a word about Andres leaving. When I returned from the shop with a third bottle of wine later, they'd already moved over to Andres's bed, and I had no other choice that night but to listen to their moaning and groaning until the morning came. Andres finally fell asleep sometime around 6 A.M., but Vika apparently heard my grumpy tossing and turning and called out with lust still lingering in her voice: "Enn? You awake? Be a darling and go fetch me a smoke, will you?"

Already then, it should have been clear to me that I'd never become a true ladies' man—the kind whose scent girls can pick up from a mile away. I'd never had a problem finding female friends, but maybe I understood them too well, because they felt like they could talk to me about everything, including other boys. Whenever I timidly attempted to touch them, they glared at me as if I was Mr. Bean—always coming and ruining everything beautiful. Even so, I did end up having a real thing with a pale, spritely girl whom I met somewhat by accident in the spring semester of my first year. We both went in the company of mutual friends to see a performance of Jaan Tooming's play *The New Devil of Hellsbottom*,[2] and it turned out that neither my friend nor girlfriend especially enjoyed it. Our friends decided to leave after the first act, but Katariina and I stayed to the end and were enthralled. We went to a few more plays together and were something like a couple. She was very modest, was studying Estonian philology, and somewhat

2 A play based on the novel of same name by Estonian classic A. H. Tammsaare. Satan strikes a deal with God that he will go and attempt to prove mankind is capable of achieving salvation, thus averting the disgruntled deity's plan to write off both Heaven and Hell.

resembled a little gray mouse, but could argue vehemently when something was important to her. Pretty much right away, I realized this "something" could only be literary or artistic: in her grounded, worldly life, Katariina allowed anything happening to her to simply happen. We went to cafés and the theater and the cinema, read Hesse and Kafka and Alliksaar together, debated Freud and Camus, and dreamed of a time when we could both stroll around Prague, Barcelona, or Amsterdam. We cared for each other. And naturally, we said   all of the words that are said in such instances, and I tried to convince myself that it really was love, that it really was happiness. Or, well, maybe I didn't—maybe it just was. What happens later does color what came before. We parted in the spring under the impression that we'd be together again in the fall. I was supposed to join a construction *malev*[3] (where I actually deeply missed her even when everyone else around me was giving their instincts free rein), while Katariina went back to her home in the vicinity of Koht-la-Järve, which she didn't invite me to visit because she had a strict religious mother who didn't want to know anything about her male friends. But when fall finally came, I found out that she had quit university. I tried to track her down and even wrote a letter that I sent to an address I got from her former roommates, but it was returned stamped: "Wrong address"; I suppose one of the numbers was incorrect. To this day, I don't know exactly what happened to her. I don't believe I played any part or that I'm to blame, but I can't be sure of it, either. In some of my darker moments, I've even asked myself whether the reason for Katariina's disappearance might have been an unintended child she didn't have the courage to tell me about, seeing how helpless she was in all practical matters. Still, it wasn't hard for me to

---

3 A malev is a traditional organized grouping of Estonian youth that gathers to socialize and conduct various paid or volunteer activities.

dispel such thoughts: no one could really be that awkward, could they? They just couldn't. And all in all, I suppose everyone is personally responsible for their own fate. To my own surprise (and what's there to hide—even a little unpleasantly), I realized before long that no matter how things were with Katariina, my heart hadn't been broken by the breakup. No doubt I would have been capable of finding her, too, if I'd made a real effort to do so.

And then came Maire.

Our natural trajectories shouldn't have intersected: I was studying biology; she, law. But life, as they say, makes its own adjustments. Our first meeting was rather run-of-the-mill, at a former schoolmate's birthday party. Maire was there with a snotty and unpleasant classmate, who acted as if he was her owner, or at least her manager, making joke after joke about how Maire nagged him incessantly and how he couldn't understand why. He commanded the attention of the entire group. Maire was no *femme fatale* then, nor was she later—at least not according to the general standard, which prefers brunettes to blondes and curls to straight hair. Even so, the gravitas and charm that she radiated lifted her several heads higher than all other girls, in my opinion—both at that birthday party and overall. She behaved as if she'd bequeathed an entirely unearned honor upon the entire city of Tartu with her presence, and so it was our duty to show gratitude for it. At the same time, she never and in no way gave the impression that anything around her was unfit or lacking in any other sense. The impression she left, suffice it to say, was tremendous. The next time I saw her was through the window of a café—she was sitting alone at a table with a barely sipped glass of white wine before her (it was one o'clock in the afternoon), reading a book concealed in a cover decorated by folk patterns. Since I didn't have anything ahead of me that day, I decided to seek out her company, and surprisingly, she didn't object. However, when I started listing options for what we could do next, she explained that the glass of wine was the only thing she intended to enjoy that day, and chiefly so as to compensate for the intellectual dearth in her reading materials from the 25th Congress of the CPSU[4], and although she might consider going to the cinema or the theater later in the evening, she couldn't be company for me in any simpler pleasures. I picked her up that night. Her parents had rented her a little two-room apartment on Kastani Street where she lived alone for the most part, although she would sometimes host friends who were in-between apartments. This likewise meant that she had a telephone, and could be called. She had an amazing effect on me. The dormant actor within me entered his golden age: with Maire around, I was able to tell even the most trivial of stories in such a way that everyone would break into raucous laughter, and I found the ability to argue the most iron-clad logic into a corner. I'd always been more cautious than impulsive, but if I sensed it might win her approval, I became capable of climbing up a drainpipe to a second-story window or chugging an entire bottle of champagne (whatever that might have proven). My monetary opportunities weren't exactly wide-ranging, but if I happened to be walking hand-in-hand with her past a flower shop on scholarship payday, then I would buy her an entire bucket of roses—even if that meant a longer diet of porridge. In short, I was in love, and harbored no doubts over what something both my male and female acquaintances tended to debate frequently back then: whether or not two people are capable of loving each other their entire lives. And naturally, I liked the person I was much more than who I'd been before, too. Maire probably did as well.

Before long, not a day went by that didn't end at her Kastani Street apartment, where an array of guests gathered regularly (the bulk of whom were, incidentally, male). Even then, Maire probably liked to think of herself as a salon hostess.

4 Communist Party of the Soviet Union

But the guests mainly drank tea, and when anyone arrived in a very spirited state of mind (which happened to me once also), it was implied rather firmly that they could leave and return some other day. There wasn't a bright future in store for that kind of a salon during our university years, and over time, only a few of Maire's more persistent admirers remained. In the end, it was just me.

It was spring. We'd already had our first kiss, and I was even permitted to tentatively reach my hand underneath her blouse, but those were the limits at first. I'm telling you all of these things mainly to clarify how different the world was back then. For our generation, the authorities had decided (in our moral interests) one was mature enough to see popular films such as *Angélique, the Marquise of the Angels* only at the age of sixteen. Back then, in 1973, it was the very first over-sixteen movie I was officially allowed to see (I'd snuck into others before), and to tell the truth, I don't understand to this day why anyone would want to see it at all. But I digress. I proposed to Maire in May, and as far as I was concerned, we could have rushed off to the Vital Statistics Department to be registered without delay. She, however, was convinced that young people should consider marriage for at least a year, and if they aren't disappointed in each other by the end of that period, then they truly can become a couple. I had no choice but to consent, because the most important thing—her hand—depended on me submitting to those conditions.

I've already written about what came next. We married in the summer of 1979, on the ninth of July, and lived together for just shy of twenty-four years. In spite of all of the arguments and disagreements that ultimately drove a wedge between us, I wouldn't be honest with myself if I didn't say: Maire was the greatest love of my life—maybe not because our love was great, but rather because there has simply been none greater than it.

Why am I addressing all this at such great length? The story isn't about me, now is it? I suppose it's as a disclaimer. That world really didn't provide me with anything to bestow upon my daughter and help her leap across the chasm. I certainly wasn't a better father than most men my age, but I'd very much like to believe I wasn't a worse one either.

I can still clearly remember the day Anni was born. It might have been one of the most beautiful days of my life. Spring came early that year, and for a brief spell in early May, Estonia was engulfed by a heat wave that could have heralded the dog days of summer. Women donned short skirts and almost translucent blouses, while men started feeling hot in their blazers. Maire was taken to the maternity hospital in Tallinn. Not the one we should have ended up at based on our place of residence, but instead under the care of the best doctor in all of Estonia. This mollified me, of course, even though there was allegedly no reason to worry, since Maire's pregnancy had gone by the book. She couldn't decide whether or not to do a caesarean, since on the one hand the whole process would be over much more quickly if she did, but on the other, it could leave a nasty scar, and then she might not be able to wear all kinds of bikinis on the beach anymore. Ultimately, the doctor told her quite bluntly that there was no reason for a C-section, and therefore her dilemma was a totally abstract one. I witnessed all of this through a window, since I naturally wasn't allowed in to see her. I could only loiter with the other fathers-to-be bunched along the hospital's façade, shouting up and trying to extract the replies meant for them from the collective and (thanks mainly to Maire and me) bilingual exchanges. Some of the cleverer couples had brought children's toy telephones, which their wives dangled from the window so they could converse in peace. I also went looking for one in the toy stores, and of course couldn't find any; but when my mother-in-law succeeded in acquiring one through her own channels, it was of no use anyway, because the hospital staff refused to accept it on Maire's behalf—she should have had it with her from the start.

It was a three-day weekend, and I'd come back from Tartu that Thursday. Maire's mother and father had taken a spontaneous trip out to Lake Võrtsjärv, so Elo and I were alone in the house. I'd gone to check on Maire the day before, of course. It was May 9th, Victory Day, and the city was swarming with veterans. Slightly boozy Russian grandpas, their chests plastered with medals, were also in full supply among the hospital visitors, which made verbal exchange more difficult than usual. For that reason, I didn't stay for very long, but instead decided to dedicate the rest of the day to homework that I'd been putting off for reasons easy to understand. I had to come back again the next day anyway. But things went otherwise: the telephone rang in the dead of night, and I was informed that Maire had started giving birth. We were asked to wait patiently. Elo and I both sat very anxiously by the phone for several hours before we finally received news that everything had gone just fine and another beautiful little girl had come into the world: 43 centimeters long and weighing 3,600 grams. We naturally rushed to see Maire the next day, but she was too exhausted to come to the window. I took oranges from home and picked up some flowers and chocolate on the way there: it hadn't occurred to me that Maire might not especially want them, but, well—at least she had something to offer the nurses to ensure she'd be taken care of.

I had a daughter. Would I have wanted a son instead? Maybe up until that moment, but the knowledge that I had a daughter erased all the earlier hopes and expectations from my mind in a single stroke. I was only able to see her a week later, when, together with my overwrought mother-in-law and my father-inlaw stoically enduring the situation, we went to pick up her and Maire. I don't remember very much from that drive. What can I say—the night before, after they'd returned from Lake Võrtsjärv, Maire's parents and I had downed a fair number of shots to celebrate the good health of the world's newest citizen. The news hadn't reached them immediately, since the local mailman who was supposed to have delivered the telegram was in the clutches of one of those sudden flus that always struck him after a long, national-holiday weekend. So there was already a good amount of agitation in the air, especially with my mother-in-law constantly instructing my father-in-law on how to drive. But we did get there, no matter that it was a few minutes later than planned. Maire, pale and strikingly thin, was already sitting downstairs in the waiting room. I was called upstairs, and a merry-eyed nurse holding a pink bundle of blanket asked: "Are you Enn Padrik? Here's a young lady who would like to meet you."

How scared I was! My whole theory of fatherhood vanished from my mind in a single moment, and my relationship with that tiny being started from scratch—from a completely clean slate. I was afraid to breathe on her (I could already tell from Maire's expression that my breath was far from pure due to the effects of the previous day); I was afraid my clumsy arms would be unable to hold her as she should be held. I stared at her, and she stared back. She had my Grandma Anni's eyes—large, translucent, and a deep shade of blue.

I'd considered naming our child after one of our grandparents, no matter whether from Maire's side of the family or mine; but now it was all clear to me. Maire had a different idea, though. When we broached the subject a couple of days later, she thought our child should be given a "cultural" name such as Madeleine or Marilyn. I reckoned the name should be something that any Estonian would be able to pronounce properly. It was a fair argument. But I agreed something more contemporary would be the best fit. Gerly, Carol, Kätlin. Perhaps Kristel. Maybe Reelika. "Yes," her new grandmother piped up. "Reelika would

be great." One of my coworker's sons had named his daughter
Reelika. "Well, it's decided," Maire said. "Not at all," I protested,
although I didn't want to wind it up into an argument either—
Maire was understandably exhausted from childbirth and
constantly irritated by every small thing. "Well, why can't she
have two names, then?" Maire's father asked, coming to my aid.
"That would be very nice," Elo also agreed. "Sure," said I. Anni-
Reelika Padrik. And that's where we left it.

She was an ideal child. It was easy for us to think that, of course,
since we saw her significantly less than parents usually do during
their child's first years. I had my last semester of college ahead
of me, which consisted mostly of an internship and writing my
thesis, while Maire had two more years to go. She didn't want to
take a year off either, since it wouldn't get any easier afterward
with a child. Her breast milk ran out after only a few weeks, so
after that, Anni was raised on the wonderful products of the
Russian chemical industry. It gave her a few allergies later in
life, but not so many as to be a bother. We had every reason to
be incredibly thankful to Maire's family—especially to Elo and
her mother, of course. Whenever we managed to go to Saue
for a few days, each moment spent together was pure quality
time. Anni would be there waiting for us, dressed in nice clean
clothes and seemingly overjoyed by our arrival (true, she wasn't
shy around people and was probably brightened up by more or
less everyone). She was so darling that it made me swoon. At
night, she cried very little and only briefly, and as soon as you
handled whatever the problem was, she'd fall right asleep again.
In short, she was a young parent's dream.

Her grandmother tended to spoil her too much, of course. It
didn't make her stubborn, but it still left a mark. She liked to be
liked; she needed each and every little thing she did to spark a
burst of delight in whoever was watching. When we were taking

a walk in the woods one time, she leapt off a tree stump, but the performance wasn't followed by jubilant applause from Maire or me, so she nearly broke down in tears. We honestly didn't understand what the episode was all about, but Anni specifically thought that the jump had somehow been (it just *had* to be, unlike all the ones that had preceded it) a total failure. And as a result, she spent that entire afternoon practicing jumping off of a rock in the backyard—only the prospect of meringue pie and ice cream was finally able to coax her away from the episode of intense personal development.

Those traits didn't disappear with time: her constant craving for acknowledgement and approval from the people around her at any point, and extreme determination when working to accomplish her goals. Neither of these were negative characteristics in the least, the way I see it; it's excellent when a person doesn't actually have any worse flaws. For her sake, I have to say, furthermore, that she never tended to be satisfied with the standards of those around her. She only measured herself by absolutes. That was also the reason why Anni, in spite of her perseverance, quit figure skating and piano lessons as soon as she figured it was possible to do so. For she'd already realized she wouldn't be the next Irina Rodnina or Teresa Carreño.

She also learned over time to conceal her thirst for recognition, since she realized that when she expected approval so plainly and openly, it could fail to come as a result. But this benefitted Anni greatly at school, since her teachers usually liked when a student wanted to be to their liking. Her picture was tacked up on the honor board already in the first grade. I do understand this was mostly because *someone* from her class had to be on the honor board, even when all of the first-year children were given top scores in every subject on their report cards because such was the teacher's educational principle. Anni was naturally a very suitable candidate to be singled out, because in spite of her overwhelming number of extracurricular activities, ranging from figure skating to piano lessons, she actually did—without a doubt—deserve it. A's in every subject; and on top of that, she was able to stress the right sections of the poetry she recited in her childish voice in front of a full school auditorium; and on top of that, she was very photogenic too.

She looked better in pictures than in real life, since although it goes without saying that she was the prettiest girl in the whole world to me as her father, if I'm to tell the truth, I must at least now, in retrospect, admit that she might actually have been a little plain in terms of appearance. Aside from my mother's blue eyes, she didn't inherit anything from my side of the family as far as looks go. Anni resembled her mother less than she did her aunt—she had the same kind of weasel-like face, although while Elo's lively personality danced across her features constantly, Anni's inner confidence kept it in check. Her deep, dark eyes likewise added a sheen to Elo's looks. Even Anni's hair was the same potato-skin shade as Elo's; they didn't contract into curls though, but were rather straight like her mother's. She was one of the tallest girls in her class—but those kinds of features can be more of a problem at that age, since she was placed in front of most of the boys in gym class, which is something boys generally don't appreciate. All the same, she got along very well with her classmates and often invited them to come over. Especially when they could still be in the garden in fall and spring, two or three of her girlfriends would always be running and squealing out there. An entire flock of them would sometimes descend during the weekend, which meant there wasn't much chance of escaping them inside either.

I'm reminded of one instance that I believe is a good illustration of Anni's character. Students were instructed to take their most precious toy to school with them the following day, then show it to the others and tell some kind of a story about it. Anni relayed this information to us, and we spent an evening in collective discussion of what her most precious toy might be. She had several fancy foreign dolls, even a few that were generally kept behind glass in a cupboard and only taken out on rare occasion so they wouldn't get dirty. And she had a little pony with thick plastic hair that would change color by way of some electrical effect when it was brushed. And she also had an old-fashioned toy car, a 1920s Packard, which might have suited a boy better, but when Anni was pretending that her dolls were going out for a walk, she would always park the car behind them, and when I asked why, she answered matter-of-factly that they hadn't gone from home to the park on foot—that would be too far. The dolls alternated, but the Packard stayed the same. And then there was the gigantic fuzzy bunny that was certainly very cute, but impractical, seeing as how she would've had a hard time dragging it to school. We even got into an argument with Maire's family over what toy would be the most sensible to take, and poor little Anni overheard us. She would gladly have taken the whole lot of them, since each of us praised our own favorite so convincingly that she simply had to agree with us all. In the end, our collective decision was made in favor of a German doll that was the right size to fit in her bag next to her school things—a doll that was extremely beautiful and rare (so there was no question that anyone else in her class might have anything like it), and that was, at the same time, something Anni had actually played with once in a while, too.

We all ended up being in a bit of a rush the next morning. It was raining and I drove Anni to school, after which I headed to work. In the car, I asked her one more time if she had her toy with her, and she replied that of course she did. But moments after I got to work, Maire called me, at a loss for what to do, since it turned out that the German doll was still back at home on the table. I told her Anni had confirmed to me that everything was A-OK when we were in the car. At first, Maire wanted to go and take Anni's doll to school, but we ultimately decided it would be better not to: if our girl had done something wrong, then let her deal with the consequences. Nevertheless, upon arriving home that evening, Anni told us her teacher had praised her presentation.

"But how can that be?" I asked.

"You left your doll at home, didn't you?"

"I had Muki with me," Anni explained. Muki was a tattered and greasy foam-rubber dog that she had slept with for so many years that one of its front legs was in serious danger of falling off.

"But why'd you take Muki?" I asked.

"The teacher said we should bring our most precious toy," she said, shrugging, "and Muki's my most precious."

By the way, she'd been lauded for her presentation specifically because she told the class about how she had all kinds of pretty dolls and a perfect old-fashioned model car and a big bunny and a pony, but the most precious one of all to her was Muki— so what that he was already old and worn-out.

We'd been lucky with Anni's homeroom teacher—or at least that's what everyone thought. She was undoubtedly an experienced educator, slightly younger than my mother but still from the older generation of teachers, and putting Anni in the other class would undoubtedly have been a worse option because none of those children took their own teacher, a grossly overweight natural history instructor, seriously. Ours, Mrs. Mäeorg, on the other hand, showed a real concern for her students, and went to great lengths to get them ballet tickets at least once a month. The children were even transported there in their own bus, since the father of one of the boys in Anni's class was the director of the city bus fleet. When I asked Anni how she liked a performance after attending, she always replied that she liked it a lot; but when the question came up once whether she might like to go to the ballet with her mother and grandmother, she was flabbergasted— for her, the ballet had been part of schoolwork, and it would have been absurd to want to do anything like that in her free time. I'd certainly heard other good things about Mrs. Mäeorg from other parents, and Anni was just as fond of her as any good student will be of their first teacher. But I had some doubts, too. Anni always spoke a little too much Soviet-talk at home after Mrs. Mäeorg's classes; would gush about the Ulyanov family's Society of Clean Plates; and before we even knew it, she started licking her plate clean after lunch. Maire and I discussed whether or not we should bring up the cult of Lenin at home, but my wife was firmly against it and of the opinion that it was still too early—if we did so, we'd ruin Anni's relationship with her teacher, and besides, operating successfully in Soviet society meant being able to maintain a normal relationship with its institutions. No doubt she would ultimately figure things out on her own.

The issue became a bit more acute in the spring of Anni's first year at school. We had decided to throw a birthday party for her, and invited almost half the class. Maire ordered a large cake from Tallinn specially for the occasion, and Anni's grandmother had busied herself preparing sandwiches and salads since early morning. I didn't send Anni to school that day either. The day before had been a holiday, and I'd decided that Anni wouldn't go to town with the other Little Octobrists to bring flowers to the veterans gathering in front of the Bronze Soldier statue. Several of the children invited to Anni's party ended up having to cancel because of that event, because Mrs. Mäeorg had demanded that the girls wear their school uniforms and white blouses—without jackets, mind you—and a number of them had caught colds in the biting wind. But the worst was yet to come. In spite of a few cancellations, Anni's party went swimmingly— there were enough guests to form trivia teams as well as to fill all the house's secret nooks and crannies with hide-andseekers just fine. The next day, however, Mrs. Mäeorg called me and demanded to know why Anni had been absent on her birthday without good cause, and why she'd also failed to show up and "defend the honor of the school" the day before. At first, I didn't understand the teacher was talking about Anni not going to greet the veterans.

"Am I to draw any conclusions about your personal views from this, Comrade Padrik?" the teacher asked. "Especially considering you're connected to a family in the position that it's in?" This was all funny to me, but it soon turned out that she really had contacted Maire's father to ask how it was possible for someone who held such an important position in the Party to merely look on calmly while his grandchild decided to spit on our veterans' heroic deed. Maybe her wording hadn't been so intense, but nevertheless, she managed to absolutely enrage my normally tranquil father-in-law. It was the only time that Anni was shamed in front of her classmates, and although they didn't take it seriously, she herself was extremely irritated by what happened and informed me that on next year's Victory Day, she would go without question to bring flowers to the heroes who'd saved the world from fascism, since her teacher told her that otherwise, she should simply be ashamed and embarrassed of herself. I felt so badly for her.

That being said, it was incredibly puzzling to hear what kind of a speech Mrs. Mäeorg gave the second-grade students the next fall. According to Anni, more than half of the children wore pins with the Estonian tricolor flag on it—something previously unheard of—when they attended the opening ceremony for the school year. That hot summer of 1988 hadn't passed uneventfully for the teacher either. Her former worldview had been replaced by a wholly new one, at the center of which were Jesus Christ and the Virgin Mary. And as you might expect, her rhetoric had turned nationalist through and through. She now permitted children to talk openly and proudly about all those things that until then could only be discussed at home in secret with moms and dads, since the back of the beast had been broken and, before long, free Christians would be able to fill their lungs with free air while walking on free soil once more. To tell the truth, I was stunned, and wanted to start checking on whether it might be possible to transfer Anni to some other school, since it made me a little sick to my stomach to think about how my daughter's outlook on life was being shaped by someone who personally lacked (or so I thought) any kind of a conscience. Maire only smirked and asked whether I really believed I'd find a school somewhere with no teachers like that. Well, true—I suppose we all know that adaptation is the key to survival. She might even have been right, but it gave me a nasty feeling all the same, and when Mrs. Mäeorg called me once, later, to see whether spiritual values were held in high enough esteem at Anni's home, inquiring if we were members of any congregation, I said flatly that she could draw any conclusions she pleased about my views, but that I wasn't about to start discussing them with her because I'd already drawn my own conclusions about *hers*. Maire took care of contact between home and school after that. Still, even she did so in a chilly but polite tone, and not long after, we moved out of Saue and Anni enrolled in a new school in Tallinn—my very own alma mater, which now bore its pre-Occupation name of Gustav Adolf Grammar School again.

I've spoken very little about my own family up to this point, which is also natural, because we did speak to Maire's parents every day for as long as we lived under the same roof, but met with mine more infrequently. Today I feel embarrassed by it. Especially when I consider my father, his final months. Now I myself am also conscious of what it means to know you're going to die. He asked about Anni whenever we spoke together on the phone, and we always agreed to get together soon, but somehow never did. My father never criticized me for it and, well, I did go and visit him on my own from time to time too. Or, occasionally, I guess. He never complained. But, on the other hand, I suppose I myself don't really outwardly project how the need for a loved one can sometimes scream so loudly that it silences even cancer.

Things were different for us after we moved to Tallinn. My father may not have been around anymore, but my mother visited us frequently. At first Anni didn't want to hear one word about relocating. Our new home was in a Stalinist apartment building in relatively decent condition on Tehnika Street, and had three separate rooms and a kitchen. The ceilings were high but the layout wasn't exactly ideal, and one of the rooms was significantly smaller than the others. Since it wouldn't do for a living room, nor for our master bedroom, Anni was the one who had to switch her spacious second-story room with its huge windows in our Saue home for the much darker, longer, and narrower chamber. Naturally, she wasn't all that enthused about the prospect. But when we explained to Anni that her old room in Saue would essentially continue being hers and that she could always go to visit her grandparents and sleep there again just like she used to, she finally made peace with the situation; or at least she stopped bringing it up. Actually, Maire didn't take to our new home very well either. That is to say she was, of course, glad in principle that we were living on our own and that nothing would disturb our privacy; and naturally, I had been lucky to get that apartment on the basis of the old waiting list, since we knew all too well that many of our friends who had similarly been biding their time to get their own living quarters for many a long year had suddenly been informed that the communist regime's presents had run out—that now, they could only acquire a new apartment if they had the money to pay for it, and this for an amount that wasn't inconsequential, to say the least.

In any case, we had the place all to ourselves. It took a couple of months to complete the renovations after we'd been given the keys, which had left us quite short on cash, so at first, we were only able to furnish it with some used pieces of furniture that we wouldn't be reluctant to dispose of later. We also raided both the shed in Saue and the attic in Mustamäe for old furnishings. In the end, we made it quite cozy. It was, at any rate, our own space where we were left alone and disengaged from the big, messy world outside, which had crept up closer than it had in Saue; beginning right outside the apartment door—in the foul and invariably piss-drenched stairwell, progressing on to the butter lines and the trams packed with stoically silent passengers, and extending from there into our terrifying imaginations, which the ever-freer press was serving up ripe and ready. I can remember to this day how, for example, in the weeks following the cruel and pointless killing of two Swedish union-leaders in January 1991, my pace quickened all on its own when I walked home down empty streets on dark winter nights, and how my apartment door seemed to swing open into a different and righter reality. At first, it was even a little strange with just the three of us there, but a television soon became our fourth family member, and everything was more or less as it had always been. It's possible that period—our first couple of years on Tehnika Street—truly was the happiest time of my life. You only realize something like that in hindsight. We lived our lives and kept in touch with all our relatives consistently, but only when we ourselves wanted it. I had a pretty fascinating job, and the world around us was going through an interesting time, in spite of everything. Life was hard during those final years of the Soviet Union, of course—shelves were empty, and if we hadn't had Maire's parents' access to the privileged grocery stores, our diet would definitely have been much more meager than it was; but even that wasn't so important.

And what delighted me even more was the fact that we could attend theater performances to our heart's content in the capital. We always needed to seat my mother next to Anni when we did, and when we got back home that evening, we would all discuss the performance at length, since she had already gone to see almost all the plays before us. That was a time when theater somewhat played the role of history textbooks and basic national-enlightenment digests. Sold-out auditoriums guzzled the words spoken from the stage more than they paid attention to the playwright's signature or the actors' performance— words that dared to say more; that dared to speak out about the deportations, and about homosexuality, and whatever else. In short, they were words that spoke about everything that had been entirely non-existent in our previous world. Understandably, every upstanding citizen had to attend such performances and see them all. I'm not talking about myself, of course—for me, theater had always been one of the things that made life worth living in the first place. I tried to pass this appreciation on to Anni as much as I could and took her to all the age-appropriate plays there were, but they didn't engage her all that much; no more than an interesting school project, in any case. Afterward, though, when we were discussing them, it was clear that Anni had watched the plays very perceptively and, even as a child, was able to differentiate between what was genuine and what was contrived in the actors' performance.

Anni and my mother got along very well. It wasn't simply incidental that for decades, she had been many a student's favorite teacher, of course. From a very young age, Anni was taught interesting secret-language phrases by her grandmother, and when she was later required to take extra lessons after switching from a regular class to a special French-immersion one at her new school, it turned out that she actually already possessed a considerable foundation—even though she'd acquired it while playing. And as soon as the opportunity came, I naturally also subscribed to the French ARTE television channel so that my own proficiency wouldn't slip away, and so that Anni could pick up as much as she practically could.

Yet another cause for delight— Anni had readily adopted our family's traditional Francophilia. Especially since France was inching closer and closer all the time. Gone were the days when, standing in front of the chalkboard at school, I had to recite in detail how to walk from the Louvre to Notre-Dame—all without any realistic hope that I would ever actually complete that route (even though that knowledge did happen to be of practical use to me once) and for a teacher who didn't have the heart to even dream about traveling to France anymore.

My mother hadn't included me in her linguistics club, for understandable reasons. My mother regarded Maire's family with mild contempt (which they either didn't notice or had simply decided not to pay attention to), although the gifts she gave them on holidays were always chosen with care and were truly relished by their recipients. Our parents encountered one another more rarely now, since we tried not to invite them to our apartment at the same time with the obvious exception of Anni's birthday, and without us, they wouldn't have had any reason to interact at all. I can't say my mother was all that bothered by Maire's parents' apparatchik past (since they hadn't pulled off anything ridiculous back then), but she wasn't exactly accepting of their outlook on life either.

Oddly enough, it was political issues that eventually sparked the first substantial arguments between Anni and us. I can't say that my own views were clearly formulated in any way, shape, or form; and as time has gone on, I've voted for different parties in the elections according to whichever I believe is lying the least. By and large, I'm merely the sort of honest, simple patriot who wants Estonia to do well, and for all its people to do so likewise. It might not be a very well-thought-out platform, but it's enough for me. Maire, on the other hand, was a very avid follower of current affairs and always ready to debate them at length. Nor was it any wonder—that world had intrigued her from a very young age. However, her views weren't especially stable. On the whole, she almost always defended the stances of whoever was in power at the time. This typically happened at night in front of the TV, and as if by a curse, exactly when the sports news was just starting. But nothing could stop her, of course. When reminded that one or another of her statements was the polar opposite of the previous government's position, which she'd approved of just months before, Maire would narrow her eyes and say it actually *had* been right from a certain standpoint, but that I needed to take a look at the bigger picture. Or something similar to that. Just like all women, she had the ability to alter her memories fantastically, and was dead certain that she'd spoken of things only in the exact way that she remembered.

This irked Anni at some point. She wouldn't leave the matter of her grandfather's Communist Party career alone.

"But those were different times that you know nothing about," Maire argued, "and you need be grateful to your grandparents for what they did. Because you had everything."

This didn't satisfy Anni. "They were who they were," she said. "I'm not condemning them; but why say you were hollowing it out from within the whole time when we all know it's a lie? It's embarrassing. And there's no point pretending to be some kind of a mega-patriot with a background like that, you know."

Maire cited a theory according to which only seven percent of people possess the ability to lead others, and that it is their obligation to do so no matter what the circumstances. Anni heard her out attentively and never raised the subject again. But when Maire once got to talking about, I think, income tax or strict immigration policies during Sunday breakfast, Anni told her about a classmate who had to move from a house in the cozy Lilleküla neighborhood that was being returned to its pre-Occupation owners to a cramped, pre-fabricated apartment in the Lasnamäe district. It was only Anni's friend and her mother there, because the father had up and left during the process and since the mother's job (typist) was eliminated over the course of technological advance, they simply had nothing to put on the table.

I have to say that, as I observed their arguments, I was amazed by them both equally: by Maire's skilled debating and flawless knowledge of current affairs, as well as Anni's improve-the-world stubbornness. And I felt that they mutually complemented each other, and that it helped them both to maintain a clear gaze. That was definitely true, to some extent. I certainly didn't share Maire's conviction that if anyone in free Estonia faced hard times, then it was entirely their own fault—that with a little bit of initiative and enough work, a leafy limb is within anyone's reach; nor, however, did I agree with Anni, who believed that society must always guarantee equal opportunities to everyone and that if someone falls behind the rest, then a common effort should be made to help him or her catch up—no matter whether or not that "someone" has managed to accomplish anything in the name of their own advancement. I wasn't totally on board with either view. No population can truly thrive if it is only capable of existing under laboratory conditions; but on the other hand, humankind isn't just any old population either. And so I played the part of a third party in their conversations very well—keeping one in check one time, and the other another. Their habit of debating faded after a while. Apparently, both sides' arguments had lost their freshness as time passed.

That brief interval during which we were financially well-off also coincided with our time on Tehnika Street—back when I took a job at a company that a friend of mine started up, which I think I already mentioned once. Over those years, we finally furnished our apartment decently, we even took a couple of family vacations to Crete and the Algarve, and Maire began looking into getting our very own house. But then I quit my job, which she didn't approve of at all, of course; even though

I got a position at the ministry that came with a completely respectable salary. Six months later, when my friend's company became tangled up in some scandal and went belly up, I was very much pleased with my decision. Maire still worked part-time at a notary's office and, all in all, we got by just fine.

In grammar school, Anni was just like children usually are at that age. She withdrew further into herself and didn't include us in her plans very much, except in those generally rare instances when she needed money. We gave her enough so that she shouldn't have to feel ashamed, but not so much that she might squander it. We didn't debate the world's bigger problems all that much anymore, but we were always clued-in to her school affairs. And she never played music too loudly in her room. What more could we have wanted?

She graduated with honors, naturally; but it's not as if we expected anything less from her. She was number one on the university acceptance list for French studies. Maire and I were ecstatic. What did I really know about my daughter at that point—about her as a person? I can honestly say: almost nothing.

3

THE SENSATION OF BEING in Paris came slowly. Every airport is, needless to say, an airport first and foremost, no matter what language its signs might be in, and there are always more foreigners on the train to the city than there are locals. I stared out the window while a woman singing arias in Romanian passed me with her hat extended, and continued staring even when three jolly black men began singing French seamen's songs, one of them accompanying the others on accordion. Because it could have been happening anywhere else, too. The same cosmopolitan hustle and bustle even persisted at Châtelet Station. I transferred to a southbound train. The hotel I'd made a reservation at online was located quite close to the Latin Quarter and I had a Google Maps print-out of how to get there, but I somehow still managed to get lost. The street names were entirely different from what they should have been and when I asked for directions, no one knew French—at least not the kind of French that I tried speaking to them. *I really should've taken a taxi from the metro station,* I thought, but according to my calculations, I was so close now that it would have been embarrassing—even if there had been a taxi anywhere in sight. I had no reason to be trying to save money, understandably; but alas, old habits are hard to break. I stood on a street corner and peered around, looking a little helpless.

It had been different the last time. When was that? Sometime around Christmas 2003, eight years ago. I was there with my mother then—I'd bought her the trip for her birthday. I knew she wouldn't like celebrating her jubilee the usual way because of the overwhelming amount of masquerading it demanded from all parties involved, at least in her mind. We had spoken about it in depth ten years earlier—right after her sixtieth birthday. Then, she felt like the preceding celebration had been an obligation that was as tiring to her former students and younger colleagues as the multiple-day process of cleaning the house had been for her, a process after which she could no longer seem to find anything at home. Some of the guests she'd especially hoped to see failed to make the trip out to Kuusalu, while some of those she hadn't especially hoped would appear ended up staying the night. And providing food had been a difficult task, too, because it was right at the time when stores already had everything, but people's pockets weren't holding very much. I wasn't reluctant to buy her whatever her heart desired, of course, but she herself didn't want anything aside from a balance being maintained: that no one regard the offering as meager, but neither for them to feel like a poor guest at a rich feast. "I won't be doing that again," my mother sighed afterward, and therefore taking her to Paris for her next big birthday seemed just right. Especially since she had been there only once before—she took a wearying bus trip to the country almost right after Estonia's re-independence, but her fellow travelers had turned out to be insufferable and preferred the Tati Department Store over the Orsay Museum. And we both, of course, wanted to see how Anni was getting along there.

We stayed in Montmartre then. I knew my mother wanted to be in that neighborhood by any means necessary, so that she could breathe the same air her beloved Impressionists had a century before. Anni came to meet us at the airport, and we didn't really care to take in much more than each other on the way to the hotel. I was amazed by her. Not even so much by how cheerful and bubbly she appeared, but by her fluidity— by her ability to handle the unfriendly automatic ticket dispensers and make her way through complex spaces—by her complete immersion into the immense and colorful whole that surrounded us, as if she really was a natural part of it. And I suppose that was true, even though she was still unmistakably our little Anni, all the same.

But that place, that great colorful whole—already then, it really was something unlike France. That is to say—it was something unlike the France my mother had taught me, from books and pictures, to love, and which her own spirit hadn't allowed to be extinguished. We saw *that* France there, too, of course; but firstly in a form packaged up for foreigners—on the trinket tables near sightseeing locations, where Africans and Arabs tried to fob it off on us. So, essentially, that wasn't really *that* France either. And we saw more of it later (a rather genuine version by that time) when Anni took us to meet her friends. But most of the time, we first had to make the best of the new version that had digested the empire's counterblow— one that mildly frightened and slightly disturbed me all at once, but which my mother was able to enjoy with unexpected receptiveness. When I tried to warn her about the risks of taking nighttime strolls, she stopped me with a soft smile and explained that criminals of all races and ethnicities are like dogs, which means they only pay attention to you when you're afraid of them. It took all the patience I had to keep calm when she struck up a conversation with some Arab miscreants having a smoke on a street corner, asking them where you could get a good but cheap meal nearby; and then I had to muster all the persuasiveness I could to convince her not to visit the place they'd recommended—a "Chez Ali."

"Why not?" she asked in sincere disbelief. "It'd be awfully interesting to try a proper couscous."

I promised her that we could go to an exotic restaurant when we were walking around with Anni on one of the following days, but insisted that we stick to European cuisine while we were out on our own. She consented (albeit somewhat disappointedly), and when we did go and order couscous at a Lebanese place in the Latin Quarter two days later, she only ate a little of it, even though I was completely sure they made it better at that establishment—or at least with not so spicy a sauce.

On the other hand, the square behind Sacré-Coeur that was filled with street artists who'd converged from all across Europe seemed quite genuine to both of us, even though the paintings being sold at steep prices weren't all that much more interesting than the watercolors on sale at any Toompea viewing platform in Tallinn. And when we were descending the wide stairs in front of the church to meet Anni by the carousel, well—it's hard to imagine any stronger sensation of being in Paris. Or at least it seemed that way then. I believe that, if I were to stand right there on that same staircase, hearing the sweet music of the carousel, the exact feeling would return to me now, even though I've started to think differently about the city in the meantime. Simply as a memory, simply as something that possesses special meaning for me—so what if it's built upon a corny cliché? That was one of the first days after the divorce when I felt like life was still worth living. But that day, then and there, I wasn't capable of experiencing that kind of feeling anymore, and therefore I wasn't planning on returning to Montmartre either. Even so, one of the addresses I needed to visit wasn't far—that of some young woman who was Anni's roommate for a short time not long before she moved back to Estonia. Her name was Corinne. I'd met her briefly on that trip with my mother, but it was hardly likely she'd remember me. I deeply hoped that she still lived at her old address, or that if she didn't, that the new residents would help to put me on her trail—even though it was slightly crazy to bet on that last possibility.

I've always enjoyed reading crime novels. Especially classic English ones—and it's never bothered me in the least that the murders committed using all kinds of clever means are somehow clean and proper, or in any case extremely far from the real world and life's actual twists and turns. And instead of grim, tormenting hatreds, they are wrapped up in crafty mysteries that the detective cracks open like walnuts while he drops witty remarks left and right. Of course, I imagined myself in that same role when I read them, though I never guessed in my wildest dreams that I'd actually end up doing something similar one day. Be that as it may, I never quite liked the kind of crime novels where the ending is revealed at the very beginning, and our job is to merely watch how it's reached. Back then, at the start, I really did think the mystery that loomed before me was no different.

I didn't believe, of course, that Paris might hold the key to explaining Anni's death, but I knew that something important had happened to her there—something which she hadn't told me about at the time. Something which might shed new light on some seemingly insignificant detail I was already aware of—something which might become a thread or reveal other connections. All in all, I needed to put together a very large puzzle without having the slightest clue of who or what the final picture was. And you've got to start somewhere.

First of all, though, I had my hands full just trying to find my accommodations. My temples were pulsing from the red wine I'd drunk on the plane, and my stomach was growling. The street wasn't all that crowded, which seemed relatively odd given the closeness of the Latin Quarter, and when I tried to address a dour-looking man—the only person to walk past me on the same side of the street in ten minutes—he didn't even stop, but just shrugged and didn't break stride. A little while later, though, a taxi pulled up next to me without being hailed. Luckily, I had enough smarts to tell the driver the address first and not lug my bag into the backseat, because he only sniggered and pointed straight ahead. Sure enough, I found the right sign a couple hundred meters away. I was greeted at the reception

desk by an exuberant and energetic *madame*, who firstly asked
if I was in Paris on business, and when I gave some vague reply,
she went on to say that I could certainly do a little bit of work if
there was no avoiding it, of course, but that the city is generally
meant more for enjoying oneself. I promised I'd do my best,
and when I handed her the key after exiting my room half an
hour later, she nodded approvingly.

The café I was headed to was the source of my second
memory set in that really real France, which I'd imagined
for myself. Anni had taken us there on that trip eight years
earlier. I'd forgotten the name of the establishment, but could
vaguely remember that it was located across from a cinema that
specialized in especially complex artistic films, and was in a
small alleyway right near the Sorbonne, just a couple steps away
from Rue des Écoles. For a moment, I felt like I should already
be in the right place, just that the cinema and the café were
missing; but then I walked on another ten meters, and found
my destination.

I entered the café, and everything was exactly the same
as it had been so many years ago. Godard and Chabrol film
posters hung on the dark walls together with quite a few that
were unfamiliar to me, a few old Jean Gabins among them.
Occupying the tables were young intellectuals with airs about
them identical to the ones in my memory—youths who
undoubtedly opposed all kinds of stereotypes, but personally
represented the stereotype of the young French intellectual in
the absolute purest form. It just so happened that the only open
table was one in the back corner—the very same at which my
mother, Anni, her friends, and I sat eight years ago. I took a seat
in the same chair I'd occupied back then, if memory served me
correctly. My mother had been sitting next to me, Anni across
and Hervé at her side, followed by Yves and then Corinne.
There had been one more girl, but I couldn't remember her
name and Anni hadn't written much about her in her letters

either. Thinking back upon that group now, I for some reason imagine a young man nicknamed "Android" being among them—a man without whom this entire story might have gone differently. And if he *could* have been there among them, then maybe he would have been a different person, also. But we were who we were, because we'd been exactly where we'd been at every point in our lives. What can you do.

Hervé was studying at the same political-sciences institute that Anni had been lucky enough to get a scholarship to attend, and it seemed like he had at least a little bit of a crush on her. But Anni wasn't interested in him. Yves was Hervé's friend and was studying philosophy at Sorbonne Nouvelle. Corinne, his girlfriend, wasn't studying anything ("For now," Yves remarked), but merely worked as a waitress in a café. What that other girl did, I can't remember. I guess she was simply there with Corinne.

Shortly after my mother and I had been introduced to Anni's friends and we'd exchanged a few words with them in our slightly stiff French, the tempo of conversation sped up so much and its content became so complex that we couldn't really keep up with them anymore—not that I would have had much to contribute to that discussion in those days. The topic was something that was stirring up a lot of passion at the time— whether or not Muslim girls living in France should be allowed to wear headscarves at school. Sometime later, when Anni was back in Estonia and living with me for a while, it evolved into one of our favorite debates—something that one of us would bring up sooner or later as an illustration when we were discussing whatever other topic. We'd forget whatever we'd been talking about before and often used the exact same arguments over and over again—to the point of fighting and weeping, depending on the situation. But that evening in Paris, I was hearing the debate for the very first time. Hervé was of the opinion that limiting what someone can wear is undemocratic, and that in a true democratic state, Muslims must be able to make their own choices as freely as everyone else. Thus, even though he himself didn't believe that the religious custom of hiding one's hair fits with the values of secular society, that secular society itself shouldn't be able to restrict the right to exercise customs either. Yves's position was a sharp polar opposite. A school is a public institution and therefore must strictly adhere to the system of values upon which the given society is built, and its separation from the Church (from any kind of a church) is undoubtedly a standard, where no concessions may be made.

"But if a non-Muslim girl wanted to wear a headscarf at school simply because she likes it—then, could she?" Anni interrupted them to ask.

"Yeah, sure she could," Yves replied. Then, Hervé made some complex point and Yves replied even more complexly and at the other end of the table, Corinne started speaking with her friend at a whisper about something else altogether. The way I saw it, the whole issue was relatively trivial. No one commanded those Muslims to move to France, now did they? I tried to say something to that effect, but Hervé and Yves both stared at me in bewilderment for a brief moment—just a moment, as if I were some kind of an alien—before they delved right back into their debate. I realized that I'd said something completely inappropriate. Now, of course, I understand this all too well; I actually grasped it before the end of that trip, and felt embarrassed. I did perceive that Anni was feeling a little uncomfortable already, since it was obvious that the boys' discussion interested her—and maybe not solely the discussion, but one of the boys as well. Yet, at the same time, she also apparently felt obligated to speak to us, and now I'd gone and said something totally out of line and indicated what kind of a backwoods place she came from. "*Alors*," my mother spoke up, "on the one hand, you can certainly reason that a school has the right to regulate the way its students dress; but when it does so, then it transforms its character and becomes similar to an army—doesn't it, now?—because it is exercising the same right by which an army clothes thousands of individuals in its uniforms and thus takes away their individuality—*hein?*—but if that's the case, then it turns out that schools are tasked not with helping people develop freely, but rather with raising subjects who are obedient to that society; so, in other words, not at all with teaching them to independently make the kinds of decisions that are simultaneously up to them and well in accordance with society's secular and democratic system of values. *N'est-ce pas?*"

To think—those thoughts would never have strayed into my mind just a half an hour ago, but now, sitting here at this table, I could recall that evening down to the last detail; and even if not all of the details were exact, nor were they of any consequence. I loved my mother. Which is to say: I love my mother. My *croque monsieur* was served, and I asked the waitress for another glass of red wine. It had turned out to be a good day nonetheless.

I'd like to think that the time Anni spent in Paris was a happy one for her. At long last, she had a chance to be entirely herself—to decide even the most minute of details all on her own, and this in one of the most beautiful cities in the world, into which she was able to directly and satisfyingly immerse herself through her university and her classmates. She told me a few things about her classes in her letters—the subjects seemed a little pointless and hackneyed, for the most part, as if they were merely trying to restate self-evident points using complex terms; but she herself was confident that this new knowledge could benefit her greatly in Estonia later on. In addition to her handful of mandatory requisites, Anni showed up to all kinds of other lectures on topics ranging from economics and leadership theory to history and journalism, and she read a great deal else on her own—at least at first, when she, like a camel in an oasis, gained access to a proper library that was able to satisfy her intellectual thirst. Since she had a guaranteed dormitory space, she generally managed quite well on her scholarship money and didn't ask us for extra funds, although we naturally sent her a little every now and then.

Moreover, the Estonian embassy occasionally offered her little translation projects, such as when someone with Estonian documentation had a brush with the authorities and needed assistance. The embassy's own employees were already up to their ears in work. The budget was scant, of course, but the country had to be represented to the fullest extent, and there was always enough funding for buying its way out of interpreting for Estonian crooks and prostitutes. The work even appealed to Anni and she was well-suited for the job, since her French was almost impeccable and what's more, it often turned out that detainees who had presented themselves to the authorities as Estonian nationals didn't actually speak Estonian at all, which left the embassy interpreters in a jam. Luckily, we'd managed to make it clear to Anni at a relatively young age that Dostoyevsky and Chekhov were in no way responsible for the Bolsheviks' acts of terror, and that if she deprived herself of the opportunity to read them in their original language, then she'd be punishing not the Russian people, but rather herself. Anni never did become proficient enough to read original Russian literature, but she spoke the language decently all the same—unlike the majority of her classmates, who used their refusal to learn all the letters of the Cyrillic alphabet as a way of expressing their patriotism. Still, I can't keep from remarking with some resentment that although Dostoyevsky and Chekhov suited Maire just fine for making a point, her relationship with the classics extended no further. For instance, when I went to great lengths one time to acquire tickets to the Vilnius Youth Theater's guest performance of *Uncle Vanya*, she was incredibly reluctant to attend—ultimately, she was very satisfied because she noticed a large number of celebrities in the audience, but felt relatively impassive about the performance itself. Not that she was unable to enjoy very much on an intellectual level—on the contrary, plenty of things that had no effect on me whatsoever revealed themselves to her; but she was only content with things of which she could be absolutely sure.

In any case, this was how Anni came into contact with girls who'd moved from Estonia to France, earning money there by picking up men on Rue Saint-Denis. She managed to be quite useful to a few of them, too, who out of inexperience (or at least that's what Anni believed) had allowed themselves to get wrapped up in a more serious affair—such as by allowing a friend to leave a backpack in their room for a few days and later finding out it contained a package of heroin. Suffice it to say, it was with Anni's help that the protagonist of that specific incident managed to avoid a lengthy jail sentence. When the girls figured out that she didn't view them as worthless trash, then they were prepared to speak with her quite openly, and even a few Russian, Polish, and Hungarian girls joined her circle of acquaintances that included prostitutes from Estonia. She shouldn't have sought out their company, in my opinion, but she'd decided to do a study on Eastern European outcasts in Paris, and speaking to those girls was necessary fieldwork. When they headed back to work at night, Anni would sit with her real friends at a café or in someone's mansard apartment and discuss what she'd learned, shocking the French with her extensive knowledge of their capital's darker side and with all kinds of particulars that those boys from good families had no idea existed. On one occasion, she even brought Father Dominic with her—an unusual priest who would walk around Saint-Denis in the daylight hours, speaking to the girls in cafés and stairwells without scolding them for their sinful lifestyles and simply offering spiritual help. The boys jeered at him, however, because it was impossible for them to imagine a Catholic capable of doing something selfless, and they naturally believed that Father Dominic was using it first and foremost to satisfy his own sublimated desires.

This infuriated Anni, because she took Father Dominic— and her own work—seriously.

"I want to know," she wrote to me, "what makes them tick, because it's impossible that they're somehow physically different from me as humans; life and the world have just made them that way. I want to know how it could have happened; and what's more, why it makes Yelena from Daugavpils place a saucer of milk outside the window of her rented mansard room every day for stray cats; or why Katalin sends not money home to Pécs, but rather rare stamps that she buys from a philatelic store for her little brother's collection."

I naturally held on to those letters, and now I also possess my own replies.

"So, that means you think that circumstances are always to blame—that life makes us who we are?" I wrote back to her.

"No, it's much more complicated than that," she replied, and gave me a rundown of a number of French philosophers whose names I've since forgotten, but whom she was reading at university and had apparently explained it all very clearly. If I remember correctly, it was something to the effect of: "we adopt the form the world believes we embody, because only in doing so can we become who we are." And then we ourselves perpetuate that form by obeying the rules the world regards as normal and forcing them upon others, and so on and so forth ad infinitum. In short—she'd thought it all through thoroughly for her own understanding.

Anyhow, Anni received a perfect score on her research along with the assurance that her scholarship would continue for as long as it took to defend her thesis in France. This was certainly fantastic news, although it came just when Maire and I were in the middle of our divorce and the atmosphere at home was fraught on account of it. Still, I suppose it also gave us both a sense of certainty that even though our life together was coming to an end, at least our daughter was on the right path. Things were just as they usually are in those instances: neither partner was entirely sure of which way things were going, neither wanted to say anything they couldn't take back, and although it was mutually evident in our everyday reality that we couldn't keep on living that way, and we discussed that fact, too, neither of us was capable of taking that ultimate step, that leap into the darkness, which determines that your whole ensuing life will take a different direction. When it finally happened all the same and we were forced to let Anni know, she was completely devastated, because until then, the news she'd gotten from home was that everything was going along just fine, the way it always had. She came back for a while that summer, but both Maire and I were still such a mess that she didn't stay long at either of our separate places—she went on a brief tour of acquaintances' summer cabins, attended a few outdoor performances, and then hitchhiked back to France.

I also stopped by the university Anni had been attending back then, just in case; but to tell the truth, I didn't entertain any great hopes. So, it came as no surprise that the main office wouldn't give out anyone's contact information and further-more—as the young woman with big, somewhat doleful eyes explained—it was hardly likely that anyone who had studied there at the same time as Anni would still be found at the same address now. I actually had the same fear concerning the address Anni's letters had been mailed from, and to which I'd sent a little money from time to time after she moved out of the dormitory. It was near Montmartre, but on the other side of the hill from the hotel my mother and I had stayed at: our metro station had been Château-Rouge, but Abbesses was the closest to Anni's old address. It wasn't all that easy to find, and walking up and down the steep streets was starting to wear me out. When I made a third pass by an Arab street-vendor's shop, in front of which he was sitting and smoking between the heaps of fruit on display, I realized that I might not pinpoint the address using my own wits after all. I asked the man for directions, and he stared at me as if I were an idiot. The right stairwell was just a few steps away. Seeing that I was empty-handed, he also expressed his astonishment that I wasn't taking a bottle of wine with me to pay a call. I bought a bottle just in case—a slightly more expensive brand, the name of which looked somewhat familiar.

I knew that I was looking for a "Corinne," and that I'd seen her once, briefly, too. But I naturally wouldn't have recognized her if she were to walk past me on the street. When I was climbing the narrow, creaking steps to the third floor of the building, a woman who might have been the right age went down past me, walking a dog, and I startled for a moment, wondering whether that might be her—still, nothing about her face looked familiar. She greeted me in a friendly and unguarded tone, and I greeted her back.

But when I rang the doorbell of the right apartment, no one came. What a disappointment.

I descended the stairs slowly, hoping to perhaps hear the sound of a door opening behind me, but there was only silence. In reality, I didn't even know whether Corinne still lived there in the first place. It'd certainly be a shame if my entire trip to Paris turned out to be chasing the wind.

When I exited the building, still holding the bottle of wine, the Arab eyed me with curiosity.

"Not home, huh?" he asked. I shook my head.

"Whom were you going to see, then?" he questioned further. "Niculescus or Corinne?"

"Corinne," I told him, heartened.

Ah," he said. "You should have said so right away. Corinne'll be coming home around six o'clock today. She has yoga on Wednesdays."

"I see," I said, and checked my watch. There was a couple of hours' time.

"Will you be coming back later, or are you going somewhere else?" the Arab asked.

"I'll be coming back," I said.

"Then you can leave the bottle with me meanwhile," he replied. "There's no point in you carrying it around with you the whole way."

He's right, I thought, and handed him the bottle. He looked at the label and nodded as if to say, "This'll do just fine." I figured I would get a bite to eat meanwhile and found a tiny, nice-looking restaurant near Rue des Trois-Frères, which was furthermore occupied by several locals, so it had to be quite good. But when the waiter, who was wearing his hair in a short, well-combed ponytail, walked lazily past me for a third time, I got the hint and left. Luckily, I found a Vietnamese deli a couple of buildings down, where the owner-woman and I both laughed mirthfully as we attempted to elucidate what she was offering and what I would like. We weren't all that successful at it, but the result was delicious, regardless of the fact that I didn't quite understand what I was eating. It was still only a little past five o'clock when I left the deli, so I ambled around to pass the time and was back at the address by around six. The Arab was occupied with his countrymen bustling to buy his wares, but when he saw me, he stopped and took the bottle of wine out from under the counter.

"She came just a short while ago," he said. "I told her you were looking for her, so she'll definitely be at home."

I knew that Corinne was maybe a couple years older than Anni, which would put her at slightly over thirty now, but the woman who opened the door could just as well have been forty already.

I could tell that she was used to getting by on her own, but had stayed human in every sense meanwhile; and she certainly didn't deny herself anything she might be able to afford, such as one more little glass on a lonely night—and those nights hadn't entirely gone by without leaving a mark. But she hadn't given up on herself. I don't believe she powders her face and accents her lips that delicately every time she stays in after yoga class; or that she wears a tight tunic that shows her slim figure in the best light when she's alone. She looked at me with bemusement, since my face didn't ring any bells.

"Hello," I said. "You and I have met once before, and my daughter lived in your apartment for a while. Anni. Do you remember her?" Recognition flashed in Corinne's black-currant eyes; no doubt Anni and I shared a similar accent, too.

"Of course. It's great to see you; come on in. How is she doing these days, anyway?"

I handed her the bottle and removed my coat. The apartment was tiny but very organized and tidy. The bigger room had a kitchenette in one corner; a couch, a dining table with two chairs, and a television in the other; and a narrow cupboard placed against the wall—there wasn't space for much more. The door to the smaller room was slightly ajar, revealing a neatly made bed with a bedspread.

Corinne gestured for me to sit on the couch, brought over a chair from the table for herself, and uncorked the wine.

"Cheese? Olives?"

I nodded and sat down. She buzzed about the kitchenette for a few moments and then set a tray that held two or three rather pungent cheeses, a few crackers, and a little bowl with wrinkled black olives on the coffee table. She popped one of the olives into her mouth immediately.

"It was very nice of you to let Anni stay here," I said. "It's amazing that there was enough space for the both of you for so long."

Corinne shrugged.

"I suppose it was just a tad cramped, yes," she said. "And, well, there was no room for privacy. But on the other hand, getting half of the rent paid was pretty important for me then, too. Up until she lost the scholarship, I mean. And it wasn't like I could kick her out after that."

I frowned. The fact that Anni had lost her scholarship was news to me, and Corinne noticed.

"You didn't know, then? It was back when she started fawning over those Muslims and practically stopped going to classes."

Now it seemed quite logical. It had been stupid of me not to ask Anni those questions back when there was still time. Even if she wouldn't have answered. But I was in the dark. And even there in Corinne's apartment, sitting on the same couch where my daughter had spent evenings conversing just like that and with the very same person, I still had a very, very long way to go before I would arrive at that knowledge. But I'm getting ahead of myself.

Corinne had poured us wine in the meantime.

"Cheers," she said. "You never told me what Anni's doing now."

I sipped my wine—it really was quite good.

"She died," I said. "Five years ago, already. She took her own life."

Corinne seemed to jolt. I knew it, that was how it often went—I wasn't the same in her eyes anymore. She put down her glass and I could see her considering how to act.

"It's a very difficult story," I tried to explain, "and I truly can't understand how it could've gone like that. When she left here to come back home, she ended up with some religious group— with some kinds of sectarians, you know, who suddenly up and decided to pay God a visit together."

"I can't believe it," Corinne said. She pulled a pack of cigarettes out of her pocket and unconsciously removed one, but didn't light it. "Anni wasn't like that at all."

"I know," I nodded. "And that's why I need to follow her

tracks; I hope it's no bother to you. I'm playing a little 'detective,' in a nutshell."

She thought for a moment, rolling the cigarette between her fingers. If I wasn't grossly misinterpreting her expression, she wasn't expecting me to leave as soon as possible, at any rate.

"No, of course it's not. But I don't really believe I'll be able to help you with anything."

She reached for her glass again and suddenly discovered she was holding the cigarette.

"Oh. You wouldn't mind if I . . . ?"

"You're in your own home," I said and smiled.

She nodded and lit the cigarette.

"I didn't know what kind of a life she was living here, you do realize," I continued. "Aside from what she wrote or told me on the phone, but that wasn't all that much. I trusted her; I was confident that she was strong, especially after my mother and I came to visit her."

"Yes, I remember that well. And she was strong—there was no doubt about that. Maybe even too strong." "What do you mean?"

"I suppose she believed," Corinne said, blowing out smoke, "that if need be, she alone could pull the wagon carrying everyone down on their luck."

Yves, whose far-reaching circle of acquaintances included all types of people, had introduced Anni to Hassan. Corinne had already met him once earlier, since the starry-eyed Yves held Hassan in very high regard—perhaps because while he himself perennially left projects unfinished, Hassan managed to accomplish undertakings that were of practical benefit to people. Corinne had found that slightly shorter-than-average Iranian, who had a coal-black beard and seemed to be in perpetual motion, very likeable, because he laughed like a free man.

"I even reckoned that *I* could have a boyfriend like that," she reminisced. "But, well, who am I kidding—I suppose we were from two different worlds, all things considered."

She remembered his story well and was happy to tell it. Hassan's family had been forced to flee their homeland not long after the ayatollahs seized power, but not because they had numbered among the shah's supporters. On the contrary— they'd been very critical of the government even before the revolution, and were worried about what would become of Iran when its villages' dark hostility and its large, well-off cities' superficial Westernness finally came to clash with each other. Hassan's father had taught French literature at a university, and his mother worked as a translator and a secretary at a company involved in foreign trade. They both lost their jobs after the 1979 Revolution, and when the morality police started wrapping women's heads in black scarves, they realized it wouldn't end well. Yet somehow, they were able to leave the country without much of a hitch. Hassan and his younger brother Hussein were still very young at the time and hadn't been to their homeland since. As it turned out, there was an unexpectedly large Persian population in Paris—an entire community; and quite a mixed one at that. Even several strict ayatollahs led by Khomeini himself had spent their exile in the city, and a few radical Islamic organizations that had supported him were still in full operation, although most of the immigrants had enjoyed golden childhoods and weren't drawn to the severe lifestyle. There were also many who, like Hassan's father, had moved towards freer air rather reluctantly—they generally believed the situation in Iran was temporary, and that they would be able to return home before they knew it. *Not too different from the Estonians who docked in Sweden in 1944*, I mused. Luckily, Hassan's father was able to find university work in Paris, now as an instructor of Persian; but what his mother did, Corinne didn't know.

"I even saw them one time," she said. "It was a Friday and

I was just hurrying home from somewhere when I saw them walking by the river. His mother and father were strolling slowly, almost like a royal couple—that's exactly how it felt—and Hassan was with them, too; I wouldn't have recognized them otherwise, of course. Hassan was talking nonstop, naturally, and it was obvious that they were too slow for him, but he was still a good son." Corinne smiled. Hassan was an eternal college student, just like Yves, and was active in a hundred different things at once. Of these, the most important to him was a network of people who helped women expelled by their families. "It's horrible," Corinne emphasized, describing how Muslims treat their children in general.

"Not all of them, of course," she disclaimed when she saw my look of uncertainty. "All kinds of people exist. Take Hussein's own parents, for example, right? Totally normal people. But, well, they're still just crazy overall. Boys are allowed to do anything they want, but if a daughter wants to live like a real person, they might put her under lock and key at home or whatever. But you've got to draw the line somewhere, you know—no father should ever be able to force his child to choose between herself and her parents, am I right? It can't end well. I remember I saw on TV one time how one girl was killed by her brothers when she wouldn't agree to marry the man her family had chosen for her. She wanted to wed a Frenchman instead. But what's so wrong about that, huh?"

As she spoke, I gathered that Hassan had worked with those very girls in danger. Within his network were several women from North Africa and even farther afield who had managed to peacefully exit the traditional social system and were now glad to be of support and assistance to others suffering the same fate— women whom the old way of living didn't want to let go without a fight. They simultaneously aided the authorities in collecting information for investigations into violence against Muslim girls. This naturally made them traitors in the eyes of fellow Muslims, but their own belief in the justice of Western society's institutions was resolute and naïve. Even astonishingly so.

Hassan's parents approved of what he was doing, but his younger brother did not. Hussein, whom Corinne had encountered only once or twice and with very unpleasant memories of the occasions, had abruptly begun rebelling against his parents' Western lifestyle during his teenage years, and had sought his roots in very different company. The more time that passed, the worse the brothers got along. Hassan had spoken of it with sadness, but without regret. Someone who stands for the right to personal choice for some shouldn't be allowed to deny it to others, and Hassan found that he himself had done nothing wrong. Nor had his parents.

This was all revealed to me over the course of our relatively long and heavily detailed conversation, which also managed to include a quite comprehensive review of the development and dissolution of Corinne and Yves's relationship. Which was also a complex story in and of itself. As I came to understand, Corinne had fallen in love with Yves simply and mundanely, but Yves had responded with something socio-cosmic—something in which the human aspect was interwoven with the global, or so much as expelled by it; and naturally, a blend like that didn't have much of a future.

"I broke up with him," Corinne continued, "when I realized that . . . well, how can I put this? That I was a project. Just one more. An unintellectual and uneducated being (it depends on how you look at it, doesn't it), who transforms under the influence of genuine emotion. Who starts to see the world the right way. Well, I mean 'right' in his and who-all-else's interpretation. That genuine emotion of mine had to be for him, of course—not vice-versa. And I felt one, too, when I realized it. A genuine wish to tell him to fuck off. Sorry." Regardless, this didn't preclude them from staying friends in the end, and close ones, at that. They were the kind of friends who continually showed an interest in whether the other was doing well, and when Yves brought any of his other projects-in-dire-straits to live at Corinne's place for a little while, she'd make room for them without putting up a fuss. That's probably how Anni had ended up staying with her, too.

"That was when Anni was already spending more time with Hassan than at school," Corinne explained. "She did try to convince herself she was doing research. But who was she really fooling, aside from maybe just Hassan? Even though it *was* her research topic in pure form: women who had gotten caught in the gears of two worlds. She knew half of the whores on Saint-Denis—you know that, right?"

"I do," I nodded. By that time, we were already half-finished with another bottle of red wine taken from her cupboard.

"So, yeah, and those Arab and Turkish and Persian and whatever- else girls had, like, totally cast a spell on her by then. She said she couldn't figure them out at all, and that she wouldn't find peace if she didn't. I, on the other hand, was confused by what there really was to understand. I guess everybody just tries to put their life in order however they know how. Even if they don't."

Again, I had no choice but to agree with her, even though I actually already sensed that things might not be so simple after all.

"Some of them stayed here, too," Corinne continued. "Such as Shirin, for instance—she hung around here for quite a while. Shirin came from Germany via Strasbourg and was only supposed to be staying in Paris for a few days and then travel on to England, but something got messed up, and she was around for a good couple of weeks. Pretty girl, but when she got here, she was covered in bruises from head to toe. She'd gone to a club with her girlfriends and that was it, according to her version. Well, I dunno. Soon as it happened, she had to pick up and leave home. Although I guess it hadn't been her first time either. The beating, I mean. Everybody's got their breaking point."

It's like something right out of a human-rights pamphlet, I thought, and shook my head. It really is amazing how banal personal ordeals can be sometimes.

Shirin apparently didn't speak a syllable of French, so their communication passed through either Hassan or Anni, because she could generally get by with English. Once in England, she planned first to find work as a nanny and then enroll in a nursing program somewhere. Corinne generally didn't put much trust in Shirin, because she believed the girl was just a big tease and an attention whore who seemed to try to flirt with everyone, both male and female.

"Well, I guess she just needed people to view her with pleasure," Corinne shrugged.

Shirin's acrid cigarette smoke and sweet perfume that clouded the entire apartment didn't bother Corinne that badly, but there was indeed one thing she didn't like at all. It was her constant praying.

"I'm not running a mosque here," Corinne declared adamantly. "I even thought about snapping at her because of it once, but I just let it go. The kid was all messed up in the head already, and she wouldn't have understood a single word of what I said, anyway."

Yet, Shirin's praying bothered Anni as well, although in a completely different way. She wasn't living in her old strict home anymore; she didn't have to pray anymore; she had broken free of that life, hadn't she? So, why did she keep on doing it? Why did the girl feel downright physically sick when she missed a prayer for one reason or another? It was baffling. "Well, Muslims are just Muslims," Corinne reasoned. "What more can you expect?" She topped off our glasses and the clever look that had foretold the finding of a new bottle the last time appeared on her face again.

Or take for example that Ayshe, who had been next to Hassan outside Corinne's door early one morning. She was at a ripe age already, older than Corinne, and from Tunisia—a chubbier older woman. And she spoke fluent French, almost a little too much. Her story wasn't so bad—she'd simply divorced her husband. He was an electrical engineer or something like that, and she was trained as a primary-school teacher. They had separated very civilly and stayed more or less friends—the man had found a younger woman. Tunisia didn't allow polygamy, of course, but this actually suited Ayshe very well, because she herself had also grown somewhat distant from her husband and would have gladly lived on her own. What's more, they had no children. But the prospect didn't suit her family one bit. If only they'd just left her alone. But no! After the separation, they made her live with her almost senile uncle, who wouldn't hear a word of her going to work and thus making her family's shame public. Instead, he envisioned her sitting at home and helping with the household chores, all through which she would be constantly reminded how thankful she should be that she was tolerated there at all. In the end, she couldn't stand it. Since women still weren't allowed to travel alone in Tunisia, she had no choice but to locate her husband and explain the situation to him. And he helped: they fled in secret from the rest of her family to Tunis, where the man helped Ayshe find a ship that would transport her to Sicily. From there, she had to somehow make her own way to Naples (which involved a lot of mishaps), where there were acquaintances waiting who would finally help her get to Paris.

Ayshe was confident she'd find a job in no time—as a schoolteacher, for example. She had no doubt about her qualifications, her diligence, or her ability to handle even the most problematic of children. Nor did she doubt there was a demand for people like her. Good teachers are needed always and everywhere. She didn't necessarily have to live in Paris—

any small town would do just fine. The main thing would be to somehow acquire documentation. She couldn't wrap her mind around the possibility that a French school, especially a provincial one, would hardly want to employ an Arab woman.

"But we're in the *West*," she said. "There's not the kind of corruption here that we have—here, there's liberal society, *liberté, égalité, fraternité*. Everyone has equal opportunities."

"And she truly believed that, by the way," Corinne now reminisced with a smirk. "Poor thing."

Ayshe managed, with her undying belief in the French spirit, to repeatedly put Corinne's patience to the test as she recited by heart an endless string of quotes by Flaubert and Pascal and Voltaire, since at least one of the three was always able to confirm any of her claims. The fact that France's laws had not been drafted according to the collected works of Ayshe's favorite authors in her mind had nothing to do with the matter.

And even so, Ayshe also prayed regularly. "Because the ability to perceive God really is what sets us apart from unintelligent animals, isn't it," she explained when Corinne and Anni were confounded by her practice. And, she alleged, Westerners' understanding of Islam as a somehow barbaric and archaic worldview was a complete misunderstanding. On the contrary—it was, in her opinion, the most rational of all religions, pure of any childish tales of miracles or confusion over whether there are three gods or just a single one. What human stupidity had done with those faiths was another matter, of course—no, there were no justifications for that either; but it didn't change the topic at hand, regardless.

Corinne didn't know how Hassan finally got Ayshe her documentation, but somehow he managed it. And the woman had barely packed her bags when a new one took her place—the most difficult of the refugees and also the very last: Leyla, with her slit, sunken eyes and sharp cheekbones. She did speak French and did understand everything that was said to her, but always replied with only a handful of words. Leyla's relationship with God appeared to be even more complex. Corinne couldn't remember her ever praying, but she did startle at every unexpected noise, and when the doorbell rang, she would shut herself away in the bedroom. Leyla had arrived at the apartment from right there in Paris, but why exactly she was on the run remained a mystery to everyone at first. Hassan would only say that Layla had fled her cruel and violent husband, who forced her to submit to unnatural sex and beat her constantly.

Corrine wasn't even sure whether or not Leyla slept at all. Maybe in the daytime when Corinne herself was out, because at night the girl would only sit in the darkened kitchen and chain-smoke. In the morning, the air in the apartment would be thick with smoke, a couple empty packs of Gauloises would be lying on the table, and the ashtray would be full of butts. And aside from about a dozen espressos per day and a potato chip or two, she ate practically nothing.

Leyla didn't stay for very long, either, and a couple days after her departure, the gendarmes showed up at Corinne's door. They had picked up her trail. It turned out that in fact Leyla had, using a shaving razor, slit the throat of a man prone to violence and whatever else. Corinne didn't blink an eye when she told the gendarmes that there had obviously been some kind of a mix-up, since her apartment was certainly no sanctuary for Arabs fleeing from the law. Even so, she resolutely told Hassan that no more women in need would be housed at her apartment.

Hassan's story ended quite differently than how I'd expected. I never did find out whether or not the gendarmes nabbed Leyla, but one of Leyla's husband's relatives apparently located Hassan. He was found in the playground of a 19th arrondissement pre-school, sitting in a climbable spaceship next to a sandbox with a knife in his ribs. Anni was in shock. Yves visited the police department several times to look into the case, but found out nothing. It seemed like Anni herself was afraid also. And, it turned out, not entirely without cause. One time, Corinne's doorbell rang and standing on the doorstep was a relatively young dark-skinned man wearing an expensive black coat. He instantly undressed the woman with his eyes and entered the room without uttering a word. It turned out he was Hassan's younger brother Hussein, who had come to collect his sibling's things. Indeed, Hassan had left behind a suitcase on his last visit and Corinne naturally had no cause to forbid his brother from taking it.

"But oh my, he was one nasty guy," Corinne detailed. "Obviously mafia. The kind of guy who's slick and cruel all at the same time. He was totally polite with me in words, but I could see that if he needed to, for whatever reason, that he'd have no problem sticking a knife into my kidney either. A lackey, you know? Carries out to the letter every order those up high hand down to him, and gives total hell to anyone weaker than him."

Nevertheless, even that unfavorable character profile couldn't explain what happened when Anni entered the room. Unexpected and completely stunned recognition flashed in Hussein's eyes, while Anni's face turned plaster-white and she gripped the wall for support. This in spite of the fact that Corinne didn't believe they had ever met before, and when she asked Anni about it later, her roommate so passionately denied having ever been acquainted with Hassan's brother that Corinne decided not to poke at the topic anymore—just in case. And in truth, not even I had known enough then to be able to pay any attention to that fact. Who knows what I might have gone and done then.

"And you are?" Hussein had asked, approaching Anni and resting his hand on her shoulder.

Anni avoided looking at him directly and pushed his hand off of her.

"She's my boarder," Corinne said. "You have no business with her."

Hussein glanced at her over his shoulder with a look that wasn't at all necessary to put into words.

"Fine," he said. "I'm going." He took Hassan's suitcase with him, and at least Corinne assumed they'd never see the man again. Just in case, they stared out the window to see him get into a very big black car and drive away.

However, things didn't go as they'd hoped.

"It might have been early December," Corinne said. "There were already Christmas decorations in the store windows, in any case. I remember there were children standing in front of the Galeries Lafayette display, staring at the moving Christmas figurines—I walked past there that day and a sort of light, delicate snow that won't stick was falling. My spirits were bright, in a way. Well, *before* it, I mean. In any case, I luckily got there right in the nick of time."

When Corinne opened her apartment door, Hussein had already managed to tear off most of Anni's clothing, and his own pants were already undone, too. Corinne immediately realized what was happening. She grabbed a vase from the table and smashed it over Hussein's head. He collapsed like a sack of bricks, and the two of them somehow managed to drag him outside. Then, a few awful minutes passed before Hussein regained consciousness and attempted to knock the door down, as furious as a hornet. Fortunately, the gendarmes got there quickly and while he was still pounding away at the door. It turned out that Hussein had already been wanted earlier in suspicion of a crime. He was allegedly the driver for some Syrian mafia boss.

"I was pretty scared for a while, to tell the truth," Corinne said. "And it's no wonder why. I was afraid he'd get out and come looking for revenge. But then barely a week had passed, I ran out of sugar one night, and I decided to go down to the shop. I usually don't buy from there because it's all a little more expensive than at Franprix, but it was raining and I didn't feel like walking any farther. And when I went up to the counter to pay, the Arab there looks at me and says he was told to tell me I had nothing to worry about. 'What do you mean?' I asked, and felt my legs go weak. 'That's all I know,' the Arab said, shrugging, 'they just said you've got nothing to worry about.' And so it was—nothing else happened. I suppose it meant Hussein was a black sheep in his own people's eyes, too."

Corinne shivered and took a small sip from her glass. I glanced over at the bottle, but we'd emptied it again.

"Anni was already gone by then," Corinne said. "She didn't dare stay here for another minute. I understood; I understood it all too well. She didn't have all that much to pack, of course—a dozen or so books and some clothes. She sent one box of junk by mail; the rest fit into her backpack."

Yes, and I already knew the story from that point forward.

I did something stupidly touristy on my last day in Paris, but more or less with the certain knowledge that it'd also be the very last stupidly touristy thing I'd ever do again. On top of that, I did it out of nostalgia. On the last day of the last time when I was there with my mother, we'd strolled from the Arc de Triomphe down along the Champs-Elysées (we walked at a leisurely pace and without allowing ourselves to be bothered by the Japanese hordes crowding and taking pictures); then sat in the Tuileries Garden for a little while; afterwards walked past the Louvre to Notre-Dame, taking a small bow before the great cathedral; and finally made our way into the culinary bustle of the Latin Quarter to eat. That walk had understandably taken longer, as I recalled, because my pace was a little slower with my mother, and that had been for the best. All in all, it was our goodbye to the city—especially for her. I suppose she might have surmised she wouldn't return again. On top of that, it had been winter and chilly at the time, and you could feel the slowness in your bones, not like now, when it's spring and warm.

I could remember that feeling clearly: I am leaving, but this city will remain, with its people and its sounds and its rhythms, and the fact that it will be left without me once again makes no real difference to it. The faces of passersby, which just a couple of days earlier belonged to people with whom you shared that large space, now seem to retreat behind a border. That space is still theirs, but it's like you no longer exist in it anymore. You see them partially through a pane of glass, behind which everything carries on the way it's always been. It's a melancholy feeling, but melancholy in a good way. I've never suspected that the rest of the world apart from me doesn't really exist, and proceeding from that thought, I can similarly conclude that all the places where I'm not in the present moment always live on independently of me and my desires. But it's one thing to know and quite another thing to feel. Especially when you've been in a strange place long enough that it almost starts to become your own, and when you leave it once again, it changes in your eyes: what has come to feel so near to you becomes distant again; and then, after you've really left, bit by bit it becomes more abstract.

I would've been glad if that same feeling had returned to me as I strolled down Paris's sunlit central boulevard this time. But it didn't. The people who walked past me were the very same as they'd been yesterday and the day before that and even before then. The city's sounds and rhythms were nearly just as close as they'd been before—or just as distant. And that's when I realized: Paris isn't the place I'm departing. I'm departing in principle. For good.

4

Maire's telephone call came as a surprise—after all those long years. I hadn't deleted her number from my contacts and when I saw her calling now, the feeling was dually strange: why just now, and why at all?

"Hello?" I answered as if I didn't know whom I was speaking with.

"Hi, Enn," she said. "It's me."

"Well, hey there."

"So, how are you doing?"

"Same old," I lied. My other option would have been: "Oh, you know—long story."

A brief pause ensued.

"Listen, I've got a little favor to ask," she continued, as if we hadn't been divorced for eight years. "You wouldn't mind dropping by Elo's place for a little while, would you? I'm really worried about her. I'd ask Arno otherwise, but he's very busy with work."

"Sure, I can," I consented, already guessing the cause of her worry and the actual reason why she couldn't ask Arno. But no matter—I'd been planning to look up Maire's sister anyway. "Is she in the city?"

"No," Maire said, "out in the country. I'll text you her address."

I'd been to her country home together with Anni once, not long after Elo returned from Sweden. Anni had been alternating between living at my place and Maire's since the Christmas after she moved back from Paris, and didn't feel very comfortable at either, because both parents wanted her as their our own ally and exhausted her with divorce-themed unburdening. I don't know how things would have gone if we'd known then the kind of trauma she actually had to live through in Paris. We would certainly have tried to offer her more support, and maybe that would've even helped to steer relations between us onto a smoother path—who knows. Maybe one of us would have been able to tell her something she so dearly needed. But I suppose Anni had already stricken both of us from the list of those who might be capable of understanding her. And when Elo then proposed that Anni come to live with her in Pärnu County for the summer, we were all pleased. Elo's husband Harald Laiksaar is about twenty years older than her, and even a good deal older than me. Harald was born to Estonian refugees abroad—he and Elo met and got acquainted at some patriotic gathering after Estonia's independence was restored, wed not long after that, and then moved to Sweden, which made her parents very proud and Maire relatively jealous. They later received a bonanza restitution of pre-Occupation assets in Estonia, including a few houses in Tallinn, one farm near Tõstamaa, and another in Järvamaa. Harald knew how to do business. By that time, he'd been made director of a Swedish company's local subsidiary that produced canned fish, and was an all-around top dog.

Still, Anni stayed at Elo's place for a mere couple of weeks. I only found this out more than a month later, when she and a couple of friends showed up at my mother's to visit. Already then, Elo's life hadn't been all that rosy.

I stopped at a grocery store on the way to pick up a number of necessities, just in case, and by doing so pushed finding Elo's property a little too late into the day. I sped past what was apparently the right turn in the evening twilight, but only realized

I'd missed it a fair amount of time later, and when I turned back around, I started driving slowly and cautiously, keeping my eye on the side of the road at all times. Regardless, I still took a wrong turn and after heading down it for a while, I had to drive in reverse all the way back to the main road along what had become an ever-narrowing cow path. What could I do—the last time I'd visited had been many years ago and during summer, but now the last remaining strips of snow still scored the ground here and there, and the trees were still bare. So, the outcome was that I arrived at Elo's house only when it was quite dark out. All of the ground-floor windows were illuminated, but no one came to open the door when I knocked. It was simply unlocked. Already from the entryway, I could tell what kind of a life she'd been living here—what I'd already picked up a little from Maire's tone. Trails of tobacco smoke and Estonian dance music were coming from the living room. I took a deep, decisive breath and entered.

Elo—who had aged much more rapidly over the past years but was attempting to conceal that truth with whatever was in makeup's power—was sitting at one end of the couch, and lounging at the other end was a man with a couple days' worth of stubble, wearing a wool sweater and a brown jacket. Another man—a little younger, with buzzed hair and a checkered shirt—was seated at the table, which was covered with china plates and crystal shot glasses, resembling the remnants of bygone glory.

"Oh, and who do I see there?!" Elo exclaimed when she recognized me immediately, which was rather surprising given her current state. She tried to stand up, but her legs buckled and she stumbled, flopped back down onto the couch, and started laughing. "Well, come on in and get acquainted. Ville," she said, gesturing towards the man sitting next to her, "and Oskar. Ville and Oskar, this is my dear brother-in-law, Enn."

Ville and Oskar stood up just in case—seemingly out of politeness, but threateningly at the same time. Ville also appeared to be quite in the bag, but Oskar was handling himself a little better. And he very obviously felt sick. "You know what, Ville and Oskar?" I said politely but with sufficient forcefulness. "Thing is that the party here's over for today."

"I don't know nothing," Ville grumbled. "Around here, the man of the house's always the one who decides stuff like that."

"And who would that be?" I asked.

"Aw, leave it, Enn; come on and sit down, huh, and grab yourself a drink," Elo attempted to interrupt, but her tongue was already tied up tight in knots.

"We're here at the lady of the house's invitation," Ville said, taking his tone down a notch. "Don't go holdin' it against us."

Oskar had already figured out what was happening. He lifted his brown jacket off the back of the chair and started buttoning it up.

"Oh, listen, come on," he said to Ville. "Let's not make a fuss."

If it had come to fisticuffs, I wouldn't have been a match for either of them in my current condition, but that didn't necessarily show outwardly, and luckily Oskar appeared to have enough wits about him to grasp what consequences a fight like that might have in the longer term. Neither of them knew for certain what Elo would remember from that night, of course; or how substantial her rights in the household actually were.

"Ah, what fuss are we makin'," Ville mumbled. "But we are still guests here, not just . . . whatever."

"Can you get yourselves home or do I need to drop you off?" I asked Oskar.

"Our bikes are in the shed," he said, waving away the offer.

"Well, there's nothing more to say but good night then," I said, ushering the men out the door and locking it behind them. Under no circumstances would I have allowed my own friends to get on the road in that condition, of course; but the way I saw it, how and whether they got home was their problem and theirs alone. I switched off the music and opened the windows.

Elo's eyelids had fluttered shut meanwhile, but they opened again when the cold draft washed over them.

"Enn, is that you here?" she murmured incredulously. "You know, there should be some cognac around here somewhere." Then her gaze clouded over again and she passed out.

I looked around the house. The upstairs rooms had tidily made beds that no one had used for a long time, but I wasn't sure I could manage to carry Elo up the narrow staircase. What's more, she'd apparently been using one of the smaller groundfloor rooms, where a thick blanket had been spread out right over the wide bedspread. So, that's just where I heaved her.

After putting her to bed, I went back into the living room/kitchen and cleaned up a little. I remembered Elo and Harald's country home as being very nice and neat during my last visit; but now that was quite hard to believe. The kitchen sink was piled full of dishes and mold had already overrun the pots and pans strewn across the stove. It appeared that the party had been in full swing for several consecutive days and would probably have lasted for a number more, at least judging by the alcohol reserves. One after another, I uncapped seven bottles of vodka and poured them down the drain, followed by two bottles of cheap Moldovan brandy and five bottles of bottom-shelf Romanian red wine. I myself drank the one lager left in the fridge. The groceries status, on the other hand, wasn't as rosy as I'd imagined. I stocked the refrigerator with the contents of the bags I'd brought along and quietly went to make myself comfortable in a room upstairs.

It took me a long time to fall asleep, but I woke up at sunrise, covered from head to toe in a cold sweat.

I went downstairs at around eight o'clock. Steady snoring was coming from Elo's room—she apparently wasn't the type of person who's woken up early by alcohol drunk the night before. I hardboiled some eggs and made some frankfurters, located a toaster in one of the cupboards, set the table with cheese, ham, and sausage, and started brewing a liter of stronger-than-ordinary coffee. My breakfast preparations were apparently loud enough to rouse Elo, because after a short time I heard her starting to move around, then visit the bathroom, and not long after that she appeared in the kitchen doorway. Now, in the morning, she looked even ghastlier than she had the night before. She'd washed off her makeup (although not entirely), and there were big, bluish blotches beneath her still-deep, dark eyes.

Her body appeared somehow limp, as if it was being lugged around against its will, and every limb was shaking. I could imagine how bad a hangover she must have been suffering, but even so, it appeared to be the kind she had already learned to live with.

She collapsed into one of the two chairs at the table. I poured her a big mug of nonalcoholic beer.

Thanks," she said hoarsely, drinking it in big gulps. "You're a real pal."

It took several minutes before she realized there was something wrong with the beer.

"Hey," she exclaimed, "don't we have any normal beer or anything?"

"We don't," I said. "Only designated-driver beer."

She fished two packs of medicine (aspirin and vitamin C) out of a large tin can on a shelf above the stove, took two of each, and washed them down with the rest of the beer.

"Nonalcoholic beer," she scoffed, still dissatisfied. "Next, it'll be plastic Christmas trees. And then inflatable women." A hazy chain of associations continued forming behind her forehead for a few moments before she looked up and caught my eye. "Want to fuck?" She seemed to read right away from my expression that it wasn't a good idea, and shrugged.

"Ah, well. Okay. I was just asking."

"Oh Elo, Elo," I said.

"What's it now, huh?" she asked, becoming a little irritated. "I've liked you since I was a kid, I really have." Which in and of itself could be entirely true, of course.

She stood and beleagueredly made her way to the refrigerator, then noticed the bag of empty bottles placed next to it.

"Wow," she said. "I guess me and the boys did a bang-up job yesterday."

"Did you really need to get so drunk here?"

"Listen," she said, laughing, "where the hell do you think I should have gotten so drunk, then?"

I didn't know how to respond. She searched through the cupboards.

"Looks like we're totally out," she said when she'd finished. "You think you could drive us over to Tõstamaa real quick?"

"We're going to go without it today," I announced.

"What do you mean?" She crossed her arms. "You're not going to stay hanging around here for the rest of your life anyway, and I can bet that the same night you drive off, one of the boys will come and see how I'm doing."

I would have lost that bet, in all likelihood.

"Still," I said.

"You could fetch a bottle of vodka for lunch, even so," she insisted. "We *are* Europeans."

"I'm not going to."

"And why the hell not?!" She was almost shouting. "Why can't I drink when I want to, huh? If that's just what I want?"

I didn't answer. A detailed description of the biochemical processes taking place in her liver would hardly have convinced her anyway.

"You think *I* give a shit about the boys, huh?" she railed on. "I could just as easily sip on a rum and Coke alone in front the TV, too. But there isn't shit on TV."

"There are clinics, you know," I said cautiously. "Really respectable places where they simply remove the toxins from your blood so that you can, well, get a fresh start on your life."

"My life?" she snorted. "You think I've got some kind of a life? All I've got is money."

She ate a decent meal, even so. I took a look at Harald's sauna to see how it worked, and discovered it was a city man's sauna—the kind where you can launch all the necessary processes with the simple push of a couple of buttons. I got it warming up.

After Elo realized I really wasn't going to be her delivery boy, she went to her room, stone-faced, and wasn't much for conversation. To tell the truth, I was a little bit at a loss. She obviously lacked any kind of willpower to break free of her current cycle, and I was very well aware that if she herself didn't want to, then no one would be able to help. But I'd have to tell Maire *something* about her sister back in the city. The truth? To what ends? I fully understood that neither Maire nor her parents would be able to do anything for Elo. Maybe they would even start nagging her, which would only make matters worse. If anyone was to help, it'd be me. But I couldn't just go and tell her that the way she was living was wrong in some kind of a higher sense. Wrong according to the rules that existed before us; that will continue to exist after us; and that man has no power to enact or annul. Out of all the people I knew, I was the least fit for having that kind of a talk with her.

And that was exactly why I was also the only one who could help her, you see? Because no matter how wretched her situation might have been, she still had a chance, in principle. Unlike me.

I knocked on Elo's door and let her know the sauna was ready once it had heated up. She didn't answer, but she did pull a clean towel out of the dresser and went. I put some ready-to-bake pork chops in the oven and started skinning potatoes.

Elo's bad temper gave way shortly after lunchtime. I reckoned that since she'd seen herself as the undisputed master of the house, she'd had no need to install caches of secret booze supplies—even my father-in-law had a couple such stockpiles hidden from the rest of the family at their Saue home. And it would have been demeaning if I'd gone snooping around or even tried to catch a whiff of her breath. Maybe she had a small bottle of cognac behind her nightstand for nightcaps, but more likely not. In any case, it appeared that she'd reconciled herself to the situation for the time being, and I suppose my company did offer a little variety compared with the locals, all the same. I told her about myself and everything I'd found out to date (which was a little more by then, and a little less than what I've recorded here so far), while she informed me about her marriage, which had been keeling from the very start. Harald hadn't actually expected her to love him—apparently because of their difference in age—and therefore hadn't made any effort to win that love either. He did desire her gratitude, however, and gave cause for it. Elo was initially content with her fate, to put it mildly, and when Maire and their parents went to visit her (Anni and I stayed home), she radiated so brightly that for several weeks afterward, Maire was plagued by chronic headaches whenever I tried to hold her in bed at night. Because immediately after she arrived in Sweden, Elo was—no wonder—overwhelmed by all the things she could ever have felt were lacking in her former life. They had a house in a suburb of Stockholm, which was accessible by a charming old-fashioned electric train. Their home was furnished with such elegance and splendor that Maire and her mother couldn't believe their eyes: paintings and graphic art by the best Estonian artists hung on the walls, while the kitchen featured the most up-to-date technology. Elo could already regale her family with impressions from trips to Paris and London, with Rome and New York coming up next. Maire's father, on the other hand, was most impressed by Harald's sailboat, which they took on a little tour of the archipelago. And naturally, Elo now also had an entire wardrobe of the kinds of clothes her status required. As she explained, Harald likewise took her attire seriously and accompanied her to department stores all around town; and rightly so, because more often than not, Elo wouldn't have even dared to dream, once she saw the price tags, about wearing the things that were ultimately wrapped up for her. She also dragged Harald to the theater on a couple of occasions—he didn't go very much on the whole, although it wasn't much of a problem because Elo herself didn't especially enjoy Swedish theater either. In a nutshell, everything as good as it could be. She'd won a white Mercedes in the lottery, as the old Estonian saying goes.

Yet, over time—as she told me now—it all began to distress her. Among other things, "gratitude" also meant that she shouldn't have any wishes aside from the ones that Harald could grant without much of a show of effort. A wish for a new coat or a trip to Miami or a bedroom renovation was right. A wish to find a job in Stockholm or learn how to drive a car or buy herself jeans—even if they were just for walking around on the island— was wrong. Harald wasn't home often, but he called frequently to check if everything was fine, and so it was better if Elo didn't leave the house for very long. Once, she simply ended up standing in the yard chatting with the woman next door, who invited her to attend a demonstration protesting a law that regulated how one can and cannot cut a dog's tail, and it turned out that Harald had called. He was snappish later that night (although he never criticized her directly, not to mention ever raising his voice), and naturally immediately ruled out any chance of her going to any kind of a demonstration, because it was "stupid, pointless activism." Not that Elo herself would have wanted to go—they didn't have a dog anyway.

It was only a couple of years later that she managed, bit by bit, to wiggle her way out of Harald's enclosure and make some other Estonian friends who were somewhat closer to her in age and interests. Quite some time later, when she was with those friends at a wedding and they all ended up getting quite tipsy, one of them was struck by a burst of candor and to Elo's great surprise, she found out that when the local Estonians had talked about her before, they'd always argued over whether she was a hunting dog or a chicken—in other words, whether she was married to Harald for his wealth and could instinctively sense that others realized and disapproved of it, or if she really was just a mindless creature who had no real need for anything more in life than the pots and pans at home, seasoned with some skimpy clothes and trips to paradise. The real-life Elo actually couldn't be farther from either version, and for a while, her life in Sweden was highly tolerable. But then her new friends and their families moved back to Estonia one after another, and she was left alone once again.

In short, when Anni visited them in Sweden about five years later, after finishing tenth grade, Elo and Harald's relationship was already quite rocky. They naturally both projected themselves as being a respectable upper-class married couple. Harald did so because he didn't actually expect anything else, while Elo followed along because she simply had nowhere else to go. She would never dream of returning home with her tail between her legs, because the way she saw it, she was the one who had done best for herself out of the entire family. In principle, she could have divorced him and attempted to go on living in Sweden, but that would have been complicated because he would be capable of mobilizing lawyers skilled enough to go against her in court, and she lacked any kind of a social network aside from the people who'd known Harald from before. Divorces weren't looked upon all that favorably in the Estonian immigrant community either. Luckily, Harald didn't demand children of her, and even his interest in sex was relatively modest.

When Anni arrived in Stockholm, Elo and Harald tried to keep their tension under wraps. Harald had gone so far as to take off work for several days in order to drive Anni around for sightseeing. Anni let him take her to visit Skansen, the Moderna Museet, and the Estonian House, where she was able to meet several living classics of immigrant-Estonian literature. She also had her picture taken in front of Riddarholmen Church. The next day, she and Harald sailed to the island and stayed there overnight, although he had business in Stockholm that couldn't be delayed the very next afternoon. Elo and Anni spent one pleasant day combing through Stockholm's department stores on their own. They had to get back home by late afternoon, however, because although it would have been financially feasible for Harald to employ a housekeeper, doing so wouldn't have fit with his convictions, and so Elo herself was required to make dinner. They bought meat from the market cellar, got onto the subway and transferred to another line, then spent the evening together in the kitchen, just the two of them. Elo told me all of this with a kind of calm and delight that made it seem as if that entire period of her life had been a happy one; but in reality, I suppose she was simply thankful for the slightly expanded enclosure that Anni's visit enabled her to have.

And, always prefacing it with the same "We *are* Europeans," Harald uncorked a bottle of red wine for them with dinner every night. Anni was poured half a glass (which her aunt recommended she dilute with water), Elo received a full glass, Harald himself drank two with the meal, and he split the drops left over in the bottle more or less equally between himself and Elo.

"One glass of wine isn't moderate consumption," Elo said. "It's an exceedingly refined form of sadistic torture."

I agreed with her on that. My custom had always been that if you're working, then work, and if you're drinking, then drink. Drink so that you can feel it a little. Understandably, I refrained from telling her that now.

Harald even drank the same exact wine all the time—a

younger Bordeaux red, of which he had about a dozen crates he'd stocked their home with during a big sale at the Systembolaget[5] under the assumption that every wine only gets better with age. Which apparently wasn't always true.

In reality, Elo didn't have to limit herself to one glass, of course. After dinner, Harald would ordinarily withdraw to his upstairs office to leaf through some more documents, since Elo and Anni's chatting didn't interest him anyway. Elo would lead Anni to the living room, sit her down on the soft, deep-sinking couch, and pour herself a glass of Madeira or cognac. She offered them to Anni at first, too, but the girl didn't like those nightcaps very much. They had more than enough to talk about— the only Estonian news that Elo was up-to-date on was what had been published in Stockholm's weekly Estonian-language newspaper, because they had no foreign subscriptions and the Internet wouldn't have been much help back then, either—even if Elo had known how to use a computer. The first glass was usually followed by a second, which sometimes even led to a fourth. Thus, there was nothing strange about the fact that Elo had a hard time getting out of bed in the morning, or that Anni herself would then occasionally fry an egg and make toast for her uncle—something he received as if that was simply the way things were meant to be.

But when Elo emerged from her room at around eleven o'clock, came down to the kitchen, made herself a family-sized moka pot of espresso, and appeared with it in the living room, she was always in a good mood and even infected Anni with her eagerness to start planning the new day together.

"Well, maybe I poured myself a little glass of Gammel Dansk or put a drop of it in my coffee every now and then— but so what?" Elo said. "By the way, the label on the back of

5 Sweden's alcohol monopoly.

the bottle says it's "traditionally enjoyed in small glasses for any occasion at any time of the day," and it's served with breakfast at Copenhagen's airport—I saw it myself one time when we had a layover there on our way to Málaga."

Anni hadn't commented on it, at any rate, because it never gave her aunt a perceptible buzz and, all in all, they were Europeans.

What seemed much more strange to Anni were her uncle's Christian practices—he didn't fold his hands to say grace at every meal, but they weren't able to avoid going to church on Sunday, notwithstanding. This didn't pass entirely without a hiccup the first time. Harald had gotten up relatively early in the morning and even Elo had been roused, although she was more irritable than on normal days. Harald was wearing a suit and tie, so Anni and Elo naturally needed to dress accordingly, which was a problem for Anni (at least on that first occasion) because she hadn't packed or meanwhile acquired anything overly formal. This mistake was corrected by the next week. Then they drove across the somewhat empty city to Stockholm's Old Town. Harald knew of a place where they could park, but to do so, they had to get there sufficiently early because otherwise, someone else would occupy the space, and then it could take who-knows-how-long to find another one. As a result, they had enough time to walk several circles around the Old Town before mass began—on that occasion as well as on the following ones—and on one especially gorgeous Sunday, Harald even took a picture of Elo and Anni in front of the church. But that first time, they went with Harald's friends to eat fish at a very respectable restaurant after the service, and those friends (who weren't driving) ordered red wine, even though white is actually paired with fish—doing so because red is better for your health. Anni had figured things out clearly enough to know that if she turned a glass down, then Elo might also be deprived of one and turn sulky, so she bravely consumed two.

Maybe she wouldn't have dared to speak up on the topic of religion otherwise. I can remember how she told the story after returning from Sweden. It was easy, of course, for Harald and his friends to write off Anni's words as the quirks of a rebellious pubescent girl, but she herself took it much more seriously and was upset for quite a long time afterward that she might not have appreciated her uncle's hospitality with the gratitude it deserved. It's also entirely possible that she was still a little worked up from the previous day, which hadn't been a total success, either. Naturally, Elo wasn't Harald's first wife. His need to form a new family arose when his Swedish wife Gunn left him and moved in with a loser sweetheart from her younger days somewhere near Malmö. Harald had a son from that previous marriage— Anders, who was just about a year older than Anni and had been invited to stay with them in Stockholm for the weekend, because in Harald's mind, Anni needed the company of peers. Anders's father had always spoiled both him and his mother rather indiscriminately over all those years and they got along well, although (as Elo told me with a light grimace), it should be crystal-clear that kind of "go and play now, kids" doesn't work at such an age.

"If you ask me, that boy was a total jerk," Elo said. "Ville times Oskar squared, just from a good family."

In any case, Anders's father gave him a sizable lump of cash to use for showing Anni the young-person's Stockholm. They were able to communicate with each other, although Anni's English was far better than Anders's—"No matter that it was her second foreign language," Elo beamed proudly. Yet upon arriving back home that evening, both were noticeably irritated. When Elo asked Anni where they had gone, she replied that Anders had dragged her from store to store to look at motorcycles and then taken her to some lousy club where he'd basically only spoken to his friends in Swedish the whole time and left her completely on her own. Anders's explanation to his father, in turn, was that

Anni was a pointless, vapid chick who was just impossible to talk to. In short, they didn't click. Anders quickly skedaddled the next morning—he naturally had no business attending an Estonianlanguage mass, given that he spoke no more than a couple words of the language, and old friends had included him in their plans.

Elo harbored a certain suspicion that something more might have happened the previous day, but neither Anni nor Anders confirmed it in any way. Still, if it really had been the case, that could also have incited Anni's behavior at the lunch table.

Although it was definitely far from polite.

Anni's own version of what happened diverged somewhat from the way that Elo told it: she made herself out to be the victim, whom her uncle had started examining on the topic of primary values in front of complete strangers. But for some reason, I feel like Elo's version might be closer to the truth, all the same. Because Anni did need to somehow justify her choice of words, while Elo had no reason to show her in any worse light in front of me now.

According to Elo's version, Harald had been telling the others at length and with the utmost pleasure about how the company he worked at was merging with another, much larger one, and that it could mean a very good promotion opportunity for him personally—if God willed it. Right when he uttered that last expression, Anni's fork— spearing a large chunk of salmon— stopped halfway to her mouth, and she sunk into thought. And then she asked: "How should that work, exactly?"

Harald had carried on speaking meanwhile and didn't understand the question.

"How should that work, exactly?" she had to repeat. "God willing you a really good promotion opportunity, that is? I mean, does an actual individual like that really exist—God, who personally sets out to make the decision and will you that opportunity?"

"Oh, that's just kind of a saying, you know; isn't it, now?" Harald chuckled in a fatherly tone.

"Yeah-yeah, sure, I know," Anni nodded. "So in other words, you don't actually believe, regardless, that God can will you something or take something away—you're just saying it for no reason?"

"What does that have to do with anything?"

"Well, we all just went to church, didn't we?" Anni replied. "I was just sort of along for the ride, but I assume that you yourself do actually believe in that God-stuff in some way, anyhow."

"You know," Harald said, "for me, the question of if God exists or He doesn't isn't as important as the fact that the Estonian Evangelical Lutheran Church does exist—for me, it's a very important part of the concept of Estonianness, and without it, there'd be no Estonian Republic. And I'll gladly leave deciding the God-question up to them."

"And those who don't—you're saying they're not, like, actually proper Estonians then, is that right?"

Harald put down his fork and knife for a moment.

"I certainly understand that you may have been raised in the spirit of atheism as a result of communism," he said. "But you could still show a little respect for those who have done so much for the freedom of our land and our people."

"And what's that, exactly?" Anni sputtered, unable to hold back her laughter. "Prayer?"

Harald briefly considered how to respond, and simultaneously realized the situation was already funny to his friends. He also wouldn't have been a successful businessman if he hadn't realized he might lose the argument to the cheeky girl's merciless logic, and so it would be better to direct the conversation onto another track.

"Freedom is a great gift to us all," he said. "Some believe it comes from God; some, from fate; and others that it comes from us ourselves. Does it really make a difference? But if we're capable of being grateful in our souls—not to anyone in particular, but simply grateful all the same—then, I believe, we're deserving of that freedom, too."

"Nicely put," Anni agreed. "Although . . ."

"Could I get a little more wine, please?" Elo interrupted. Harald sprang to carry out her wish with unusual zeal, promptly asking a friend to hand him the bottle and then holding it up to the light to check and see whether there was still enough left, and Elo told him to go ahead and pour it even if there was only just a little drop, and then Harald filled her glass and was very careful to make sure that sediment didn't carry over from the bottom of the bottle, and when the whole operation was over, Harald hastily asked his friend's wife whether there had been any progress with the restitution of her parents' pre-Occupation property, and that's where the God topic was left.

"It's strange," Elo said now. "When Anni was here with us that last summer, she had an entirely different opinion about those things."

"Is that so?" I asked.

"I wouldn't say that she herself had turned religious," Elo explained, "but to me, it seemed like she was jealous of them."

I actually already knew that. When she was living with me, our arguments perpetually revolved around the topic of religion, which cropped up sooner or later after something reminded her of her experiences in France (although, as I now know, she'd only informed me about a carefully selected portion of them). Faith, she said, was the only thing that set Middle Eastern women who had fled their families apart from the Eastern European street girls—in the sense that none of them had a way back to their former lives. The difference in practice, however, was immense. No matter what kind of trouble any of Anni's female Arab or Iranian acquaintances might have ended up in, never in their entire lives would they have been capable of making mental peace with the fate adopted by the Eastern

European girls in her study.

"Is it simply faith, or maybe just Islam?" I asked, not at all certain about the truthfulness of her claim.

"Simply faith," she asserted. "Although I don't mean, of course, the Christianity that's made itself so convenient for everyone." Apparently, a Polish prostitute she had visited once had a large poster hanging on the wall of her room that read: "Dear Virgin Mary, who got pregnant without sin, help me to sin without getting pregnant." This, Anni said, summed up contemporary Christianity quite nicely.

"Yes," Elo agreed when I told her this. "That's exactly what Harald's Christianity was like, too."

Elo and Harald's relationship took a sharp turn for the worse after they moved to Estonia. Firstly, because they were now on Elo's home field, so to say, and Harald no longer had any opportunity to stand between her and the world. Elo had just about as many acquaintances among repatriated Estonians as Harald did, and on top of that, she still had countless old friends. Secondly, because although the Swedish tinned-fish industrialists had chosen Harald to run their Baltic subsidiary precisely because he spoke the language and knew the customs, he actually wasn't all that familiar with the customs (or at least not the rules that governed the business world), and it cost him dearly on occasion: he was unable to wrap his mind around some situations, not to mention make them intelligible to his Swedish superiors, and the mistakes were measurable in very concrete numbers.

"When I heard about one debacle or another," Elo said, "then I thought—Christ, why the hell didn't he ask me? I could have explained it to him in just a few minutes. He could easily have had me work for him, totally without pay, and then things might have gone more smoothly for us, too." Nevertheless, Harald wasn't the kind of man who might need his wife's help at work.

And thirdly, as Elo acknowledged with a certain bravado ("And so what, huh? I had to do *something*, didn't I?!"), she also tended to empty out their bar cupboard quite rapidly back in those days, even though the brands it contained were significantly more refined than the ones that she had learned to consume in Ville and Oskar's company. Even when she told me this now, she somewhat had the eyes of a domesticated wild animal that will make a break for freedom as soon as the cage door is left open a crack.

Understandably, it wasn't exactly the right atmosphere for a mixed-up girl who officially should probably have been readying herself to go back to university. Anni was no longer drawn to French philology, but political science—which had intrigued her when she first went abroad—no longer appealed to her either. "Too general," she said. Instead, she had put social work in her crosshairs. And then it turned out that since it would be a different academic department, she would have to re-enroll and start her studies from scratch, and what's more, she would have to pay for it as well. I would gladly have provided the money, but she didn't want to accept it. Then she considered going back into philology all the same, but while simultaneously attending social-work lectures and afterward trying to somehow transfer or even defend two theses. It would have demanded an immense amount of work, of course, and maybe even advanced knowledge of theory—in short, she was in quite a mess as far as her future plans went, and ultimately, as we know, she never went back to university. This naturally wasn't Elo's fault, but it wasn't like the high-strung environment and coals of discontent smoldering beneath the ashes lent any kind of support, either.

Their property was far enough from the sea that a walk to the beach took at least an hour, and since Elo had never been able to learn how to drive, they were dependent upon Harald, who spent weekends there that extended from Thursday evening until Sunday or occasionally even a Monday afternoon. Harald undertook that journey a couple of times, too, but he obviously was no beach bum, so the women mostly had to settle for tanning in the backyard. Harald would meanwhile plug away at projects here and there—fixing the shed's roof, doing yard work, and appearing to enjoy it all with every cell of his being. Still, it got on his nerves that Elo didn't want to do anything for the common good with her time.

"But, I mean—I was just tired," Elo said. "I wanted to rest a little. All in all, people don't have a country home so that they can slave away their time, but so they can just *be* there."

Harald's opinion seemed to differ, but to his credit, it must be said that he didn't let it show in any way aside from some slight irritability. For the most part, that is. Only when a household chore that—without a shred of doubt—fell into the female sphere of responsibility was disregarded would he sometimes appear in the yard and sarcastically inquire when the "madams" might care to consider washing the dishes, or when they intended to call him to lunch. Alternately, Elo and Anni spent the days that he had to be in the city in a state of blissful chaos, having espresso for breakfast, raw salad for lunch, yogurt for dinner, and unlimited white wine as a snack for whoever wished. Elo would only turn off the tap for herself on Thursday and wash the dishes that had collected in the sink while Anni ran a mop over the downstairs floors. In the afternoon, they peeled potatoes and waited for Harald to arrive.

"When I think back on it now," Elo sighed, "it feels like it could have even been a pretty sweet life."

But it wasn't. Although their marriage trundled on for several more years, it had apparently missed all of its healing opportunities by that very summer. I'm accustomed to viewing their conflict according to Elo's perspective, but I'll admit that no matter what Harald might have done wrong before, the final lap of his second family wasn't easy for him, either. Striving at any cost to maintain the outward appearance of being a smart, healthy, successful Estonian, he went to great lengths to ensure that Elo still had everything her heart might desire, and more: they never missed a chance to vacation at the finest resorts of some warm, exotic country in fall and winter (even though Elo wasn't all that likely to make it past the hotel bar), and they held elegant receptions at their city apartment, to which a few politicians and celebrities of the art world were most certainly invited. On each of those occasions, Elo kept herself in check until the guests arrived, and those who left at a decent time always had the impression that the evening was a success; but when an outsider who had gotten into gear strayed into a later hour of the festivities, they also had the chance of seeing a different kind of host sometimes. The longer this went on, the more infrequently Harald organized such gatherings in his home.

That summer, Harald kept up before Anni the façade that everything was in the very best shape, even though he was well aware that Elo and Anni's own conversations caused credibility to seep out from the image. He should have maintained more trust in his niece-in-law: before long, Anni didn't want to hear Elo's sob-stories anymore and whenever the weather allowed, she tended to take long walks alone in the woods nearby instead, leaving Elo to sun-tan on her own. And for the most part, she carried a Bible in her bag.

On the day that Anni finally left, Harald had brought a nice, big fillet of salmon that they marinated in ginger, honey, and lime juice, then grilled at low heat until the flesh began whitening. It was outstandingly delicious with a side of goat-cheese and olive salad, even the weather was wonderful, and after lunch, the three of them sat for a while in reclining garden chairs on the spacious veranda, sipping a slightly bitter white wine in glasses that Anni and Harald stuffed full of ice cubes. And it felt like, actually, everything was just fine.

Elo couldn't remember how the argument began anymore. Either one of them might have made a comment that somehow ruffled the other's feathers, after which the latter knocked the ball back into the former's court, and before they even knew what was happening, the idyllic scene was irrevocably ended. Elo spoke intensely and with no tolerance for interruptions about how she couldn't keep on living that way and had to break free of that "fucking jail" (which there had been no rationale for in a long time), while Harald likewise raised his voice to declare that he toiled incessantly for the good of their home but had gotten absolutely nothing in return. They didn't even notice when Anni stood up quietly to go to her room meanwhile, realizing what was happening only when she came back downstairs wearing her backpack.

She stopped and stood in front of Harald first.

"She's your wife," Anni said, gesturing towards Elo. "You've chosen her. Remember that."

Then she looked at Elo and gestured towards Harald. "He's your husband. You've chosen him. Remember that."

And then she addressed both at once: "I truly wish you could understand how two people are capable of loving each other their entire lives."

With those words said, she walked out the door.

"What was that supposed to mean, then?" Harald exclaimed while Elo ran outside after Anni.

"Do you have bus money?" she called out.

Anni stopped and glanced back towards the house.

"All I can say to that is: I've got even more," she announced, then turned around and walked on in the direction of the closest town. Driving past at that moment was a local rig, which stopped as soon as Anni lifted her thumb.

They never saw each other again.

I stayed at Elo's place for one more night, and she already looked significantly better by the following morning, even though she was still a little peevish. I didn't conjure up any grand illusions of it staying that way for long. "Stay strong, then," I said when I'd hauled my things to the car after breakfast. Elo came to the door to wave. I committed to memory the way she stood there—it's not as if I could know whether or not we'd ever see each other again either.

I met Erik one early evening in an empty club, where his band had just finished doing sound-check. The bare concrete walls and floor (which looked filthy despite having undergone a proper scrubbing) were both a little misleading, and I probably appeared even more ridiculous to myself in those surroundings than I did to him. Their band wasn't all that bad, I might add, although they might not have needed to be so generous with the decibels. Now he and I were sitting at the sturdy bar counter, both holding a mug of coffee that was a little on the weak side.

He looked a little older than he should have been by my calculations, and was much taller than I am; but there isn't anything unusual about that, of course. And he had strong hands— not a musician's hands at all. They were the first things to leave an impression, although his somewhat crude facial features and honest grayish eyes suited him well, too.

"It's weird of you to ask me that just now," Erik said. "I got together with Mona a couple of days ago—totally randomly— so we had cause to reminisce about the old days."

Mona was a girl Erik had fallen hopelessly in love with five years before, just like all the other boys who formed the ensemble that accompanied her singing persona at the time. Erik played bass along with three more identical unfortunates: i.e. keyboard, guitar, and percussion.

"She was still as dopey as she's always been," Erik continued, "but she's gotten over that Christian quirk. No more 'gates of paradise' or anything. And her voice has gotten deeper and hoarser somehow, too."

"That comes in handy for some," I reckoned.

"My thoughts exactly," Erik agreed. "She could sing some pretty sweet blues, no problem. Still, it seemed like she's actually up to her ears in some eco-thing, and apparently doesn't even do music anymore. Too bad. Of course, it's not like I'd want those days back or anything, either. We really sucked it big time, back then." He laughed with no bitterness in his voice.

I'd tracked Erik down to find out something about the Christian youth camp Anni ended up at after leaving Elo's place. His contact information came from my mother, with whom she'd stayed for a couple of nights along with a few acquaintances after leaving the countryside. I found some details about the camp online, but only a few. It was run by some Finnish sectarians at a former coastal Pioneer camp that had been converted into a resort, and Mona with her band were among those invited with the aim of attracting a young audience.

"It was a pretty depressing place, otherwise," Erik told me. "There wasn't even any beer, and you weren't allowed to smoke on the premises, either. Luckily, the food was all right and, well, you could head to the beach during the day and, all in all, what's there to complain about—there've been way worse summers than that. But I was so wild about Mona back then, and I guess that left its mark. Totally messed up, I mean. I just looked at her and my whole body trembled, you know? The other guys were just the same. And she enjoyed it to a T—she played us like a fourperson instrument. She'd smile at one, take another by the arm for a minute, ask somebody else for help buttoning up the back of her costume. Ooohh . . . It was like an electric shock when your fingers touched her body. But none of us got any more than that."

I kept silent, waiting for him to steer the conversation more towards the camp again, and he could probably sense it, but just couldn't help himself.

"The campers went to hang out under Mona's window sometimes, too—boys, mostly. The scrawny, pimply-faced types—and she'd do a little God-talk with them then. I didn't really know how serious she was about all of it, of course. 'Cause she dressed real cool back then and didn't really look all that Christian on stage, either. She had these tall, soft, silver-colored boots—big platform-heeled ones; and she wore a long white wig. Ahead of her time, you could say now. Sort of like a Lady Gaga look. And her dress wasn't too long or anything, and she wore a real tight-fitting top. But for her, it was more like a matter of principle. That faith doesn't mean you've got to turn into some kind of a nun right off the bat. That, well—Jesus loves you just the way you are. It does sound pretty reasonable, all in all, though personally, I'm not too crazy about that God-stuff, and neither was I then."

"I can understand," I nodded.

"There were all kinds of people there. Some were still full-on minors, fourteen-fifteen-year-olds or what have you. And the oldest, I guess, were college theology students—they held their own talks and discussion sessions there, but I don't know too much about that since we were beach-bumming it all day, for the most part. Only Viljar—that was our guy on keys—he went to listen to those sermons, too, but I'm guessing he just wanted to impress Mona by going."

Judging by Erik's smug expression, it was clear this hadn't worked out for Viljar.

"All in all, it felt like the people living there were sort of lost souls, mostly. I myself couldn't really figure out why they were there. Some came out of curiosity, while others were sort of like a bird with a broken wing. But, well, once they were already there, they had to convince themselves and each other of how supercool it was. 'Cause otherwise, their summer would have been a total bust, you know. Maybe some of them really did believe it in the end. That it was cool, I mean. Some of them might have believed it from the start, of course. But those campers must have been totally terminal, then. We were there for longer than anybody else, you know—three shifts in a row, so there was time galore for it to make you jaded."

"So, it went in shifts like that?" I asked. "The way I understood it, you could just come and go as you pleased, if you wanted."

Erik nodded and sipped from his mug.

"Most of the campers were, yeah, still shift-based. But a few did have friends come and visit and then split again. I was told that no one had to pay for anything out of their own pocket—the sect covered it all. So, there was, like, no problem. The Finns didn't make a big deal of that in-and-out business, but just said everybody had to sign in. The camp was pretty big and there were open spots available all the time and there was always food left over, anyway. And then everybody in charge was able to impress their bosses afterwards, too."

I can't imagine how Anni might have felt there. It certainly didn't sound like her kind of a place, based on what Erik said. It was my understanding that she had let someone invite her along, someone whom she'd met randomly while hitchhiking. How long she spent there, I didn't know.

"Then, once every shift, we held a dance competition there. Mona was the judge along with some old Finnish guy. Another Finn—the one who spoke Estonian—was the DJ and played records—that kind of spiritual rock—and he'd made a special slideshow where pictures and Jesus's message flashed up on the wall so that there was no way in hell anyone'd forget what the whole thing was all about. Boys and girls signed up separately and were paired at random (well, sort of making sure that their age was the same), and then each pair had a minute on stage and were scored. It was unfair in the sense that the couple was given points and if one was pretty good but the other sucked, the total score was still shit. They hadn't, like, thought it out really well, in my opinion. But it was a total hit with the campers.

And they weren't, like, disappointed when they lost. Christians, right? The grand prize was Mona singing you a song. Oh shit, she was good. She'd wrap her arm around the boy's shoulders and look him in the eye while she held the girl's hand like they were best friends. She did it the same exact way all three times, and on each of them, the couple looked as if they'd hugged an angel when they walked off stage."

I wasn't all that hopeful when I described Anni to him, and it was no surprise that he shook his head regretfully.

"Sorry. There were so many of them there that not a lot of them stuck. I've only got, like, a definite memory of one girl in a wheelchair. Or more like a memory of the wheelchair, not the girl—heh."

What's more, it was the past, of which he was now free.

I don't know why I decided to track down the girl in the wheelchair. It wasn't very hard, in any case. For some reason, the sectarian manning the information line wasn't suspicious at all of why someone would be trying to find that exact person without knowing her name, and she gave me the girl's address and home telephone number without greater ado. I doubt she would have been as helpful if I'd said I was looking for a blonde with big tits. But Godspeed to her. Or, well—that goes without saying.

As soon as I saw Kelly, I realized what connects us. There was no doubt. It wasn't about the ability (or inability) to accept a misfortune that's befallen you: it was something completely different—when an irreversible thing has happened and you know that's simply the way things are now, that it's not merely a stroke of fate, but the kind of problem that from here onward is yours and yours alone, and that defines you as a person both from within and without, because your chances aren't unfettered—oh, no: what can happen is no longer pure coincidence. It's happened to you already, and that's the way it's going to stay.

That, *that* is what is unbearable; *that* is what wakes you up in the middle of the night or pierces you on an otherwise mild evening, when you've nearly managed to forget the how and why.

Kelly's mother extended a smile to me as she opened the apartment door: she apparently didn't have the slightest trace of distrust for strangers that tends to rather be the norm these days. Or else that's what she wanted me to believe. On the way there, I donned a tie for some reason and bought some small cakes just in case, which she accepted, asking whether I'd like to have coffee or tea. I said I'd take whatever was easier—because I hadn't come for the refreshments, of course—but no: she demanded softly but firmly that I clearly state my preference, and then had me pick from several different kinds of tea before she led me to Kelly's room.

Kelly barely turned her head to look when I entered. I sat down on an empty chair and said nothing, simply breathing in her room and her loneliness. The furniture was simple, the books on the shelf not so much.

"Well, get it over with already," Kelly said. "The clock's ticking."

Later, when the two of us had been conversing for a while, I found out that she'd been expecting the next subsequent Biblebanger and had even watched some Hitchens and Dawkins videos on YouTube to prepare her counterattacks. When she realized that I had no intention of redeeming her, we got to chatting with relative ease, even though it didn't fully dispel her prickly attitude. I suppose nothing could. In any case, she was entirely different from what I'd expected. And much more memorable, I'll say. But let's be honest—if you had been handicapped in a motorcycle accident six years ago, not at all by your own fault, and now lived with your mother, who held the firm belief that you yourself are rejecting the simple solution to all your problems, a certain prickliness is incredibly understandable.

Because of the way things had gone, Kelly's accident somehow managed to ground her mother's life in place almost as much as it did her own. Namely, her mother had decided that she herself was being punished. At first, the punisher was simply abstract fate, because Kelly's mother had never had any ties to religion before. But then a distant relative came to help them out for a period of time: until Kelly had more or less learned to cope with her inevitable mobility needs within the bounds of her new limitations. That relative himself had recently come to know Jesus and never tired of talking about it, to the point that even Kelly's mother allowed herself to get caught up in it, and not long afterward, she discovered a new life for herself, too.

"The fact that this is the way I am now is all a consequence of her sins, you understand," Kelly explained. "And I'm just the instrument that delivers the message. Can you even imagine a more iron-clad logic than that?"

Specifically, a short time before Kelly's accident, her parents divorced after many years of fighting. There might have been a slight, indirect connection between this circumstance and why she was speeding around on a motorcycle, of course, because Kelly loved her father dearly and didn't approve at all of her mother's resolution to show him the door.

"I believe that a marriage can't be dissolved and a home can't be sold," Kelly informed me. "If that idea crosses your mind, consequently it wasn't a marriage, but an economic agreement. If that idea crosses your mind, consequently it wasn't a home, but a piece of real estate."

"Well, to each his own," I tried to argue.

"I'm guessing you're that type, too?" she said, seeing right through me. "A proper family expert *you* are."

Kelly's mother re-arranged her own personal life rather quickly, and perhaps that played its own part in the woman's religious awakening. All those years, a sectarian pastor would occasionally spend the night at their house—a man whose wife had up and left with some Australian evangelist, but without divorcing first, so he wouldn't have been able to make his relationship with Kelly's mother official. Furthermore, her mother explained, that relationship was above all spiritual.

"Spiritual my ass," Kelly said. "The walls here are paper-thin."

The man left Kelly alone after a couple attempts to call her to his flock, but her mother hadn't lost hope, instead inviting an endless stream of new soul-catchers to show Kelly the true light. It was no surprise that she thought I was another one of them at first. But later, I no longer got the impression that she was awaiting my exit, either. It was only when I told her about Anni's death that she compressed her lips into a thin rift and refused to say anything for a while, causing me to believe that I'd broken our connection. But I hadn't.

For she remembered Anni well. The camp experience as a whole had been a relatively depressing one for her, since she couldn't find anyone to have a conversation with anywhere around. There were a couple of exceptions, and Anni was one of them. Not that their worldviews corresponded, necessarily. But when Kelly made a couple of sharp atheist remarks to Anni and my daughter didn't roll her eyes at them, but instead countered them with calm and amiable arguments, Kelly was impressed. On top of that, there was no one else to talk to there, anyway.

"We didn't see eye-to-eye, of course," Kelly disclaimed. "But she was no religious schizo, either. She told me about the categorical imperative. You know what that is, right? I totally get it; just that in my opinion, there's nothing divine about it. Why do we believe that if humans themselves have agreed on something, it can always be changed? And yet, if some god has signed it with his golden quill, that law is holy and inviolable?"

"It's certainly easier for some to be good people that way," I shrugged.

"Yeah, but maybe we could also talk about those for whom

it's easier to be bad people that way—huh?" Kelly countered. "I definitely believe there are, like, tons and tons more atrocities committed in the name of God. Starting with the Crusades and the St. Bartholomew's Day massacre up through all kinds of fucked-up human relationships. Don't even start talking about human goodness here, all right? I've already been there."

"Maybe we could talk some more about Anni," I prompted. The more time that passed, the more time they spent together. Anni would push Kelly's wheelchair to the beach and then sit on a rock, where they would stare out at the sea together and sometimes talk, sometimes not.

"Sometimes I couldn't even tell which of us was the sick one, anymore," Kelly said. "She'd gotten hurt really badly somewhere, you know. But she was really strong, and that's why it didn't show. Some luckless love or something like that, I think."

If I'd have known then, I believe I might have told her. But maybe not.

"That's how little those people get it," Kelly continued. "That there's no such thing as luckless love. That if there's love, there's happiness, too; it's just that there's all different kinds of happiness. And if there isn't love, well, there just isn't."

At that moment, Kelly's mother knocked on the door and entered. The tray she was carrying held a teapot and a plate with the cakes I'd brought, sugar, and two unattractive pinkish mugs adorned with chubby flying cherubs.

"Everything's going well for you two here, I hope?" she asked, not directly addressing either of us.

Kelly looked up and glared, but her mother just placed the tray on the desk and stood there, waiting for a response.

"The door," Kelly finally said. "Close it."

Her attitude caught me by surprise. With a look in her eye that seemed apologetic, Kelly's mother retreated from the room and swiftly closed the door behind her. Kelly had already noticed the astonished look of disapproval on my face.

"Oh, I don't give two shits about what that slut-of-the-Lord thinks about world affairs," she snapped.

"Hey, are you really sure a person can talk about her mother that way?" I asked.

She shrugged. "Accepting gifts from someone who loves you without hoping that relationship will last forever is just a form of prostitution."

I didn't know what to say to that. Or did I?

"You know," I said, "sometimes life is far more complicated than it seems, but by the time you grasp it, there's nothing you can do about it anymore."

"It shouldn't be, then," she replied. "If I ever do understand it. You know, there's just not a single square centimeter in common between her world and mine."

"And this world is somehow better, then?" I pointed to a Dale Carnegie book protruding from a stack on her desk. "*How to Win Friends and Influence People.*"

She started laughing.

"What, you think I'm reading that for real? It's just for defense, buddy. So that when any of those dudes start laying wisdom on me that they learned from somewhere in those pages, I'll be ready."

"Is that right."

"For instance, I found out there why they use my first name all the time. Like: 'Look, Kelly, did you know?' 'This is how it is, Kelly.' 'Kelly.' 'Cause that old guy thinks that people *like* it. That to them, their name is the most beautiful word in the world. And if you repeat it over and over to them, they'll buy more of whatever you're selling. Fucking retard. *He* apparently wasn't named after some brainless chick somebody saw in some brainless TV show."

I couldn't help but be reminded of the arguments Maire and I had when we were naming Anni, as a result of which I was sadly unguarded for what she said next:

"You know, Anni and I were like reflections of each other, in some sense. Or more like the same photo, just that one was the positive and the other the negative. And because of that, since she died, I've got to live."

The next times I went to visit her, we didn't talk any more about Anni, or if we did, very briefly. But I hope that I played my own little part in the fact that over time, she gradually started making amends with her mother.

I hadn't gone to visit my own mother all that often lately, but not because I hadn't been thinking about her. Both of us knew the way things were going and that it's not natural for sons to depart this life before their mothers, and neither of us desired the kind of atmosphere where that knowledge hung over us. Once, I made the mistake of inviting her to attend an opera in Riga, and she naturally accepted. The opera was indeed fantastic. We went to see *La Traviata*—I hadn't realized in a very long time how greatly I missed the opera, because those kinds of performances aren't given in Estonia. And I'd booked a hotel in the Old Town—everything in Latvia is so cheap because of that fiscal crisis, I guess. We had one of those semi-luxury rooms with a ton of space and a good feel to it. Even so, it had been a mistake. Or at least that's how I felt. Every silence at the end of a sentence, every pause that trailed a simple question sliced into me like a scythe. I personally tried to keep up the act that there was nothing wrong, although I realized, of course, that I wasn't fooling anyone; still, my mother didn't let it show. It was nice to be near her, naturally, and vice versa—if only we'd have been able to limit ourselves to the present moment at each moment.

But I went to visit her from time to time, of course. I liked Kuusalu, and she did, too: you could still perceive the proximity of the city (I suppose most people there commute to Tallinn every day for work), and therefore it didn't feel like you were in the middle of nowhere, although at the same time, it wasn't as if a high-strung electricity was sizzling through you either. Mother, in any case, had still managed to maintain her habit of going to the theater while living out there. Although she didn't drive, she could always find someone to give her a ride there or back, and when she stayed at my place overnight (which lately had become a much rarer occurrence than before), it was often because she had something else planned in Tallinn for the next day. If I'd had a reason for making future plans, Kuusalu would be a stable setting for them. Why lie—right now, the town is only an episode.

Naturally, I'd called ahead to my mother, which at least meant cake. That's why I brought a bottle of wine along, too—not so much for drinking as for the immediate implication that I would be staying the night. She was glad of it. We chatted about this and that for a while; or, well, what "this and that"? About the books either of us had read recently, of course; about the music we'd listened to; about the everyday political scandals that darken your mood. It was a currant-and-gooseberry cake (berries which could be found year-round in her freezer) that had a crispy glaze lightly dashed with cinnamon. She served herself a small piece only out of politeness, since her doctor had warned that her sugar level was a tad too high.

"And, well, I'll gladly have a look around this place a little longer—for as long as I'm allowed," she concluded, looking me in the eyes—she was well aware she could talk to me that way.

Then we were silent for a little while.

"Actually, I'd like to talk about Anni," I finally said. "She came here to visit you once that summer, too—right?"

"She sure did," my mother nodded. "She had a couple of friends she knew from that sectarian camp along with her—a boy and a girl. I can't remember them all that well, but they were, well, you know—two souls a little messed up by the world the way it is today."

This was true. I'd actually already spoken to both of them by that time, without finding out anything interesting.

"Then they left here to go see that 'Beekeeper,'" my mother continued. "I think Aivar is his name, actually. He's a nice man otherwise, just a teensy bit bizarre. But, well, you know—those were the kinds of people she was drawn to then. There's always a girl living over there at Aivar's, each one twenty or so years younger than him and always prettier than the last. They help him keep the place in shape and, well—you know."

I do know.

"He was a pastor once, back when he was younger," my mother hastened to specify. "What might he have been, now—probably about your age. Fifty years behind him, in any case. I saw him one day at the grocery store in Kuusalu: he lives a ways on from here, by the way, out in the middle of the woods; does his beekeeping there. Back in the day, he had quite the shock of hair—sort of yellowish-red—and his beard's just spectacular to this day, although his head's already shiny. He'd been kicked out of the Church when he started preaching his own personal beliefs from the pulpit, and told the old ladies who were demanding some good old Jesusing to beat it. But from that time onward, those lost little lambs started pouring into his place from each and every direction. He was quite the handsome man when he was younger, too; now he mows them down more with charisma."

Mother glanced over at me to make sure her words hadn't been grating, but I was already long past that danger.

Anni did stay over there for a while. Then she came back here for a spell, and told me she'd be heading to somewhere down south in Mulgimaa next. Oh, she was a restless soul, that daughter of yours—you know how she was. Couldn't stay in place anywhere for very long if she didn't feel like she was needed right there. I made them dinner, and afterwards Anni and I spoke for a while, just the two of us, for almost the whole night. We drank tea and she got a whole lot of things off her chest . . . Or, well, that's what it seemed like then."

My mother was silent for a short time, as if weighing what parts of what Anni had said she might be allowed to tell me, and what parts not; apparently, it had been a little like a confession that not even death allows to be discussed.

"She really was awfully mixed up," my mother confessed. "She had grown up made for one world, but had to live in another. And maybe she also understood that other one far better than the people who felt good living there. I can't say— I've always had to defend my own living environment; my war has been a defensive one, and I've never felt the need or even the desire to go and fix other people's worlds. Not, of course, counting those who personally come to me for help."

"Isn't that a little odd coming from a lifelong teacher?" I questioned.

She nodded and smiled sadly.

"I myself have only realized it over the last few years, yes. There was a time when I thought—likewise, I suppose—that I was doing things for the sake of my students' souls. And that that's what made me me—what justified me being the way I am. But you know what? I was nothing. I can tell you that. I'm no missionary. But those, yes, only those who planted themselves in my flowerbed—*those*, I truly watered with care. And when any of them withered regardless, it was all the more painful. They themselves were already a part of me—that's why."

She looked over at me and then served the last piece of cake onto my plate without asking. There was something final about the movement.

"But we were talking about other things," she sighed. "You know, I've wondered very often what really happened to Anni then. Whether I might have been able to do something differently—to prevent it. Whether at that time, she already had that 'something' inside of her that later consumed her. To tell you the truth, I don't know. It troubles me. It troubles me horribly."

"Oh, stop it now," I said. "You don't have the least reason in the *world* to blame yourself."

"I know," she replied. "And I'm not, or not in that sense. And there was hardly anything I could have done, even if I had seen what was coming. And I didn't know anything about that artists' farm down near Viljandi, either—what kind of people were there or any of that. I suppose she didn't know, either. One group had passed through the Beekeeper's place with some kind of a plan to head there, and the way they talked about it, she thought it sounded like a pretty cool place."

And what else could someone have really thought in that case, right?

I knew their type well: when I was in high school, they were the go-betweens to get your hands on Uku Masing[6] poems and essays on forming a connection with the higher spheres of consciousness by way of Tibetan yoga, typed ten sheets at a time onto sheer cigarette paper. In short—weirdos, and not necessarily harmless ones. Back then, I'd been highly indifferent about those kinds of hobbies, and I wasn't all that convinced of their reasoning even now. But of course, the Beekeeper of today wasn't like men of his type were back then, either. Parked in front of the house was a maybe three- or four-year-old Volvo SUV in good condition, and the fence was freshly painted, as is proper for a respectable middle-class homeowner. I bet he had a home page and a blog, too. And he does have to make a living

6 Uku Masing (1909–1985) was an Estonian theologian, oriental-ist, philosopher, poet, folklorist, and ethnologist.

somehow—maybe he sells organic honey; maybe he writes EU grant proposals for his non-profit. But, well, he can't be blamed, because it's not as if he himself came up with that world to suit his purposes. Before I saw him, I was unable to guess whether I would find him pleasant or unpleasant, because I still had no clue whether he actually believed in what he told others. Or if he'd at least be able to give me that impression.

He didn't know I was coming. But I suppose that to this day, strangers weren't required to inform him of their arrival in advance, either. When I opened the gate and called out a hello, a tall girl stuck her red-haired head out the doorway, and a few moments later, the Beekeeper himself emerged too.

"Well, come on in," he said without taking much of a look at me. His voice was full and resonant, strong but with a deep timbre that could have been trained into a respectable operatic bass once. "The tea's just ready. Reet, be a darling and find us another mug."

There were three places set at the table inside—seated there in addition to the Beekeeper and Reet was a boy with a chalk-white face and coal-black hair. He was dressed all in black and had his shirt buttoned all the way up to his throat, which made it look as if the shirt had been what choked him pale.

"Hanno," he named himself instead of saying hello. His voice had a slightly singsong quality to it.

"Enn," I replied, and then had to clear my throat.

"Well, and what are you standing there for, Enn?" Reet asked. "Would you like sugar or honey? We drink it more with honey here, I might add."

"I suppose I'll have honey, then," I said. I couldn't help the fact that I liked them.

My reason for coming and what I needed didn't seem to interest them at all. They were presently in the middle of a discussion on Buñuel's films, which they cheerfully continued. The Beekeeper was attempting to explain to his two younger listeners that in spite of all of Buñuel's atheism and anticlericalism, he had always been Catholically-minded; or, well, if not Catholically, then Catholic-ish (whatever difference that might make). However, Hanno was heatedly disputing the point. I myself had a rather poor recollection of Buñuel's films, so I spectated the exchange more with sports-pub enthusiasm. Reet didn't especially interfere in their conversation—she comprehended marvelously that her not-at-all modest contribution to the debate's complexity and inarguable elegance was brought home by her mere presence. And therefore she hovered around the entire time.

"Fine, fine," Hanno said. "I might even understand what you're calling 'Catholicism.' But in that case, you're the only person who uses the word that way. So tell me now, honestly: what's the point in creating complicated systems of meaning that no one else understands the exact right way? In making a sort of world map that doesn't help anyone else travel around a territory, and perhaps even conceals it from them, too?"

"That *is* the only thing that still has a point to it," the Beekeeper shot back. "After all that postmodernism has swept over the world the way it was before."

"And *that's* your mistake," Hanno remained persistent. "You see yourself as a Christian, don't you?"

"I don't see myself as one—I *am*," the Beekeeper corrected.

"Yeah, well, not a single Christian church has the same opinion as you on that little issue," Hanno replied. "Okay, I get from your theory that God is a sign that points to something within me, not some kind of a being or a will or whatever. That's a super-cool theory, in my opinion, but let's be honest: not one church has approved of it."

"That's not my problem," the Beekeeper shrugged.

"On the contrary," Hanno disagreed, "that's *exactly* your problem. That's the exact reason why you've got to assert yourself all the time, no matter who you're talking to at that moment, because you're not really trying to seek communion with others—a common, systemic background. Instead, you want everybody else to understand the world the way that you stipulate. You do realize, of course, that by doing so, you only end up talking to people weaker than you?"

The conversation was fascinating to me, but apparently not to Reet.

"By the way, Enn, are you staying for lunch with us?" she asked.

"It depends," I replied.

"Well, decide then," she said. "I need to know how many servings to make."

"Actually, I came to speak with Aivar," I said. "On a very specific topic."

"Oh-ho," the Beekeeper said, turning to me and apparently enjoying the chance to escape Hanno's offensive. "What's it about, then?"

Hanno stood up without a word and left the room.

"Do you remember Anni?" I asked.

"Anni?" He frowned for a moment—a fair number of girls with her name might indeed have passed through that place. "Maybe we should go and continue this outside; we'll only be a bother to Reet with her cooking."

"You won't in the very least," Reet announced. "I'd actually be very intrigued to hear you two talk about Anni."

"It was quite a while ago," I explained. "She was here for a couple of months in the summer of 2005."

"Of course I remember," the Beekeeper said, and stood. "The girl who'd come from France."

"She's the one," I confirmed, standing up as well. We went outside.

"Of course I remember her," the Beekeeper continued. "She was very special."

"Aren't they all, then?" I asked with slight sarcasm. He didn't answer, only staring at the path for a few moments.

"You're her father, aren't you?" he then asked. I nodded. "What did you actually come looking for here?"

"I don't really know," I shrugged. "Memories. Anni's no longer with us."

The Beekeeper stared at me in silence for a long while.

"You know, it might be painful for you to hear this, but that actually doesn't surprise me," he said. "Anni was one of the most heroic people I've ever met. The kind who'd be the first at the barricades in every revolution, prepared to sacrifice herself in the name of the idea, if you only gave her one. And I believe that because of that, you've got reason to be seriously proud of her, no matter what else might have happened. But in this age of ours, the accountants lead the revolutionaries, too; no wonder that she didn't feel herself at home here. If Joan of Arc'd had to write a grant proposal first, Paris would be part of England right now." That last sentence sounded like something he'd said earlier and in other contexts. Which didn't mean it was any less on the mark.

"We completed each other, you could probably say," the Beekeeper continued. "But our worlds didn't actually match, in spite of it. I believe she might have gotten bored here. I don't want to change anything, you see: I only want to understand, and that's quite enough for me. Not for her. I was toothless, the way she saw it."

"I can see that," I said. "That she could think that way, I mean. I just don't understand why she wasn't searching for justice anymore. Only God."

"But that's so logical, isn't it?" the Beekeeper reckoned. "Everyone who perceives the absolute arrives at it sooner or later. Whoever doesn't quits partway there."

I shook my head—that kind of argument seemed too convenient. I said so, and he shrugged.

"People with ambitions are inevitably disappointed in life," he continued, "because at some point, the time comes when they aren't capable of achieving their next goal. Those, on the other hand, who really only dream at an average level aren't capable of anything other than that average. But if there does exist a kind of person who is capable of assessing both herself and her life so exactly that she can avoid both dangers—that, I don't know. I'm not that strong."

Reet and Hanno had prepared a vegetarian meal, but it was filling. And then they offered me an upstairs room, and I stayed. The Beekeeper made a fire in the fireplace and discussed with Hanno the whole evening through the topic of whether you can make ethical judgements of people themselves or rather of the acts they commit, and we drank white wine mixed with warm apple juice and cinnamon. That night, I felt like I could have stayed there for good. A tempting thought flashed in my mind: what if, in this life, I'd stayed together with my first-year college girlfriend Katariina, who would have undoubtedly felt at home in such company? Could my world have then ended up much closer to this one, too? Could I, perhaps, have also been able to freely and naturally think thoughts entirely different from the ones that have consumed my life? And what's more: when I arrived, I was afraid that maybe it was here that Anni had been infected with some kind of a virus from beyond. When I left in the morning, I was disappointed that wasn't the case.

II

BIRCHBACK

5

NEXT, I NEED to tell you about people I've never met in person, and whom I haven't even tried to find, especially. On this journey, I've naturally also come across those who have regarded me with clear hostility and haven't wanted to speak to me at all; that's why you won't encounter them in these pages. But I've personally tried to approach all of them with as open a mind as possible. The person whom I'm going to tell you about now is an exception. I'm unable to think positively about him. What I know about him has been pieced together from many stories— from everything that those who have suffered at his hand have told me—in other words: from all those who have had any more extensive interaction with him at all. I've likewise seen a number of relatively poor-quality photos. Still, I've formed a much clearer mental picture of him, which over time has also mingled with another memory, one entirely independent of him.

Once, when I was still a schoolboy (I might have been in seventh grade), I stood a long time waiting for Trolley #3 at what was then the Victory Square stop (now Freedom Square) on a sniffly November day. Standing among the crowd was a very strange figure—a boy who was in his last years of high school or had graduated a couple years earlier at the most; tall and with narrow, hollowed cheekbones. His unwashed hair hung down to his shoulders, and his eyes were piercing, almost burning. He was thin and wearing a jacket, which was a little too light for the chilly weather that day. He carried a briefcase, and his somewhat grubby jeans were tucked into his tall rubber boots. Yet, it was all merely a casing—a thin shell hiding a single pure, clear nerve. Before long, he realized that I'd been goggling at him, even though I tried to avert my gaze every time he looked in my direction. As soon as he wasn't watching anymore, I was forced to stare at him again as if against my own will. There was nothing pleasant about him; I had absolutely no desire to get acquainted. It was like he was from a completely different world, and yet, penetrating deep into my bones was the feeling that the man knew something—something about which I hadn't the slightest clue, but of such importance that it could change my life or the life of someone else.

After a long wait, Trolley #3 finally rolled up to the stop. The man glanced over, noticed that I didn't intend to board it, then walked up to me with long steps and said: "We're having a youth night over at St. Olaf's on Thursday. Come check it out!" And at the last second before the doors clapped shut, he hopped onto the trolley.

I didn't go, of course. Not because I had anything against the Church as such—oh, no: by then, I'd extensively read both my mother's pre-Occupation religious readers and a little of her school Bible, too. But I somehow sensed—instinctively, maybe; like an animal that knows how to avoid traps—that this was something different. I didn't think much more about it, and neither did I mention the episode to my parents at home. Because for some reason, I was ashamed—I couldn't even have told you why.

I never saw that man again, but everything I've been told about Android summons that impression—that spell I felt at the trolley stop, which was a mixture of horror and disgust.

He naturally wasn't nicknamed Android after the telephone— that didn't exist yet. And I'm guessing he didn't even have a telephone; it wasn't his style. One of the people who spoke to

me about him reckoned he might have gotten the nickname
from a Philip K. Dick book, but maybe his real name was just
similar in some way; I'll never know. He was from somewhere
in eastern Estonia and grew up with a single mother, who was
a little hysterical and completely incapable of contact with the
world, as well as a strict religious grandmother—Android apparently spoke about both of them with a hint of bitter derision
from time to time. He knew nothing about his father, or if he
did, he never mentioned it, only making the occasional snappish and disdainful remark about fathers as a species. Nor could
anyone say whether he'd received any education at all, and if he
had, where that seemingly awe-inspiring but actually cursory
and spotty knowledge had come from—he knew a little more
about everything than a popular-science magazine could expect
its readers to know, but not so much about anything that he
could be regarded as an expert. He likewise never spoke about
a single university in a manner that implied he had attended it,
but since he regarded all institutions with contempt (including
those from which he had benefitted), it actually didn't mean
anything either. With the self-confidence of an independent
studier, he was able to posit grounded claims on anything at all
or inform people of facts they knew previously with such pomp
and circumstance as if he himself had come up with them right
then and there for the very first time. His remarks were actually
quite exact and intelligently worded on some occasions, because
he undoubtedly *was* very talented; but on some occasions, they
weren't.

Even so, his instinct was almost unfailing. He was always
able to read on his interlocutors' faces the effect his words were
having on them, and if he made a gaffe, he instantly turned it into
a clever joke that naturally wasn't directed against himself, but
rather against the overall obtuseness of the world. He generally
refrained from systematically presenting his own views for the
exact same reason. Even so, there were rare occasions on which

he still did—attempting to engage his audience in dialogue from the very start. That way, he was able to keep an eye on what his listeners expected from him. Or, to be more exact: what wasn't expected from him, but he could say regardless—and that's just what it would be. All of this resulted in his inarguable authority among the social circles he frequented. And it made him *look* for the circles where such authority could be invoked. They weren't hard to find.

The first time I heard about him was from two youths who had been at Birchback that summer. Kaupo was maybe a couple years older than Mailis, and they were perfect for each other: one strong and trustworthy, maybe a little simple but all the more predictable because of it; the other delicate and vulnerable, perhaps slightly unbalanced but with a wider range of emotions as a result. Kaupo was someone easy to both meet and part with: he had an athletic build and a sincere face with what was almost a built-in smile; more a man of acts than of big words. His hair was buzzed short, but the natural intelligence reflecting from his eyes betrayed the fact that his talents weren't limited to the weight room; even though he could excel beyond many a person there as well. After graduating from grammar school, he spent a couple of years traipsing around Europe and working random jobs, then returned to Estonia and started looking for new acquaintances. Mailis was cut from an entirely different cloth. She was a little taller than average—her head well over Kaupo's shoulders, who was by no means short—but at the same time as fragile as could be; it felt like even a strong breeze could have swept her up into the air. She had glittering light-blue eyes, brunette hair that sprung into curls just a tiny bit, and at the same time a suresounding voice just a little deeper than one would expect. Mailis had gotten into the Estonian Academy of Arts on her first try, which indicated that she had true talent, and had graduated in textiles. Nothing bad happened to either of them at Birchback, but something good certainly had—that was where they had met, and by now, they had been living together for several years. Kaupo had managed to finish a degree in IT meanwhile and even had his own start-up—it appeared that things were going very well for him, at least judging by the home address I was invited to for our chat.

Entering the foyer, I noticed a pair of leather gloves on a small table. They were the exact same as a pair I had bought just recently, so I knew how much they cost. But I have no more use for money, anyhow. I did, however, stick my own pair into my pocket just in case, so that they wouldn't get mixed up. I saw Mailis notice this and at that moment, I thought she was no doubt also aware of what they cost.

When I was shown into the living room, I observed that their standard of living was visible but not ostentatious: the lamps and designer furniture came from the very best shops and the stereo system alone—which was set up on a low, dark-colored table—likely cost more than my car. But they were the kinds of possessions that simply made you feel good, and taking them in, you hoped it really is true that two people can be capable of loving each other their entire lives.

All they knew about the Birchback fire was as much as had been printed in the papers—meaning the deaths, too. Still, it was only the general facts, and I didn't start enlightening them in greater detail. And they had positive recollections from that summer, because it had been a very important one for them. They elaborated on each other's stories in a well-meaning way, and when either one occasionally interrupted the other, it was only to pick up the very same sentence while the other took a mental breather.

That summer had been Mailis's second at Birchback, and so she was able to compare it with an earlier one. Kaupo had been there for the first time, however, having come along with random friends who promised he would see all kinds of weirdos—for it was precisely the weirdos whom Kaupo missed the most after having hitchhiked home from Germany to Estonia.

"And there really were some oddballs there, too, of course; you remember—that guy with unwashed hair and round yellow glasses," Kaupo said. He startled for a moment when he looked over at me, because mine were almost a little similar and it's hardly likely that he had intended to associate us in any way. But, well, I wore them for medical purposes—not to look cooler somehow.

"You mean Android," Mailis said.

"Yeah, him," Kaupo nodded. "That was one special bird."

I couldn't tell whether it was meant as a compliment or sarcasm, or even both at once.

"Yep," Mailis agreed. "Android was totally a case in and of himself."

"Anyway, I've got no reason to speak badly of him," Kaupo remarked, putting his arm around Mailis's shoulders. "If he hadn't tried to get Mailis under his control, he wouldn't have pissed me off in the first place. Nor would I have come to her rescue. But, well—here we are now."

"Android had this habit, you see," Mailis explained, "of like having to mark all the girls for himself. It was pretty disgusting. No, not in that sense at all, I mean—he just needed them to lock their eyes on him and nod along to his every word."

"And they'd feel guilty if they tried to think with their own brains," Kaupo added. "He tried to put all the guys in their place, too, but a little differently. Sort of like a stray dog, you know—so that they wouldn't trespass on his territory. 'Cause he was the only one allowed to be the great leader and teacher."

"Oh, yeah," Mailis said. "But he arrived later, didn't he. Maybe it's best to start from the very beginning."

I've been told about what happened at Birchback by altogether five people, each of whom held a very different attitude towards what transpired. Whoever said whatever in particular shouldn't be all that important in the grand scheme (and what's more, several of them told me most of the same things), but I'll make a distinction wherever it's important. I'll attempt to tell the events chronologically and compose the story as neutrally as possible, but I suppose I haven't quite been able to entirely exclude my subjects' personal judgments, especially when only one person told me about a specific point; nor have I been able to prevent a modest contribution by my own imagination, which has naturally been required to assemble all those viewpoints into a homogenous whole and elaborate where logic has had to fill some gap. It's not at all impossible that I've sometimes given fantasy too much leeway and imagined more than I should have. Yet, it can't be helped—by going over and over all those events in my head, they've started to live their own lives inside of me. Which is inevitable, I suppose.

Of course, I realize I won't be able to recreate the conversations at Birchback in the way they might have happened in real life. But I can't stop myself from trying. I ask that you don't blame me for either.

Anyone who hadn't been to Birchback before probably wouldn't have been surprised by the property's new look, but in reality, the transformation it had undergone since early the previous spring was truly radical. First of all, it was clean everywhere. Those arriving by car (such as Kaupo) were pleased by the fact that an overgrown patch of land along the road leading to the house had been mowed and paved with gravel, so a good dozen or so cars could easily be parked there. The lawn had likewise been cropped to barely a few centimeters high. But that was just the beginning. All the musty old junk that had filled the main house's upstairs rooms had been hauled out to the sheds, and all the filth that had collected on the windows left unwashed for years had been scrubbed off, so it was a gleaming white everywhere, Mailis told me approvingly. The large wood-burning stove in the kitchen had been scoured to a shine, even though it was long since anyone had used it for cooking. Secondly, everything was now state-ofthe- art. The filthy, ancient Soviet gas stove had been removed and a proper Zanuss put in its place (electric, of course); there was now also a microwave, and a dishwashing machine had been installed next to the sink. Next to the old stove in the sauna, which had taken hours and hours to heat before, another had appeared—a powerful city-slicker's electric stove, which heated the relatively spacious room to 100°C in under an hour and a half 's time. The ground floors of the former barn and a shed had also been turned into bedrooms and equipped with portable electric radiators so that they would still be habitable in the chillier fall season. And there was a coatrack in every bathroom.

"Why do you need a coatrack in the bathroom?" Kaupo had asked Joel once they'd become acquainted.

"So that if the Wicked Witch of the West happens to be flying through, she'll have somewhere to hang her broom if she's really got to go," Joel replied. "Or at least that's how it was explained to me."

However, two new structures constituted the greatest update to the property. One of them was a one-and-a-half-story-high cube that had no visible windows, was constructed of transparent- varnished boards, and lit by a glass ceiling. The cube sat on the edge of the property, "bizarrely outside of its own time and place like a UFO," Kaupo laughed. At first glance, even the entrance was hidden from sight to the unfamiliar eye. And its purpose remained just as ambiguous from within, because the empty space had no partitions and didn't contain a single piece of furniture—only the floor was covered evenly by a thick reed mat, on which outdoor shoes weren't allowed. White slippers in three different sizes had been placed on the runner along the wall for those shy of being barefoot or in socks.

The second new structure was more straightforward. It was a circular pavilion set in the middle of the spacious yard, built on a stacked stone foundation, and included a circular table and a grill in the center of the ring. Anyone could hazard a guess off the top of their heads as to its purpose, and it didn't take much effort to imagine sitting there in the company of friends, holding a plate of juicy pork chops or sausages and a glass of red wine. An image, which—let it be immediately clear—wasn't quite correct; but I'll get to that later. In any case, one could see that life at Birchback was taken much more seriously than it had been before.

There was a relatively uncomplicated explanation for all the changes at Birchback. Simply: the hive had a new queen. The property's owner and operator, Joel, had wed the previous fall. His bride Veronika was a jewelry designer just like Joel himself, but in addition to their immense, honest, and mutual love, it was probably the only thing that they had in common. Joel, who was slow- and primitive-natured, had always been somewhat lazy and easygoing—he liked to putter around on his own. And his jewelry, which was primarily valued by somewhat older and more heavyset women—pieces that had a softly shamanist appearance but were still fully contemporary brooches and clasps—contrasted with Veronika's lavish, firework-like, and unspeakably finely threaded necklaces and earrings in a way that was identical to their own contrast as persons. At first glance, it appeared as if Veronika walked just a smidgen off the ground in general—she was so light and airy and at the same time graceful and swift, while her voice had a lightly singsong and faintly dreamy, almost hypnotizing quality to it. But she wasn't happy-go-lucky. She even wore her long, flowing hair that was nearly a transparent shade of blond in a bun wrapped tightly at her nape, because it was easier to maintain that way. Yet that look was misleading, because behind her large, brown, childlike eyes lay an awe-inspiring expanse of intelligence. Unlike Joel, she was able to make quick calculations in her head and knew the prices of things; she was brilliant at writing grant proposals, drafting budgets, and holding negotiations—in short, she possessed all of the skills crucial to being a successful artist these days—skills more crucial than talent, in the opinion of some. And she had gotten quite far, indeed. Veronika had studied in the US for several years and had even put up her own exhibition at a small gallery somewhere in Philadelphia. Several of the most elegant female members of Estonia's parliament wore her jewelry at formal engagements, and they were even popular among ambassadors' wives—and not at all without reason either, because they were truly wonderful.

Naturally, she had been to Birchback before—back when it was still filled with the traces of Joel and his friends and their numerous friends and chance acquaintances. Mailis also remembered Veronika and Joel's darling budding relationship from the previous summer, but since Joel had had a new "favorite" every summer, she was unable to expect it would progress so far. I imagine that Veronika, being a clever woman, had simply expressed her enthusiasm for everything in Joel's world back then while initially keeping all the thoughts that came to her on the old property to herself. But she began executing these plans right after the wedding. The squalid bohemian colony was to transform into a center that was livable and functioning year-round, and she herself was happily prepared to take her place at its heart. She applied for support from the Ministry of Culture and rural-support funds, went to speak with various sponsors, and as a result of all her endeavors, she managed to gather up enough money to re-shape Birchback into a place where people would start practicing healthy lifestyles and art-therapy, as well as engaging in psycho-physical exercise and meditation. In this way, the artists' summer commune was meant to get its second wind and a more stable form, in addition to (according to Veronika's original concept) turning into a source of income, since all those benefits couldn't be shared with the greater public at zero cost, of course. However, Joel resolutely locked horns with her over that final point. No numerical prices or weekend packages of any kind! The people who could come would either be his friends or his friends' friends, and he wouldn't start treating them like customers, and he didn't want any outsiders at his country home, either. The financial arrangement in summers would likewise remain the same: everyone would go to the store according to their own means, and would eat from the refrigerator and the dinner table according to their own needs. Especially given the fact that while Joel alone had enabled that system with his income before, now—with the wages of two people—there shouldn't be any problems at all. With a little bit of grumbling, Veronika decided to come to terms with the situation for the time being; but people's opinions can change over time, can't they? Especially when they haven't had to defend them very angrily.

Yet in spite of this, the atmosphere at Birchback had changed, too. Veronika pushed through a strict vegetarian policy in the communal kitchen, and whoever wanted pork or sausages had to get them on their own. And the picnics on the meadow that Veronika similarly loved to arrange could easily consist of simple cheese sandwiches, fruit, and hard-boiled eggs. Joel was, of course, a little disappointed that the expensive, top-of-the-line new grill he had bought for the yard was now only used for zucchini and eggplant, but marital bliss meant something to him, too. Even so, Veronika would have been risking her own health and home had she tried to ban alcohol—something she naturally grasped straight away. She herself was no teetotaler; still, drinking was only permitted in "public spaces" starting from their six o'clock dinnertime. Needless to say, she was unaware of what went on in people's private rooms. But when, for instance, a friend of the painter Oleg was discovered with a beer in the cooloff room during morning sauna, Veronika made it unequivocally clear to him that he was no longer welcome at Birchback, and although Oleg went to plead his friend's case with Joel, it was for naught. Oleg announced that if he and his friends were going to be treated that way at Birchback from now on, then he for one would never return, and the pair left angrily. Still, he was back again less than a week later. Oleg didn't bring up the incident again, although it did somehow come up in conversation that he and the friend had gotten into a fight in the meantime, because the man was totally clueless about art and artists. Nevertheless, there were also others who departed quietly and without a fuss— giving the excuse that they had pressing matters to go take care of, but never coming back. And those who remained were well aware that there were certain rules, which had to be honored.

Veronika had notably less success promoting her own lifestyles and worldviews. For instance, she declared any kind of swearing to be "undesired" (one could still say "damn" or "shit," although she very visibly disapproved), and everyone did at least try to abide by the ban in her presence. As if that was enough, though! The way Veronika saw it, Birchback's guests should have followed a strict daily schedule beginning with a sun salutation on the nearby knoll called Dickens Hill, where everyone would hold hands and listen to her recite a poem, which would be followed by psycho-physical exercises and then a morning sauna, concluded with green tea and a healthy meal. And so forth. Early risers grateful for the warm morning sauna weren't scarce, but there were also those (unfortunately including her husband) who didn't emerge from bed before midday out of principle, and then wanted to have strong coffee, eggs, and potatoes fried with mushrooms and onions, since bacon and hot dogs were, of course, banned. Those who had been there longer told stories about how immediately after they arrived at Birchback, sometime before midsummer, Joel really had tried to act according to his wife's fancy, adhering to her schedule and menu for an entire week, which had apparently been an utter disaster. He had been hungry and drowsy for days on end, couldn't remember anything asked of him, forgot everything he was told on the spot, and during the hours designated for independent creative work, he simply sat in his studio and did nothing aside from perhaps napping a little. He simply gritted his teeth and suffered through the evening meditation sessions, because while his legs wouldn't flex into the correct seated position, the position he *was* actually able to bend them into caused him unspeakable pain. Veronika, on the other hand—for whom her personally devised regime was an ideal fit—blossomed and at first didn't even notice that she was causing others any suffering. Yet, when the first few friends informed her they probably wouldn't be staying for the whole period they had intended, she started opening her eyes a little and realized that compromises were necessary in the interests of communal living. From that point onward, the greater part of her daily schedule was made voluntary for everyone else, and she even put up with the men's collective ham-and-cheese sandwich instances in Joel's studio.

I have to admit that I might be treating Veronika with somewhat unjust irony here, because over the course of my life, I've come into more than enough contact with those sorts of active organizers and go-getters, and some part of me sincerely hopes that if she and I had ever personally met, I'd have a different impression of her. But things are the way they are now.

Veronika also envisioned boosting Birchback residents' spirituality in a specific and systematic way: she had an entire series of lectures planned for the summer. The opening one was given by an acquaintance of hers—a meditation teacher brought from the US using grant money, who was said to have

made a very strong name for himself in his own circles. Veronika
drove to Tallinn to pick him up at the airport, and on that day,
Joel and Oleg brazenly grilled cherry-marinated pork chops
and thick sausages on the pavilion, which were served with red
wine at the early hour of two P.M. Veronika had allegedly even
given her permission, since she was ecstatic about the arrival of
a visitor from so far away and believed it would also be for the
best if the other guests received him with an open mind. By this
line of reasoning, they shouldn't be tense, and if that indeed
cost the life of an innocent little piggy, then—farewell. What
was important was that it didn't happen with her presence or
participation. Thus, all were able to take part in the feast without
having to worry that they were eroding Veronika's authority by
doing so, even if some of them believed that a more significant
erosion might be necessary.

Veronika and her guest arrived early that evening. The
meditation guru turned out to be a man in his early forties,
properly shaven but with long hair, tiny round glasses, and a
slightly whiny voice. He was wearing a somewhat worn denim
jacket, jeans, a T-shirt that read "MAKE LOVE, NOT BABIES,"
and Nike sneakers. He had brought a massive suitcase, which
Kaupo and Jaagup heaved up to a large upstairs bedroom that
had been reserved for him. Veronika had indeed asked Joel
to take care of it initially, but he was already rather drunk
by that time and Oleg was nowhere to be seen. The lecturer
was bewildered—apparently, the fact that Veronika had wed
meanwhile and that the property he was presently on belonged
to her husband was news to him, since Mailis, for one, was
certainly given the impression that the man had undertaken
the long journey under entirely different assumptions. Neither
could he wrap his mind around how it was at all possible that
the slightly tipsy collective in the yard of a country home "out
in the middle of nowhere" had been able to pay for his plane
tickets and daily stipends, but Joel patted him on the shoulder

and told him Estonia simply was that kind of a country, whatever that was supposed to mean. "In-fuckin'-deed," the guru agreed, which made those in earshot slightly flinch.

The guru was a vegetarian, of course, and therefore it wasn't at all a problem that the pork had run out by the time he arrived. There was enough wine left over, on the other hand, and he enjoyed a little glass of it while Veronika warmed up some canned beans for him in the kitchen. After eating, however, he went up to his room and didn't appear again until the following morning. That time he and Veronika did their sun salutation alone, because everyone else had worn themselves out the night before by continuing to rigorously prepare their minds for the lecture—even those girls like Birgit, who didn't partake in all that much wine, but had stayed with the rest of the group to the very end for company.

When she returned from Dickens Hill, Veronika was already highly irritated, in any case, probably because none of the other guests cared much about her meditation guru. She went knocking on everyone's doors to remind them that they were to gather in the auditorium in half an hour—whoever had time to clean themselves up should clean themselves up; whoever had time to eat should eat. By "auditorium", she meant her large cube. They all got themselves up and to the event somewhat against their will, although in reality they were curious enough to actually want to know what the American had to say. However, he wasn't even present at first. Veronika stood before the audience wearing tight work-out clothes and directed everyone else to sit down barefoot on the floor. They weren't required to take their meditation positions, but could sit however was most comfortable.

"Now we'll prepare ourselves to receive his message," she announced. "We'll close our eyes and all say *mmmmmm* in chorus. This is important. It'll have an effect even if you don't believe. Your whole body will echo back, your channels will open up, your consciousness will become a whole. So: one, two, three, go."

"MMMMMM," everyone hummed together. She hadn't said when they were allowed to stop, but they did so one by one even so, last of all Joel, who was a little embarrassed by his behavior the previous day, so Veronika had to wordlessly walk up to him and tap him on the shoulder to signal it was enough.

When they opened their eyes again, the guru had taken a seat in the front of the auditorium. Veronika had positioned herself by the door. According to Kaupo, it was apparently so that no one would think of entering or exiting the space during the session. The American's change from the previous day was astounding. He wore a long, light-blue gown with wide lapels and odd ornamentation sewn upon them: it reminded Kaupo of the priestly robes of a made-up religion from some sci-fi film. His hair was bunched up under an amorphous beanie.

"My sincere greetings," he said with a practiced mannerism. The audience murmured something unintelligible in collective reply.

"After that," Mailis told me, "he took stock of us for pretty long. I guess he was trying to figure out the most reasonable way to treat us."

"I suppose I know," he ultimately drawled, "why you're here. It is because you have decided to find yourselves. Maybe it's not a conscious choice that dawns as clarity on some beautiful morning—a knowledge that this is the way things are; that now things can't be as they were. But in any case, you're not those who hide their problems from themselves, who compensate for the empty space that yawns in place of true *being* with new clothes and electronic doodads and what all else."

"Or he said something to that effect, so at first it wasn't all that bad," Mailis explained. The more he talked, however, the more carried away he became. Out of all those who told me about Birchback, she was the only one who attempted to somehow summarize the American's long lecture for me. Janne hadn't arrived at Birchback yet. Birgit, who out of everyone else thought most highly of the American and, she claimed, even tried for a while to practice the exercises he taught them, nevertheless allowed herself to later—after she had moved on—forget his "wise theory," because it was a little too skillful and insufficiently deep for her all at once. And Kaupo, seeing the way Mailis strained to bring the man's words to mind, interrupted her before long and asked me whether it was really all that important to know.

It wasn't—that much was already clear to me then. The American had simply presented a drawn-out, complicated, and (at least in my opinion) not exactly original theory about man as a multi-level system, in whom the physical and the spiritual are interwoven in ways that are beyond common understanding. After receiving my diagnosis, I myself had researched enough self-help literature of every kind to immediately recognize the majority of his ideas as Mailis told them. And the way he described human life as a journey into your inner core was just clichéd. All of that lasted for a couple of hours. The only noteworthy aspect of his theory was that he never appealed to a higher power even once—not to anything divine or spiritual, with which man should learn to communicate. His whole talk fit into the bounds of a strictly scientific worldview, so to say; upholstered with not-at-all-false claims that what goes on in our heads greatly affects what happens in our bodies, and vice-versa.

The practical exercises that he guided the Birchback community through next were supposed to draw on that particular fact. These required sitting in the already classic position—straightbacked and cross-legged. For the first exercise, he instructed them to gather together inside of themselves everything they'd like to be liberated from; to imagine it as a brown, negative mass that seeps from points all over your body and brain and into your mouth; and then to expel it with a strong exhale, leaving it about a meter or so away on the ground in front of you. The second exercise had you imagine that mass of energy gradually taking a new shape, transforming into a tiny self, staring back at you. And the third, most important part was to receive the light falling upon you (this was supposed to be possible even in pitch-black darkness, but the fact that the cube's roof was made of glass was only an advantage for the beginners), to condense it into a point with hair coiling around it, to allow it to penetrate your skull and scorch your mind to a state of clarity, and then for it to project out through your eyes so that the beam destroys the being of brown energy across from you. All of the participants practiced for a good hour or so, until the guru was satisfied with the results. Joel and Oleg suffered the most since the seated pose caused them both excruciating pain, but the guru explained that the sensation of pain is even a good thing—it shows that your body is becoming more and more aware of itself. Furthermore, just five minutes was supposed to be enough daily practice from then on. All of this, the guru explained, was the first step in a seven-step journey, and whoever was interested in what came next could buy his book. That's what his large suitcase had been filled with. Jaagup bought one out of politeness.

Veronika's eyes clouded more and more as she observed them. No doubt she realized that the American's talk hadn't made a very deep impact on the group, Kaupo believed. In any case, her reaction was lightning-quick. There was no cell-phone service at Birchback and it hadn't had an internet connection in quite a long time, so while the others were having lunch, she scaled Dickens Hill (where you could at least get some reception in nicer weather) and booked the guru a hotel room in Tallinn for that night. Then she told him to pack his suitcase and drove him to Viljandi to board a bus. "Old Tallinn is not to be missed," she explained as if it had been her plan all along, reassuring him not to worry and that everything had been paid for by credit card. Still, she'd seemed to mention earlier that the American would be working with people on a one-on-one basis the following day. Veronika was understandably anxious about whether the incident might bump her from her position as queen bee, because she had only spoken about the guru as highly as possible before then. Perceiving that someone would make the remark anyway and that it was only a matter of time before people's politeness would fail to hold it back any longer, she herself declared openly that the man had been a disappointment, but that his talks in America—which were given to very large audiences—had always been highly inspiring. Maybe it was jet lag, maybe it was something else, or perhaps he was simply losing his touch. But it was an interesting experience all the same, wasn't it? She spent the next day reading Dostoyevsky in her room.

Veronika came up with a new way to pass the time by that evening. A fire was made in the fireplace, everyone was told to take a seat around it—some in armchairs, some on pillows—and the storytelling began.

"Each and every one of us has something in our lives that we'd like to get rid of," Veronika explained. "Or something shameful that we always keep to ourselves because we're afraid to show it to others. But fear only makes us weaker. It's only when we overcome it that we're able to turn it into love. Until we're able to stare our memories in the face, they have power over us; they're able to dictate who we are. And we change. Maybe we want to change into the person we remember ourselves as being in our most beautiful memories. But the truth is that we change into whomever we want to hide from others, and even from ourselves. And when that happens, we aren't able to become ourselves, to *be* ourselves, entirely."

"Whose theory is that, then?" Jaagup asked, at which Veronika clicked her tongue.

"I'm telling you all how I *feel*," she clarified. "It's no theory.

And I feel like each of us can become stronger and more liberated if we're capable of speaking about the most shameful moment of our lives in front of others. Because that's the only possible way to erase it from our lives. All right? Psychologists have actually written about it, too, of course."

"And the whole Catholic Church is founded on it," Carola backed her up. "And the early Buddhists also practiced public confession."

"And the Maoists, too," Anni added suddenly. "Which doesn't mean, of course, that it might not work."

"So, should we give it a try?" Veronika then asked more confidently. "If someone wants to volunteer, for example?" She looked around, and her eyes finally rested on Kaupo.

"Well, okay—I can start," Kaupo said and smiled. "But I hope you'll all still be talking to me after."

"There's no worry," Veronika nodded, and the others murmured in agreement.

"Here goes, then." Kaupo took a deep breath and leaned against the back of his chair, as if preparing himself. "I do have a story like that, which comes to mind every once in a while ... I don't even understand how it happened the way it did. I was in probably sixth grade. We'd gotten a new classmate in the fall, a boy—Raido. He was a little shorter and had kind of a rough voice and wore glasses. He was a totally normal kid, maybe just a little more uncoordinated and awkward than the rest of us were in general. Even so, not because of that, but because I-don't-evenknow- why, I had an awful dislike for Raido from the first time I saw him. Sometimes that's the way it goes—without any kind of justification. As if we'd been at odds in a previous life or something, as they say. I tried not to let it show, of course—to not be nasty to him, but I couldn't help it. I even made a few attempts against my own will to strike up a conversation with him—he was just as friendly towards me as he was to everybody else, you know. People don't go picking fights with you right away when you join a new class. But I just couldn't do it. We had an honors English-language class; Raido had been in the regular class before and studied independently outside of school. He got along pretty well, for the most part, but the teacher still thought someone should be his study-buddy and help him out a little bit and whatnot, and I hoped the teacher would pick me, because then I'd just have to get over my aversion and because I was one of the best students in our English class, but she picked Merike, as always. I was disappointed, but what could I do? Raido worked all the kinks out soon enough, anyway.

"The story I want to tell happened a little before Christmas. There was a boy in our class, Aivar, whose father was some high-ranking police officer, and so he always had all kinds of gadgets. That time, it was a watch. It was some kind of special extreme-athlete's watch—you know, one that doesn't break when it's dropped or gets wet, and which had three little dials inside of the big one. Aivar had gotten it for his birthday late that November, and was showing it off to everyone proudly. One time in the gym, when we were getting dressed for class, he let us chuck it against a brick wall. And so we did. The watch was fine. Aivar offered to let Raido do it, too, but Raido said he believed him already. What was there to believe—it'd been proven over and over again right then and there. Raido was busy getting dressed—on days that there was PE class, all of us wore clothes with zippers on them so that it wouldn't take much time, but he had a ton of buttons and laces for some reason, so he was the last one left puttering around the locker room while we all ran out into the gym.

"After class, I ended up being the first one to finish showering and return to the locker room while it was still empty. Aivar's watch was laying on top of his pile of clothes. I didn't give a second's thought to why I was doing it, but I picked it up and stuffed it into Raido's satchel—I stuffed it way deep down, under his textbooks. I regretted it the very next moment, but it was already too late by then, because the other boys were coming out of the showers and we started getting dressed. When Aivar discovered that his watch had disappeared, he made a huge to-do about it, naturally. A teacher came to see what had happened, and Aivar demanded that everyone's things be searched immediately because someone had pocketed his expensive watch. He couldn't find it under the benches or in any of his own pockets or anywhere else it might have fallen on accident. The teacher really dreaded the potential fallout—everyone knew all too well who Aivar's father was, and so we all had to give the teacher our bags to be checked. And, of course, the watch showed up in Raido's satchel. The kid went pale and swore that he hadn't put it there. The teacher told him to reconsider his answer—the whole case seemed quite clear to her—but Raido refused to apologize and change his story. Of course, everyone remembered that Raido had been the last one out of the locker room, but no one started calling to mind who had been the first to leave the showers. The rest of us were sent away in the end, but Aivar told us later what had happened: they had both promised Raido that the whole thing would be put to rest if he apologized. But he wouldn't. He hadn't taken it, and that was that. I was the only one who knew he was right.

"Aivar's father turned out to be a man of principle and succeeded in getting Raido expelled from school. Not, however, as a thief and a liar—the school's official reason was that he wasn't getting by in his English class, because Raido's father also came out in support of his son and said he believed him. Furthermore, he added, it would have been extremely stupid of Raido to steal the watch under those conditions, because it was impossible to reckon that Aivar wouldn't notice its disappearance. And extreme stupidity was something of which his son certainly couldn't be accused. So, the teacher ultimately decided that he wouldn't start ruining the boy's life just yet, even though she wasn't very convinced by the man's arguments.

"I randomly saw Raido again about a year ago. I didn't even recognize him at first. And absolutely any sort of antipathy I'd had towards him was gone. I said hello and he said hello and then we both stood there too long to just part ways without doing anything more. I can't actually remember which one of us proposed that we grab a coffee when there was time. He's doing great. He graduated from grammar school with outstanding grades, did a couple of years at the Tallinn Polytechnic, then a classmate invited him to partner up together, and now they make designer furniture. The friend comes up with the models, Raido directs the business end, and they've got a little workshop set up near Jõgeva where locals manufacture the pieces. They made them for rich Estonians at first; now they export more to Germany and the Netherlands. On top of that, things started going so well for him that when his classmate wanted to take out a loan a while back and had to show the bank he had a steady income, he sold Raido his half but stayed with the company as a salaried employee, so the whole business now belongs solely to Raido.

"The whole time he was telling me this, I was thinking that I should confess about the trick I'd played on him. Because, well, without it, he wouldn't be the owner of a furniture factory now, would he? He would have no reason to be angry at me. But I didn't," Kaupo concluded.

"Why not?" Anni asked. "I mean, if you wanted to erase it from your life?"

"And there's hardly a chance you'll get together with Raido all that often anymore," Mailis added.

"I dunno," Kaupo admitted. "I was embarrassed. What else."

"Well, then," Veronika said. "There we are for starters. And what can we conclude from Kaupo's story?" she asked, answering herself immediately: "We can never know what our actions actually mean. We think we're doing good, but we're actually doing bad. We do something bad, but actually, good." She looked around the room: "Are there any more volunteers?"

"Sure, I'll be next, then," Jaagup said. "I've only got one story to tell, anyway."

Everyone shifted themselves to listen.

"Or, well, it's not even really a story," he continued, brushing his fingers through his curly beard. "More like a kind of inner feeling. It was three years ago or so. I should probably start by saying that my mom fell down the stairs. Or, wait. No. With the fact that I had a girlfriend then—a really great girlfriend, just sort of, a little, depressed. Meaning that occasionally, she'd short-circuit and then lose it all the time, but it'd blow over pretty quickly and then she'd be herself again. In any case, I knew my parents wouldn't have liked her all that much. Or, well, that's what I think, but she never came to visit—we actually hadn't known each other for very long yet, either. Right. And then there was that Rammstein concert in Tallinn back in the day, you know, and we both really wanted to go, but when I finally went to buy tickets, they were already sold out. 'Course, you could get them from scalpers, too—for a higher price, of course. But, well, that wasn't, like, a problem. Then a friend of mine told me he basically had four tickets and that I could have two of them if I wanted, and of course I did. Well, and that same day, my old man was out of the country somewhere defending the honor of our nation and people, as usual, and my mom came home from the grocery store and fell. We were still living in our old apartment back then, up on the third floor. I was at home at the time, thinking about how amazing the night was going to be, when I suddenly heard an awful racket coming from the stairwell. I open up the door and there's Mom—I guess she'd slipped on something and fallen. She was carrying heavy bags, too, so she couldn't put out her hand to block her fall, either, and got knocked up pretty badly.

At first, I thought that maybe I'd have to call an ambulance, that maybe she'd broken some bones and what have you. But she was, like, as right as rain—I helped her get up and get in the apartment, and she said everything was totally OK. Like, not even the wine bottle smashed in her bag. She still had bruises afterward. But, well, I started feeling a little shit- . . . um . . . a little bad about it, then, about going to a concert and leaving her lying there all alone, but she said it wasn't a big deal, that I should go ahead. 'Honestly?' I asked. 'Sure,' she said. Well, it wasn't like I'd actually have happily given up going, either. So, I met up with a friend and his girl—and you know, she was one super cool chick. She had long black hair and feral eyes and long fingernails with dark red nail polish. A little like our Birgit here, just with an awesome leather jacket."

"Uh, *sorry*," Birgit said, but Jaagup had meant the comparison as a joke and barked in laughter.

"Well, yeah—and then my girlfriend got there, too and she was the total opposite of that chick. Pretty quiet in general, you know, and blond, and didn't really wear makeup. And then my head got all messed up for a minute. I guess my friend was actually just being polite and whatever, asked her who she was and what she did, but I sort of felt like he was totally hitting on her. But it, like, didn't even make me angry at all. You know why not? Because knowing that I'd left my mother home alone was still gnawing at me. Well, okay—there wasn't really anything wrong with her, but maybe she would have liked it if I'd simply stayed at home, maybe chatted a little and sort of been around for company. But I was there, at the concert. You know what I mean? And I realized that with the kind of girlfriend I was with then, I would've had to stay home. But with the kind of girl my friend was with, I should've gone to the concert. You know what I mean? That if I myself was so wild that I'd left my mother home alone, then a wild girl was, like, a better fit for me, too. And then, all of a sudden, I started picking on my own girlfriend. Asking why she was quiet when she was quiet, and why she made stupid comments whenever she opened her mouth. That other girl was having a riot hearing it. I mean, she figured out that I was showing off in front of her, of course. Women *always* realize that right away.

"I don't remember all that much about the concert other than it was totally sweet, because that other girl had already gotten under my skin. When it was over, the four of us left and were standing out in front of the concert hall. The weather was abysmal, but we couldn't seem to all go our separate ways. I couldn't just leave that chick there without trying, you get me? I had to have her, come what may. My friend reckoned we could all go somewhere for a drink. I said my mom was at home, that she'd fallen and gotten hurt, and I had to go see her. My girlfriend said she'd probably just go home, too. My friend asked where she lived, and it turned out they were sort of going in the same direction. I asked him, "Oh, would you mind maybe taking her home?" He stared at me for a few seconds, but I guess he'd already figured out what was going on. So, they left that girl and me standing there together. "My mom's sick at home," I said, "so we can't go there—what if we go to your place, maybe?" She giggled and took my hand. It turned out she lived in a little Soviet-era studio apartment right nearby, so we went and I did her so hard there that both of us could hardly breathe. I can't remember screwing anyone else like that ever since."

"And you still want to erase it from your life," Birgit interjected sarcastically. "I don't even know what to think of myself now."

"Just wait a minute," Jaagup said. "When I got home in the morning, my mom was already making breakfast in the kitchen—she was as right as rain. 'I hope you had a pleasant evening,' she said, and I realized of course that she was mocking me, but what did I care. That's not what it was. Anyway, my friend and I had switched girlfriends. Or, well, I guess that chick wasn't actually really with him. I mean in the sense that there wasn't like anything serious between them. In any case, my friend didn't hate me or anything because of it—we get along to this day. On top of that, he was really into that ex of mine; they were together for six months or so after that. It didn't take more than two weeks for my relationship with that wild chick to get all messed up, on the other hand. And it wasn't at all her fault, by the way—she would've gladly kept going out with me. But me—I simply realized all of a sudden that I'd, like, slipped off onto the wrong track. That my life should've gone a different way. That the girl I'd dumped—she was actually the one for me. That in reality, I shouldn't even have gone to that concert in the first place; that when my mother fell, it was like sort of, like, a sign or something. But I couldn't do anything about it anymore. I tried calling her a couple of times again, but what's broken is broken. You know? And things didn't turn out between her and that friend of mine, either; I reckon probably for the same reason. We'd had our chance, but I'd fucked it up."

"Jaagup!" Veronika exclaimed.

"Sorry. Screwed it up. Well, anyway. If I hadn't left my mother home alone that night, I'd be a different person than I am today. And I probably wouldn't be sitting here."

"But then you really can't say that choice only brought something bad along, now can you?" Veronika said with forced chipperness. "We're all glad that you're here with us, anyhow."

"You might all be glad," Jaagup shrugged, "but I'm just here simply because I don't know where the right place is for me."

There were no more volunteers, and Veronika decided that they'd draw lots to decide the next speaker. This turned out to be Anni.

(I've heard this story three times. Each time, the storyteller first asked me whether I really wanted to hear it. I did. A myriad of details was held back from me on the first occasion, and that's why I needed to hear it a second and a third. At some point, I'd developed a masochistic itch that demands more and more details. I don't know what they must have thought of me. For the most part, my knowledge is based on a recording transcribed from the mouth of one person. If you were to ask me right now whether she said "her" or "me" in regard to Anni on that tape, then to tell the truth—I don't remember. And I'm not going to go check, either. In reality, I'm actually still trying to convince myself that she imagined the bulk of the story just in order to rile up Veronika. Not that it holds any real importance anymore, of course. It takes a lot of strength just for me to write all of this down here, and if I had any reason to believe in the continuity of my own world, I'd hardly make the effort. I can hear Anni telling the story in my mind, in that tone so familiar to me—a tone that is calm and practical, but slightly mocking, because that was the only way she could nudge everything a little closer to nonexistence. And I write, and only I myself know that each and every one of my words is screaming, but I write, because that's the only way to force it out of me a little . . . Not convinced? Then imagine that this is just a show of respect from me as a person to my daughter as a person, regardless of all that may connect or divide us; the same kind of show of respect as the descendants of Estonians who were deported to Siberia may make to their grandfathers and grandmothers by committing their difficult memories to paper and print. But what am I saying. Just read.)

"It happened the first year that I was in Paris," she began. "I was very young back then and still going to university, studying all kinds of philosophy and political science and what all else; and I thought I was oh-so smart and capable of understanding the world from top to bottom. I was writing about Eastern European prostitutes for a research project then. I'd interpreted for some of them at the police station before, and it seemed like an interesting topic—the girls there were sort of like me, I guess: they'd also ventured into the big wide world to seek their fortune, in a way. I studied them from a sociological perspective, and just in general. They thought kindly of me, on the whole, because they were able to speak rather freely to me about all kinds of things. The trade wasn't controlled by the mafia so heavily back then: if you managed to rent yourself a room in the right area, you could go totally freelance, if you wanted; no one else would be pocketing your earnings every day and no one went around beating up independent sex workers, either. The rooms were certainly a good deal pricier in those areas, and if you'd been stable there for a longer time, you'd develop your own half-boyfriend, halfpimp, too. But even so, the market was significantly more liberal in places like that overall, and the prices were really low—especially after Eastern Europe's borders opened up. So, those girls also thought they'd come to make a little money and then go back to their own country. Some had a boyfriend waiting back home, some planned to set up a sewing shop, some wanted to go back to school—each one had her own plan.

"In short, I got along really well with them—some were like full-on girlfriends; or, well, almost. I knew all of their life stories and dreams or, I should say, *illusions*, because there wasn't really much hope for them, you know. It showed. Sooner or later, they'd start using or they'd get AIDS or get into some other mess and it'd snuff out their lives. But I didn't go around telling them this, of course. And what's more—who knows? They, on the other hand, hassled me—saying I was strong in theory but had zero experience. It didn't really bother me, though. They were right.

"But once, when I was invited to one girl's birthday party— she was a Pole named Danuta who had made an impressive feast for the occasion and had gathered up all the better girls from the street—we all drank pretty heavily and they started taunting me in mixed French and Russian. One said I'd have really good chances out on the street; another that I didn't have the guts to do it; while someone else said—hey, listen, leave her alone, she's about to cry, come on, she's our theoretician. And it was really weird for me, because I couldn't understand why they were teasing me like that—was it hard for them to include someone so different in their social circle? But if it was, why'd they invite me to come over in the first place? 'You know what?' said Katalin, who was a Hungarian girl, 'You don't understand us, anyway. You don't understand what kind of a life this is, so maybe it'd be best if you didn't come around anymore.' Stubbornly, I said, 'I do understand. I understand magnificently.' We were already pretty drunk by then. 'So, does that mean you think a social worker who helps addicts should do heroine herself, huh?' I asked. 'Because otherwise, she won't understand what they're feeling?' Sasha, who I think was from Ukraine, said, 'Totally, yeah. Because if she doesn't, she'll have no idea what a proper *lomka*[7] can do to a person.' She was speaking from experience, by the way, even though she was clean then. 'Oh, come on,' I protested; but the other girls agreed with Sasha. And then I don't know what came over me—I simply couldn't let them win. Who did they think they were? What right did they have to talk that way? So, I said: 'Okay, dress me up and I'll go walk the street once, too.' *All in all, why not?* I thought. *At least I'll understand what it feels like to stand there while men walk past and undress you with their eyes.* 'You're crazy!' Danuta exclaimed; but the others just clapped. They put together a really decent prostitute outfit between them all—Danuta lent me fishnet stockings, I got lingerie from

7 "Hit" (Russian)

Katalin, and Yelena gave me a pink shirt and a leather skirt that barely came up over my belly button. I put it all on and then they did my makeup, too, and when I looked in the mirror, I was . . . well, as whore as a whore can be. They all laughed like it was the funniest joke in the world, and up until that moment, it all still felt a little like a game to me. I drank another good mouthful of wine and went out onto the street with Katalin and Sasha. Even then, I still didn't really believe a man might actually buy me. The plan was that if the situation got out of hand, they'd get me out of trouble.

"But what happened instead was that Sasha was picked up first of all—it was one of her regulars and she knew she'd be back on the street after fifteen minutes with him, and she didn't want to send the guy out to other hunting grounds. And that's when the man came—some Middle-Eastern guy who was walking down the street like he was inspecting a meat counter, then stopped in front of me. He was a nasty-looking guy—sort of slick, but his eyes were cruel. A little like the Devil's lackey. '*Viens,*' he said, '*allons-nous y.*' And he gripped my arm hard enough that I wouldn't be able to tear myself away. Katalin ran after us for a couple of steps and tried to holler, I think she even offered to take my place, but the man shoved her so hard that she fell into a puddle. Like I said, we were both pretty drunk by that point, too. The guy turned off into some alleyway, where a big black car was parked. He opened the door and shoved me into the backseat. A fat old man was already sitting in there; he looked a little Arab, too. He was about my dad's age or even older. '*Bonsoir, mademoiselle,*' he said, but that's as far as his French went. The rest of what he said was in some Arabic language, but he illustrated with gestures, so I got a general idea of what he wanted from me. The guy who had brought me started the car and drove off. I tried to, like, protest, but they only laughed and the old man petted me like I was a dog. And what could I do about it, really? We drove to some hotel, I don't exactly remember where, but it was more than a one-star, in any case; maybe even a three-star. *They'll never let me in here—not in these clothes*, I thought in relief, but the guy in the backseat had a coat with him—a sort of long, expensive leather jacket that goes down to your heels—which he ordered me to put on. The driver went first, I was in the middle, and the old man was behind me, and that's how we got through the lobby. I asked myself what would happen if I were to start screaming, but I didn't, even so, and then we were already in the elevator, where there was an old American woman who gave me the kind of stare that made me feel like I wanted to sink into the ground."

That was the point at which people's versions of Anni's story diverged. Therefore, I don't really know how much she told them, or what. Or what they tried to spare me from hearing without realizing that imagination does its own work in the places they kept silent about.

Did I now know why Anni always went white in the face when some sports broadcast came on TV after she'd come back from France? Why she refused to sit facing a wall? Why she didn't let anyone touch her head? Or were they merely little quirks of hers? Quirks, a few of which all of us inevitably develop over the course of our lifetime? I don't know.

Out of those who told me that story, Mailis spoke about the pressure of the present. About the impression Anni's story had left: all of it is happening to me in particular, right here, right now; it's no longer simply a possibility that I'm abstractly aware of, and it's not something that leads tension right up to its climax, but then stops and goes away. You're forced into a corner, and your corner remains exactly that. The feeling was all too familiar. But Birgit described it a little differently: as a perception of how in a single instant, you're not *you* anymore, because nothing like that could ever happen in your world. You're suddenly split into two: one part is the former you as you were, but the other undergoes a grotesque journey through an imaginary world where the rules are different, and you yourself are different for as long as it lasts—and until that point, your task is to not let yourself confuse your identities; to not allow the former you to identify with the character in whose head and consciousness you're experiencing all that horror so closely and as if it were real.

The third version of the story was different in turn. "There are events," Anni had said, "which divide your life into what was before and what is now to come. That's what every occurrence is like, in reality; it's just that we usually don't notice. Well, and it's not like every moment transforms us into such a noticeably different person, either. But sometimes, you simply *know* when an idea or a plan that you might have had just a couple of days earlier has become impossible in a single instant. Not because the trains don't run anymore or the milk has gone sour, but purely because you yourself are no longer the same. One door or another has now closed. And maybe, even though you yourself don't notice it just yet, maybe a window somewhere has opened.

"I was so ashamed," Anni continued her story. "I was totally warped, turned upside-down—believe me, you don't want to know what it felt like. And you can't either. When I made my way out through the hotel lobby in my—or what do I mean 'my'—in *those* clothes then, the porter raised his eyebrows a little, but he didn't start giving me any grief when he saw the look on my face. Who knows what kind of trouble there could have been—I was clearly leaving, too. I couldn't go home in those clothes, so I simply had to get back to Danuta's place. I stumbled my way there using side streets, and everybody who saw me drew their own conclusions. I couldn't take the subway or a bus or a taxi either, looking, well, the way I did then. I finally got there somehow. The girls were still hanging out, because only a little over an hour's time had passed—unbelievable, right? They were in even higher spirits and even more drunk than they'd been before, but when they saw me, they were suddenly silent. 'I'm sorry!' Danuta shouted, almost in tears, 'I'm sorry!' The others didn't say a word. I got dressed again in my own clothes, waved goodbye, and left. I never went back there again.

"The next morning, I went to go find Father Dominic—he was a priest I knew from the neighborhood, who did a round of the cafés where the prostitutes went every morning and talked to them. I told him everything that had happened—or, well, not in detail—and he consoled me. He said that many women have made that mistake, that they'd been unable to draw a line between themselves and the world, and have gotten hurt as a result. And that if I truly wanted to help, I had to be capable of staying an observer. I handed him the hundred euros I'd been given and asked him to spend it on the right thing, which he promised to do. Then I went home and read through my research paper again. It'd already been submitted and the teacher had it; otherwise, I'd have just deleted it, set it on fire—it was that kind of full-of-yourself blah-blah-blah, just disgusting to read. Well, I decided I wouldn't show up for my discussion section, in any case; but a day or two later, I realized that on the contrary—I *would* go and do all those things that were going on in my world, because it was the only way I could get over it and be capable of being me again. I got a perfect score on my paper and presented it convincingly in the discussion section. I did know what I was talking about, of course."

Everyone was silent for a while. But what were they supposed to say, really?

"You . . . haven't done anything wrong," Carola (we can guess) finally stammered.

"I know," Anni might have replied. "It didn't kill me. Consequently, it made me stronger, don't you think?"

"But Father Dominic . . ." someone spoke up (we'll presume it was Veronika).

"Father Dominic didn't get it at all," Anni's judgment might have sounded. I'm highly certain of it. "Father Dominic was a buffoon, whom they tolerated having around because his performances gave just a hint of color to their world."

"But he *helped* you," Birgit exclaimed then, just as she had to me. "You shouldn't talk about him that way!"

"He got a hundred euros from me for it, too," she remembered Anni having replied. "So we were beyond even. I'd go so far as to say it was a fair amount easier for him to earn that money than for me."

"In any case, that was the story you chose for what you'd like to erase from your life the most," Veronika said at one point, hurriedly trying to wrap up the conversation.

"Why do you think that?" Anni asked in surprise. "We had to tell either the most shameful story of our life or one that we'd like to erase from it. It's totally clear that those two expressions can't mean the same thing. If you're not a little kid, at least. As for me—there's nothing about my life that I'd like to erase."

This made Veronika pause to think for a moment, but she couldn't come up with anything to argue.

"Fine," she finally said cautiously. "I suppose it's already a little late to continue for today. But maybe we could pick tomorrow's speaker right away? Then they can prepare and consider things a little."

"Well, why don't *you* tell a story tomorrow?" Anni asked in a syrupy voice.

"Me?" Veronika asked incredulously. In truth, she probably hadn't planned to take up that role personally. "Why me?"

"Why not?" Anni persisted. "Are you trying to say there's been nothing shameful in your life, then?"

"Well, um," Veronika mumbled. "Of course there has. I suppose we'll see."

But naturally, an entirely different kind of event unexpectedly popped up on the schedule for the next evening. A big bonfire was lit and Oleg stood in front of it reading symbolist poetry in Russian, which no one really understood, but his performance was extremely expressive. A large clay goblet was passed around the bonfire and constantly refilled with an aromatic drink made from rum steeped with honey, pepper, and herbs; and so the general consensus was that it was a much better way to spend the evening than storytelling. On top of that, it was Friday evening and more people had come from the city to spend the weekend at Birchback. They brought some shady-looking pills along with them, and when Veronika saw Jaagup taking one, it resulted in quite the scandal. Veronika demanded that he clear out that very instant, but even if she had managed to get her way, there wasn't anyone left who was fit to drive by that time. The wrongdoer solemnly promised to never do it again and claimed that he hadn't known there were new rules in place at Birchback, so Veronika ultimately agreed to let him stay. Jaagup, however, spent the rest of the night sitting on a stump and chatting with a broom leaning against the woodpile.

I'd already left the building when I heard the stairwell door bang behind me. Mailis was standing there holding a pair of gloves.

"Those aren't mine," I said.

"I know," she replied. "But I told Kaupo that you forgot your own and that his are in the car."

I waited.

"I don't want him to know," she continued. "But I think that maybe it's important. That guy Android, you know . . . he was a little more important to me than I said before."

"I understand," I nodded.

"He's an awful person, you know?!" she suddenly exploded with the kind of force I wouldn't have expected from her. "Just terrible! I'm not saying it because he dumped me or anything. I myself . . . I finally tore myself away from him, but it felt like

I had to wrench him out of me completely along with pieces of my own body. But he did that to everyone. Like a cancer. His instinct was sickeningly dead-on when it came to people; he knew exactly what buttons he needed to push with each person to get them under his control."

Everything I heard about Android later only confirmed that judgment. Even now, Mailis was peering around nervously, as if merely talking about the man had somehow put her in danger. Or else she felt like Kaupo could still see her through the brick walls; like what she was doing was wrong.

But she spoke to me about Android regardless, rapidly and heatedly, even though at the time, I thought it was due to her own frail imbalance. Only later did I start to believe that everyone must have been like that, and even *that* was hard for me to understand.

"I have to go now," she ultimately said. "But if you'd like, I can give you a couple more numbers. Two girls who knew Android . . . and Anni, too, of course."

I took a notepad out of my jacket pocket and tore off a page. She wrote down their phone numbers, using my back as a hard surface.

Birgit and Janne.

6

I CALLED BIRGIT first, but found out that the number was out of service. Janne, on the other hand, listened to what I had to say and then invited me to come to her place the very next evening. She lived in Tallinn, somewhere around the Uus Maailm neighborhood and not very far from my old home on Tehnika Street. Her voice already left a warm impression on the telephone, and as soon as she opened the door, I realized that was exactly what she was, entirely and uncompromisingly: a warm person. She had a slightly plump proportions, very light-colored hair, and a pale face with eyes that were brimming with pure joy, despite being slightly narrowed. Eyes that it wasn't hard to believe had also done their share of crying over her lifetime.

That warmth—Janne as a whole—seemed faintly familiar somehow, but I couldn't say from where.

"Come in," she said. "I hope you'll eat with us."

The living room table was set for four. Also seated there were Janne's four-year-old son Priit and her mother, from whom she very obviously hadn't inherited her *joie de vivre*. After lunch, Janne's mother took Priit, who was fidgety and cast suspicious glances at me from time to time, for a walk, promising that they might even go to see *Toy Story 3* if there were still tickets and he behaved himself.

Janne and I were left alone. She served us tea. I wondered how to begin the conversation, but it turned out to be very easy. She was one of the few people I'd encountered over the course of that journey who agreed to speak about their Birchback memories and experiences without any trace of tension or hesitancy.

"It all seems so distant to me now," she began without prompting. "But you have to understand—that was a very difficult time in my life. It lasted for years and years, and I couldn't seem to get over it. You see, what happened was that my father drowned when the *Estonia*[8] sank. Yeah. And all of a sudden, my whole life was empty and bleak."

I didn't say anything.

"I was, what, just sixteen at the time. It was a difficult period in general, you know." She laughed for a moment. "You know how it is—first loves and that. And several all at once. And then, *bam*—taking a blow like that." She gulped. "I'd never had any interest in religious stuff before, you know; I'd read horoscopes in the newspaper every now and then, and they were dead-on, of course. But then I started having those dreams.'"

"Mm-hm," I nodded.

"You remember how it went: for weeks after the *Estonia* had sunk, some people kept believing their relatives had made it out alive somehow; so what that they weren't on the lists? Some believe it to this day, maybe. But there seemed to be, like, cause for it at first, too—maybe somebody didn't have any ID on them and was too weak to say anything; maybe one name or another had gotten mixed up by accident; had been overlooked; had been lost."

I suppose she didn't actually expect me to comment at all.

"Before very long, my mother realized that was how things were going to be. And she started thinking about how to move The on. She's a strong Estonian woman like that; you know how they are. I understood it logically, of course; but I still

8 The MS Estonia ferry sank in the Baltic Sea in 1994, killing 852 passengers.

didn't believe. And that's when the dreams started up. Night
after night. My father came back to me in those dreams and
said: 'Janne, my little girl, don't believe them. I haven't gone
anywhere. I'm still here.' In those dreams, though, I was the one
who knew he was actually dead. 'But you *drowned!*' I'd cry out.
He'd dismiss it with a chuckle like he always used to do. 'So what
that I drowned,' he said. 'I'm here—touch my arm if you don't
believe me.' I gripped his wrist and, true enough, I felt his hand
in mine—for real. I suppose actual touching like that isn't all too
common in dreams, is it? And then I woke up, sweating from
head to toe. I was totally convinced that it'd been him talking to
me for real, no matter that it was a little different in some way."

"I understand," I said softly.

"I believe you," she nodded. "Something's always like that
when you lose someone close to you. But I myself was especially difficult back then, too. And I cried all day long, of course.
Well, and that's when I started gaining an interest in that stuff. I
went to St. John's Church and to the Catholic church and even
attended mass at the Russian church in Old Town, but none of
it was quite right, all the same. They all wanted to console me
for my loss. What loss! I wanted to know exactly how things
were for my father. I read some books on clinical-death experiences and even a little bit of Tibetan stuff. My mom didn't
really approve of it; well, I guess she would have understood if
it'd been the Lutheran church, but that wasn't the right place for
me. Still, she did, of course, grasp that it'd at least be better if I
had something to help me cope with my despair. I didn't drink
or smoke or do anything that might've left a mark, you know."

I wasn't about to start telling her that everything leaves a
mark.

"The dreams stopped after a while, but by that time I was
already pretty deep in that stuff—I knew people and what have
you. I can't really say for sure whether or not I, like, actually
believed it, too; but I certainly wanted to. Oh, yes. I wanted

more than I even knew how to. I was more like a researcher at first— kind of like what our history teacher told us when we had to write a paper at school: don't believe what someone says; instead, check out a number of books that contradict one another and put it all together, then you'll understand. Like how scientists do. Well, so I went and looked at different systems and discussed them with other people, saying *if it's like this, it should also be like this, but not like that,* and everyone told me about their own experiences. We did these kinds of exercises, you know—we lay real still and allowed all our muscles to relax. The idea was that your soul would be able to pull free from your body for a little while and float around on its own and experience reality just the way it is. Weird, right? Now, it certainly seems like half of them just imagined their experiences to make themselves look important. It didn't really, like, work for me personally, and on top of that, I was afraid that if my soul really had gone and left my body for a moment and then my father was there, maybe I wouldn't *want* to return to it anymore, but then that'd be a whole disaster, too . . . My body out in the world without me and no one able to explain to my mother what had happened, either. Yeah—I suppose I wasn't thinking all that clearly."

She laughed again.

"Well, and then, at some point, I met that guy." The trace of a smile disappeared from her lips instantaneously.

"Android?" I asked.

"Yeah, him. He really was incredibly intimidating, I've got to say. He was quite the proper authority in those circles. I'd heard about him before, of course, but when I saw and heard him for the first time, it made me weak in the knees—what could I do? You know, I always felt this little shred of doubt with those others to the very end, wondering whether they were just taking me for a sucker; whether they'd maybe all conspired to, like, royally mess up my brain, or that they were, like, each trying separately to impress the others. With Android, there was no question at all. He was totally genuine. Genuine for me, in that moment. One hundred percent. When he opened his mouth, it was like shivers ran all down your body all at once. Just like that. Whew."

She stood up and walked over to the cupboard.

"Would you like a little whiskey, maybe?" she asked. "Or are you driving?"

"No, why not," I shrugged.

"Irish or Scottish?"

"You've even got a choice here!"

She laughed again. "Veiko—he's my boyfriend right now— he says that Irish whiskey is, like, better and smoother. But Priit's father, on the other hand, believes that Scottish is the right stuff. So, yeah, I've got both."

"I'll have the same you're having," I said.

She took a one-liter bottle of Tullamore Dew out of the cupboard and poured two glasses.

"Would you like ice? Or a drop of water?"

I shook my head.

"The way things've gone somehow now, I'm—yeah— definitely drawn more towards whiskey-lovers," she said with a laugh, and raised her glass to cheers. "Android certainly never touched a drop. He was a teetotaler, just like I was back then. But that wasn't what, like, clicked with us from the very first moment, of course. When was that? I think I'd already graduated from high school. I hadn't quite decided yet what I was going to do with my life; I sort of felt like I could go on to study something—my GPA hadn't been too shabby—but on the other hand, I couldn't figure out what that might be. And that's when I thought I'd have a little look around the world first. I was working at, like, a travel bureau, selling the Canary Islands to neurotic fathers and Ibiza to rich chicks. I suppose it would have been hard for my mother and me without my salary, being alone and all."

Now I remembered.

"At Hermann Travel?" I asked. "Across from the Drama Theater?"

"Exactly," Janne nodded. "How'd you know?"

"I bought tickets to Paris from you once, a long time ago," I said. "And then you helped me to pick a hotel, too. In Montmartre."

"And you can remember that even now? I'm flattered."

But truly: never before or since have I encountered such service. The young woman across from us at the counter had managed to create the feeling that we ourselves were standing in that far-away city and she was showing me that world, which she knew front and back from her own experience, even though (as she later told me) she had never actually been to Paris. But each and every one of my choices, the possibilities I voiced as alternatives that were even slightly worth consideration—*That hotel? Or a different one? What's the price? How big are the rooms? Is there a good view? Is breakfast included in the price?*—earned her unhesitating approval, followed by an honest list of problems that might crop up. And later, everything in Paris really was just as she had promised.

She splashed more whiskey into our glasses.

"Where'd I leave off?" she continued. "Oh, yes. On the very first night when I met Android, he was sitting with a group of people and imposing his views on them, as usual. He had a habit of doing that. He never drew attention to himself except for when it was the two of us alone. But he'd shoot down everyone else. No matter what anyone said, you could clearly tell from the way Android acted that it was crap. Even if he didn't speak. And whoever was talking's voice would gradually start to waver—they weren't sure of themselves anymore; they tried to argue their point with all their might, even though they themselves realized that whatever they were saying was totally

ridiculous, or else boring and pointless. Everyone who was
listening would seem to gradually switch over to Android's side,
even though there weren't any sides in the first place; but you
know what I mean. It was really strange that anyone wanted
him in their group of friends at all, in that sense. But everyone
did. It was like a mark of quality, right, because the very next
day, someone else would be talking about how Android said
this and that yesterday. It was a total mystery how he did it.

"Well, yeah. And so, at one point, Android stood up, looked
over at me, and announced: you're coming with me. 'Me?!' I
exclaimed. 'Yeah, you. Let's go already.' Afterward, I heard he
apparently did that often. He took me by the hand, or rather,
he wrapped his hand around mine. He had long, strong fingers
that he, like, enclosed my hand in—meaning I was completely
trapped, like a bracelet that wouldn't slide off. He only released
his grip once, when we were putting on our jackets. And then
we left. I had no idea where we were going, but even so, it didn't
even seem to cross my mind to protest. He didn't say anything,
just walked at a rather brisk pace past Hotel Tallinn and then
up and over Toompea Hill, then down the Lühike Jalg shortcut
to St. Nicholas' Church. 'Where are we going now?' I asked,
but he just took keys out of his pocket and opened the door
to the church—it turned out that he worked there as a night
watchman back then. It was already dark out and quite spooky
in the empty church, and then he went and opened the tower
door, pushed me through, and ordered me to climb the stairs.
He showed the way with a flashlight from behind me. My heart
was beating like a drum. The staircase was dark and steep, and
I was horribly afraid of slipping and falling back onto him—or,
well, I was simply *afraid*. It was the first time I'd ever been in a
situation like that. I couldn't even understand why I was going
along with all of it, as if I didn't even have my own will. But I
suppose I really didn't in that moment. And then we reached
a window, from which you could see the rooftops of the Old

Town far below. The window was open. I stopped; my legs were shaking. I'm generally afraid of heights. But Android climbed up onto the windowsill and reached out his hand—or, I should say, grabbed mine—and pulled me along, so I had no other choice but to clamber up next to him.

"'Would you believe it if I told you that you can leap down from here, stretch out your arms and soar over the city, and that nothing would happen to you?' he asked.

"'No, I wouldn't,' I mumbled back.

"'Oh, is that so? And if I were to say that I'll show you, that let's jump together, hold hands and soar over the city, and nothing will happen to us?'

"'I still wouldn't.'

"'You're absolutely right,' Android said, and then climbed down off the windowsill. He was totally calm, as if he'd simply asked me what time the next bus left or something. I jumped down after him. 'It doesn't pay to believe all kinds of stuff that strange men try to tell you.'

"We felt our way back down the stairs and I still couldn't figure out what it had all meant. Then we were back in the church again. He walked up to the *Danse Macabre* painting and bowed low to each panel. Then he looked at me as if puzzled by why I was still there, and walked past me in silence. I followed him. We circled the church and then descended to the basement level, down to the watchman's booth by the ticket counter.

"'I've got to read a thing or two now,' he informed me, removing Hesse's *The Glass Bead Game* from a drawer. To this day, I remember that was the book, because I tried reading it myself later, too. I didn't find it all that interesting and didn't finish it. 'Leave me your number.' And then he remembered I needed to be let out of the door and he walked out, but didn't even say goodbye."

"That's quite a bizarre way of getting acquainted, I'd say," I couldn't hold back from commenting.

"Well, that's the way he was," Janne said. "And the impression he left on me was quite a deep one, in any case. It's hard to even explain what it was about him. Over the following years, he entered and exited my life—sometimes more frequently, sometimes less. In reality, it started to seriously torture me after a while, because I couldn't develop a single normal relationship: Android was back on the scene again after a period of time, and then almost all of my friends seemed ridiculous, boring, and materialistic next to him. They, in turn, weren't able to put up with the relationship he and I had, which was understandable." She apparently noticed my questioning look.

"No, we weren't like that. I think he wasn't interested in girls at all that way. He was totally content with just controlling their souls."

"Cruel fate," I said.

"Yeah," Janne agreed. "There was a girl there at Birchback, Carola, who said once that Android is asexual and that's why you can't sell him on anything. Pretty spot-on, right? Well, and that's why he was able to behave with people the way he did. It took me, in any case, an immense amount of strength to tear him out of my life, and I was really happy that I finally managed to do so. But you know what?"

She stood, walked over to the cupboard, and rummaged through its drawers for something. She handed me an old cassette tape. "He had a habit of recording his voice for the girls to listen to," she explained. "So they wouldn't grow apart from him, so to say. It's pretty sickening to think about now—sort of keeping people on a leash like that. But if you want it, you can have it."

Of course I did.

"I'll have a listen and then bring it back," I said.

"No, don't bring it back," Janne said, not laughing. "That way, I can be rid of him for good."

We chatted on for a long time that evening, until Priit and

his grandmother returned from the cinema, and then for a little longer, and then Veiko came, and then we chatted some more, but by that time about everything else in this world; so, when I finally left, I was a little sentimentally drunk and took a walk past the windows of my old home, and I saw someone else's light illuminating them.

The next morning it took me a while rummaging in the bottom of a cupboard before I found an old Walkman that still played cassettes. I put on the headphones. I don't know what I was expecting, exactly. I guess pretty much what I heard: esoteric statements made with demonic theatricality, which on the one hand were seemingly meant to have an impact on the listener, but on the other to convince her of the speaker's exceptional, towering intellectual strength. The recording quality wasn't the best, but it could have been worse, too. Android's voice was powerful and piercing, occasionally sounding a little hoarse, although that might also have come from the background noise. He would occasionally pause for a few moments, and if the given message allowed, he'd sometimes end a sentence with a sarcastic snicker. I tried to imagine myself as Janne, playing the same recording back for the umpteenth time.

I'll remind you, Android began, *that you're only capable of seizing the reins of your own life once you've released yourself entirely. You've got to give yourself up to gain yourself. I know that you want, that you* need *me to remind you of this. Otherwise, you wouldn't be listening to my voice right now. Only those who know how to destroy time are able to achieve eternity. Everyone else just comes to an end. You've seen them: some have been ensnared by their beauty, some have been killed by their intelligence, some have such great bodily strength that it has beat them senseless. All of them are dead. Not one of them has set out to do what they were born here on Earth to do. But I suppose you know what that is, even so. Don't you? Maybe you're wondering right now what I'm feeling when I sit here like this and speak into a microphone, as if it were you. Think, think! The turkey thought, too, until it was made into a soup, as they say. That's what my mother always told me. Actually, there's nothing odd about a person speaking alone. Maybe you're the strange one if you don't? Huh? Maybe you should sometimes tell yourself the things that shouldn't be forgotten? Say them in a loud voice. In my voice. You might think that you've already achieved something. Don't! What's more, there's no difference between whether you have or you haven't. You've got to keep doubting, all the way to the end. If that doubt disappears, it's over. Finito. You're just as dead as those other folks.*

And therefore, it's absolutely crucial that no matter how pretty, strong, or smart you might be, you understand that your beauty, strength, and intelligence aren't your friends, but rather your enemies. Some people think they're able to control and govern them. To put them to service. But that's only a trick. Have you ever heard of a rich man who is capable of ruling his money, not vice-versa? Beauty. Strength. Intelligence. Of course they offer themselves up as aides on your life's journey. Whores. They want you to depend on them; for you to not be able to get by without them. Until they've turned you into mincemeat. Until they've done it to your soul, which would have been capable of everything.

You doubt just like the wavering of a candle's flame. That flame is the candle's life, but that doubt is your life. You're nodding? Are you sure? It's so nice to think that, oh—I'm the biggest doubter there is. But are you, really? Maybe you even believe that doubt is somehow harder to pretend to yourself than those other things. And maybe it is, a little. Athletes have medals, a pretty girl stares in the mirror, and a sharp guy is pleased when only a few others like him are able to understand his clever words. But in the end, they all melt away. Go take a look at a girl who chased after all the boys in sixth grade, because she was one of the first who took dance lessons, and so she stood out at parties. Would you, perhaps, want to trade places with someone like that now?

That doubt, the one I'm talking about right now—it grips you when you stand onboard a sinking ship and wonder: should I jump? A cold wind blows, stormy black seas crash below you, and you don't know, you can't know whether anyone will save you from them.

What a bastard, I thought when I heard that part. *He must have known how Janne's father died.*

But here, above—nothing is waiting for you here, either. Every second you delay the decision only brings you closer to your doom! Your time will be up in an instant if you don't jump! But if you do jump, then jump so that you stay floating in the air; so you don't fall down into those waves; so they don't close in over your head. Abandon that tiny surface, but don't hope to land, because you exist nowhere else but in that jump. There—there is where you are alive.

But what came next slowly covered me in a cold sweat.

And then there's that one feeling. It's the feeling that you get when you understand the body, which you've believed to be your own, like a home, isn't really yours anymore; that it has rooms hidden behind corners, and someone else has moved into one of them; someone who is basically a different kind of being; and he has nothing against you personally, of course—oh, no; but if you get in his way or stand as an obstacle to him in his existence, then he won't let it rest and there's nothing you can do about it, either. He comes and he takes. That's just the way he is. You can even try to act to his liking so as not to bother him, but you can never be certain that what you do

won't have the completely opposite effect. You're startled by every
slightest buzz, every tremor in your physical state that wouldn't have
even scratched the surface of your consciousness before now: could it,
perhaps, be the next sign that a new process has begun within you?
One that won't pass through you without leaving a mark?

That was the exact same way I'd viewed my illness. I couldn't
understand how it was possible: how it could be possible that
a person whom I was connected to by nothing—absolutely
nothing— had found me as if by way of some invisible under-
ground threads; and not the "me" I'd existed as at the point in
time when those sentences were recorded; but rather that very
same me who I am now—sitting at home, wearing headphones,
and listening to a recording that an almost complete stranger
gave to me yesterday. How had that voice seen inside of me?
Because in that back-room chamber, Android continued, *that is
your God. You have no other, and you cannot come any closer to
Him. Should I tell you now to just deal with it?* Au contraire! *Don't
deal with it! Do you hear me? Don't deal with it for a single second,
because if you do, you're finished!*

Android was almost screaming. I pushed the stop-button and
took off the headphones. I couldn't keep listening to that crap.

Janne had arrived at Birchback in the very best of spirits, but her
mood was ruined in the first half hour of being there, because
among the others who came outside to greet her was someone
whom she could have least hoped to meet there out of all the
people in the world. Jaagup. He had the same curly beard and
restless eyes, the same awkward gait. Naturally, several years had
already passed since that unpleasant concert incident, and all
wounds had healed since then; but even so, she couldn't imagine

exactly how she was supposed to spend the coming weeks there. Because Jaagup had once been very important to her, in spite of everything—his slightly coarse demeanor and ability to not ask stupid questions at the wrong moments. Whatever he was like now didn't interest Janne. But she couldn't leave, either, because she had promised Android she'd wait for him there. *And why should I hightail it again?* she reasoned. *Let Jaagup leave if it gets complicated for him.* All in all, Janne hadn't been the one who'd screwed it all up in the first place.

Yet, she kept her calm on the surface, simply saying hello to Jaagup as if they'd only been briefly acquainted at most. Jaagup greeted her back and Janne could immediately tell it wasn't easy for him, either. *Good*, she thought. And then Veronika came outside, introduced herself, and offered to show Janne to her room, which had been set up in the auxiliary building. "We'll turn the radiator on high if it gets chilly at night," Veronika said. "Lunch is in an hour. We're all vegetarians here—I hope that suits you." It did, indeed.

Veronika was a little luckier with the next lecturer: a historian who lived in Haapsalu and researched old religions. On this occasion, everyone who wanted to could bring a paper and pencil with them into the auditorium, although only a scant few took advantage of the opportunity. Janne had heard from Android that there would be lectures, because Android himself was supposed to give one of them and therefore she had brought a notebook and a pen with her to Birchback. The lecturer was a little irked upon arriving: it turned out that he had prepared extensively illustrated slides and intended to present a wealth of factual materials, but Veronika's auditorium didn't even have a chalkboard, not to mention a projector or a screen.

"Yes, we here old-fashionedly rest our hopes on the living word," she explained to the historian with her distinct charm.

Somewhat awkwardly, the man fished some notes out of his greasy portfolio and started speaking.

His lecture was fascinating in every respect, but would have been better suited for an entirely different audience. He assumed his listeners possessed knowledge of very many things, commenting on a number of insignificant details with fatiguing comprehensiveness, and at least once every five minutes he would say that a picture should be displayed at that part of the lecture, but unfortunately couldn't for technical reasons. His voice was likewise rather monotonous and seemed rusty from underuse. These aspects didn't reduce the value of the talk's substance, of course; it simply made following the speaker's points a relatively trying task. Even so, Janne had several pages filled with dense notes by the end of the lecture, and when perhaps the most interesting portion began—a Q&A dialogue with Jaagup—Janne wrote down almost just as much more.

"I threw that notebook away later, all the same," she told me now. "I came across it while cleaning one time and I saw that everything in it had gone so far somehow, and I really didn't long to have any of it back, either. On top of that, I simply didn't have a place to put it." Which was disappointing for me, of course.

The speaker didn't stay for dinner, but instead finished his paperwork with Veronika, got into his tiny car, and started the bumpy journey back to Haapsalu.

However, time passed rather quickly at Birchback even without the educational events. Janne read during the "self-expression" time slots meant for more creative personalities, and at one point was even afraid that she had brought too few books along with her, until she compared her stocks with Birgit's and discovered that although their interests matched, the contents of their suitcases differed. She likewise found this and that in Birchback's main library, primarily works by sci-fi and fantasy authors: a little bit of Estonian-language, but mostly in English.

Although her English reading proficiency wasn't very high, they had the ability to sometimes draw her in so deeply that afterward she couldn't even remember the language in which she had read them.

The weather was nice, of course, and would occasionally just tug the residents outside and away from indoor activities. Everyone went swimming in the lake once or twice during the day, mostly in twos or threes, and Janne had to always be careful to ensure she wouldn't end up in the same cluster as Jaagup. In the shed were a couple of older bicycles, which Oleg had checked out and confirmed they were in shape for riding. Oleg himself biked about a twenty-kilometer circuit every day and Janne tried to accompany him on it once, but realized she wouldn't be able to keep up with the boy's speed and didn't want to hold him back either. So from then on, she explored the surroundings on solo bike trips, pedaling up and down the hills of Mulgimaa and through villages, where people were mowing lawns or caring for gardens, and when she rode past them, they would stop for a moment and stare at her. She would call out a *Hello!* in a bright voice and they would greet her back, scowling and suspicious as Estonians always are.

Veronika introduced the third lecturer as the Director of the Institute of Cosmology. He was a stunted man a little older than his listeners (though not by much), who paced nervously back and forth at the front of the auditorium and tended to get so worked up about what he was talking about that he simply had to visibly express his points with wild gesticulations. The points themselves, on the other hand, remained a little vague for the most part. And it similarly turned out that the "Institute of Cosmology" was a relatively modest undertaking composed of just the speaker himself; not a serious scientific institution, as the title would otherwise have one assume.

"But how was *I* supposed to know that?" Veronika cried, even though the "institution"—whose only contact with the outside world was a Tele2 mobile number—could certainly have stirred justified suspicions.

Unlike the historian, the cosmologist stayed not only for supper, but overnight. It was a warm evening and the table had been set outside with long benches on either side. The cosmologist sat himself down next to Birgit and persistently refilled both his own and his neighbor's glass with wine, not especially concerning himself with the rest of the group, and after not very much time at all, he even snaked his arm across Birgit's shoulders. It rested strangely in place there at the same time as his other hand continued drawing diagrams of cosmic vibrations in the air—their coincidences with the patterns of human karma were supposed to define both the instances of the greatest danger and the greatest opportunity in her life.

"And, naturally, also man's chance of meeting his soul mates," the cosmologist added, squeezing Birgit's shoulder.

When Birgit stood up from the table shortly after and excused herself momentarily, the cosmologist also stood up and meant to accompany her. However, Birgit fended him off by saying that Birchback only had a one-person toilet. The cosmologist sat back down to the sound of the group's laughter, filled his glass to the brim again, and then started making eyes at Mailis.

"But I'll tell you all this." he announced. "You've got to be awfully careful handling that field of science. Awfully careful. There's all kinds of crap going around. All those Antero Allis and Igor Mangs and you know what I mean. Oh, all they do is explain and explain! And they don't get it one bit, themselves, not one little bit. Swindlers, I tell you! Charlatans! They should be outlawed."

It didn't take very long at all before Joel hauled him to his room, and he was taken to board a bus already before breakfast.

"I suppose I don't need to give much of an introduction for our speaker today," Veronika said, beaming. Indeed: aside from Carola and Anni, everyone there had either met Android before—no matter how fleeting the encounter was—or had at least heard of him. Or, like Janne, they were at Birchback primarily *because* of him. Observed opposite the listeners seated on the floor of the bare auditorium, his scrawny frame appeared even taller than it actually was. His gaze pierced his tiny rounded yellowish glasses and flitted from one person to another as if assessing the situation on a chessboard, and when Veronika finished speaking, Android only gave her a slight nod and then sat down amidst the others.

"I've been invited here to speak to you about anything," he began in his penetrating voice, "and that's exactly what I intend to do."

Everyone was on the edge of their seats waiting for Android to continue, but he stared off into nothingness for a while, as if only considering just then what he was really going to lecture about. The only sound in the silence was the steady rustling of Mailis's cassette recorder. She had to be certain she would capture the entire lecture; just recording it on paper might not suffice.

"There are only two questions capable of interesting someone of full spiritual worth for more than a fleeting moment," Android continued again. "They are God and death. Camus managed to join these together and said that the question of suicide is the only philosophically intriguing problem there is. Even so, I would keep them separate. Why death should interest us—I suppose that's self-explanatory. It is the only one of the great changers that we all encounter. Inevitably. You might go without experiencing love; ecstasy and happiness may never appear; and if suffering fails to surface, then all the better. But death, *death* will definitely come in the end. 'Death and taxes,' as Brad Pitt once said. Well, I don't actually know anyone who truly fears the tax board the same way. Death is death. All of us must take that leap into the unknown at least once in our lifetime, and naturally, we would like it to not be so very unknown.

"God is the more interesting question. Vercors, a French writer, says that the presumption of God is what makes us human and differentiates us from inferior species. Vercors was his pseudonym, of course. His real name isn't important. In his novel, a creature that lies exactly between human and ape is discovered, and leads to the question of whether it has human rights, so to say, or whether it can be put to work like a domesticated animal. Vercors says he's human if he believes in something higher than himself. I agree."

Mailis asked how the writer's name was spelled, and Android told her.

"But now we have a reason to consider why this is. Let's take an atheist's standpoint here for a moment: people imagine God because they're unable to handle their world otherwise. There is too much randomness and unexplained phenomena. But based on that, one should seemingly conclude that things will go better afterward. And do they, then?"

It was a rhetorical question.

"If they did, then the atheists could go keep their traps shut forever. The problem is that the world is the exact same mishmash it is both with God and without Him."

Carola coughed, and Android's eyes flicked over to her for a brief moment. It had just been her dry throat, however.

"Followers of religion are, of course, relatively skilled at finding an answer to everything in their closed system; and they do so in a way that every conceivable argument made against them only strengthens their own belief. But the same goes for atheists, doesn't it! Though I certainly don't know what it strengthens for them. Are you familiar with Lourdes? It's a place in France— millions of pilgrims travel to it and quite often, someone who is hopelessly ill is suddenly cured there. Or so they say. A religious person will see miracles there, but take any feisty atheist to Lourdes and he'll only see a flock of mixed-up souls, some of whom are even in such a mess that they're capable of replacing one psychosomatic ailment with another. Well, maybe every once in a while it's also possible for someone to go there unbelieving, but to then come away knowing his inner confusion. That psychosomatic thing, by the way, can be incredibly powerful sometimes. There are doctors who believe that more or less all diseases are psychosomatic. All it takes is a big cleansing upstairs, and they're gone. Who knows."

Then Android stood up again and started walking among the listeners, occasionally pausing and staring directly at one or another. Mailis's notes also became spottier accordingly, because the speaker's voice wasn't very audible when he moved further away.

"But now let's leave behind the grouchy atheists, the Sunday churchgoers, and all the rest of the accountants' race," he continued. "Let's talk about things the way fit for an open-minded individual. Why is it that a belief in something higher than us makes us the way we are? Huh? Can someone tell me?"

He commanded the auditorium so that if anyone really did doubt what he was saying they didn't let it show. Although on this occasion, Android's pause was so long that Mailis managed to quickly shake out her hand, which was cramped from writing, and Birgit even got the sense that he really was waiting for a response, so she attempted to formulate something into words. But she ran out of time.

"My answer to that question is as follows," Android announced. "Deep down in our souls, none of us are able to make peace with our own finality. With our limits. And that's how simple it is. You go and you go and you go and all of a sudden there's a wall in front of you. Not just in one spot on the road before you, but totally in front of you, no matter where you turn. So, what do you do? Do you hire the A-Team, huh?" He snorted. "They won't come. They'll say that you have to deal with the problem yourself. And they're right, by the way. And we already know that, by the way. We simply aren't able to come to terms with it. And that's why we need a reason for why we should rise above ourselves. We're all Michael Jacksons: we can sing or move perfectly, all peaks have been summited, the masses are falling over themselves for us, but hey—it's the wrong color. 'Shit happens,' right? You know, that's a pretty good example, since it helps to explain why people are split into two groups. Let's call these 'patients' and 'parachutists.' The patients are those whose diagnosis is Michael Jackson and whose treatment is plastic surgery. You think you'll go buy yourself a new face and you *will be* a different person. The one you want to be. Or, well, you go and acquire a new gadget, car, girlfriend—there's no difference. Of course, it's not a treatment that might fix them, but rather a treatment that they themselves have chosen. And which, for the very same reason, cannot help them. Their illness isn't at all untreatable like, for example, well, I don't know—diabetes or homosexuality. They simply don't *want* to treat it. They don't set a goal of rising above themselves, although they sure do act like it. They attempt to stretch closer and closer to their ideal, but along with everything they've got, without giving themselves up. Without giving up that image they have of themselves: a good person, an honest citizen, a decent father. Hah! Not to mention their house and their junk and their bank account. And then they feel like they've actually achieved their goal. But have they, then? As if! They've simply been sold something again, something which they still haven't been able to crack open. The existence of those kinds of people is the very reason why intellectuality has just become the next big business, so 99% of what's stuffed into you is sort of like 'Made in China.' And I'm not talking about Taoism." He'd gotten on a roll, and paused to steady his breathing. "But that suits the patients just fine. You're asking: do I think I have the right to regard myself as better than them? And I reply: yes, I do. Just like you. Since you and I are that second type of person. The parachutists. Because it's the parachutists and the parachutists alone who are capable of leaping into the darkness without knowing what awaits them down below."

His gaze slid across the faces of his listeners and then lifted upwards for a moment, through the skylight and up into the sky, as if soaring across it at that moment was a plane, from which one could leap into the unknown.

"A parachutist is never sure of himself—don't go thinking that," he continued after the pause. "Being a parachutist does mean the readiness to forgo yourself and your whole world, but not because there's anything wrong with them. Or that no matter what you might see there before you, it'll always be better. Far from it! When he makes that leap, the parachutist knows all too well that he could lose everything. Therefore, a parachutist can never become a good revolutionary who is wonderfully aware of what a righteous new world should look like. But unlike Catholics, he will never say: *Ora pro nobis, pescatoribus.*"

"*Peccatoribus,*" Anni corrected him with a faint smirk. I can imagine it vividly—I do remember how she demanded accuracy with those kinds of things, although she was probably the only one at Birchback who had two semesters of college Latin behind her and was personally acquainted with a Catholic priest. Or who knew very well how the Hail Mary actually sounded in Latin.

It appeared that Android had accounted for that possibility. Mailis said he didn't even look over to see who had interrupted him when he pointed his index finger towards its source.

"Here, you can hear the way that sense and order speak," he said, and only then looked in Anni's direction. "Yes. Of course, they say *peccatoribus*. Pray for us, the sinners. But they mean *pescatoribus*. For us, the fishermen. What did Jesus say to Peter? You will all be fishermen. You'll start catching people's souls. Every Catholic is a fisherman. And at first, they are, of course, themselves a caught fish. That's why I believe the fish is such a good symbol for Christianity. A net would be even better, naturally, but I have no clue what the first letters of that word in Greek could offer together."

Anni glared at him with bare antagonism. I'm quite certain that by that time, she had already managed to categorize Android as a smug cryptomnesiac and truly believed he had said it incorrectly on accident.

"One French literary scholar has written a book titled *S/Z*," Android continued. "It's about Balzac and how to read him and so forth. You switch one letter at the right moment and everything that's hidden surfaces. Certainly a very important topic. But that's not why we remember it . . ." He snickered. "If I were to write a book about Christianity, I'd title it *S/C*. Truly, truly, I tell you: rather great things may come forth from behind a single letter. Because language, you see, is simply a technology. And systemic men of every suit are very adept at taking advantage of it. It's so typical how they've hidden their intention—oh, not only their intention, but rather their imaginary divine right to force their god, who is documented with extreme precision, onto others (i.e. the S in our diagram)—behind an image that is seemingly humble, but in sales-strategy is highly important— one depicting them as imperfect. C, in our diagram. Or, if it's easier, we can also use the words 'mission' and 'sinner' in place of those letters. But why, may I ask—why should I try to learn how to live correctly from people who personally believe that they're constantly getting all their own actions wrong?"

He peered around the room as if he truly intended to ask the question. Mailis busied herself with scratching down notes.

"Now you may be thinking," Android continued, "that I want to write off Christianity completely. Like some Nietzsche or Marx. Far from it! Even though all churches could go, in my opinion. I mean, of course, the institutions, not the buildings. Please don't touch the buildings. Architects and artists are behind those, not priests and bishops. I mean the institutions, the systems, the regiments, the rules, the pointless wars over whether the divine and the human were together or separate and how many fingers you should use to make the sign of the cross and what have you. It's unbelievable—what's there to deny—*unbelievable* how, time and time again, Jesus has it in Him to still turn the other cheek after all those knocks over the head that the popes and the patriarchs have competed to dole out."

He took a slight theatrical pause, giving the resounding sentence time to sink in.

"So, yes, we truly do have reason to take heed of Jesus's words. If they reach us. And if they echo back. Those who humble themselves will be exalted. There's a genuine ring to that. I came to bring a sword, not peace—no shit, Sherlock. But even so, we have reason to keep our guard. Because sense and order have certainly taken care to see what's worth showing to the masses, and what might get them mixed up. We've got no real reason to reckon that, just like my little evangelist here," (he had walked up to Mailis and stretched out his hand, as if intending to lean against the crown of her head, although he retracted it at the last moment) "so did Matthew and the other boys who recorded Jesus's words just as well or as poorly as they understood them. But we likewise don't have much reason to believe that one smart old man after another hasn't pored over those texts later and thrown out everything that seemed the slightest bit dangerous in their opinions. And we do only have four gospels in the New Testament, don't we? How many others were left out? At least fourteen! And it's obvious why this is. Because their message was too intense for the men of sense and order. So the Christians' current Bible isn't even a 'best of ' the original thing, but a 'greatest hits' at most."

At this point, Mailis's story (which is my most credible source for the lecture) became a little disjointed, because she was so swept along by Android's words that she forgot to keep

an eye on her recorder, and that was when the first side of the
cassette tape unfortunately ran out. As a result, her reports on
what he said further are only based on her relatively sparse
notes. On top of that, it took some time for her to get used to
the idea that fourteen more gospels exist. Janne later threw her
notebook away, of course, and couldn't remember much of it
at all, while Birgit's own recounting of the lecture only helped
to confirm a few hazy parts. And so, by the time Mailis had
managed to re-hone her thoughts, Android had already moved
on and was speaking about Faust, who he believed was similar
to Jesus. Jesus as the human incarnation of God and Faust's pact
with Satan were both parachutists' leaps into the unknown,
according to his logic.

Quite a lot of people have spoken to me about Android, and
all of them (including those who had managed to very painfully
extract him from their lives, such as Mailis) still believed that he
himself was one of those "leapers into the unknown." However,
I dare to doubt that, at least on the basis of what I now know.
Maybe because according to his terminology, I'm one of those
accountants, patients, and decent fathers, who really hasn't
yearned for something higher in his life. Nevertheless, I'm
presently standing before a leap that I inevitably must take.
And observed from this perspective, I have an entirely different
picture of Android in my mind than those who readily allowed
themselves to see him as being better than other people. To me,
it feels like he wouldn't have been capable of taking the jump
personally, and that's exactly what caused him inner torment.
Which, in turn, was why he wanted to make everyone else jump.
Because for him, that was the only way to be close to jumping.
And as much (or, rather, as little) as I knew my daughter, I
believe that she also grasped that fact relatively quickly. But now
I'm starting to digress once more. Android has a thing or two
more to say. Mailis also now finally turned the cassette over.

". . . we mainly have Goethe's book going around, don't we?

Do you still remember it? But Faust's story itself is much older. And even Goethe, who was indeed a man of sense and order— well, at least in his old age—nailed it pretty adequately. Or, let's say, he gives a couple of clues to those who are capable of seeing. Take Mephistopheles, for example. What does he say about himself? 'Part of that Power which would the Evil ever do, and ever does the Good.' This is worth considering for a minute. First of all, he says it 'would' ever do evil. Does it mean that which we're taught to regard as evil? You don't need to go to the crossroads of three merging paths at midnight on a Thursday with a full moon. It's enough to just close your eyes and listen in the silence. And boom—there he is. But 'ever does the Good.' Come on— that would be too easy! There's something up here. What is it, then—you would do good and you do carry out evil? Just like the saying that the road to Hell is paved with good intentions. Then the secret of life would be nothing more than to just read through the instructions and do the exact opposite. But, hey—it really is much more complicated than that."

Everyone hung on Android's words, enchanted, with the exception of Anni, who was fidgeting. However, there was nothing she could do but continue listening. It turned out that in Android's interpretation, Mephistopheles represented and channeled uninhibited creative energy that, being chaotic and powerful, could both create and destroy, and in doing so was just as blameless as nature itself. Because good and evil exist only in the contrasts that go on in people's heads, not in reality; thus any kind of creative act is unavoidably both good and evil at once. "Would evil ever do, and ever does good," can thereby be explained by saying creative force erupts from a desire to replace what exists (i.e. to destroy), but can only achieve its goal when it is capable of surpassing that which exists—of managing to do something better and higher than that (i.e. create).

"But if someone tells you that, first of all, you need to do a SWOT analysis, draft a budget, apply for funding, perform your activities, and then write a report—then spit in that person's face," he continued. "In the beginning, there was no SWOT analysis. Faust already said it, no matter that it was through Goethe's mouth: 'In the beginning was the Act.' And when I say 'act,' I mean something capable of changing the world— of changing it in a way that nothing is as it was before. Well, maybe not for everyone in the world. Maybe not for the whole world. But at least for the person who has managed to execute the act."

"Was 9/11 an 'act' from that point of view?" Anni suddenly spoke up once Android left the next theatrical pause in his speech.

"You mean, is a fanatical terrorist also a parachutist? I certainly understand what you wish to achieve." Something akin to a smile spread across Android's face. "If I say yes, I'm agreeing that a true act may bear evil within it, and if I say no, that isn't an act, what's the point of everything I've been saying up to now?"

"That's about right," Anni nodded. "So was it or wasn't it?"

"That's not quite a yes-or-no question, all the same, as I see it," Android answered.

"It is as *I* see it," Anni said, not allowing him to continue. "Was it or wasn't it?"

"Maybe we can leave questions for afterward?" Veronika proposed. "Let's listen until the end of the lecture."

"No, why not—certainly I can answer promptly," Android pronounced slowly after his eyes had made a round of the auditorium. "Do you know what Stockhausen said about 9/11? That German composer—do you know him? He said it was the greatest work of art possible in the whole cosmos: that's what he said. But, hey—I don't agree. Yes, 9/11 was undoubtedly a leap into the darkness. But *only* that. The creative side was lacking. And even more importantly: those who came up with that act of terror and those who executed it weren't the same people. Blind obedience and the ability to do what you're told with a slave-like mentality—that does not produce acts. Devising schemes without the courage to carry them out personally and leap into the darkness—that does not produce acts. Do you agree?"

"I do," Anni said, and although Android left her the opportunity to debate it further, she remained silent for that occasion.

Android continued, now without interruption, and took up the subject of faith and belief next, as well as how the "men of sense and order" sitting on either side of an argument are unable to get by without hating each other, because that is the inevitable outcome of sense and order's agenda, all while in reality, the exact same experience lies behind or beneath all religions. Rising above oneself, the severing of apparent ties, and becoming one with that original energy of chaotic creation—the sole thing worth striving towards. The "Power," which Goethe had associated with Satan in *Faust*, instead gained, bit by bit, a godly definition in Android's lecture. He spoke fervidly and compellingly, and anyone listening to him attentively was unable to maintain any doubt that in spite of the spectacular variety of faiths around the world, one true God stood behind them all, and Android was His Mephistopheles.

The lecture was followed by a dinner, as always. Janne told me that everyone presumed an interesting debate would take shape, but Anni quickly emptied her bowl and vanished to her room. As such, Android had an uninhibited chance to enjoy the entire group's attention. This didn't dampen the mood, of course: Joel kept bringing more and more wine up from the cellar, so he himself along with Oleg and Kaupo got rather drunk as the hours passed, and even Veronika erupted into unrestrained laughter every short while, so much as slapping her palms against her knees as she did so. Android himself didn't drink alcohol, of course, but it seemed like the buoying collective mood alone was having such a positive effect on him that his attitude and behavior didn't differ much from everyone else's. And he specially divided his attention between the girls seated around the table—or, to be exact, between Birgit and Mailis.

"But you said girls didn't interest him?" I asked Janne.

"Well, not in that sense," she said with a melancholy smile, taking a sip of whiskey. "He still needed them, just in a different way. And that's how he'd branded me for his flock already before Birchback."

Then it slowly started getting darker and chillier outside that night. Carola and Birgit were the first to leave the group, followed by Jaagup, and it seemed like the night was coming to a close.

At that moment, Android stood up. He didn't start walking towards his room, but rather seized Mailis by the wrist.

"Come along," he said. "We're going now."

Mailis, stunned, allowed herself to be dragged along, especially since no one was paying them any attention and it would have been somehow embarrassing to suddenly protest, to say nothing of starting to scream for help. Android tugged her up the forest path to the crest of Dickens Hill, from which they could see the whole cloudless sky pricked full of stars and a bright full moon—all of which was truly very beautiful.

But that wasn't the reason they were there. Android pulled a long, sharp butcher's knife out of his coat pocket, which he had apparently taken from the kitchen. Mailis suddenly couldn't take her eyes off of it, as if hypnotized. Moonlight glinted on the long, razor-sharp blade as Android raised it high above his head, pointed straight up towards the heavens.

"There are the stars and the endless sky," he said almost tenderly.

Mailis's eyes turned upward together with the blade. There was no denying that the distant expanse managed to take her breath away, but her heart only pounded wildly in her chest that moment because Android still had her wrist clamped in his iron grip.

"The universe, with which even we are one," Android continued.

Mailis tried to break free of his hold, but simultaneously realized with exceptional, astonishing clarity that no matter what might happen in the coming moments, it would take place exactly and only in the way Android wanted, and she herself had absolutely no chance at all to influence it in any way.

"What could one person yearn for more than to receive messages from it?" Android asked, looking over at Mailis. "Huh?"

"What messages? Let go of my wrist."

Android didn't let himself be bothered and when he continued speaking, his voice was still soft and reflective.

"What if I were to say to you now: in my heart, I am as sure as can be that God has spoken to me, like he once spoke to Abraham, and has commanded me to make a sacrifice?" Android asked nonchalantly. "Just like how He asked Abraham for his son Isaac? What would you do then? Entirely free, by your own will? Would you then bare your neck to me and say: here I am?" Android uttered all of this without any tremor in his voice, as if he was simply intrigued by the question.

"You're joking!" Mailis said.

"Not at all," Android smiled.

"You're insane!" Mailis felt like she might collapse at any minute.

"Yes or no?" Android demanded.

"*No*, of course!" Mailis yelled angrily into his face.

"And that's entirely right," Android said, released her wrist, and slid the knife back into his pocket. "Consequently, I can count on you. I hope you'll remember this: there's no point believing in all kinds of crap that others try to persuade you to believe."

Mailis's head was spinning, her vision blurred, and she felt like she was going to throw up. But there was nothing there to lean against except Android's shoulder. "What's your problem, you asshole?!" she yelled. "I almost had a heart attack!"

"But you didn't," Android said, shrugging his other shoulder. "Whatever doesn't kill you makes you stronger."

They stood there like that for a few moments. Mailis's chest felt tight; she clenched her hand into a fist and thought she simply had to punch Android—she even raised her fist, but couldn't bring herself to do it.

"You really, truly are totally messed up in the head," she ultimately said, gradually regaining her self-control but still trembling from head to toe.

"Take me as an opportunity given to you," Android spoke. "As a door, to which you have the keys. Only you know whether or not you'll open it. Whether you'll just remain an evangelist, or whether you yourself will become a part of the message."

He started walking away, and Mailis followed, shaking. It was dark beneath the trees and the path was difficult to see. But from that point forward, she couldn't help herself: whenever she heard Android's voice, it penetrated through all of her defense mechanisms and went straight into her veins like cold, strong medicine that rips away the world's curtains.

Hanging on the wall of Kaupo and Mailis's living room was a small piece of poster art, which had seemed a little pale and oddly placed before; but now a red beam of setting sunlight struck it directly, which suddenly transformed the cadaverous faces in the picture into a lively, excited scene.

"What a total bastard he was!" When we were seated at the coffee table, Mailis had only told the story in broad strokes, which was why I couldn't understand right away why Kaupo—who had only met Android once in his life—suddenly became so irritated. But even later, outside, when I'd heard everything,

I still wasn't entirely convinced. Not until I remembered the spindly man at the trolley stop, but that was later.

"You should have called the police. Or told me about it immediately, right there. You don't just let things like that go."

"Oh, who cares about him," Mailis said with a wave of dismissal. "You'd have gone and broken his nose, too."

"Still!" Kaupo shook his head, slowly regaining his composure. "As hard as I could have. And for the right reasons. And to think I invited him to come visit, too! Well, luckily he didn't."

"No, he didn't," Mailis repeated like an echo, her eyes locked on her teacup and her spoon stirring in sugar.

Mailis came down to breakfast a little late the next day (everyone except for Anni was already there), and when she did, the open spot furthest away from Android was next to Kaupo. And that's where she sat. And whenever Android looked in her direction, she instinctively grasped Kaupo's hand. Android was presently telling some story about his teenage years—about how his grandmother, who had poor eyesight, had him read her the Bible aloud, and how he would alter the story as he saw fit.

"I made it more contemporary," he said. "So that the message wouldn't be out of touch with the modern day, you could say." Android's grandmother had been partial to the psalms and the *Song of Solomon*, but her favorite at the time was, without a doubt, the *Book of Revelation*. The two struck a balance, where he always read her a little from here and a little from there, but the boy didn't leave his grandmother's favorites entirely untouched. In his version, for instance, the angels never appeared as choirs singing songs of praise, but rather sped around on motorcycles. "That can't be right," his grandmother protested. "No, no—it's just a new translation," Android explained.

"On top of that, I wanted her to take that stuff about loving your neighbor seriously," he added. "Back then, some bikers would meet up in our courtyard every night and make an awful racket. You know—those Russian bastards who believed that the louder the noise your instrument produces, the more impressive you are."

"Oh, we know," Oleg said. "I was one of them, more likely than not."

"Oh, really?" Android said, looking at him attentively. "Well, then you'll be glad to know that I specially had the angels in my grandmother's Bible whiz around on motorcycles so that you and your friends wouldn't get her pissed off. Otherwise, she would always tell my mother to go yell at them to shut up from the window."

"Yeah, well, we *were* the Angels of Death," Oleg laughed.

"Makes no difference," Android replied. "An angel is a species; the address is secondary."

Everyone laughed. They were in high spirits, because Android had just announced he would stay at Birchback for a little while longer. Everyone except for Anni, perhaps, who appeared to be running unusually late, because she was ordinarily up and at 'em before the others on most days. As it turned out, she nevertheless had been that day as well—moments later, she entered the room, but from the front door. She had gone for a walk in the woods and gathered a large bouquet of wildflowers, which she now handed to Veronika.

"Thanks!" Veronika exclaimed, getting up to find a vase. "Should I make you some more salad?"

Anni peered into the bowl and dumped the entire contents onto her plate.

"No need," she said, "but I would like some tea."

Both Janne and Mailis later told me that the exact same thought crossed their mind at that moment. Android stared at Anni with a look that burrowed into her and her alone, and both of the girls admitted they simply couldn't imagine how he might ever yank Anni along to test her with an extreme, just as he had tested them. Anni seemed to be standing outside of his reach. But it wasn't anything that they regretted. On the contrary: they felt sorry for Anni, as if the incapacity to undergo the same trial that was now behind them was rather a defect or a disability in some mysterious way, something that set Anni apart from the rest of them. Nothing that could be perceived clearly, like a stutter or a big birthmark on her face; but rather, an inner ailment— something akin to color-blindness or a mild allergy that prevents you from eating fresh fruits.

"What's the plan?" Anni asked after she had cleaned her plate. "The weather's nice—we could do something outside."

"You don't think we'll get chilly?" Jaagup asked doubtfully.

"There's always tools for countering a chill," Joel reckoned. "A picnic would be pretty cool."

And so, they decided that day's lunch would be eaten outdoors. In spite of Veronika's searing glares, Joel announced that as an exception to the rule, anyone who wished could also have meat and wine at the picnic, and then drove to the store to pick up disposable grills, pork chops, and sausages.

It truly was an exceptionally beautiful day, which in almost no way felt inferior to a July heatwave. There was a picnic spot beneath a lone tree on the meadow, which offered a little bit of shade on hotter days; but on this occasion, they sat smack-dab in the sunlight. The girls spread out a blanket and set an array of bread, butter, and cheeses onto it, while Joel went straight to determinedly uncorking two bottles of red wine, explaining that they needed to breathe a little. Jaagup and Janne preferred Coca-Cola (a detail that connected them, which caused Jaagup to sigh wistfully as he raised his glass), while Carola had brought along a small bottle of vodka, still hoary from the deep-freezer. Joel set up the disposable grills and Veronika got the coals going while Birgit and Oleg opened the packages of meat and sausages. Veronika stayed true to her principles and packed a large container of marinated vegetables (which she promised to share with anyone who wanted a helping), while Jaagup's backpack held a towel-wrapped pot containing freshly boiled yellow rice.

"Seems there's no reason to worry anyone'll go hungry," Joel remarked, sizing up the spread and pouring the wine. "Cheers, then."

No one spoke for a while, simply enjoying the moment. Even Veronika took a small sip from her wine glass and appeared happy about it. Birgit let down her voluminous black hair, which cascaded freely across her shoulders, while Oleg leaned back on his arms and angled his face towards the Sun. "Oh, it was a gorgeous day," Janne recalled. "If only Jaagup hadn't been staring at me the whole time."

"It's such a shame the summer will be over before we know it," Mailis said. "I don't want to go back to the city at all."

"I know," Kaupo said. Although he had nothing waiting for him in the city, he had still decided to head back together with Mailis.

"No worry," Veronika said. "Next year, again."

"And then the next, and then the next," Mailis said with a smile. "And then the next."

"Until summer's turned into a nasty routine," Android jabbed, "and even the thought of someone's face from here makes you sick."

There was a long silence after he spoke.

"Well, you just had to go and ruin everything nice, didn't you?" Jaagup finally grumbled.

"Why's that?" Android shot back. "I'm telling it how it is. That's the primary mechanism that puts human life into gear. Buddha knew it: most of our efforts are spent on making the absolute happiest state we're capable of achieving last forever, and as soon as our wish is granted, we start searching for opportunities to break out of that routine somehow."

Birgit laughed.

"We're *in* a routine," she reckoned. "Constant change can turn into routine the very same way. Every night, a new party; a new group of friends; new names and new faces. Just like it is for some jetsetting multi-millionaire: a new city, a new hotel, new opportunities. Doesn't take all that long before it gets monotonous, you know."

"Precisely," Android said crisply. "That's just what I said. Routine is routine. It's like a ribbon around your neck. If you don't break out of it, in the end it'll choke you. And without you even noticing, I might add."

"Oh, let's leave the philosophy aside for today," Mailis said. "It's too nice a day."

"Why's that?" Android pressed. "Does my little evangelist not have her pencil and paper for writing down my words?"

Mailis shot him an irritated glance.

"Hey, leave her alone," Kaupo snapped. "She hasn't done anything to you; what are you picking on her for?"

"On the contrary," Android corrected him. "I'm very grateful to her. Each and every person wants a disciple, someone to write his teachings down on paper; but not everyone gets to enjoy that in real life."

"Only the worthiest, right?" Kaupo didn't realize that Android was luring him into a trap. The yellow-spectacled man looked around to observe everyone's faces before replying. Oleg's eyes were still closed and trained towards the sunlight, but Carola was glaring at Android and Anni was pretending she hadn't even heard what was going on. It wasn't the best standing for him.

"Oh, not in the least," Android continued amiably. "I was simply glad that she took notes during my lecture—that's all."

"Is that so," Kaupo growled, but Mailis placed her hand on his and he stood down.

"Looks like I've got a few sausages ready over here," Joel announced, placing a bowl in the center of the blanket. Veronika handed out paper plates and plastic forks, while Anni searched the picnic basket for a tube of mustard. Only Carola kept to Veronika's vegetarian diet—everyone else stuck their fork into a sausage. It was all just wonderful except for the fact that the scent of food had attracted a swarm of wasps, which made repeated attempts to land on the tips of the sausages and weren't even deterred by the mustard.

"Does anyone have any bug spray?" asked Mailis, who was especially allergic to stings.

"What're you going to do with it—spray the sausages?" asked Jaagup, who was also bothered by the insects.

"No, I mean to make some kind of a stench that'll just drive them away," Mailis replied while fruitlessly trying to swat two of the angry creatures off her plate, which she ultimately abandoned on the picnic blanket.

However, no one had considered the threat of wasps beforehand. Someone reckoned they would probably go away on their own.

"Let's just be happy that nothing is perfect," Oleg stated ceremoniously, and poured himself more wine. "It means we've still got something to look forward to."

"Exactly," Android said, raising his glass of juice in a toast. "At least we still have chance to look forward to."

"Well, there's always some kind of a chance, now isn't there?" Oleg said. "Even when you've screwed everything else up royally."

"And what will you do, then?" Android questioned. "Frame your chance and hang it on a wall?"

"That's right," Oleg smirked. "And then I'll light candles in front of it."

"Just like they do in Russian churches, huh?" Android smirked. "The Orthodox faith has always been skilled at making healthy people bedridden invalids for life in the event of a health problem."

Oleg only smiled at the comment.

"But you know what?" Android said. "Don't put out candles. Put out a piggy bank instead. My mother told me to do that once, when I was begging her for a bicycle. She told me we'd put a piggy bank on top of the cupboard and whenever I went to the store and had change left over, I could drop it in there. I went and did our shopping for a whole year like a good boy, voluntarily; sometimes, I even asked to see if maybe we needed something extra—lozenges for Grandma or anything. And then, in the spring, we had a piggy-bank-opening ceremony."

"What happened then?" Birgit asked. Android shrugged.

"Might have been enough in it to buy a reflector and a spare inner tube," he said. "My mother simply didn't know what bikes cost."

Android picked up a fork and fished a wasp out of his glass of juice.

"Nevertheless, I'm grateful to my mother for it," he said. "It cured me of capitalism. So what that it was with the mind of a child—I still realized: if you start wanting the things that have been made for you to desire once, you'll keep wanting them forever."

"You sure lucked out, then," Birgit said. Android flicked a glance over at her, but the girl had meant it without any shade of sarcasm.

"Ten points, navigator Birgie," Android nodded. "I sure did."

"It took me longer," Birgit said. "Maybe because I didn't actually want anything that couldn't be acquired."

"Well, then you simply weren't sick enough," Android replied. "I had severe asthma, you merely had a chronic cold."

"Maybe," Birgit agreed.

"Oh, fine," Carola spoke up. "All that pointless junk, that 'Made in China,' that trash that's slowly turning the planet into an indestructible piece of waste, and that advertising biz surrounding it—it's obvious to the naked eye that the whole system is rotten through and through."

"Yes—you see?!" Android cried out. "And it's people like you whom the rich people cry over."

Everyone laughed.

"Oh, come off it," Jaagup said. "Bashing capitalism is a hoot, but it's, like, inevitable. Unless someone here can propose anything better?"

"Of course I can," Carola huffed, although she didn't start describing anything in greater detail.

"I'd like, of course," Veronika remarked, "for us to leave our children a better world than the one our mothers and fathers left us."

"You said it," Jaagup nodded. "But first of all, we eat up our fathers' shit and our children eat ours. That's just how the saying goes," he added when Veronika glared at him.

"Fathers . . . Yes," Android murmured, "that's a species in and of itself."

"Who our fathers are doesn't make us who we are, though," Jaagup remarked. "If I'm good for anything, I'll be capable of stepping over my father at any hour."

"If that's your goal, you're sure shooting low." "I, no—that's not quite how I meant it."

"Ah—but it is, indeed," Android said. "You meant it exactly the same way that your father did before you, and his father before him. That is the problem you all have. You don't need to learn how to lie on the coals the right way. You need to stand up and let your urine splash down upon them."

"Hm," Anni huffed, who had been listening to the preceding conversation with an absent expression.

Android glanced over at her and then at Jaagup, then decided to put what was undoubtedly a tried and true expression of his into play: "When everyone is counting money, count poetry stanzas; when everyone is speaking justice, speak the truth."

"Nicely put," Birgit nodded.

"And that's exactly what your problem is," Anni spoke up. "Everything you say is said nicely. Or, well, almost everything. You even mean it quite nicely, occasionally. Just that it doesn't feel like it comes from the heart."

"And what do you know about my heart?"

"Yours? Nothing," Anni replied. "But I know a fair amount about my own, on the other hand, and this is the picture it's formed: I think you're a fake. Maybe the best brand, yeah; but also sort of 'Made in China.' You try to teach people how to swim, but you've only read about water in books. You talk about flying, but you're looking at the sky through a window. I do fully believe that you really want to be the person you're trying to look like. And when you manage to convince others of it, you almost start believing you *are* that person. But you know what? It's time somebody told you: you yourself, *you*— you yourself aren't capable of it, you never have been, and it's hardly likely you will be in the future, either."

That's my girl, I mused when Janne told me this.

"Let's not go overboard, okay?" Birgit reproached her.

"Well, well, well—now our cards are on the table," Android chuckled. "And what of it. I've always known that when it comes to fighting, your respect for someone else suddenly becomes your weakness. You look them in the eyes, wondering how you really can throw that punch, and by then, they've already hit you."

"Sorry," Anni said, lifting her wine glass to her lips and taking a big swig. "I really wasn't even thinking of fighting with you. If that's the way it looks, I'm very sorry. I simply said what I had to say."

It appeared that Android wasn't listening to her at all, however, but only staring attentively at a wasp that was probing a dab of mustard smudged on the corner of his plate. Then he picked it up between his long, boney violinist's fingers, and held the insect in front of his eyes.

"Hello, little creature," he said to the wasp. "We're angry, aren't we now? Don't worry—your anger will remain long after you."

And with those words, he stuck the wasp into his mouth and bulged out his cheeks. In the momentary silence that ensued, the picnickers could clearly hear the wasp's furious buzzing in the cavity of his mouth, but then Android swallowed, and it was gone.

The effect sunk in undisturbed for a heartbeat, but Anni wasn't impressed, all the same.

"I'd consider it," she said, nabbing another wasp from the picnic blanket, popping it into her mouth, and swallowing it without further ado. "Although I'd rather have sausage, for the most part," she added.

The second tray of meat was just coming hot off the grill.

Kaupo and Mailis left Birchback for the city the next morning. Classes would be starting for Mailis before long, and it was simply the right time to go. Kaupo had written his mobile number down on tiny scraps of paper that he handed out to everyone instead of business cards.

Mailis wrote everyone's numbers down in her notebook. Their luggage was already packed and stowed in the trunk of Kaupo's car and it was time for them to hit the road, but Mailis was still looking around searchingly. Then she spotted Android coming from the direction of the lake. Birgit walked a couple of paces behind him with an enraptured look blanketing her face, the train of her skirt wet and sandals dangling from her hand. Seeing that the others had gathered around Kaupo's car, they likewise walked directly up to the group. Mailis wrote down Birgit's telephone number and Kaupo handed Android his own.

"Don't hold a grudge, now, you hear?" he said. "And call if you ever end up in town."

"Of course," Android nodded. Janne had been generally

trying to avoid being left alone with Jaagup with the same amount of care as he was taking to seek out the opportunity. But as one might guess, she wasn't able to keep away from the boy forever. A few days after the picnic, Carola, who was scheduled to wash dishes with Janne after lunch, had cut and bandaged her finger, so she asked whether Janne might manage without her, and Janne was fine with it, especially since Carola promised to fill in for Janne the next time. Thus, she had nowhere to run when Jaagup showed up in the kitchen, and—as luck would have it—no one else was there or entered, either.

The way Janne told it, this is how things might have gone. And I believe I'm able to more or less imagine how it seemed from Jaagup's point of view.

"Well, what do you know. Seems like we haven't gotten a chance to chat yet," Jaagup said.

"Not really, yeah," Janne agreed.

"So, how've you been lately?" Jaagup asked. "All right, I suppose," Janne answered.

Jaagup was apparently expecting Janne to ask how things had gone for him in turn, so that he would be able to say "not so well." But she didn't.

"Guess that's how it is, yeah," Jaagup remarked after a pause. "It's weird meeting you again here, of all places."

"What's so weird about it?"

"I mean, well—just that it's this sort of a place. I wouldn't guess that you'd find it, like, interesting here."

"Same here," Janne nodded. "It's as far away from your world as you can get, the way I see it."

"Don't say that," Jaagup said, offended, and scratched his beard. "I guess time's passed meanwhile, too, and . . . That's not really who I am anymore."

"Okay, okay," Janne quickly interjected before Jaagup could start explaining what he was like now. "We all change. It's the exact same with me."

"Uh-huh," Jaagup murmured awkwardly. He was briefly silent, but didn't leave, either. Then he coughed.

"You know, I'd like to tell you I'm sorry," he finally spoke.

"Well, then say it, I guess," Janne replied.

"I really, truly was an awful pig back then," Jaagup continued. "I feel really bad about it. I hurt you."

"You did," Janne agreed. She wasn't about to start flaunting her tear-soaked pillows in front of him. Jaagup probably knew about her and Erki, but maybe not the fact that she had only talked to Erki so that she wouldn't feel so empty, or that nothing had happened between them other than telephone calls and walks. Erki was well aware of what had happened and didn't even make any advances.

"So, that's that," Jaagup said. "Now it's over, I guess."

"Yeah," Janne concurred; but Jaagup still didn't leave.

Are you able to forgive me?" he finally asked in a somewhat strange voice.

"You know, Jaagup," Janne said, putting down the bowl that she had been scouring intensely for the last couple of minutes, "I forgave you for it a long time ago already. Honestly. If I hadn't, I might not be who I am today or standing right here at all. But what was, was. It happened. And, let's be honest—it did take you a pretty long time to find me again."

"That's true, yeah," Jaagup agreed uneasily. "But even so."

"You think I could maybe wash these dishes now?" Janne asked. "You're bothering me."

"No, of course, yeah," Jaagup said, and sat down at the table—not actually leaving, but not speaking anymore, either.

Then Anni peeked into the kitchen from outside.

"Well, *there* you are," she said to Jaagup. "I'd like to borrow something. Come on!" And she vanished from the doorway. Jaagup stood and followed Anni with emphatically sluggish steps.

Now, more than five years later, Janne was silent for a moment after recounting the memory, and took a small sip from her glass.

"I know that he stayed there," she said, "and I'm very sorry for it, but I'd feel just as sorry for whoever else might have been there in his place."

It wasn't my place to argue with her.

Instead of an evening by the fireplace, Veronika informed the group, everyone was asked to come to the auditorium today, where Anni had something to tell them. When they gathered, they found Anni sitting on a stool in the middle of the empty space. She wore a work jacket taken from the shed, and her head was swathed in a large scarf, as if she had just come from the sauna and her hair was still wet. Everyone removed their shoes and sat around her in a circle.

"Today, we'll continue the same topic that has interestingly come up in a few earlier lectures," Anni announced. "And that topic is the *act*. But we won't approach it very theoretically, especially since that's already been done before. Even though we could. I suppose we all wore down the school benches a little back in our day."

She looked around the space, smiling. "But, no. We'll ask frankly and without overly complicating things: what is that 'act,' anyway? Is it something that stands out so suddenly and visibly from the rest of our arc in life that we spot it immediately, both in ourselves and in others; or could, perhaps, just any old kind of everyday task also end up taking that role?" She looked around at their faces, not expecting a reply. Everyone stared back at her with the exception of Janne, who was peeking over at Android.

"Here, opinions diverge," Anni continued. "Luther, for

example, believed that we must serve God specifically through daily work and austerity. The consequence, as we now know, was capitalism. Kierkegaard speaks in turn about a leap, as a few others here have also done. He says we cannot become who we are without taking a leap into the unknown. I believe we can freely infer here that Kierkegaard's jump was that second type of act. Or take, for instance, André Gide and his 'gratuitous act'—the kind that we perform without any goal or reason, simply to ensure that we're capable of totally free self-expression. Is shoving a complete stranger off of a train an 'act'? I mean, the kind of act that we want to consider here today? I'd dare to doubt it. But neither is it a possibility that I'd like to offer you, especially since we all know the trains don't run in these parts anymore. I'm going to make an entirely different kind of proposal."

It appeared that Android meant to interrupt, but Anni raised her hand to stop him.

"Let's change the subject for a moment, though," she continued. "Let's talk briefly about something much more proximal and earthlier. Like hair, for example. Why is it that almost all faiths with monasteries inhabited by monks and nuns have made cutting off your hair a rule when you join? Do you think it's for the same reason as people are made to do so in the military or in jail? To prevent fleas? Not in the least. Even though by using the flea excuse, the military and prisons are able to tear people away from their previous condition by removing their hair. Humans certainly aren't completely identical when their heads are shaved, but they're definitely more similar than in ordinary life. Aren't they? Especially women."

Anni pointed at Birgit's impressive mop of dark hair.

"The answer to this question can be found in Asia, in the Buddhist monasteries," Anni continued. "There, they have a custom where when someone leaves the world behind and takes up monkhood, his whole head isn't shaved bare at first.

They leave a clump for a little while. According to their belief, hair constitutes the thread that connects us to the world. Not figuratively, but in the very meaning of the words. And for as long as a novice is unable to break all mental ties to his former life, so long must he wear that dumb-looking tuft as a sign of it. Shaving one's head isn't a disciplinary measure, you see—it's a privilege. It shows that you've crossed a boundary. That is an act."

She slowly rose from the stool and looked around. Then she removed the scarf from her head in one swift pull. She had shaved her head. Well, not entirely, to tell the truth, because although her level of determination was beyond a shadow of a doubt, buzzing her hair to the skull using Jaagup's electric beard trimmer hadn't been all that simple.

"Welcome!" she exclaimed theatrically. "Greetings from the Padrik & Friends Salon! You *are* my friends, aren't you? Today, we have an exceptionally good discount for all who please! We'll free you of the chains that bind you to the emptiness of the world at no charge at all! We do speedy and top-notch work! And what's more: it's guaranteed protection against fleas!"

She removed Jaagup's trimmer from beneath her jacket and looked back and forth around the room.

"Well? Who's first?"

Gradually, it dawned upon everyone seated in the auditorium that she truly was offering to shave their heads. They exchanged slightly uneasy looks. Then Oleg stood up—his hair was buzzed to an almost nonexistent length, anyway, so he had nothing to lose from continuing the performance.

"I guess getting a little trim wouldn't be all that bad," he said with a smile, peeked over at Android, and then sat down on Anni's stool. She laid a towel over his shoulders and got to work.

"Voltaire was said to have gone to a barber one time," Anni spoke while shaving, "who believed that he had to cheer up each and every one of his clients by chatting with them. The barber

asked Voltaire: 'How would you like it cut, sir?' 'In silence,'
Voltaire replied. What do you say?"

"No, go ahead and talk," Oleg laughed.

"Maybe we should raise the stakes a little?" Anni reckoned.
"In addition to the salon, we'll open up a bookmaker named
Padrik and Prokhorov? Because each and every one of us does
believe that they know their friends. So, it really would only
be fair to allow people to earn a little money off of it, too—
right? Who'll bet ten kroons that Jaagup will allow his ties to the
world to be broken? Or that Birgit won't give up her pretty little
do, against all odds? Huh? Well, maybe it's not a very good idea,
after all. I can just feel how we'd clean out each other's pockets."

As soon as Oleg had stood back up, Carola came and sat
down resolutely in his place.

"Our salon has gotten popular!" Anni crowed cheerfully.
"Maybe we should start considering an expansion? Birchback,
Tallinn, Tartu? London, New York, Paris? Place yourself under
our care and we'll make you free! And by free, I actually mean
free."

She was remarkably skillful with Jaagup's trimmer. Carola's
matte locks dropped one by one onto the towel and the floor,
and then it was done. Jaagup's eyes turned to Janne as if
searching for support, and then he stood up. But Veronika had
beaten him to it. I suspect that by that time, she had already
realized that no one at Birchback saw her as Android's importer
anymore—on the contrary, she saw Android as a possibly
dangerous contender for her leadership position, which Anni
quite obviously wasn't seeking. After Veronika came Jaagup,
and after him, Joel. Anni just kept chatting on and on while the
heaps of hair encircling her stool grew and grew.

When Joel stood up, only Janne, Android, and Birgit were
still left. Anni's eyes locked on Birgit's.

"Drumroll," she said. "The flashes are popping. The suspense
becomes unbearable. Only one knows the answer. Will she dare

to leap over the boundary? Will she relinquish her blinding beauty? Or will the sacrifice be too great for her, regardless?"

Terrified, Birgit looked over at Android. He shrugged.

"Your hair," he said, "your decision."

Birgit rose unsteadily and stepped towards Anni, placing one foot directly in front of the other as if she was walking along a tightrope.

"Let the little children come to you?" she asked as she sat down on the stool. "Or is it more like lambs to the slaughter?"

"Who cares anymore," Anni said, "once the die has been cast?" And with that, she drew the trimmer in a single stroke starting from Birgit's forehead and arcing across her skull, leaving a light streak.

Janne observed what was happening in horror. She didn't intend to relinquish her hair, even if it meant she would be the only one. She certainly realized what Anni was doing, and even why she was doing it. But it didn't mean she approved of the way in which it was being done. She similarly decided she wouldn't plan on staying at Birchback for any longer, and would drive back to the city the next day.

Even bald, Birgit was still very beautiful, although she herself didn't know it yet, because Anni had no mirror to offer. When Birgit stood up from the stool, Anni looked towards Janne.

"Well?" she asked. "What'll it be?"

"No," Janne replied. "No, thanks."

"Ah-ha!" Anni exclaimed almost triumphantly. "There's also one among us who still regards the ropes tying us to the world as important! Well, what can you do. We live in a free country. No one can force anyone else to do anything. And so, all we have left is the million-dollar question," she said, turning towards Android. "Do you, our great and benevolent soul-keeper, also wish to stay chained to the world of passions?"

Android stood up. He was visibly agitated. He had spent the entire time considering what he would do at that decisive moment, and had apparently counted on Janne also allowing her head to be shaved. Then there would have been a sense of style to his refusal. But not anymore. And now he was unsure of how to answer, although he had to answer fast.

"Well, what is it?" Anni asked. "It's just the next yes-or-no kind of question."

Android didn't say a word. He looked towards Janne for a moment, then around the others' faces for another, appearing to calculate all of the risks and possibilities in his head at lightning speed. Then he paced rapidly up to Anni and sat down on the stool.

Whether it really was harder to work through his oily mane, or whether Anni was simply buzzing off the hair with steady enjoyment—in any case, it took her a good deal longer to shave Android's head than even the time it took for Birgit's. It might also have been due to the trimmer's battery starting to run low, because the sound it made while burrowing into Android's hair was a little weaker and whinier. But finally, it was finished. Still, Anni didn't remove the towel from his shoulders just yet, but took a couple of steps back to admire the scene. Without his hair and his little yellow glasses, Android truly looked quite ridiculous.

"Well, do you believe me now?" she asked.

Anni walked back up to Android and placed both hands on his shoulders. For a moment, it seemed as if they might embrace each other the very next second like sister and brother. But that moment didn't arrive.

"I have one more story to tell you," Anni announced. "It goes something like this: two old Zen masters once got into a debate. One said he understood the meaning of a blank sheet of paper; the other didn't believe him and said he had no clue what it meant. The room was full of their students, and the debate became rather intense. 'Well, fine,' the first master said. 'I'll prove it to you. Light a candle, I'll enter a deep state of meditation, and when the candle burns out, I'll be dead. Okay?' 'Well, let's give it a try,' the other master said. A candle was fetched and lit; the first master settled into his meditation pose and folded his hands in his lap. The candle burned down; everyone was holding their breath. And then the candle burned out. One student walked up to the master and looked for a pulse. There was none. The man really was dead. His students sighed in relief, even a little victoriously. But the second master said: 'Well, he died. So what? All of us are able to do that.' But he still had no clue what the blank sheet of paper meant."

Android was staring straight at Anni as if hypnotized. Anni, however, lifted her hands from his shoulders and slapped him across the face so hard that both he and the stool fell over with a bang.

It came as a shock to everyone. Android was apparently hurting very badly, but he promptly leapt up to his feet, regardless. He was breathing heavily and unsure of what to do next. It almost looked like he meant to attack Anni, and then it didn't. He staggered around the room a little, then finally just exited, slamming the door behind him.

"Well, looks like he and I aren't going to be a Bonnie and Clyde," Anni said, shaking her shaved head. "Not in a million years, try as you may."

In the morning, Android came down to breakfast with his backpack already packed.

"I've stopped to stay here in your company for too long," he announced. "I need to go prepare for the coming of darkness."

No one paid him any heed.

"I always do," he clarified. "Starting in fall, I reduce any kind of contact with other people bit by bit, and then at some point, I don't speak to anyone at all anymore. I listen to music. Not Christmas songs, of course. Mahler and Pärt and Shostakovich, mainly. And I re-read a few books—the kind that never age."

"Wow, I'd so like to be you," Jaagup said.

No one spoke up to point out how Android had been seen here and there just early the last winter, for instance.

"I believe that was the moment when I realized I could and wanted to expel Android from my life," Janne said. "Because he truly wasn't the person he pretended to be. Not in my eyes, and probably not in the eyes of a few others, either. He'd been beaten. Anni had maneuvered him into a corner, and instead of straightening his back, he'd allowed himself to be twisted. He and I left together—Joel drove us to the Viljandi Bus Station. I actually needed to go to Tallinn, too, but when Android started to buy us both tickets, I told him I was going to see a girlfriend in Tartu instead; and so I went."

7

Birgit wasn't at home when I tracked her down at an address in the little town of Türi, an address I'd gotten from Janne. The apartment door was opened by a cheerful older woman, who turned out to be Birgit's grandmother. They lived in one of those awful gray brick buildings that were built in Estonia's lovely little garden towns in the 1970s and were intended to attract young, fresh-out-of-college specialists with their private (albeit tiny) apartments—buildings which for the most part hadn't been renovated since then. As soon as she retired, Birgit's grandmother had swapped her larger dwelling in Tallinn—the upkeep of which had overwhelmed her—for the Türi apartment, because the fresher air and more peaceful rhythm of central Estonia suited her better. At the same time, she hadn't wanted to give up the comforts of an urban apartment, even though a duplex with a nice garden a little closer to the town's lake would have been available for about the same price. She explained this all to me before I'd had a chance to tell her why I'd looked them up in the first place. Birgit wasn't home yet—she worked as a simple sales clerk, although (as her grandmother informed me) she could have easily gotten much better paying and better overall work at a hair- and manicure salon with her cosmetology degree; but, well (her grandmother continued), "the kid's just a little bit tough, you know?" The coffee she offered me was relatively weak, but the cinnamonraisin cookies, on the other hand, were very good.

I didn't have to wait very long, regardless. I heard a key turn in the lock and the door unbolt, and then someone removing their shoes in the hallway. Then she entered the kitchen and set a large plastic bag of groceries down on the table. She nodded at her grandmother first, wordlessly, then observed me for a few moments before also nodding in my direction. She was dressed all in gray—a gray shawl hung across her shoulders, under which spread a gray blouse and a gray skirt that spilled down over her knees to her ankles, which were topped by gray socks. Only her slippers were black, just like her buzzed hair. She wasn't wearing any makeup. Even so, none of her appearance dampened—to the very least extent—the immense, suppressed force that she radiated. No matter that her eyes were chilly and her lips compressed into a narrow slit. She moved as smoothly as a dazzling predator and made just about as little sound.

"Birgit," her grandmother said, "this gentleman came to see you."

"I can see that," Birgit replied. Her voice was deep and a little raspy, as if she was suffering a slight cold.

"Maybe I'll leave you two here to chat a little, then," her grandmother said, standing up to leave the room.

"He's come for naught," Birgit announced. "I have nothing to say to him."

"Just listen," her grandmother said in exasperation. "Maybe you'll just have a little listen to him first, huh?"

"I have nothing to say to anyone from this world," Birgit declared. Yet, if her statement had been meant to carry a theatrical effect, it sounded a little hollow and ridiculous, which she herself immediately realized. "In short, I'm tired from work and would like to rest now."

"Birgit," her grandmother insisted, "I'd like you to speak to this gentleman."

It appeared as if something clicked inside of the girl at that moment, and she sat down on the chair.

"Well, let's talk, then," she stated, staring into my eyes.

"Should I pour you a cup of coffee, too?" her grandmother asked cheerily.

"I'll do it myself," Birgit said without taking her eyes off of me.

"Fine, fine," Birgit's grandmother said, leaving the kitchen and closing the door behind her.

"Well? What are you and I going to talk about, then?" Birgit asked. "You've already got the mark of death upon you over there."

I'd just regained my composure when she pulled the rug out from under me again. It couldn't be possible that my health was written across my face so clearly, but you really don't joke about those kinds of things.

"I'm looking for my daughter," I said, my voice unsteady. "Anni Padrik."

"Anni's your daughter?" she asked without any note of astonishment. "I could have guessed. But you're searching for naught. She's gone."

Birgit raised a fist in front of her face, opened it, and blew on her palm.

"I know," I snapped. She had no right to speak to me that way.

"You know nothing," she replied. "Anni was already gone when I first saw her. At Birchback. She'd already given up by then. Given up searching. Everything else is just the natural course of things."

"Hey, listen," I said, losing my politeness. "There's nothing natural about four young people taking their own lives. If you really are capable of saying crap like that, then sorry, but I'm not going to take that big, holy faith of yours seriously."

She was taken aback.

"Does that mean Anni's dead, then?" It was the first thing a normal person would say that I'd heard from her. "I'm sorry. I didn't know."

"Yeah," I said. "It's been more than five years already."

It turned out that she truly hadn't heard anything about the Birchback tragedy. After leaving, she had moved in with her grandmother and renounced all acquaintances on top of everything the world might have to offer—from television and newspapers to any books that weren't one of about a dozen spiritual treatises or the Bible, in addition to conversing on topics that didn't involve everyday activities. She allowed no one to violate that boundary, including her grandmother.

"I breathe, eat, and sleep here," she said. "But I'm there."

The door that had been kicked open by news of the deaths of Anni and her other former commune members soon began to creak shut again. I could see that Birgit was unsure of whether to tell me about her memories (which would, however, have also required her to personally return to those moments—something she clearly didn't desire) or be the kind of person who drives a grieving father from her doorstep without helping him the slightest bit, even though it would be in her power to do so. It appeared that living with the latter feeling would have been more difficult for her, all the same—especially since she'd disregarded Anni so cruelly before me just a moment earlier.

We drank many more cups of coffee that evening. The longer she spoke, the less theatrical her behavior became as a whole, and although she couldn't help but stick a truth shouted from a mountaintop into her story every once in a while, she gradually evolved (clearly against her own will) into a confused and somewhat helpless girl, who was furthermore scared to death at the present moment. For she understood all too well that if she hadn't left Birchback at the right time, then her grandmother might have been going to care for her grave now instead of her being the one caring for her grandmother.

As far as I understand it, experts on religious psychopathy often say that the tendency to turn to religion is simply a human trait that some have and others don't. Something like musicality or mathematics skills. That's complete bullshit. No one is protected from it. Someone simply appears in your life at the exact moment you've hit a dead end, presses the right buttons (comforting some, questioning some, or simply being near others), and then even the most rational mind, the most cheerful spirit is capable of withdrawing from his or her former principles. Perhaps not starting to believe at that very second, but *wanting* to believe, really *yearning* to believe—and that's already the first step, which is closely followed by a second and a third. And it's pure chance whether or not what is now going to become your highest truth ends up being an old institutionalized religion—something which, in the best of cases, teaches people to be nice to one another—or a deranged cult that believes your ultimate manner of self-accomplishment will be to blow yourself up at a busy market, carry poisonous gas into a subway, or commit collective suicide at a picturesque farm near Viljandi. What's more, poison can be distilled from even the most peaceful of religions, just as every shade of fundamentalist and sectarian has proven over and over again. Of course, more or less anything can be taken fundamentally—climate change, free trade, a curious mountain people's quest for freedom. Even a famous singer can be bowed down to. Yet, paradoxically, this is perhaps exactly what differentiates an exceptional religious predisposition from anyone's chance to be reborn in faith. If you possess a tendency to believe, your belief doesn't necessarily have to be in God. Yet, it is God who, in spite of your own character, may strike when something has irrevocably shifted your world from its foundations, resulting in you readily accepting the knowledge of a higher power whose mysterious acts return logic to the greater picture; return course and content to life.

And then, you yourself already carry the virus or are like a vampire: transformed by someone else's bite, but now the one who bites others.

This awareness had been dawning upon me slowly and steadily, but I understood it swiftly and clearly when I spoke to Birgit. I can't imagine a less suitable candidate for heroic religious deeds than her, and even so, serving God had become second nature to her in its own bizarre way.

"Whether God actually exists, so to say, and if so, in what way exactly has no importance whatsoever in regard to how I've chosen to serve Him," Birgit said. "Nor for how I ask His forgiveness for the acts I've once committed. Except, perhaps, for the way I see it, no one else (meaning no one here in this world) has the right to judge me. It might be difficult to understand, but that's the way it is."

Birgit had first arrived at Birchback in the company of friends back when Joel was running his modest artists' colony alone. Therefore, she had also happily agreed to go for a short period the next year when Karl-Anton invited her. Karl-Anton was attending drama school and Birgit was infatuated with him, but they slept in separate rooms. Birgit and her ex-boyfriend had broken up a short time earlier, and for the last several months her lifestyle had been a good deal calmer than it had in earlier days. Sometime around Christmas, she happened to run into a couple of former classmates at the shopping center by complete chance. One of these girlfriends had come home for the holidays from Brussels, where she was working at some international organization (in a relatively unimportant position for the time being, but an impressive feat, regardless), and the other—who had once been the biggest bookworm and intellectual in their class—was just walking around the mall with her very nice-looking husband. They were pushing a darling little daughter in a stroller, and a second child appeared to be on the way. Over the course of their conversation, they both mentioned twice to Birgit that they were now Catholics. She needed to do something with her life, and the theater could certainly be her path—not the stage, of course, but rather the makeup room, because she was no worse at the job than a Rakvere Theater makeup artist she had met the previous year at Birchback, who had asked Birgit to fill in for her one time when the troupe was doing guest performances in Tallinn.

She had been dating a boy named Vambola for a little while around that time. Vambola had a baby face and rosy cheeks, worked as a stagehand at some theater, rode a motorcycle, and played drums (more just for fun) in a post-punk band. He certainly didn't quite fit Birgit's conception of a stable life, but even so, she was fascinated by spending time in the band's practice space tucked away in the cellar of a house in Nõmme inhabited by one of Vambola's friends. There, she always felt like she was witnessing the birth of something new. And a potpourri of people came and went there all the time, chatting about interesting things—occasionally, the band didn't even get much playing done. That was also where she had seen Android for the first time. Back then, she couldn't find a better word to describe him than "freak," but their meeting had also been brief—for a while after, Android didn't surface again in her life there or anywhere else. Not that there was no one else to talk to at the house. One girl, for example, stirred a huge debate one time (she studied philosophy and was therefore familiar with such topics). The subject was one of the band's songs, the lyrics of which spoke about God's funeral and how it was drizzling and the five of us were standing around His grave. Birgit thought the lyrics were great, but the other girl said something about Nietzsche and the symbolic meaning of the number five and wanted to look awfully smart in general. The band's guitarist, who had written the lyrics, was a little irritated by her

comments, and they argued for a while. Vambola ultimately
threw up his hands and went to grab a couple bottles of wine
from the store, but Birgit had started getting quite intrigued by
the debate meanwhile and afterward asked the girl if she could
borrow some Nietzsche to read. She hadn't read anything in a
very long time (at least nothing like that) and the text seemed to
outright scorch her, although it also got on her nerves. Because
the way she understood it, Nietzsche believed the Superman was
the one who was supposed to sweep his path clear of old, worn-
out idols. But if you take today's world, then there's nothing
for him to do anymore because such idols are long gone. Now,
the Superman could instead be someone capable of clearing
his path free of malls and shopping centers and television
and all the political parties and politicians and their clueless
talk of competitiveness and economic growth, and who could
replace them in his world with pure values that need nothing
and depend on nothing. And when she said that to Vambola,
he was thoughtful for a while and said: you know, Birgit, I'm
proud of you.

Nevertheless, Birgit and Vambola didn't stay together for
very long, because the boy found some new chick during a
concert tour, on which Birgit hadn't accompanied him. But,
well, Birgit couldn't go—she had to graduate from cosmetology
school. She wasn't very disappointed by the development
either, because by then she had moved from post-punk on to
post-post-punk— meaning a state where Vambola's band and
its music and members could no longer offer her anything
significant, and unlike before, she had started to feel that two
people really are capable of loving each other their entire lives.
Even if she was one of those two, no matter who the other
might be. She began reading instead, and sought the company
of other readers. She read quite indiscriminately—anything
anyone happened to recommend. She didn't understand half of
the works, but others in turn struck her like a razor blade used

to try to shave off nerve endings protruding from the skin. She didn't read with her head as much as she did with her heart, and whatever the heart understood was ultimately grasped by the head as well, one way or another. It took her quite a long time before she figured out that what she actually needed wouldn't be found in books. By then, however, she had already read a fair amount. And her circles of friends had changed drastically. It had taken place gradually—some of her new acquaintances lingered and brought others along with them, while other old friends popped up in unexpected places. Generally, however, Birgit primarily socialized only with very fresh acquaintances then, all of whom were connected to the theater scene in some way or another. The more time she spent with them, the more convinced she became that it was the place for her. Back when she was with Vambola, she had heard incredible tales told of theater's monumental democracy—that any stagehand could speak on familiar terms with a world-famous director right from the beginning and freely booze with him at theater parties, and that most of the famous actors behaved very simply and naturally. But most importantly: that in theater, anyone could voice the wildest and most fascinating ideas, and that he or she wouldn't be seen as annoying or not the sharpest tool in the shed for them. Of course back then, Birgit still couldn't access the bigger theaters in any greater capacity than as an audience member or, in the most extreme of cases, by crashing acquaintances' workshops. She occasionally also ended up at one party or another in the company of mutual friends, but even that—along with the stories they shared—sufficed. She did, on the other hand, easily adopt the theater scene's periphery as her very own, doing makeup for one troupe and helping out a little with their costumes. These were students from the Viljandi Culture Academy, who were doing a pantomime show along with a poetry program. It allowed Birgit to be with the participants throughout the entire rehearsal period, which was a compelling experience.

Thus the second time she went to Birchback was as an entirely different person. Among other changes, she took the daily selfexpression time slot very seriously. She didn't know what to do at first, but after a short time, she, Carola, and Veronika came up with a very interesting project. It emerged almost accidentally when Birgit and Carola were the only people to attend Veronika's psycho-physical exercise class one day. They tried to perform the stipulated exercises for a little while at first, but then started to chat, and it turned out that they had almost the exact same interests. They spoke for hours about the Doors' music and poetry by Betti Alver and Uku Masing and Peter Greenaway's *The Pillow Book* and Gibran's *The Prophet* and what all else. The result was absolutely mystifying. From that day onward, they took over the auditorium for the duration of creative slots and got down to work on jointly creating something that was their very own. The plan was to conjoin movement, light, and body painting, all on the subject of "perfection." A photograph was going to be the final result of the collaboration. That was Carola's task. Veronika was the primary model, but Birgit would also model a little, and finally the two of them talked Carola into it as well. Then Birgit photographed and Carola complimented her great eye for framing. It was only when Veronika tried to take pictures of Carola and Birgit that nothing turned out, because she apparently didn't have such an eye, and they didn't know how to move so precisely on their own part. They read from works by female mystics (a collection of which could be found in Birchback's library) during breaks in the photo sessions: Mechthild von Magdeburg and Caterina da Siena and Teresa de Ávila; and they listened to the music of Hildegard von Bingen—naturally not the stupid version processed by a drum machine, but the original. They lost track of time on several occasions (none of them was wearing a watch); Veronika was completely naked, as was Birgit most of the time, and Joel would go knocking on the locked auditorium door to tell them it was mealtime again.

And so, those days mainly leaned towards serious work for Birgit, with lectures and picnics and other such events simply wedged in-between for relaxation, just as it was for Oleg, who painted, and for Joel, who crafted jewelry in his workshop and observed his wife's project a little skeptically, since she also had a whole lineup of moneymaking commissions waiting for her. Still, Veronika had her priorities set firmly in place, and just like in all other matters that didn't demand too great a contribution from him, so did Joel give in to her now without putting up a fight.

The longer she was there, the better Birgit grasped that no matter what one might call the endeavor that Birchback's residents had undertaken, it was an altogether worthy one. The fate of their art project in the greater world wasn't actually so important to Birgit as it was to Carola, for one, who so much as submitted a grant application to the Cultural Endowment (because there wasn't any money for quality prints of their photographs) and gave serious thought to possible exhibition spaces. Of far greater importance to Birgit was rather the cognitive aspect that reading those mystics (no longer with her head and not even her heart, but with her whole *body*) meant for her. She apparently even asked to borrow a few meditation books from Veronika and tried what was written there for a little while in practice, too, but ultimately gave it up. For while her thoughts really did turn incredibly lucid after each seated attempt she made, and while she could then understand complex matters as if they were child's play, before very long, she could feel herself becoming irritated and a headache slowly coming on if she didn't adopt her meditative pose again straight away. She didn't want that either, and figured she had probably done something wrong or at least done it in the wrong order; but she had no one credible enough to ask how to do it the right way. Instead, she started speaking to God in private, or at least that's what she called it. God didn't answer back, of course, but she hadn't actually expected Him to. "It's just like all of us," she explained to me. "Sometimes, we talk to ourselves about things as if we were speaking to someone else—to a totally real person every once in a while, you know? And by explaining something to them in your thoughts, you figure it out for yourself." This was exactly how Birgit spoke to God—i.e. to a perfect, all-knowing imaginary conversation partner, from whom she expected no feedback, but before whom any kind of deception was impossible. And these conversations were not held sitting quietly in cross-legged position, but instead during long walks in the woods, which she relished to an unimaginable degree.

By the time that Android arrived at Birchback, Birgit was more than ready for his message.

Over that period of time, she started getting along better and better with Carola, who taught her the basics of photography and composition. But they spoke of other things, too. Everyone else regarded Carola as a quiet, closed person, but Birgit knew how she could be during photo sessions: incredibly brisk and passionate, able to seize upon another person's thought on the fly, and, most importantly, not only having a very sharp eye, but also a very exact way of wording things. She simply felt distressed when she ended up being the center of attention in even the slightest public space. And her ideas of perfection and purity greatly coincided with Birgit's own. Birgit and Carola spoke quite a lot about politics as well, which didn't especially interest anyone at Birchback aside from them and maybe Anni. Or, to be more precise—not particularly about political affairs, but about the way the dominance of money and power has impacted the world. Birgit carried only abstract disdain for that world—she couldn't tolerate a system that had tried (with near success, incidentally) to raise her and others like her into brainless bimbos, but she didn't dedicate much more rigorous thought to the world's future. Carola, on the other hand, was certainly capable of digressing into those topics heatedly and at length if she was only given the chance.

"In short, it was a beautiful time," Birgit summarized.

She and Carola only fell on different sides in the conflict developing between Android and Anni. Carola uncompromisingly upported Anni, and not at all because she was a woman, but because she found the way Android treated all women as simply unacceptable. Like a vampire who, while certainly dependent upon them, tosses them aside once they're drained of blood. And it was absolutely right for Anni to come out against it—she, Carola, wouldn't have dared. Birgit, on the other hand, didn't agree with Anni's harsh judgement. "There is so much I have to be thankful for to him," she told me. Birgit and Android had even communicated a little after she left Birchback. In truth, Android might have been the last person she finally cut off contact with, apart from her grandmother.

"And you can think what you want, but in my opinion, it was just another 'who-will-trump-who' game to the very end for the both of them," she told me. "That Anni was no cleaner than Android, you know."

"What now?" Jaagup asked one morning, and by doing so actually expressed with very fine precision the question that had been forming in the heads of almost everyone at Birchback. It felt like things had run their course already. Summer had turned to fall, and fall to winter. Those who had other obligations waiting for them elsewhere had all gone, and only those who had nothing else to do with themselves were left. Everyone except Jaagup was living on the last cents they had, and it was somehow embarrassing to be living on Joel's dime, even though it seemed like he had nothing against it.

"Well, I suppose we should get packing," Carola said. "Are

you kidding?" Joel said in surprise. "You're all staying at least until Christmas."

"Honestly," Veronika added. "Joel and I will go crazy from boredom with just the two of us here."

"Well, it's not like that's all that hard to do as a group either," Jaagup said. "Guess we should, like, go and do something, then."

"True," Veronika said. She hadn't arranged any more lectures, and it wasn't as if the previous ones had been very successful, anyway. And there was no point in offering to play board games with them by that time either, even though she had bought a whole load of them the previous spring, most of which hadn't been opened to that day. They weren't the same people they'd been before.

By that time, they had gotten used to one another's shaved heads, and although there was seemingly no need for it anymore, they continued to buzz one another's sprouting stubble using Jaagup's trimmer.

"We could go skiing," Oleg reckoned. "Take a little ski trip?" However, he himself probably immediately realized how harebrained the idea was. On top of that, they had no skis and not all of them even knew how.

"What if we tried to put on a Christmas play?" Birgit roposed.

"For whom?" Jaagup asked, not finding it to be a very good plan.

"Well, why not for the village kids?" she answered. "Yeah, I'm *real* sure they'll come out here to watch it," Jaagup scoffed.

"No, that's definitely an option," Anni argued. "And do we necessarily need an audience, anyway?"

"What do you mean?" Jaagup asked. "We are talking theater here, right?"

"But we won't be *performing* ordinary theater," Anni said. "We'll act, yeah, but it'll be our own mysteries, meant for us alone."

"Right, right—I know what you mean. Like Grotowski!" Veronika chimed in. "I had that planned for next year, by the way."

"Wait, wait," Joel broke in. "Tell me, too—won't you, now?"

In Birgit's opinion, her original good idea was certainly starting to spiral out of control, but it appeared it was the only way to get everyone else on board, so it couldn't be helped. And when Veronika started telling them about different experiments aimed at bringing theater back to its ritualistic roots and using it as an active form that leads to spiritual freedom, Birgit herself finally started to feel like there really could be something to it. It would be a performance experienceable solely through participation; only by you personally occupying the same space and by your movements having a chance to alter it; and in doing so, you would begin to better understand yourself, your partners, and your world through your own movements. It was also clear that the performance truly couldn't have an audience, nor a long rehearsal process or a definite script. But sets and costumes and makeup—certainly. And, well, they would naturally have to agree on the sequence of events. They had no way of getting their hands on any of Grotowski's writings, but Jaagup remembered that he'd seen the selected works of Mati Unt on a shelf in one of the rooms, and late that afternoon they all took turns reading his short story "Via regia."

In the evening, they lit a fire in the fireplace and worked their way through discussing possible topics. The traditional tale of Jesus's birth and the Magi coming from the East was immediately ruled out, as were all the rest of the Christian stories. "Because," as Jaagup remarked, "Christmas is no Christian holiday—the birth of light is much more ancient and critical." Everyone agreed. After a long debate, they decided that "escape from darkness" would need to be the focal point of their performance. That's when someone suggested Orpheus.

"But why only Orpheus, then?" Jaagup pressed. "Let's go and take on all the old guys who've gone through hell and lived to tell the tale."

"There are more of them than there are us," Joel said
doubtfully.

But, no—Anni fully agreed with Jaagup on that occasion.
What was important was the very idea that someone can pass
through Hell and escape from it into the light, and that every
culture has someone who has done so, if not several of them.
Orpheus. Gilgamesh. Jesus. Odysseus. Dante. "Even Faust,"
he reckoned, "counts in some sense." And to top them all off,
Estonia's own Kalevipoeg as well.

And so, it was decided: the performance would emerge from
how that archetypal figure (who else than the doer of the Act)
overcomes death and reaches the light. Whether this journey
was one going backward or forward was left open for the time
being.

I'm very disappointed that Carola's photographs from the
project weren't preserved, even if they might have felt like pictures from a stranger's party to the outside observer. I would very
much have liked to see what they all looked like (and Anni most
of all, of course) in order to try to view them and understand
whether anything in their expressions might have betrayed—
even then—the path that stretched before them not long after
those moments transpired. I hope there wasn't.

The first thing they decided was that the hero to be
chosen (and no one, not even Carola, disputed that one of
the boys should have the role) would abstain from all of the
preparations—for since there would be no rehearsals and only
one performance, the actor's surprise would have to be genuine.
Secondly, since there was likewise no audience slated for the
event, Carola's camera would need to take on the role. Her own
job was to be the hero's personal assistant and PR figure. As
with Dante, the hero would have a personal guide in Hell—

someone who in their project had to figure in somewhere between Virgil and Lucifer. After some protest, Jaagup agreed to it. Everyone else—Birgit, Joel, Veronika, and Anni—would take turns playing all the rest of the parts.

At first, Oleg was very satisfied that he'd been made the hero, because it meant there was no written script for him (and he wasn't especially good at acting, anyway). Still, the situation soon made him rather glum, since he was essentially disconnected from communal life. After breakfast, the others would rush straight off to the auditorium (which was heated to a tolerable temperature with electric radiators) to continue working, whereas he was forced to fill his time as well as he could manage. The snowy woods were beautiful, of course, but the weather outside was nevertheless too cold for long walks, there was too little light for painting, and he'd never been all that attracted to books or even music. On top of that, Jaagup's iPod—which had the largest music selection in the entire house—was with its owner in the auditorium, because they used it to look for tracks to play during each specific scene. When he complained to the others about his boredom over dinner once, Carola promptly voiced the opinion that he could relieve it by taking over everyone's household chores. Oleg stopped grumbling and from then on did indeed wash the dishes every day, although he reckoned that no one, not even himself, would likely want to eat the meals he was capable of preparing for lunch.

The days passed much more interestingly for the rest of the community. Jaagup quickly overcame his initial doubt and became wholly engrossed in the project, which was a great benefit for all because he knew more about Hell-going legends than anyone else. It was a bit of a hindrance, too, of course, because he kept coming up with new stories that he believed should absolutely be inserted into the performance.

Birgit thought differently.

"Hell is no museum," she explained. "No matter who of us ends up there, we won't be meeting any . . . I dunno . . . musty spirits from the back rooms of history, but rather the same ones who sour our lives right here on Earth."

"Exactly," Carola also agreed. "When an anarchist ends up in Hell, he'll be surrounded by bankers and lawyers." She giggled. "And vice-versa."

This viewpoint ended up winning out, although Jaagup was still able to wangle a few of his favorite characters into the script—especially since the role of presenting all of those stories in the play was already his. The rest had to remain mute, or almost mute. It made no difference, all in all, because it wouldn't show in the pictures anyway.

When the plot was more or less sketched out, the participants started thinking about set design. The original idea to perform the entire play in the auditorium was axed almost immediately. Poor Oleg was now exiled from the main house as well, because the others started refashioning it into the underworld. Everyone also had to move into bedrooms in the auxiliary building— with the exception of Joel and Veronika, whose master bedroom was nevertheless left out of Hell. Oleg, who now had to sleep in the same room as Jaagup, made an intense effort every night to squeeze out any information on what they had in store for him, but Jaagup resisted stoically.

The group spent one entire day poking around Birchback's attics and sheds, trying to find all kinds of old odds and ends that could be used in the performance. And they found quite a few. In addition to pieces of farming legacy (a spinning wheel, looms, fishing nets, a couple of backup oars, as well as—scattered amongst them as markers of "newer culture"— an old-fashioned phonograph with its large horn and a fully functional Singer sewing machine), a lot of other things had accumulated in the trove, such as junk that there hadn't been room for in Joel's parents' city apartment: a large, somewhat faded globe and a Tallinn souvenir lamp, along with things Joel and Veronika had bought from antique shops purely for the sake of having them. Carola was ecstatic about a few old cameras they found. Oleg, whom it would have been impossible to keep away from that phase of the undertaking, even found a lighthouse lantern and foghorn packed away in a large crate—items that seemed entirely out of place so far inland. Anni came across a large tattered tote bag containing an unwieldy Jewish menorah wrapped up in thirtyyear- old newspaper. And Jaagup discovered a whole range of oldfashioned suitcases (only much smaller than normal size) from perhaps the 1950s lined up on a high shelf. He opened one and found it was full of notebooks with the name of an unfamiliar former schoolchild penciled on them.

They initially lugged all of the junk that could be of some use in the performance into the auditorium, and then started to put back one by one the things for which they were unable to think up a function. These ended up numbering many, and unfortunately, several of their most bizarre finds were left without a part to play, such as a large flour weight on wheels and a roly-poly toy that was missing its eyes but would still briskly and musically charge back up to a vertical position—simply, no one was able to think up a way to fit them into the myth.

Next came the costumes. Standing in Veronika's bedroom was a gigantic wardrobe filled with a sundry of clothes, some of which had almost never been worn. Over the previous years, those passing through Birchback had assembled a small communal collection of clothing that helped them get by in various types of weather, and for Veronika, this had also been a convenient excuse for occasionally buying the kinds of garments that she simply couldn't pass up otherwise at regular and secondhand shops' "everything-must-go" sales, even though the sizes were either too large or small for her. The collection was diverse. True—each particular item's suitability for the project was greatly determined by how quickly it could be put on and taken off, because the scene changes couldn't be too long. But given the selection, this didn't pose any great problem.

These activities were great fun to almost all—only Anni didn't appear to be very interested in the whole project. She did earnestly participate in all of the preparations, volunteering for several parts in the play and making constructive remarks every once in a while; but even so, one got the impression that she was only acting halfheartedly.

"It was always like that with her," Birgit remarked bitterly. "She was only interested in doing the things she herself had come up with, or which she was at least leading. She was able to play along in a team setting, but she didn't put her soul into it."

I'd lost count of the number of cups of coffee we'd already drained, and Birgit's grandmother had come in a couple of times to ask if we shouldn't, perhaps, have ourselves something more substantial to eat. It was nice of her to inquire, of course, but nothing would have gone down for me that night, and Birgit herself only picked at some lettuce and slices of bell pepper, as was apparently customary.

Birgit seemed slightly embarrassed when she spoke about the actual performance—it had apparently been somewhat of a disappointment for her, all the same. The things she told me didn't impart much of a Grotowski-like impression; but let's not kid ourselves—*none* of them was a Grotowski. Birgit busied herself with all of the actors' body painting starting in the wee hours of morning, and ultimately did her own as well as she could manage in front of the mirror. Oleg was brought his breakfast in bed so that he wouldn't see the others' new faces too early. They had all been dining in the main room of the auxiliary building, boiling eggs on a small electric stove because the main house had been decorated from top to bottom. And after breakfast, the event commenced with the ceremonial opening of the front door to Oleg, who was ushered in by Carola's constant camera flashes and Jaagup majestically declaring his welcome. Oleg was firstly offered the opportunity to take a Dead Sea cruise on a fantastic luxury yacht operated by Charon Travel, where the pipepuffing Joel tried to talk him into buying an oar. After that, he had to play dice with Anni and acquaint himself with Sisyphus/ Veronika, who was rolling a giant beach ball up and down the stairs. Oleg's first proper shock came when Jaagup gave him the chance to rescue from certain peril his soul and those of his friends, which had taken the form of little paper sailboats placed in a washbowl. All the ships had a picture of the corresponding person drawn on them along with their name, because everyone's sketches were identical. But when Oleg reached out to pick one up, the water in the washbowl burst into flame, since a thin layer of gasoline had been poured over the surface. Jaagup had cast a flaming match into the bowl and the poor spirit-ships all caught flame, so Oleg only had time to snatch his own out of the blaze: a choice for which the others later poked fun at him, even though it was hardly probable that anyone would have rushed straight to saving their friends first either. There were several other numbers, but Birgit couldn't remember what they all were anymore. At least not up to the point of Oleg's meeting with Fate, which took place on the second floor.

Oleg entered the master bedroom upstairs with Jaagup by his side, and saw three girls dressed in sackcloth. Birgit was seated behind the spinning wheel, Veronika was measuring out yarn, and Anni was holding scissors. The room was cold, which was no wonder, because the window behind Anni was ajar.

"This here is Clotho," Jaagup announced, pointing to Birgit. "She's spinning the yarn of life." Birgit nodded. "And this is Lachesis, who measures the lengths of our lives." Veronika nodded. "But she who cuts them with the scissors of death," he said, gesturing towards Anni, "she is Atropos."

"Also known as Eurydice," Birgit added.

"And Beatrice," Veronika added, just as she and Anni had agreed upon.

Anni didn't speak, only spreading her arms wide for Oleg to embrace her. And then she pressed her lips against his.

Oleg yelped and leapt away from her as if he'd been bitten by a snake. Carola promptly snapped a picture of them both and their faces, as well as the expressions of the other two Fates and also Jaagup, who was gaping vacuously at the scene before him. Anni, however, burst into hysterical laughter—the kind of laugh from beyond the grave that crazy people erupt into in movies.

"What just happened?" Jaagup asked, out of character.

Oleg strived to muster up a smile and laugh as well.

"What a girl, huh?" he spoke awkwardly. Without either of the other Fates noticing, Anni had reached through the open window, broken an icicle off of the eaves, and stuck it into her mouth, so when she leant in to kiss Oleg, her lips didn't emit the warmth he had expected, but rather a biting iciness.

"He who approaches his fate with open mouth must know what he's risking," Anni shrugged.

They spent the afternoon cleaning up the house, which was done in a generally cheerful atmosphere. Everyone made a point of asserting to each other how well the project had gone, while simultaneously trying to convince themselves of the same. Only Carola wasn't very satisfied when she started checking the pictures on her camera's miniature viewing screen. There was nothing there that came anywhere close to the girls' previous project. Alas, no one but Birgit shared her disappointment.

And the more days that passed, the more they talked about Christmas. Jaagup cautiously re-raised the topic that they should all maybe get going, even though he himself claimed no one was really expecting him anywhere: he naturally wouldn't be turned away from his father's new home, but the man's young wife and Jaagup's two-year-old half-sister would certainly have preferred to celebrate the holidays in their own family circle. Jaagup's mother had moved in with her spinster younger sister after the divorce. Although Jaagup's presence would also undoubtedly gladden her, it would, on the other hand, have meant for him the obligation of cooking up a full-scale Christmas lunch, just as they had done back in in his childhood—something he certainly wouldn't plan to do otherwise.

"But, well, vegetarian Christmases don't, like, really rock, either," he ultimately said, putting the main issue into words.

"Oh, come now," Veronika countered, perking up. "I've got a recipe for bean-based sausages, and you can have cranberry jelly and gingerbread and oven-baked potatoes and all that stuff as much as your heart desires."

"Yeah, well, everything has its limits—doesn't it," Joel said, butting into the conversation. "Vegetarian food is great and all in summer; I get that. But we do live in the north. At Christmas, you've got normal sausages and pork and whoever wants to have it, will; and whoever doesn't, won't."

"When you all try my recipe, you won't *want* any kind of pork," Veronika huffed in offense. "But I guess you'll go ahead and eat whatever you please."

"A woman of her word," Carola backed her up. Birgit listened to the exchange in disbelief. Had everyone started forgetting why they were there in the first place? Joel and Veronika's reason was clear enough. She believed she knew why Carola was there, too; and why shouldn't everyone else think the same way? Now, however, it turned out for instance that Jaagup was at Birchback because he didn't really have anywhere else to go, although he was ready to try his luck elsewhere if the food served no longer satisfied him. But what about Oleg? And Anni?

She was just passing by Anni's room. The door was open a crack, so she peeked in.

"Hey, I'd like to ask you something."

Anni looked up from the thick French-language book in

tiny script that she was partway through reading.

"Go ahead," she nodded.

"Don't you feel like, well . . ." Birgit began cautiously, "that . . . like, our life here has somehow come to a standstill?"

Anni cocked her head.

"You mean since Android left?"

Birgit herself hadn't formed the thought in so many words, but when she considered it now, then ... Yes, that was it.

"Not exactly," she said. "But you can't deny he gave us momentum. I mean if we're not just here on vacation, you know. We're here for some kind of a purpose."

"When a traveler stops," Anni replied, "then it's only to let his horses drink. I guess my horses haven't had their fill yet."

"Oh, go to hell," Birgit snapped in exasperation. "You got what I was trying to say." And with that, she left Anni's room.

They didn't seek each other's company much after that.

Oleg came up with the next idea. Days of silence. "Just like the Trappist monks," he explained, "so could we go without saying anything at all for a while." The thought had come to him once when, after lunch, he tried to remember what exactly they'd talked about during the meal and who had said what, and he couldn't. "If we'd said anything important," he reckoned, "then I'm sure it'd have stuck in our minds." Carola and Joel thought it wasn't a bad idea. Jaagup and Veronika weren't very enthused, but agreed to try, being in the minority. Anni was off walking in the woods just then, but when she was informed of the decision the group had made after she got back, she accepted it with unremitting calm. Birgit also welcomed the idea—she needed a little bit of time to let her inner confusion settle, and such things go much more smoothly in silence. There weren't very many matters to be settled beforehand. Everyone was already clear on the cooking and cleaning schedule. The decision was made to place a thick packet of paper and a pen on the kitchen table, so if anyone had something to tell the others, he or she could write it down. Meaningless sounds would be permitted, such as crying out in pain, and everyone would be called to eat by banging a ladle against a large pan, which reverberated like a gong.

"I wonder how long we'll be silent for, then?" Veronika asked.

"Until it's time," Anni stated, and made no further comment. Oleg nodded, while Jaagup just shrugged.

That evening, they made a fire in the fireplace and chatted for the last time. The old clock on the wall had been wound and set to the correct time, and the consensus was that when it struck midnight, everyone would fall silent, even if they were in the middle of a word.

"It's the strangest thing," Birgit mused, "how little of the chatter that we're constantly accompanied by actually changes our world. For instance, when a long moment of silence occurs in a group, it's usually downright torture. Everyone feels like it's indescribably long, but if you actually measure it, maybe fifteen or twenty seconds at the most have passed without voices. After that, there's always somebody who can't take it any longer and says something, even if it's pointless." Before they'd even made it to the afternoon of their first day of silence, almost every one of them had been forced to raise a finger to their lips to stop one of their companions from speaking, only to accidentally end up in the same situation a moment later. And it was just as strange how words truly weren't necessary for resolving the problems that make most people talk—a point, nod, or shrug was enough to make anything clear. Birgit didn't know what the others were feeling, but by that evening she was overcome by an inexplicable euphoria—a sense of happiness, the likes of which she hadn't felt in ages, as if the state was ordinarily flushed out together with all the words of no consequence. But that feeling hadn't come from the silence—far from it. That trick wouldn't have worked in solitude. It arose namely from knowing that she was silent *together* with others, and that everything they needed to understand was understandable without words— or, well, that if they didn't in the end, perhaps it wasn't worth understanding anyway. And naturally, she started up her talks with God again immediately. In truth, however, it wasn't actually a conscious decision, telling herself: well, then—now I'm going to start speaking to God once more, even though we're not out in the woods right now. That habit of speaking to Him swelled from within, almost by its own doing, and didn't cease this time. There was enough silence all around Birgit for her soul to raise its head and fill the girl to the brim with immense inner strength, and everything that had revolved around the confusion within her before, tugging her in different directions all at once, now somehow converged into a single point without her even noticing, causing her to realize: that—*that* was who she was.

This was the way in which she moved through the space she should have already known like the back of her hand over her long duration at Birchback. Things surfaced in the silence. Before, she'd always passed by the big stove in the kitchen, the windowsill in the hallway, the snow shovel leaning next to the front door with either someone's just-uttered words echoing in her head or occupied with forming her own response to something someone might ask; never in that silence. *Those Trappist monks really knew what they were doing,* she thought. *Silence isn't a punishment or a test—it's a privilege. And it's also the reason why we have to be followed by that incessant racket in a supermarket or a department store, for instance—noise, which doesn't let us remember what we came there to get. Nor who we are in reality, which, from the store's standpoint, really might be one and the same.* When it was Birgit's turn to wash the dishes, she rested a long, silent stare upon each plate and mug that was cleansed by her hands, as if the object had just come into the world at that very moment. And every night before she went to sleep, she stared at the ceiling for a long time before turning off the light.

At least a week passed in that manner, although she wasn't counting the days.

The knowledge that she had to leave Birchback alighted upon her suddenly and surprisingly, but as soon as she realized the fact, it seemed so simple and natural. She'd received her present. To stick around after it had been given would constitute a lack of respect. But she, Birgit, was grateful, and should thus show her gratitude by departing the place that had given her so much.

So, you could say that God really did answer her—with silence, which she now knew how to hear.

She decided to go and stay with her grandmother for Christmas. The old woman was certainly accustomed to solitude and probably even wanted it, but Birgit could be silent in her company, too. Gladly. And who knew what would happen next.

When she packed her bag and went downstairs, the others realized what she was thinking and gathered at the front door. She waved to them.

"Bye," Anni said.

"Bye," Birgit answered. Both their voices were a little raspy from disuse.

"Does that mean we're allowed to talk again?" Veronika asked, then turned to Birgit and said, "Bye."

"Yes," Anni replied. "For her, it's departure. For us, though, it's a sign."

8

I CALLED ON Inspector Männik twice. The first time I was on my way there, knowing only that the individual I was seeking was named E. Männik, I imagined a gloomy, balding man who was my age or even a little older—someone beneath whose rather dull appearance hid a sharp analytical intelligence, peppered only a little by his chilly sense of humor. What might his name be? Egon? Ervin? Evald? Hardly an Eduard, "Eddy" to friends. To my great surprise, E. Männik instead turned out to be a chipper woman named Epp, about ten years my junior—she had a warm face and teasing curls, and listened to my story with the kind of tactfulness and compassion that I'd never before encountered in any government institution. Naturally, she provided me with as much assistance as she possibly could, and we agreed to meet again once I'd concluded my own investigation.

I eagerly awaited our second meeting. I believed that my work was complete, and I was looking forward to sharing the results with her. For by then, I already knew a thing or two about the case, maybe even more than I'd initially hoped to find out. Of course, I still didn't understand what had happened in the end, how the situation at Birchback had spun out of control the way it did. Even so, I reckoned I now knew more about the case than the police did. I even wondered whether it might be appropriate to invite Inspector Männik out for a coffee, but figured that I'd make myself look like a fool if I did. A nice woman like her undoubtedly gets those invitations every day from men much bolder than me.

She received me in her office and promptly told me she had time—her next meeting wasn't for another hour. The greater part of it passed with her listening to my story. Still, I kept a lot of things to myself. I didn't want any of the people I'd met on that journey to ever encounter any problems because they'd confided in me; and although I wasn't afraid of Inspector Männik making it her duty to reprimand them out of an uncompromising or excessively law-abiding nature, it was better to be safe than sorry—because, you see, I didn't yet know whether the person I imagined to be within her actually even existed.

Männik listened, only interrupting to ask a few practical questions. Delicately and without prying too deeply.

"You know," she said after I'd finished. "I've actually got one more address for you."

"Is that so?" I asked in surprise.

"Do you remember the fifth suitcase? There was actually one more girl at Birchback when the unfortunate incident took place. One who got away with her life. I didn't mention her the last time because she was in a very bad state after the tragedy and refused contact with absolutely anyone at all—she even managed to legally change her first name so that no one would be able to find her. But when you showed up last time and told me why you needed to know; well, in short—I contacted her and asked if she might agree to meet you. She was a little unsure of it at first, but in the end, she gave her consent. I know she would never give me the full details. But on the other hand, I feel like she herself actually needs to talk to someone, too. And I believe, by the way, that she realizes it as well."

She handed me a folded piece of paper, on which was written a telephone number and a name that meant nothing to me.

"You know her as Carola," Inspector Männik said.

In her previous life, Carola (if I may, I'll continue calling her that here) had been a photographer, working for newspapers as well as being hired to take pictures at formal events. She'd picked up her old job again in the small town where she now lived. She ran a tiny photo store and darkroom where people could have passport pictures taken, bring their own pictures for quality printing, or hire her for photographing weddings or funerals. She told me to come by in the evening, once the store was closed. Her family was accustomed to her occasionally staying late at work when she needed to finish a large order.

I arrived a little early, so I took a stroll around town. I found a cemetery behind the church and passed most of the time there. For as long as I can remember, I've had the habit of walking to a graveyard whenever I'm in an unfamiliar place, and while one might guess that inclination would disappear after Anni's death, it was actually the opposite. And while one might guess that I'd give it up after the diagnosis, that would be wrong, too. Even so, I now walk cemeteries with a different knowledge. I presume that people who don't visit cemeteries to see their relatives' graves or to pay respects to a favorite celebrity at least partially do so not to be reminded of their own mortality. But while for most of those people (at least in my generation), it remains at first an abstract problem that can be delayed—something you can make your own assumptions about—I personally observe tombstones in about the same way as someone getting ready to go on a trip checks out hotels at their destination or flight timetables online. Or like someone comparing different restaurant menus to organize a company banquet. I read the unfamiliar names carved into gravestones that pockmark cemeteries in small towns and know that nothing connects me to them. For now, that is—but before long, I'll also possess the same kind of clarity regarding questions of the afterlife as do all who have gotten there before me. And I can't say those places depress me, because there, I feel not so much the closeness of death as I do longing. That which belongs to the abandoned, and which I myself have felt for years: a burning, consuming longing that really isn't grieving in the exact sense of the word, because grieving already includes the inevitability of departure, whereas longing denies it, is unable to recognize or make space for it. Longing is incapable of accepting the empty space, which the world's onward grind should refill as time passes. Rather, it screams out against any kind of touch—wordless, thoughtless, pointless, simply in unadulterated pain. Longing lies near in graveyards, but it is covered by a rug of silence. The scream isn't gone, but it has flowed out from the heart—beneath the green pines, between the sandy paths.

If I got anything out of those walks, it was self-confidence. After returning from a cemetery, I would no longer be bothered by passersby's greedy, stupid faces. The whole human race would be divided into two groups for a while: those who were still here, and those who were already there; and to tell the truth, I hadn't much in common with either of them.

When I finally located the right place again and knocked on the door of the darkened shop, it took some time before Carola came to open it, peering back and forth nervously. I'd apparently made more noise than necessary.

"Please, come in," she welcomed me. Light seeped into the space from the rear of the shop, where there was a windowless room that contained a large, softly humming photo printer and a computer desk piled high with CDs. Two large mugs of tea were already waiting on another table.

"I hope you do drink tea," she said, gesturing for me to take a seat. Then she sat there taking me in for a while.

"Epp told me a little about you. That you're Anni's father. And I understand you've got a special reason for finding out what actually happened back there."

"Yes," I said. "I'm ill. I might have just a few months left."

She nodded.

"I thought it might be something like that. Fine, then."

We sipped our tea.

"I haven't spoken to anyone about it since Birchback," she said. "Afterward, everybody tried to locate me—everyone who had ever been there and especially, of course, those who had been there just recently. But I couldn't. I thought I'd never be able to."

"I know," I said.

"I have a life again, now," she said. "A husband and a kid, too."

"I know," I said.

She was silent for a few moments.

"You know, I've always felt weird when a criminal is caught in some film and there's a look of relief on his face," she said. "Because there's nowhere for him to run anymore, you know? This whole time, I'd believed they were making that stuff up. But there's some truth to it." She shivered. "And I guess I can understand what they're feeling, you know? I don't even want to think about it."

Was I capable of feeling happy for her? Of course, I'd have wanted it to be my own daughter sitting on that chair, or on any chair at all, anywhere, telling her father what I didn't already know. Or at least that's what I thought then, and the thought embarrassed me. It's even more embarrassing now.

"But, anyway," she continued, "in order to resolve our problems, we need to see them from the outside—when they've grown *through* you; when they *compose* you, every attempt to be rid of them is like laying a hand against yourself. So, it's not like this is easy for me."

She started to tell her story. I asked whether I could switch on a small recorder that I placed on the table in front of her, a recorder I'd bought at the beginning of the journey and always used whenever permitted. So any type of pain that might hit me wouldn't detract from my ability to understand the speaker.

I promised her that no one apart from me would hear the tape, and that when I was sure her words had sunk in for me completely, I would erase the recording. She hesitated for a moment, but then gave her consent. Now that she'd come this far, there was no point in stopping—right?

I allowed her to tell her story at her own pace, and didn't attempt to interrupt or lead her with questions in any way. At first, she spoke for a while about what I already knew and what I've written about here already. This all helped her to achieve a certain momentum, with which she finally arrived at the days and months that were the reason why I was there.

"No one said it out loud," Carola spoke, "but we all knew it. We policed one another. Mobile phones, for instance. Earlier in the summer, no one cared who went up to Dickens Hill to make a call or how often they did it, and 'officially,' so to say, no one cared back then, either. But for some reason, we all ended up setting our phones on the entryway table, so that everyone could see right away when someone went to make a call. And we did make calls, at first. No one said anything about it. But I can clearly remember the moment when I thought about calling my brother to see how he was doing one time. Just to chat, without any ulterior motive. So, I went and picked up my cell phone from the entryway table. And I put it back down. It was the same for the others. And there, their batteries softly died one after another, and no one went to re-charge them.

"But it was like that with all kinds of other things, too. Except for when we were sleeping in our own rooms at night (at first, that is), we always tried to make sure that someone else could see us. I don't know why. Not that being by yourself seemed wrong or somehow suspicious to anyone. On top of that, Joel would sit in his studio working on something for a couple of hours each day, too. All the rest of us had creative development scheduled for that time, and that *is* something that's best done in solitude, isn't it? But all of our projects were either finished or left incomplete. One time, I'd just sat down in the living room with a book when Oleg came in carrying his painting box. I got up, thinking that the light in there was just right for him or something. 'No,' he spoke calmly, and said that me being in the living room was the very reason he'd come there to paint. And I understood him; I understood him well.

"At the same time, we didn't just chat about anything even when we were in each other's company. But it wasn't like how things had been during those days of silence, either. I guess we'd lost the habit of saying something just to talk. Well, I guess every once in a while we'd still chat at dinner like we used to before. At first, we'd kind of make fun of those who had left Birchback. Anni would always laugh the loudest. But then, she could suddenly turn so silent—so abruptly that everyone got embarrassed. We'd gotten into the habit of holding each other's hands before eating. Just for a second, and a squeeze. We formed a circle around the table with it. I don't even know why. It might have been like a mealtime prayer for some of us. Like—we were here, and we were together, and we trusted and supported each other. It was a good feeling, to tell the truth.

"One time, Veronika proposed that all of us go and do a sun salutation the following morning. Summer was already long gone, of course, and sunrises were late. Anni reckoned it was a good idea. I could tell that made Veronika extremely happy, because she was probably afraid that she'd hurt Anni's feelings somehow. Or, that wasn't it. More like that Anni didn't respect her. Actually, the way I see it, it was nothing like that. All of us had already long abandoned those kinds of emotions by then. Maybe with the exception of Veronika herself. There was even no need for a wake-up call in the morning—everyone came downstairs at the right time all on their own. And up on Dickens Hill, we followed along in a yoga exercise that

Veronika showed us. It's called a sun salutation. Oh, it's still burned into my musclememory today! But when she tried to recite a poem afterward, Anni told her to be quiet. There's only one poem, she said, that she knew was fit for that moment. St. Francis's 'Canticle of the Sun.' Jaagup remembered he had a book with the poem in it by total chance—one he'd gotten from a historian who had come and given us a talk. We didn't have a proper translation, but it really did sound grander in Italian. There was a whole explanation of its meaning in the book, too. Soon, we all had it memorized. We'd walk up to Dickens Hill every morning in silence, not even greeting each other first, and when the sun lipped up above the horizon, we'd do the exercise and recite it softly, murmuring, in unison: *laudato sí, mi Signoré* . . . I can remember how it goes, even now: *laudato sí, mi Signoré, per sora nostra morte corporale.* Praise be to you, my Lord, through our sister Bodily Death. Maybe they're right: if you repeat something for too long, it'll come true in the end.

"We all had a sauna together then, and all at the same time, every night. We usually didn't heat the woodstove—we turned on the electric one, since it would have taken too much time to heat otherwise. And too much wood, of course. We did have a whole ton of firewood, though. Joel and Veronika mostly went in private at first, but not after a while. Well, and who was really staring in there, anyway? Nothing separated us from anyone else there anymore. Joel and Veronika still slept together in their own room at that point, and, well—all the rest of us were alone; like, in every sense. It was only later that we all moved together into the master bedroom upstairs, and were all alone together there. But even so, any contracts that had been sealed with the world as its witness—marriage, purchase-sales agreements— they'd all lost their point. For instance, we were all total equals in ownership at Birchback. It didn't even cross my mind to ask for Veronika's permission before I went to cut up her bedsheet to make swaddling for the clay dolls. And, well, that's how it was with everything else, too. Altogether, we were one, not six.

"One night, when Anni came into the sauna, we all sensed there was something very different about her. And there was. She'd shaved herself totally smooth everywhere. Her eyebrows, her armpits (naturally), and between her legs, too. She was like a little girl—in the body of an adult woman, of course. But she didn't say anything about it and we didn't ask, either. The next day, everyone was still the same as they'd been before, but the day after that, Veronika also came to sauna shaved from head to toe. And then I looked at myself in there and felt so *disgusted* by myself. I'd just finished fully shaving myself the next day when Oleg came into my room. He asked if I had the cream you use to shave hair off your legs. I did. Oleg's chest was incredibly hairy— it was just one thick black bushy clump—but that night in the sauna, he was just as naked as we were. Jaagup, likewise, although he'd managed it with his beard trimmer. 'Damn perverts,' is what Joel said when he saw us. The next evening, though, all his own hair was shaved. We really didn't look human anymore—we were like some kind of aliens: halfway from here, halfway from there.

"Maybe I'm giving the impression that we walked around totally full of ourselves the whole time. Far from it. In some sense, life at Birchback carried on just about the same way it'd been before. We cooked and washed the dishes in pairs. In the evenings, we lit a fire in the fireplace and talked and talked for hours. Maybe our conversations were a little different from before. At first, Joel still went to the store once a week, too, and sometimes Anni went with him. Veronika would sit in the corner on those occasions, her nose all scrunched up, as if she thought Anni wanted to win over her husband. She should have realized how absurd that sounded. And maybe she did—sometimes, she would walk around and busy herself, making sure that everyone saw how truly on top of things she was. But later, they decided going to the store was too difficult.

It tore them away from Birchback too much. Veronika would've gone totally berserk, I think, which was why she wasn't taken along. And people in the village stared at them like they were some kind of freaks, too. Then, on one trip, they brought back a 100-kilogram sack of rice and another of flour, and two suitcases filled with preserves and enormous quantities of sugar and tea and salt and buckwheat and a crate of matches, and a good ten or so loaves of cheese and all kinds of other supplies; and that previous fall, we'd filled the cellars with jam and salted mushrooms, and Joel had bought twenty kilograms of honey from a guy in the village, and on and on. And our medicine box was stocked with forty big jars of vitamin C. 'From here on, we're on our own,' Anni said. 'We have everything we need, and if there's anything missing, we'll find it inside ourselves.'

"In reality, we had a really poor diet—or, well, a monotonous one. We baked white bread or a kind of barley bread, and lunch was always rice with canned vegetables. I remember—it might have been sometime in January or in February. Not all that long after Christmas, in any case, but already when we weren't going out anymore—I got really dizzy one time. My ears were hissing and buzzing and the light suddenly seemed totally strange. Before I knew it, I could feel just how weak I was and I sat down for a while, then went and got two vitamin-Cs and made a pot of herbal tea and drank a big mug of it with honey. Maybe I also exhausted myself more because I was dancing a lot. I was absolutely sure then that it was my way of talking to God. I wasn't like Birgit, who could handle it at any moment—I needed a jolt. And I was able to be alone then, too. I didn't care whether or not the others watched. When I was dancing, they simply disappeared. But it completely wore me out, of course. And then I was sitting there with that mug of tea in front of me and thinking that I was definitely very weak, but in an entirely different sense. Who knows what I missed seeing or experiencing—aren't I aware that saints and ascetics have starved themselves in that same way over the ages so that their spirit can become stronger than the flesh and extend to see things that are otherwise hidden? But it didn't happen to me again. Of course, it was like we were all in a light fog all the time, anyway, even though we didn't drink any wine and we didn't even have beer by the fireplace after sauna anymore; only pu-erh tea. But it was something else, all the same. 'Why is it,' I asked once, not towards anyone in particular, 'that I call out to God from the depths of my soul, but He doesn't answer?' Jaagup reckoned that the same question troubled Jesus on the cross. And Anni said, 'God only speaks to those who are capable of speaking to Him themselves; and I guess that means we *aren't* capable yet.'

"'Or we can't hear His reply,' Oleg added. To me, it felt like they were all right, and that they all understood it better than I did.

"We hardly slept at night. First of all was that routine sitting in front of the fireplace. We had a sort of system where every day, one person spoke at the beginning, and then the others asked questions. It was just about the same as we'd done at the start—back when Veronika wanted to pressure us into telling embarrassing stories. But in a different way. When you talked, you could talk like you were talking to yourself and to the others all at once. It felt fantastic, I'll say honestly. And you could speak about anything. About your earlier life, if you wanted, although no one especially wanted to. It was always more about what you'd felt and experienced over the last few days, and what you saw now that you hadn't before. And then there was one day where everyone spoke over one another. There were six of us, right, and we kept count of the weeks that way; still, it got all mixed up later and in reality several weeks had passed. We didn't keep a tally on the doorpost or anything, you know.

"But those evenings stretched out awfully long. It was like a rule we had—the first to stand up would be the one who'd spoken that evening, and the others wouldn't go to bed before it happened. Because otherwise, it'd be like they weren't respecting him or her, right? And then, what happened was—partly as a game, and partly a competition—we developed a sort of habit where whoever was talking tried to keep on going for as long as possible, if only they could manage. It was nasty, actually. And especially hard at night. You know that the others want to go to bed and you do, too; but you simply don't. Well, you did in the end, of course. But sometimes, there'd just be a short while left until dawn and needing to go up to Dickens Hill again to sing the sun-song. On top of that, we touched each other while we all lay there sometimes. I mean everywhere—you know? But it wasn't anything like what you might be thinking—or, well, I don't know, I guess. For me, what happened was I felt something communal passing through my body and the body of the person I was touching; the one that was touching me. As if we had the same blood circulation. Or something even more powerful than that. And afterward, I'd have insomnia again, of course. There wasn't a single moment during the daytime when you could catch a wink, either; there was always someone there to see you and even though they wouldn't say anything, you simply felt embarrassed. Sometimes, a quieter fifteen minutes or so would pass like you were half-asleep. I guess that made the world shimmer before your eyes after a while, too.

"And that was how we all spurred each other onward. Would I have been able to leave that place if I'd wanted to? Naturally. Whenever I wanted, I mean. Birgit had gone for whatever reason. We didn't talk about her anymore, but not because we blamed her for anything. That's the way she was, and that's the way we were. And *that* was the last thread that tied me to Birchback. No one was forcing me. Everything I did, I did myself. I knew that I was there voluntarily; I was there to try to do something; to try to *prove* something, if only to myself—and I knew that it was all my own personal free will. And naturally, if I'd realized I was unable to continue, then I could always give it up and no one would criticize me for it. And that was exactly why leaving was entirely impossible. I firmly believe that the others felt and thought something very similar. Yes, we were policing each other, but not as prison guards—rather, we were helpful companions; or, I guess, something like alpinists who are afraid that their friend tied to the same rope might fall and pull all the others down with them. And each and every one of us convinced ourselves at every hour and at every minute for both our own sake and that of the others that, no—*I won't fall.* And at the same time, we so much as felt ourselves progressing. Progressing in the way that we were. It made you feel incredibly proud to take a step in the right direction and have the others approve of you. And, naturally, it helped to dispel the doubts within—wondering whether there was really any point to it all. Did I have doubts back then? I guess not. At least not in the usual sense of the word, you know? I had conscious, rational doubt. It was more like from time to time, I felt like I was a moth fluttering towards the light—without my own will, without the force of a higher power. And within me totally existed that person who realized *she* wasn't the one wanting to go in that direction. But if anything, that understanding was what forced me to just keep on soaring faster and faster. Because in that case, it was even better if you were being led by a force higher than yourself. It meant that, consequently, it did actually exist. And you might not even feel fear, but simply follow it. Wherever it might lead. And if that was a new direction, then— great. You were a step ahead of the rest, then, and they wanted to follow you! So, I guess it really was like a competition, too. Or a game. Everyone wanted to be the first to take a new step.

"In retrospect, I can't remember anymore who came up with the clay-doll idea first. I think it was one of the boys. Joel's studio was stocked with materials for all kinds of projects, and a ton of clay, too. He liked to shape little clay figurines from time to time—kind of like those madonnas from ancient times, faceless and with big breasts. He had a whole shelf full of them, and although Joel himself generally didn't take them seriously, Veronika tended to give them to people as gifts— trinkets, sure, but still the work of a well-known artist. And so, he'd accumulated a lot of clay. Then, one day, we decided that each of us would make a clay doll of ourselves so if anything happened to us, they'd be there in our place. Whatever that might have meant. The project's idea was as bright as daylight to me back then. Joel taught us how to make them; he came around to each of us and showed us how it went. The shaping process seemed to go smoothly and simply under his hands, but when I tried it, nothing turned out. 'Maybe Joel could do all of ours, what do you think?' Jaagup proposed. He was even worse at it than I was, but Veronika objected, saying it was work that each person had no choice but to do him- or herself, and Anni only nodded along.

"We plugged away at our sculptures for a whole morning and an afternoon. Joel finished his own first and then went around helping everyone else, so the other figures still had his handstrokes, actually. Still, none of us were satisfied by that evening. So we wrapped our clay dolls in damp cloths to continue working on them the next morning, and the day after that, they all turned out to be more or less something we could be contented with. Oleg explained that it wasn't important for the doll to look like you. What was important was that it resembled you in terms of *mood*. And his own figure illustrated that wonderfully. I'd always liked Oleg's paintings—they were sort of surreal, but on the other hand a little like Russian icons, and there was always a kind of melancholy humor to them. Although Oleg himself didn't look the part at all—he was a little crude and awkward and kept his hair buzzed; you'd guess he was an athlete, not an artist. And when I saw his figurine, I could understand exactly what was going on inside of him. Because you can only choose a little of how you might seem to others, right? And then you've got habits and customs that show, too; but who you are *inside*—that's still yours to be above all. Otherwise, we wouldn't have been there at Birchback, now would we? Oleg's clay doll was molded so precisely that you could understand that it was him, unmistakably; but at the same time, it was also like a character from his surrealist icons—like one of his St. Nicholas the Wonderworkers, who wouldn't even imagine doing his tricks to amaze pagans or heal the sick or whatever, but who performed his bizarre acts purely out of love for the act itself, and *that* was the God-given gift inside of him. Oleg wasn't very good at speaking, but when I saw that figurine, I understood him so much better in a single moment—as if he'd read an entire book about himself out loud. That idea to make clay dolls really was a good one. Even though I guess my own didn't say all that much to the others. Or, well—who knows.

"After that, whenever we were going around and doing whatever in the daytime, those clay dolls would sit on our chairs next to the fireplace. And when we ourselves took our seats there in the evening, each person would hold it on their laps. It was like a part of our evening ritual. And then we started lugging them along with us to Dickens Hill in the mornings, because we couldn't leave them out of the sun-song ritual, now could we? Right now, it's so weird to think back on that. 'I know what it is,' Jaagup said that evening, since it was his turn to talk. 'And the Word became Flesh.' And Jaagup became Clay. For from earth you are taken, and to clay you must return.

"I realize that it sounds weird, but in the end, we truly did feel like those clay dolls were a part of us in some baffling and mysterious way. It wasn't like what most people believe, where you've got one person, one body, one soul. We'd transcended the bounds of the flesh. Naturally, that wouldn't have been possible if we'd had hair growing on us, but we *didn't*. And there wasn't any on the clay dolls either, it goes without saying. We treated them so tenderly—like if something might have happened to them, it could have had an effect on us, too, or, well, sort of like voodoo magic. How could we have believed that kind of crap? You know, a person can believe even the most absurd things imaginable. At least when everything she might have believed otherwise is taken away from her.

"One time, I got mad at Joel; I can't remember why anymore. I'd totally lost it, but instead of saying anything to him, I went up to his clay doll and I told it: 'Don't you understand what you did?' He saw what I was doing and went completely pale, then went up to my own clay doll, got down on his knees, stroked it gently, and said: 'I'm sorry; I was being stupid.' It was the most bizarre feeling—I realized he was saying it with complete sincerity. From then on, we always did it that way, and I've got to say that, occasionally, it truly was easier to talk to a clay doll than it was to the person's actual body. But, of course, it did only work when the real body was also somewhere close by.

"When Anni told us what was going to happen next, it seemed shocking and stunning at first; but in reality, we all realized the inescapable logic of that step.

"'We're going to burn them,' she said.

"*Yeah*, I thought, as soon as the true meaning of her words finally sank into me. *We'll burn them. Something that's made from clay really isn't complete until it's gone through fire. Only fire is capable of burning away all that is unnecessary and wrong with them, so they'll stay themselves forever.* Veronika was unnerved and tried to read our faces to see if only she felt that way. Jaagup also seemed to be at a loss for what to think of the idea, but when Oleg started shouting, 'Yeah! Yeah!' right away, then he joined him. 'We don't have a proper kiln,' Joel said. 'The whole world's our kiln,' I reckoned, and Anni nodded. 'It will be a trial,' she said. 'A trial by fire. What breaks has been broken since the beginning; what stays whole was worthy of a whole fate.'

"Birchback's midsummer-bonfire pit was located just a little way away from the main house. It was cold out and there was snow on the ground, but even so, we all bravely busied ourselves with stacking the pyre. Luckily, our firewood stocks were so full that we might've even had enough for two winters, and the result was quite an impressive stack. I took a picture of it, too, using a timer so we were all positioned in front of the pyre, holding our clay dolls, our cheeks blushing. But I don't have it anymore.

"We wrapped our dolls back up in cloth—in white linen. And each of us wrote a message on the linen in thick marker to go along with the doll. I don't remember what I wrote on mine, exactly; I think something like: 'I'm burning with you, and you're burning in me.' Depressing. No one told each other what they wrote, exactly, but I noticed that Oleg made a drawing instead; and the point of his drawing was pretty much the same as that of my note. This feeling shot through my heart—like we really *were* all one. And if we weren't yet, in reality, we certainly would be after the dolls had been torched.

"We placed the dolls in the middle of the pyre and then built a sort of pyramid-like dome on top of them, too. Jaagup told us something about pyramids and why it was good. It all seemed entirely logical and rational. We had the whole stack ready by sometime around midday, but understandably, we had to wait until evening to burn it. We were all walking around with blissful looks on our faces the whole day and pretended to talk and think about anything else. And multiple times I caught myself thinking about going to look at my clay doll and check on how she was doing. Well, I mean to the living room, naturally—I was used to her always just being there. And then I remembered where she really was, and I thought: *Be strong and resist it.*

"That night just wouldn't seem to come. I tried dancing, but there was no music in my head. My thoughts were with my clay doll the whole time. I was terribly afraid that she'd shatter when she burned. I would have been so ashamed then. Even though there wasn't, like, any reason to be. I'm no sculptor, of course; there's no way I could have molded her any better. The others were fretting just like I was. It was one of the few days I can remember when we had leftovers after lunch. Veronika practically didn't eat a single mouthful, and I couldn't keep anything down, either. Only the boys ate with as healthy an appetite as they always had.

"Finally, it slowly started getting dark, and Anni said it was time. She'd had Joel siphon a little bit of gas out of his car's tank and pour it over the pyre so that it'd definitely ignite. It was damp outside, although the firewood was dry. And we needed it to light with the very first match, of course.

"And it did. It was quite the fire—we stood as close to it as we could so that it warmed us. We had to keep rotating our other side to face it every little while, because it was just like it always is next to a bonfire in cold weather—the side facing the flames is too hot, and the opposite one is frozen. But there was a sacred feeling to it, somehow. The white linens around the dolls caught flame and started sizzling soon, and then it kind of stank, but we didn't care. I knew that my message and my doll and that fire and I all formed a single whole, and at that very moment, it felt like the most beautiful day I'd ever lived.

"We'd built a really good pyre with a sturdy structure that stayed standing for a long time, so we were able to stand there and watch the clay dolls in the center of the blaze for quite a while. You felt like you were staring into a mirror. And like your doll was staring back at you, seeing your reddened face glowing in the light of the fire with the darkened forest beyond. It was like I was observing myself, and seeing myself with my very own eyes. The sensation descended on me for a moment, and then disappeared just as quickly as it'd come. I was glad. I realized that for a split second, I'd seen the way things actually are. And I wasn't at all sad that it'd only been for a moment: I was simply happy that I'd seen it at all.

"The upper pyramid was the first to collapse; the lower

structure held up for a while longer. But by then, the burning logs had hidden the clay dolls from sight. We stood there for a while longer, anyway, with no one saying anything. I noticed that Jaagup was mumbling something to himself—maybe a prayer or a mantra, or maybe he himself didn't realize he was doing it. I suppose we hadn't really thought it would take that long. If our little religion had had its own real priest, he would have ushered us back inside and told his altar boys to put out the embers at the bonfire pit. But we didn't. Nevertheless, Anni had enough sense to see that if we stayed out there until it had gone out, then we'd freeze. So, we took each other by the hand and started to dance. It warmed us up a little and tired us out, and when we finally stopped, we started laughing our heads off all of a sudden. The laughter just kept coming and coming and coming from some inner reserves. None of us had laughed like that in such a long time. It was like when somebody tells a joke, and you get so hyped up that any meaningless story can set you off like that— where you laugh and you laugh and you just can't seem to quit, no matter what. I remember how one time, some friends and I were leaving some place and were in that same kind of a state, and then we got into a cab and kept on laughing—we somehow managed to tell the taxi driver where we were going through our laughter, and then we just kept on laughing the whole way there. It made the driver really uneasy, which was awfully funny to us, too, of course; and then we arrived, paid our fare, and the laughing fit still wouldn't pass. Well, it was something similar that time at Birchback. We laughed like we were totally out of our minds. And that was the last time I've laughed like that. When we finally did run out of laughter, the enchantment was gone. 'Inside, now!' Anni told us. The boys stayed behind for a few more minutes to heap snow onto the fire. We went ahead and made everyone mugs of hot tea with honey in the kitchen. We were happy."

"After our sun-song the next morning, Anni wouldn't let go of my hand, and so I of course wouldn't let go of Jaagup's, and then we just all kept standing there like that for a few more moments. Then Anni repeated one line from our poem again, and I guess that was the first time I realized what was to come.

"*Laudato sí, mi Signoré, per frate focu.* Be praised, my Lord, through Brother Fire.

"The previous night had been a rehearsal. The dress rehearsal."

"I don't know whether or not anyone else figured it out. None of us said it aloud, of course. It was certainly a new step—a very big one—but no one wanted to take the honor. Maybe it was simply too early. In any case, I didn't speak it. We went to check on the clay dolls at the bonfire pit. 'They've called on God now,' Anni said, and we all nodded. Naturally, they hadn't undergone the trial by fire entirely without harm, no matter how much we might have hoped for it. Oleg had gotten off easy—his was only missing an arm, while my own doll had a dark crack snaking across her neck. One of the legs had come off of Jaagup's doll, and he said bitterly: 'It is written that if your arm or leg offends you, then tear it off and cast it away.' He didn't like that, understandably. But against all expectations, Joel's clay doll had suffered the most damage. A large crack ran straight up and down the figurine, cutting it almost in half. Nowadays, I think it happened because he'd rushed while shaping his own doll—he did have to come and help all the rest of us afterward, you know. Maybe he'd been a little too self-confident, too. I didn't say anything. Only Veronika's and Anni's dolls were completely intact.

"We left them there. We went back to see them later, of course; but not all at once. I certainly went, and one time I saw Oleg returning from the bonfire pit when I was on my way there. We exchanged sort of awkward smiles. When I got to the pit, I saw that he'd put the detached arm back in place and supported it with a little piece of coal. Even so, he had to go and reposition it every once in a while.

"Veronika fell ill the next morning. We all woke up together (we were sleeping in the same room by then), and you could tell immediately that she had a fever. I guess she really had gotten cold out by the bonfire. She wanted to be brave and get up to come with us to sing the sun-song, but we told her to take it easy. Joel stayed with her, made her some raspberry-stem tea with honey, and gave her aspirin and vitamin C; there's no other way to treat something like that, anyway. She started coughing a little later, so we made her some tea out of cup lichen, too. It's not like any doctor would have been able to do much more for her. And Veronika's family doctor was based in Tallinn, anyway. But she lay in bed for almost the entire day, sweating and awfully hot; I think she was murmuring deliriously for a while, yelling about how hot she was and then insisting she wanted to go outside, and tried to throw the covers off. Then she fell back to sleep. We took turns being at her side—mainly Joel, of course, but I was there for a while, and then Anni, too. Oleg came in later and said that a sauna would do the trick of driving the fever out. Veronika was awake at the moment and murmured: 'Yeah, sauna, definitely, and sprigs for lashing, too.' We'd tied extra bunches of birch sprigs for using in the sauna the previous fall. They were bone-dry and hanging in the shed. I guess we'd forgotten we had them, or else we simply hadn't used them because then we'd have had to sweep out the sauna all the time, you know? But we naturally went and took some down to treat Veronika. I was afraid we were hurting her when we whipped her with them, because the leaves were totally dry and had even fallen off in some places. Veronika said it was no problem, that the pain was helping, and we didn't protest. That night, we heated the sauna up way hotter than usual. Veronika lay down on the top bench and said: whip me now, and don't hold back!

It was just Anni and I at first, lashing her the way you always do in sauna, but she kept yelling: harder, harder! We weren't strong enough, though. Then she got mad—or, well, *irritated*—and said we didn't know how to do it right, so she told us to let the boys come in and do it, Jaagup and Oleg. And so, they came in to take their turn. To tell the truth, I was feeling too hot already, too, because Veronika kept demanding that we pour more and more water on the stones. Jaagup and Oleg started lashing her so hard in there that it was painful to hear. She didn't allow Joel to do it, because she thought he'd hit too weakly, just like us. But finally, Joel couldn't take it anymore—he burst into the sauna and told them that was enough. Oleg and Jaagup couldn't argue, either. Joel just scooped Veronika up, tossed her over his shoulder, and carried her to the bedroom. Her back was almost bloody by that time, too. We ran upstairs after them, figuring they might need some help or something, but no— Joel wrapped her up in the sheets and Veronika appeared to be totally out of it and just kept whispering: *more, more* . . . Anni told me to go downstairs and make some tea while she and Joel stayed there talking to Veronika. I don't know whether or not she could understand anything, but, well . . . Then the water came to a boil and I brought Veronika a strong herbal-tea mixture and stirred a big spoonful of honey into it, too. She drank it and finally calmed down again.

"And the next morning, believe it or not, Veronika was as healthy as can be. Her fever was gone and her eyes were clear. She did skip the sun salutation, but when we came back down from Dickens Hill, she'd made us all breakfast. She thanked us for healing her pure. That's exactly how she put it—*pure*. It sounded kind of dumb, in my opinion, but I guess that's how she must have felt. I've got to say that illness—albeit a short one—had transformed her. Or she had simply transformed on her own and I'd only noticed it then. Whereas in the beginning (well, I'm not talking about the *real* beginning, but, you know, *earlier*), she was super high-strung all the time, worried about if everything would go just the way she'd planned, and whether everyone had actually paid attention to what she was saying. Now, that had completely disappeared. She was the humblest of us all. She almost never talked anymore, only replying when asked a question. When it was her turn to talk in front of the fireplace, she spoke about the joy of surrender. About how you have to give yourself up entirely—not in order to become yourself, like that darned Android had once told us, but simply to *give up*, to dissolve without even sweeping away your own tracks, and not so that you'll understand somehow—because that would mean there'd be no one who understands anymore—but just to be *beingless*. It might not sound very convincing, but by that time, we were all a little muddled by what she was saying. If we'd, like, wanted to say anything, you know . . . but we all knew each other as if there were hyphae connecting us. Yeah, hyphae—you know?

"Then there was one day when someone came and knocked at the door. It hadn't happened in so long that we didn't even think it was real at first. But then the knocking came again, although we still didn't actually believe we were all hearing an otherworldly sound like that all together and at once. I'll say it honestly: for the first time, I felt like they'd come to get us. But actually, it was a telegram for Joel. It wasn't very good news. He went and picked up his mobile phone and started charging it and when there was enough battery power to make a call, he sprinted up to Dickens Hill. When he came back, we realized right away that something was very wrong. 'Shit, shit, shit,' he kept on repeating—you could tell from that alone. His mother had been the one who sent the telegram: Joel's father had been hospitalized after having a heart attack, and if Joel ever wanted to see him alive again, he had to head to the city immediately. 'Shit, shit.' 'Of course you have to go,' Oleg said. 'That's really important.' 'But what about us?' Joel asked. *Us,* not *you*. 'We'll get by somehow,' Oleg reckoned. 'This is messed up!' Joel exclaimed. 'This is messed up!' Veronika offered to ride along with him, but Joel didn't want to hear a word of it. Then Anni took him by the hand and spoke to him for a long time, soothingly, really nicely, and treating him like a person. She said he had to go by all means, because although he meant a lot to us, he still came into this world as his mother and father's son. And that's more important, and we certainly understood that he wanted to stay, but even if he were to stay, a part of his thoughts would still be with his father all the time anyway, and it would hold him back. No matter how much he maybe really wanted to go all the way, it was entirely possible that he wouldn't have the guts, and that might even hold all the others back. Joel just nodded the whole time while Anni talked. I could see he didn't want to go at all, but her arguments were clear and rational. And when she finally said: 'Look, Joel—everything you've experienced and perceived up to now could somehow help your father in his final moments, and might even help your mother afterward,' then that decided things. He went upstairs, packed a few things in a bag, and put it in the car. Then he came back inside one more time and hugged each of us, one by one. 'Godspeed,' he said to everyone. 'Godspeed!' As if he knew we weren't going to see each other again. But I think he was just trying to say that if he tore himself away now, he would never reunite with us again in the way we were at that moment. I don't know why he didn't take Veronika with him. She didn't get along with his parents very well (that topic had come up once), and maybe it would have been strange for her to be with him at that time, but not with us; not here, but rather on that sad journey that Joel was facing. Well, in any case, Veronika stayed behind. And then there were five.

"Joel vanished from our pattern of communal existence as if he'd never even been there at all. When we went to check on the clay dolls in the bonfire pit the next day, there were only

five of them left, too. I don't know who removed Joel's. Maybe
he did himself when he came back from making his call, but
I really doubt it. And I don't know where the doll ended up.
Anyway, we didn't think he'd return. And we didn't talk about
him anymore. It was better that way. His departure had been
an inevitability and we had to come to grips with it as fast as we
could, to keep from holding on to him as an invisible figure in
our midst. Trapped. I believe that Veronika thought about him,
but she didn't mention it, either. That was understandable. The
whole time, it'd been a little weird for me that in our midst was
a couple, who were husband and wife to each other foremost,
and only then travel companions like the rest of us were to each
other. Maybe it was even easier for Veronika afterward. I don't
know.

"Our weeks were a day shorter after he left, too. But there
weren't all that many of them remaining. It might have been a
day or two after he'd gone that Anni finally voiced aloud what
stood before us. 'We're going to follow them,' she said, and
everyone understood what she meant. Isn't that what makes a
person a leader? Being capable of saying something clearly and
intelligibly which has only drifted through others' minds as a
hazy hunch? Our clay dolls were still out there in the bonfire pit
(except for Joel's, of course), and, well—when I'd visited them,
I also felt like they were *expecting* something of us. For us to do
something in return. Now they were hard and pure. No matter
how pure Veronika might have regarded herself as being after
the illness, they were still purer. And now it'd finally been said
out loud: we're going to follow them.

"It was strangely liberating to be able to call things more or
less by their proper names at last. For a while we'd talked about
going the distance: since the previous summer, essentially. It was
the reason we were there. But where or what that distance, that
end, would be—none of us had ever said it outright. Jesus went
the distance—that, we all agreed on. It was, in our eyes, what

set him above Buddha or Muhammad; not his divinity with its suspect value. Socrates went the distance. And Jim Morrison and Kurt Cobain. Janusz Korczak went the distance—the Polish writer and teacher who walked Jewish students into the Treblinka gas chamber so they wouldn't be afraid. They all died. Was dying a part of going the distance? Not necessarily. It could be something that allows you to start living only just then. Gandhi went the distance. Mother Teresa went the distance. It actually has nothing to do with death at all, you know. Because whoever allows himself to be sent to a pointless death hasn't really gone the distance, but has gone in the opposite direction.

"This is how I understood it: going the distance means continuing to be totally honest with yourself all the time, until you crash into a kind of wall that would have made mincemeat out of you under ordinary circumstances. But it's not impossible for you to crash into it with such momentum that the wall is the one that collapses. Even so, you're indifferent at that moment—you don't calculate or even hope that: oh, if only things would go like that. There's no other way to knock down those walls. And we'd chosen the walls that stood inside ourselves. No one made the choice for us. And it should have been clear to us from the exact moment we chose it: only one solution is possible here; going the distance this way carries its own price. It's impossible to perfectly comprehend that greatest of mysteries, which defines all of human life: death, if you don't enter it with full awareness and a straight back, yourself, if you don't approach it as an equal. Or that's close to what I was thinking.

"In a nutshell: we knew then that we were going to die. It wasn't a problem for us. Because it wasn't possible for us to get to where we'd decided to go without dying. We realized that we'd made that decision a long time ago already; only now it had been brought out into the light. Totally absurd! And yet, I felt just as confident about it right then and there as all the others did. But you can't argue with the absurd, now can you? Maybe there'd been some lingering doubts about it before, but when Anni stated out loud what was to come . . . All those doubts were gone by then at the latest.

"We talked it all out in detail. We chose a day. Now that it was all clear to us, there was no point in delaying it for too long. It just had to be clear to us that we were ready. It took a little bit of time, but not very much. We decided that Birchback itself would be our pyre. We'd go into another room, lie down on the floor, and wait for the smoke to take us. It was a worthy fate for the farmhouse—an honor only bestowed on select buildings. Veronika proposed that, logistically, the way we could do it was to turn on an iron on the ground floor and set it on top of some piece of cloth that would catch fire easily. It was a good idea. There'd be an investigation into it later, anyway, so it would turn out that a household accident had occurred, just as they tend to sometimes. Less of a problem for those left behind.

"And then the day was at hand. I can remember that morning well. I woke up with the definite knowledge that I wouldn't be laying myself back down to sleep again that evening, and I felt indifferent to the idea. We went and sang our sun-song. *Per sora morte, per frate focu.* We'd decided to die with clean bodies, so we heated up the sauna first thing that day, too. I stared at my travel companions' naked bodies and realized that I loved them all. When we came out into the changing room and they started to dry themselves off, I went and hugged each person one by one—male and female alike. There was nothing sexual about it, and it wasn't actually a goodbye either, because we were all going forward together. But it was a goodbye to those bodies.

"They understood. They all took turns hugging each other, too, and we were silent, because what was there to say?

"Anni and I were supposed to cook the last meal. The others packed up their suitcases. Jaagup had remembered those little old suitcases we'd found in the loft of the shed. We realized they possessed incredible symbolic power. It turned out there were exactly five of them. If Joel had been with us, too, we would've been short. They were really dusty—unfit for our purposes in such a condition. So, Veronika and the boys cleaned them until they were spick-and-span.

"We made rice and beans. Then Anni told me to wait in the kitchen for a second, went down into the cellar, and brought back up some herbs and a jar of mushrooms. They were some kind of special ones she'd been saving for that very occasion. I chopped up all the green onion we had growing on the windowsill— there was no point in keeping them anymore. And we added ginger, honey, red pepper, and a ton of lemon balm to the sauce. It was going to be the very best meal we'd had in a long time.

"Even so, when we sat down at the table, I suddenly had no appetite at all. Not because of nerves, I think, but simply because of the desire to not weigh myself down. Although, logically, it would've made the whole thing a lot easier. I'd had carbonmonoxide poisoning once: back when I was still in school, a girlfriend and I were at her summer home out in the country, we had a fire in the fireplace, and we closed the flue too early or the wrong way or something. I woke up that night with my heart thumping dreadfully in my chest, I felt sick, and I'd just had some horrible nightmares. Otherwise, I might not have woken up the next morning. The room reeked with smoke—I opened up the windows at once and woke up my girlfriend. She had a weird look on her face, which was sort of greenish, and she went straight to the toilet to throw up. I went, too, after she was done. In short, I had some idea of what was ahead of us.

"But at that moment, I sort of felt like I was walking through a cloud and the food really wouldn't go down. It was outright embarrassing—I, too, would have wanted all of us to have been composed of a little of the same stuff when we set off on our journey. The boys ate their fill, and Veronika and Anni did as

well, although generally, both of them—especially Veronika—
had very light appetites. But, well, it *was* tasty, and they knew
that it was going to be the last time. And it was like a ritual,
too, all the same. As if by doing so, we *were* all finally going to
be one. And prepared. Anni looked over at me and even asked:
'Carola, why aren't you eating? Is something wrong?'

"'No, no—everything's fine,' I said and stuffed a few forkfuls
into my mouth. Still, I left more than half of it uneaten. I even
felt ashamed before Anni, since she'd made such an effort to
cook it and I apparently couldn't appreciate that.

"We washed the dishes and tidied everything up. Then Ani
handed us sheets of paper and told us what to write. 'Why?'
Jaagup asked, but then he also remembered the messages we'd
sent along with our clay dolls. *I, Carola Seling, have settled all
my debts in this world and can go before God with a pure heart.*
And that was the complete, honest truth. "Then we put the
iron in place and went upstairs. We checked to make sure all
the windows in the house were shut tight. Before, Joel and
Veronika had both slept on the edge of the bed, but Joel was
gone now and so I was in his place. Lying on my other side was
Oleg, then Anni, then Jaagup, and then Veronika. We set the
suitcases under our heads and placed our hands on our chests,
each person holding their letter. We closed our eyes and began
to wait. Before long, I thought I could hear a soft hissing sound
coming from downstairs. But it felt like it was still too early,
and there didn't seem to be any stench at all. Then I heard Oleg
suddenly start convulsing next to me. Some kind of a cramp
had come over him. I sat up. Veronika was completely blue
in the face at the other end of the bed, and was also writhing.
Jaagup's eyes were open and it looked like he wanted to say
something, but he couldn't because of a lump in his throat.
'What is it, Carola?' Anni asked, which wasn't at all easy to do
for her anymore, either. Everything in my head was suddenly
all jumbled up. I didn't know what to ask, exactly, but I didn't

need to, because she murmured it herself. 'We had to be certain, didn't we?' And that's when I realized: the mushrooms she had brought up from the cellar; the mushrooms she'd used to cook us our last meal—they were no ordinary ones. No ordinary mushrooms at all.

"And then, suddenly, a painful line of thought sliced through my mind. Suddenly, everything was different.

"You see, that whole time, I'd had no doubt about going the distance. I wasn't afraid. It was me, personally, by my own free will, by my own personal choice. And now that choice had been taken away from me. If I died right now, I realized, that death wouldn't be my own—it would be a pointless death, a death totally for naught; it wouldn't raise me up or cleanse me or reveal to me anything I might hope to see in my final moment. I was already quite weak, but my mind was suddenly crystal clear— clearer than ever before—and I realized how absurd it all was; how I'd fooled myself into believing something out of a great will to do so and had helped others to be fooled; and now it had crossed all boundaries. And I wasn't sure in the very least that I could manage to drag myself back.

"But I tried, regardless. I tried, using the same strength I'd had within for going the distance. I stood up and staggered my way down the stairs. The living room was already full of smoke and the curtains had caught fire. I noticed that I was still holding onto my letter and my suitcase for some reason—I tossed them aside and stumbled out into the open and fell down onto my hands and knees and I retched. And I retched until there was nothing to retch anymore; I drank water out of a puddle next to my head and I retched it right back up again, and repeated that over and over. And then I passed out.

"Well, you know the rest of the story, anyway. They all perished, even though the fire was put out promptly and the house was left more or less intact. I was taken to the hospital in Viljandi and my stomach was pumped as empty as can be, and I guess I was so utterly weak in every other respect that they fussed over me and let me convalesce there a little. The doctors wouldn't let the police anywhere near me at first, and later, when they did, then I pretended like I didn't remember anything and, well, in the end, I *did* have to talk to them, of course, but I'd already decided by that time to say as little as possible. Well— that we were religious and we'd decided to commit suicide to go before God, but that I'd chickened out at the last minute. And that was it. Nothing illegal about that, now is there? Ha-ha.

"I've never actually told anyone else that entire story. I know that Joel tried to find me afterward, but to tell the truth, I chickened out then, too (there's no other way to put it), and I avoided him. He never did find me. I felt embarrassed later when I heard he'd died in a car crash. I didn't believe the story that it was an accident, of course. He followed them—I know it. So, I'm the only one still left out of all of us. I was still totally mixed up at first—I spent some time in a psych ward and then, when I got out, I was on some pills for a little while longer, but I finally got it more or less under control. And today, I'm as right as rain. I've got a family now, too, of course, and … I don't know how I would have made it without them. You don't forget things like that, you know. But even so, it's like they're someone else's memories that appeared in my head in some weird way. That person there wasn't me; not the me I am now. She's more distant from me than the clay doll was from her. Don't think I'm trying to justify myself or anything—I'm just telling it how it is. Whatever else, you can certainly believe that I'm still being totally honest with myself."

9

It was already late evening when I left Carola's photography shop. "Drive carefully, now," she called out. I promised I would. I'm in no hurry.

I got home only around two o'clock in the morning. Inspector Männik had left a message on my answering machine. "Hi . . . Epp Männik here." She cleared her throat, as if she didn't know what to say next. "I just thought I'd call and ask if . . . Did you find what you were looking for, then? Just out of human curiosity, you know . . . So, if you'd like, then call me." I wrote down her mobile number. If it had been anything else that Carola had told me, that call might have boosted my spirits in a heartbeat. But she and I did meet up, all the same; and then again, and then again, and I'm very grateful to her for these last couple of months.

Even so, I harbor no illusions. I know that with cancer patients, it's common to develop an overwhelming thirst for life right before the end. Along with a belief that they'll definitely get better. That an operation will help or some new drug will be invented, or that their body will simply defeat the disease in some mysterious way. I haven't felt anything like that. Maybe that means the end isn't so close just yet. For me, it's been enough to just have these weeks, over the course of which I've managed to organize my notes and write them pure.

I, Enn Padrik, have settled all my debts in this world. Period.

Over the course of this story, you've probably already wondered why it took me five years and why I had to receive the diagnosis before I began unraveling the ball of yarn that is my loss. I hope that you understand now. It was my own leap into the darkness, which I kept on delaying, though certainly not suspecting that a coin like this might emerge from the heart of the ball of yarn. But nevertheless, just in case.

What else is there to add? I went for a walk around town on Sunday morning and happened to pass by the doors of a church just at the moment the service ended. A mass of people flowed out, both young and old, and the former in especially large number. It came as somewhat of a surprise. I'd always been accustomed to thinking that churches were the waiting room to a cemetery. But no matter. I can't help if it seems overly sentimental and moralizing, but it's hard for me to forgo summary. Over the span of my whole life, even back when Anni and I would argue about religions, I'd most likely have said that, in the end, faith is each person's personal matter. Then, at the point when I decided to undertake my journey a little over half a year ago, I'd probably have said that if the old faiths with their long histories really have no other function in our society anymore, then perhaps it can be to protect us from new forms of madness. Yet, now that I know what I know, I can't help but say (and I realize how ironic it is that I'm saying it together with Harald and Birgit, although certainly not drawing quite the same conclusions they do): in my opinion, it's not important whether the things we believe are necessarily true. Whether God exists; whether there's global warming; whether two people are capable of loving each other their entire lives. What's important is the kind of people that makes us. I can condemn neither the will to be unreservedly true to oneself, nor an uncompromising desire to go the distance. But as soon as mercilessness and contempt raise their heads behind them and some god is at stake—no matter whether young or old or how beautifully it preaches love for one's neighbor, but all the while being the type that calls us unto itself without reserve—it happens without fail: for me, a line has been crossed. The only faith and hope I need for the fleeting time I have left lies in the ability to become a better person than the one I am now, even if just slightly.

I guess that's all.

Still, one more thing. Elo called me a couple of days ago. She said she's sober. She has been for a while now. The day after my car drove out of sight of her doorway, her old chums showed up just as she'd expected and asked whether she might need anything from the store. So they went to the closest town and got themselves some proper supplies, and by the end of that same evening, everything was just the way it'd been before. But the next morning, Elo herself kicked them out. "I just realized that, you know—if you're capable of handling all your problems, then I can handle mine, too." The hardest part for her had been asking Maire's help in finding a clinic, but Maire grasped the situation and helped without making any remarks. Now Elo lives in Tallinn and has even found a job at a translation bureau—there's always a demand for Swedish speakers there.

"Thanks," said Elo.

"You're welcome," I replied.

REIN RAUD was born in Estonia in 1961. Since 1974, he has published numerous poetry collections, short stories, novels, and plays. For his works, he has received both the Estonian Cultural Endowment Annual Prize and the Vilde Prize. Having earned his PhD in Literary Theory from the University of Helsinki in 1994, Raud is also a widely published scholar of cultural theory, as well as the literature and philosophy of both modern and pre-modern Japan.

ADAM CULLEN was born in Minneapolis. In 2007 he moved to Tallinn, Estonia, where he currently resides. His translations of Tõnu Õnnepalu's *Radio* and Mikhel Mutt's *The Cavemen Chronicle* are also available from Dalkey Archive Press.

MICHAL AJVAZ, *The Golden Age.*
The Other City.

PIERRE ALBERT-BIROT, *Grabinoulor.*

YUZ ALESHKOVSKY, *Kangaroo.*

FELIPE ALFAU, *Chromos.*
Locos.

JOE AMATO, *Samuel Taylor's Last Night.*

IVAN ÂNGELO, *The Celebration.*
The Tower of Glass.

ANTÓNIO LOBO ANTUNES, *Knowledge of Hell.*
The Splendor of Portugal.

ALAIN ARIAS-MISSON, *Theatre of Incest.*

JOHN ASHBERY & JAMES SCHUYLER, *A Nest of Ninnies.*

ROBERT ASHLEY, *Perfect Lives.*

GABRIELA AVIGUR-ROTEM, *Heatwave and Crazy Birds.*

DJUNA BARNES, *Ladies Almanack.*
Ryder.

JOHN BARTH, *Letters.*
Sabbatical.

DONALD BARTHELME, *The King.*
Paradise.

SVETISLAV BASARA, *Chinese Letter.*

MIQUEL BAUÇÀ, *The Siege in the Room.*

RENÉ BELLETTO, *Dying.*

MAREK BIENCZYK, *Transparency.*

ANDREI BITOV, *Pushkin House.*

ANDREJ BLATNIK, *You Do Understand.*
Law of Desire.

LOUIS PAUL BOON, *Chapel Road.*
My Little War.
Summer in Termuren.

ROGER BOYLAN, *Killoyle.*

IGNÁCIO DE LOYOLA BRANDÃO, *Anonymous Celebrity.*
Zero.

BONNIE BREMSER, *Troia: Mexican Memoirs.*

CHRISTINE BROOKE-ROSE, *Amalgamemnon.*

BRIGID BROPHY, *In Transit.*
The Prancing Novelist.

GERALD L. BRUNS, *Modern Poetry and the Idea of Language.*

GABRIELLE BURTON, *Heartbreak Hotel.*

MICHEL BUTOR, *Degrees.*
Mobile.

G. CABRERA INFANTE, *Infante's Inferno.*
Three Trapped Tigers.

JULIETA CAMPOS, *The Fear of Losing Eurydice.*

ANNE CARSON, *Eros the Bittersweet.*

ORLY CASTEL-BLOOM, *Dolly City.*

LOUIS-FERDINAND CÉLINE, *North.*
Conversations with Professor Y.
London Bridge.

MARIE CHAIX, *The Laurels of Lake Constance.*

HUGO CHARTERIS, *The Tide Is Right.*

ERIC CHEVILLARD, *Demolishing Nisard.*
The Author and Me.

MARC CHOLODENKO, *Mordechai Schamz.*

JOSHUA COHEN, *Witz.*

EMILY HOLMES COLEMAN, *The Shutter of Snow.*

ERIC CHEVILLARD, *The Author and Me.*

ROBERT COOVER, *A Night at the Movies.*

STANLEY CRAWFORD, *Log of the S.S. The Mrs Unguentine.*
Some Instructions to My Wife.

RENÉ CREVEL, *Putting My Foot in It.*

RALPH CUSACK, *Cadenza.*

NICHOLAS DELBANCO, *Sherbrookes.*
The Count of Concord.

NIGEL DENNIS, *Cards of Identity.*

PETER DIMOCK, *A Short Rhetoric for Leaving the Family.*

ARIEL DORFMAN, *Konfidenz.*

COLEMAN DOWELL, *Island People.*
Too Much Flesh and Jabez.

ARKADII DRAGOMOSHCHENKO, *Dust.*

RIKKI DUCORNET, *Phosphor in Dreamland.*
The Complete Butcher's Tales.

RIKKI DUCORNET (cont.), *The Jade Cabinet.*
The Fountains of Neptune.

WILLIAM EASTLAKE, *The Bamboo Bed.*
Castle Keep.
Lyric of the Circle Heart.

JEAN ECHENOZ, *Chopin's Move.*

STANLEY ELKIN, *A Bad Man.*
Criers and Kibitzers, Kibitzers and Criers.
The Dick Gibson Show.
The Franchiser.
The Living End.
Mrs. Ted Bliss.

FRANÇOIS EMMANUEL, *Invitation to a Voyage.*

PAUL EMOND, *The Dance of a Sham.*

SALVADOR ESPRIU, *Ariadne in the Grotesque Labyrinth.*

LESLIE A. FIEDLER, *Love and Death in the American Novel.*

JUAN FILLOY, *Op Oloop.*

ANDY FITCH, *Pop Poetics.*

GUSTAVE FLAUBERT, *Bouvard and Pécuchet.*

KASS FLEISHER, *Talking out of School.*

JON FOSSE, *Aliss at the Fire.*
Melancholy.

FORD MADOX FORD, *The March of Literature.*

MAX FRISCH, *I'm Not Stiller.*
Man in the Holocene.

CARLOS FUENTES, *Christopher Unborn.*
Distant Relations.
Terra Nostra.
Where the Air Is Clear.

TAKEHIKO FUKUNAGA, *Flowers of Grass.*

WILLIAM GADDIS, JR., *The Recognitions.*

JANICE GALLOWAY, *Foreign Parts.*
The Trick Is to Keep Breathing.

WILLIAM H. GASS, *Life Sentences.*
The Tunnel.
The World Within the Word.
Willie Masters' Lonesome Wife.

GÉRARD GAVARRY, *Hoppla! 1 2 3.*

ETIENNE GILSON, *The Arts of the Beautiful.*
Forms and Substances in the Arts.

C. S. GISCOMBE, *Giscome Road.*
Here.

DOUGLAS GLOVER, *Bad News of the Heart.*

WITOLD GOMBROWICZ, *A Kind of Testament.*

PAULO EMÍLIO SALES GOMES, *P's Three Women.*

GEORGI GOSPODINOV, *Natural Novel.*

JUAN GOYTISOLO, *Count Julian.*
Juan the Landless.
Makbara.
Marks of Identity.

HENRY GREEN, *Blindness.*
Concluding.
Doting.
Nothing.

JACK GREEN, *Fire the Bastards!*

JIŘÍ GRUŠA, *The Questionnaire.*

MELA HARTWIG, *Am I a Redundant Human Being?*

JOHN HAWKES, *The Passion Artist.*
Whistlejacket.

ELIZABETH HEIGHWAY, ED., *Contemporary Georgian Fiction.*

AIDAN HIGGINS, *Balcony of Europe.*
Blind Man's Bluff.
Bornholm Night-Ferry.
Langrishe, Go Down.
Scenes from a Receding Past.

KEIZO HINO, *Isle of Dreams.*

KAZUSHI HOSAKA, *Plainsong.*

ALDOUS HUXLEY, *Antic Hay.*
Point Counter Point.
Those Barren Leaves.
Time Must Have a Stop.

NAOYUKI II, *The Shadow of a Blue Cat.*

DRAGO JANČAR, *The Tree with No Name.*

MIKHEIL JAVAKHISHVILI, *Kvachi.*

GERT JONKE, *The Distant Sound.*
Homage to Czerny.
The System of Vienna.

FOR A FULL LIST OF PUBLICATIONS, VISIT: www.dalkeyarchive.com

JACQUES JOUET, *Mountain R.*
Savage.
Upstaged.
MIEKO KANAI, *The Word Book.*
YORAM KANIUK, *Life on Sandpaper.*
ZURAB KARUMIDZE, *Dagny.*
JOHN KELLY, *From Out of the City.*
HUGH KENNER, *Flaubert, Joyce and Beckett: The Stoic Comedians.*
Joyce's Voices.
DANILO KIŠ, *The Attic.*
The Lute and the Scars.
Psalm 44.
A Tomb for Boris Davidovich.
ANITA KONKKA, *A Fool's Paradise.*
GEORGE KONRÁD, *The City Builder.*
TADEUSZ KONWICKI, *A Minor Apocalypse.*
The Polish Complex.
ANNA KORDZAIA-SAMADASHVILI, *Me, Margarita.*
MENIS KOUMANDAREAS, *Koula.*
ELAINE KRAF, *The Princess of 72nd Street.*
JIM KRUSOE, *Iceland.*
AYSE KULIN, *Farewell: A Mansion in Occupied Istanbul.*
EMILIO LASCANO TEGUI, *On Elegance While Sleeping.*
ERIC LAURRENT, *Do Not Touch.*
VIOLETTE LEDUC, *La Bâtarde.*
EDOUARD LEVÉ, *Autoportrait.*
Newspaper.
Suicide.
Works.
MARIO LEVI, *Istanbul Was a Fairy Tale.*
DEBORAH LEVY, *Billy and Girl.*
JOSÉ LEZAMA LIMA, *Paradiso.*
ROSA LIKSOM, *Dark Paradise.*
OSMAN LINS, *Avalovara.*
The Queen of the Prisons of Greece.
FLORIAN LIPUŠ, *The Errors of Young Tjaž.*
GORDON LISH, *Peru.*
ALF MACLOCHLAINN, *Out of Focus.*
Past Habitual.

The Corpus in the Library.
RON LOEWINSOHN, *Magnetic Field(s).*
YURI LOTMAN, *Non-Memoirs.*
D. KEITH MANO, *Take Five.*
MINA LOY, *Stories and Essays of Mina Loy.*
MICHELINE AHARONIAN MARCOM, *A Brief History of Yes.*
The Mirror in the Well.
BEN MARCUS, *The Age of Wire and String.*
WALLACE MARKFIELD, *Teitlebaum's Window.*
DAVID MARKSON, *Reader's Block.*
Wittgenstein's Mistress.
CAROLE MASO, *AVA.*
HISAKI MATSUURA, *Triangle.*
LADISLAV MATEJKA & KRYSTYNA POMORSKA, EDS., *Readings in Russian Poetics: Formalist & Structuralist Views.*
HARRY MATHEWS, *Cigarettes.*
The Conversions.
The Human Country.
The Journalist.
My Life in CIA.
Singular Pleasures.
The Sinking of the Odradek. Stadium.
Tlooth.
HISAKI MATSUURA, *Triangle.*
DONAL MCLAUGHLIN, *beheading the virgin mary, and other stories.*
JOSEPH MCELROY, *Night Soul and Other Stories.*
ABDELWAHAB MEDDEB, *Talismano.*
GERHARD MEIER, *Isle of the Dead.*
HERMAN MELVILLE, *The Confidence-Man.*
AMANDA MICHALOPOULOU, *I'd Like.*
STEVEN MILLHAUSER, *The Barnum Museum.*
In the Penny Arcade.
RALPH J. MILLS, JR., *Essays on Poetry.*
MOMUS, *The Book of Jokes.*
CHRISTINE MONTALBETTI, *The Origin of Man.*
Western.

NICHOLAS MOSLEY, *Accident.*
Assassins.
Catastrophe Practice.
A Garden of Trees.
Hopeful Monsters.
Imago Bird.
Inventing God.
Look at the Dark.
Metamorphosis.
Natalie Natalia.
Serpent.
WARREN MOTTE, *Fables of the Novel:*
French Fiction since 1990.
Fiction Now: The French Novel in the
21st Century.
Mirror Gazing.
Oulipo: A Primer of Potential Literature.
GERALD MURNANE, *Barley Patch.*
Inland.
YVES NAVARRE, *Our Share of Time.*
Sweet Tooth.
DOROTHY NELSON, *In Night's City.*
Tar and Feathers.
ESHKOL NEVO, *Homesick.*
WILFRIDO D. NOLLEDO, *But for*
the Lovers.
BORIS A. NOVAK, *The Master of*
Insomnia.
FLANN O'BRIEN, *At Swim-Two-Birds.*
The Best of Myles.
The Dalkey Archive.
The Hard Life.
The Poor Mouth.
The Third Policeman.
CLAUDE OLLIER, *The Mise-en-Scène.*
Wert and the Life Without End.
PATRIK OUŘEDNÍK, *Europeana.*
The Opportune Moment, 1855.
BORIS PAHOR, *Necropolis.*
FERNANDO DEL PASO, *News from*
the Empire.
Palinuro of Mexico.
ROBERT PINGET, *The Inquisitory.*
Mahu or The Material.
Trio.
MANUEL PUIG, *Betrayed by Rita*
Hayworth.

The Buenos Aires Affair.
Heartbreak Tango.
RAYMOND QUENEAU, *The Last Days.*
Odile.
Pierrot Mon Ami.
Saint Glinglin.
ANN QUIN, *Berg.*
Passages.
Three.
Tripticks.
ISHMAEL REED, *The Free-Lance*
Pallbearers.
The Last Days of Louisiana Red.
Ishmael Reed: The Plays.
Juice!
The Terrible Threes.
The Terrible Twos.
Yellow Back Radio Broke-Down.
JASIA REICHARDT, *15 Journeys Warsaw*
to London.
JOÃO UBALDO RIBEIRO, *House of the*
Fortunate Buddhas.
JEAN RICARDOU, *Place Names.*
RAINER MARIA RILKE,
The Notebooks of Malte Laurids Brigge.
JULIÁN RÍOS, *The House of Ulysses.*
Larva: A Midsummer Night's Babel.
Poundemonium.
ALAIN ROBBE-GRILLET, *Project for a*
Revolution in New York.
A Sentimental Novel.
AUGUSTO ROA BASTOS, *I the Supreme.*
DANIËL ROBBERECHTS, *Arriving in*
Avignon.
JEAN ROLIN, *The Explosion of the*
Radiator Hose.
OLIVIER ROLIN, *Hotel Crystal.*
ALIX CLEO ROUBAUD, *Alix's Journal.*
JACQUES ROUBAUD, *The Form of*
a City Changes Faster, Alas, Than the
Human Heart.
The Great Fire of London.
Hortense in Exile.
Hortense Is Abducted.
Mathematics: The Plurality of Worlds of
Lewis.
Some Thing Black.

FOR A FULL LIST OF PUBLICATIONS, VISIT: www.dalkeyarchive.com

RAYMOND ROUSSEL, *Impressions of Africa.*

VEDRANA RUDAN, *Night.*

PABLO M. RUIZ, *Four Cold Chapters on the Possibility of Literature.*

GERMAN SADULAEV, *The Maya Pill.*

TOMAŽ ŠALAMUN, *Soy Realidad.*

LYDIE SALVAYRE, *The Company of Ghosts.*
The Lecture.
The Power of Flies.

LUIS RAFAEL SÁNCHEZ, *Macho Camacho's Beat.*

SEVERO SARDUY, *Cobra & Maitreya.*

NATHALIE SARRAUTE, *Do You Hear Them?*
Martereau.
The Planetarium.

STIG SÆTERBAKKEN, *Siamese.*
Self-Control.
Through the Night.

ARNO SCHMIDT, *Collected Novellas.*
Collected Stories.
Nobodaddy's Children.
Two Novels.

ASAF SCHURR, *Motti.*

GAIL SCOTT, *My Paris.*

DAMION SEARLS, *What We Were Doing and Where We Were Going.*

JUNE AKERS SEESE,
Is This What Other Women Feel Too?

BERNARD SHARE, *Inish.*
Transit.

VIKTOR SHKLOVSKY, *Bowstring.*
Literature and Cinematography.
Theory of Prose.
Third Factory.
Zoo, or Letters Not about Love.

PIERRE SINIAC, *The Collaborators.*

KJERSTI A. SKOMSVOLD,
The Faster I Walk, the Smaller I Am.

JOSEF ŠKVORECKÝ, *The Engineer of Human Souls.*

GILBERT SORRENTINO, *Aberration of Starlight.*
Blue Pastoral.
Crystal Vision.

Imaginative Qualities of Actual Things.
Mulligan Stew. Red the Fiend.
Steelwork.
Under the Shadow.

MARKO SOSIČ, *Ballerina, Ballerina.*

ANDRZEJ STASIUK, *Dukla.*
Fado.

GERTRUDE STEIN, *The Making of Americans.*
A Novel of Thank You.

LARS SVENDSEN, *A Philosophy of Evil.*

PIOTR SZEWC, *Annihilation.*

GONÇALO M. TAVARES, *A Man: Klaus Klump.*
Jerusalem.
Learning to Pray in the Age of Technique.

LUCIAN DAN TEODOROVICI,
Our Circus Presents...

NIKANOR TERATOLOGEN, *Assisted Living.*

STEFAN THEMERSON, *Hobson's Island.*
The Mystery of the Sardine.
Tom Harris.

TAEKO TOMIOKA, *Building Waves.*

JOHN TOOMEY, *Sleepwalker.*

DUMITRU TSEPENEAG, *Hotel Europa.*
The Necessary Marriage.
Pigeon Post.
Vain Art of the Fugue.

ESTHER TUSQUETS, *Stranded.*

DUBRAVKA UGRESIC, *Lend Me Your Character.*
Thank You for Not Reading.

TOR ULVEN, *Replacement.*

MATI UNT, *Brecht at Night.*
Diary of a Blood Donor.
Things in the Night.

ÁLVARO URIBE & OLIVIA SEARS, EDS.,
Best of Contemporary Mexican Fiction.

ELOY URROZ, *Friction.*
The Obstacles.

LUISA VALENZUELA, *Dark Desires and the Others.*
He Who Searches.

PAUL VERHAEGHEN, *Omega Minor.*

BORIS VIAN, *Heartsnatcher.*

LLORENÇ VILLALONGA, *The Dolls' Room.*

TOOMAS VINT, *An Unending Landscape.*

ORNELA VORPSI, *The Country Where No One Ever Dies.*

AUSTRYN WAINHOUSE, *Hedyphagetica.*

CURTIS WHITE, *America's Magic Mountain.*
The Idea of Home.
Memories of My Father Watching TV.
Requiem.

DIANE WILLIAMS,
Excitability: Selected Stories.
Romancer Erector.

DOUGLAS WOOLF, *Wall to Wall.*
Ya! & John-Juan.

JAY WRIGHT, *Polynomials and Pollen.*
The Presentable Art of Reading Absence.

PHILIP WYLIE, *Generation of Vipers.*

MARGUERITE YOUNG, *Angel in the Forest.*
Miss MacIntosh, My Darling.

REYOUNG, *Unbabbling.*

VLADO ŽABOT, *The Succubus.*

ZORAN ŽIVKOVIĆ , *Hidden Camera.*

LOUIS ZUKOFSKY, *Collected Fiction.*

VITOMIL ZUPAN, *Minuet for Guitar.*

SCOTT ZWIREN, *God Head.*

AND MORE . . .